ECHOES

Book Surge ISBN: 1-4563-1570-6

www.bluespikepublishing.com

Printed in the United States of America

To Bob Mitchell

Author's Notes

While I was writing my first novel, *The Quarter Boys*, I was thinking of it as a one-off. I figured that if I ever wrote another novel it would be completely unrelated. It never occurred to me that I might be writing the first book in a series.

So what changed? There's a moment near the end of *The Quarter Boys* (don't worry, I'm not going to give away any major plot points) where Sassy talks about something that happened during her rookie year that cost a little girl her life. It was just something I improvised on the spot because I wanted Sassy's empathy for Michel to feel credible (it's amazing how many of those improvised moments turn out to be fortuitous later on). But a week or two after I finished writing I found myself wondering what had actually happened. I was intrigued by it, and so the idea for a sequel was born.

The fact is that I love writing Sassy and Michel, so the opportunity to bring them back was exciting. Of course it still took me two years before I actually started writing, but the germ had been planted.

I imagine that all writers have some stuff they love to write and other stuff that they don't. I love writing the character scenes: those moments where you just have two or more characters talking, whether it's about the crime, their personal lives, or something completely arbitrary. It's fun because I get to step into the characters' heads.

The parts I don't enjoy writing are the procedural and technical stuff. Part of that is that they just don't interest me very much (I watch *CSI* and *Bones* for the characters, not the crime solving), and part of it is that they're outside my area of expertise (despite the fact that I'm called on almost daily to solve murders in my day job as a graphic designer, of course). It's also because I find it really tough to write the technical stuff in a way that's interesting. It's too easy to get bogged down in the details and bring the narrative flow to a screeching halt.

Unfortunately, for this book I came up with a plot that required me to learn more about investigative procedure, evidence collection, blood typing, etc...than I ever wanted to know. Still, I make no claim whatsoever to an expert in any of these areas.

Here's the way it works for me: I come up with an idea of what I'd like to have happen, then I do some research until I found a source confiming that it's possible, then I quickly stop doing research and start writing. Is that lazy? Sure. Does that mean that I might have found information contradicting what I wanted to do if I'd kept looking? Probably. I'm sure that any police detective or medical examiner would find lots to quibble about in my work. But as I said, the technical stuff really doesn't interest me that much so you may have to cut me some slack. Let's just say that while I've striven for plausibility, in no way have I been a slave for absolute authenticity.

I'm indebted to the following websites for information: atneworleans.com, loyno.com, science.howstuffworks.com, 3dchem.com, webmd.com, faculty.ncwc.edu, wikipedia.com, dukemednew.duke.edu, surrealcoconut.com, stphilipneri.com, gospelsonglyrics.net.

Thanks to the folks at CreateSpace for helping me bring my writing to the masses (if you can call a few hundred people the masses). Thanks to Mark Leach at Now Voyager Bookstore in Provincetown for being the first to carry my books in an actual bricks-and-mortar store and for pushing *The Quarter Boys* to his mystery customers. Remember, support your local independent bookstores! And thanks to Ernie Gaudreau and Bart for getting out the word to other gay mystery fans on Amazon.com and for your amusing emails.

Thanks to all my family and friends for your continued support and for pimping my books, and special thanks (again) to Bob Mitchell, Vion DeCew, and my husband, Brian, for your proofreading, comments, and encouragement. I appreciate it more than I can adequately express.

D.L.

OTHER BOOKS FROM DAVID LENNON

The Quarter Boys

Second Chance
(Available April 2011)

Blue's Bayou
(Available October 2011)

Reckoning
(Available April 2012)

ECHOES

A Novel

DAVID LENNON

Chapter 1

She could hear soft crying. She lifted her head from the cool hard floor and looked around in the darkness. Far off she could see a small circle of light. As she watched the light began to grow larger and brighter, taking on the shape of an open doorway. For a moment someone was standing in the doorway, but she couldn't make out any detail. There was just a heavy shadow, and then it was gone.

Now she could see a young girl on the far side of the door. She was seated on the floor against a wood post, with her arms stretched above her head. Her wrists were held in place by a thick rope that encircled the post, and a dirty white cloth was tied around her mouth. The girl had long blond hair that hung limply around her face and onto her shoulders. She was dressed in just panties and a camisole t-shirt. At some point they might have been pale pink, but now they were a dingy gray.

Even at a distance she could see the girl looking at her, imploring her for help with her eyes. She tried to push herself up to her feet. Pain exploded in her abdomen and she gasped, rolling onto her back. She put her right hand onto the small mound of her stomach and felt warm dampness. She lifted her hand and brought it close to her face. Even in the darkness she could make out the blackness of the blood on her fingertips. She felt her throat tighten and began to fight for air as a convulsive sob escaped her lips. In the distance she heard a phone begin to ring.

Alexandra "Sassy" Jones sat up in bed with a start and looked down at her right hand. Although she'd had the same nightmare every night for twenty five years, she always awoke wondering if it was real. Even in her confusion her right hand began to move reflexively for the cell phone on her nightstand. She could still feel the phantom sensation of the small round hole in her stomach that her fingers had traced thousands of times. She cleared her throat and brought the phone quickly to her ear.

"Yes?" she said calmly.

"Sassy, it's me." It was the voice of her former partner, Michel Doucette.

"Michel," she said. "Are you okay? What time is it? "

She felt suddenly anxious. Michel had been on a leave-of-absence from the New Orleans Police Department for the past six months and she'd grown unaccustomed to hearing his voice on the phone in the middle of the night.

"It's Carl," Michel said.

For a moment Sassy was confused. Why had her ex-partner said that he was her ex-husband? She tried to make sense of the words and wondered if she was still dreaming, somehow bringing together the two most important men in her life.

"This is Carl?" she asked tentatively.

"No, Sassy. It's Michel." Michel said.

"But you said…"

"I'm sorry," Michel cut her off abruptly. "Carl's dead."

Suddenly the pieces of the conversation fell into place and Sassy came fully awake.

"How?" she asked slowly. Her words seemed to come from a distance and echo in her head.

"It looks like a suicide," Michel responded gently.

Sassy was silent for a moment. It had been a year since she'd spoken to Carl and 5 years since she'd last seen him, yet he'd been a part of her life every day for the past twenty five years.

"Are you still there?" Michel asked.

"Yeah," Sassy responded slowly. "It was our anniversary."

"What?" Michel asked, confused.

"Yesterday," Sassy said, "It would have been our 25th anniversary."

Michel paused before responding, suddenly understanding what Sassy meant: Carl had killed himself because it was their anniversary.

"I'm coming over," he said finally.

"Okay," Sassy replied blankly.

She placed the phone back on the nightstand and turned on the small lamp next to it. She stared at the wall in front of her for a moment, then willed herself to get up and get dressed.

Chapter 2

When Sassy opened the door Michel was surprised by her appearance. For the first time since he'd met her five years earlier he'd expected her to look something less than her best, but the solid woman in the doorway looked as though she were ready to go to dinner or the office. She was dressed in slacks and a short matching jacket that were the same chocolate brown tone as her skin, though two shades deeper. Under the jacket she wore a deep plum silk shirt with a wide spread color, and a delicate gold necklace draped her throat. Her short dark hair with its few silver threads was neatly brushed and her subtle make-up was perfectly applied. As always the effect was both simple and stunning, and Michel wondered not for the first time if Sassy ever just rolled out of bed and slummed it in sweat pants and an old t-shirt.

As Michel walked in Sassy hugged him warmly and gave him a kiss on the cheek. Although their partnership had long ago developed into friendship, it was an unusual gesture of affection and Michel sensed that Sassy's composed appearance was deceiving.

"It's good to see you," she said softly.

While Sassy poured them coffee, Michel walked into the living room and settled onto the plush burnt orange sofa that separated the seating area from the dining room. He'd always felt that Sassy's home was a perfect reflection of her as a person. The room was warm and welcoming, yet devoid of clutter or excess. The rich cocoa walls were tastefully accented by smaller black and white photos with simple black metal frames, and larger, more colorful paintings—all depicting either the Crescent City or African-American culture. The white built-in shelves along one wall were lined by well-thumbed books on a range of subjects from psychology to religion to history to music and art. Here and there were small sculptures or artifacts that Sassy had collected during her travels in Africa and Western Europe. In addition to the sofa, there were two deep-seating chairs covered in pale sage twill. The centerpiece of the room was a coffee table consisting of a large, square glass top that rested between four thick burled olive bases. The overall effect was simple, yet with rich detail that told you everything you needed to know about the home's occupant.

Michel noticed a small silver ashtray on the coffee table directly in front of him and smiled. Not only had Sassy thought to put the ashtray out, but she'd correctly anticipated exactly where he would sit.

"How did you find out about Carl?" Sassy said as she walked into the room carrying two large white ceramic mugs.

She placed one in front of Michel and settled next to him on the couch. Michel knew without asking that she'd put three sugars and more than a little cream into his coffee.

"Al Ribodeau called me," he said as he lifted the mug and took a small sip. "He took the call and thought it would be better if you found out about it from me."

"How did he know Carl was my ex-husband?" Sassy asked, giving him a genuinely puzzled look. "You're the only one in the department who knows I was even married."

"He saw your pictures."

"Pictures?" Sassy asked, the look of puzzlement growing.

"Carl had a wall of photos of you," Michel said carefully. "Al said it looked almost like a shrine."

Sassy took a deep breath and let the image sink it. She'd closed her heart to Carl long ago but suddenly felt fresh sympathy for him. She imagined him sitting alone in a room, staring at the reminders of their life together.

"When was the last time you spoke to him?" Michel asked, bringing her back suddenly.

"366 days ago."

Sassy could see the surprise on Michel's face at the precision of her answer.

"Carl called me every year on our anniversary. Usually around 10 pm after he'd got a few drinks in him."

"And last night?"

"I unplugged my phone," she said matter-of-factly. "I didn't feel like talking to him this year. He didn't have my cell number."

"And you think that may be why he killed himself? Because you didn't talk to him?" Michel ventured.

Sassy shrugged.

"I don't know the man anymore...*didn't* know him anymore."

Michel took her hand, watching her face carefully to make sure it was all right.

"You're not blaming yourself, are you?"

Sassy met his eyes and gave a sad smile.

"I don't know yet," she said. "I haven't had time to process it. I know logically it's not my fault. I don't have any illusions that I have that kind of power. Carl was angry at me, but I don't think he would have killed himself over me. Not after 25 years."

"What makes you think he was still angry with you?" Michel asked.

He noticed Sassy slowly withdrawing her hand from his as she looked away, focusing on a spot directly in front of her.

"The calls," she said with a weary sigh. "When Carl called, he'd tell me what a cunt I was and how I'd ruined his life by leaving him."

Michel was shocked by both the bluntness of the response and the fact that Sassy had allowed the calls to continue for so long. It seemed out of character.

"Why didn't you change your number?" he asked.

"I don't know," Sassy said, looking back at him. "I guess I figured he needed to vent and it was harmless enough. Maybe I was worried that if he didn't have that opportunity he'd do something more drastic."

"Like kill himself?" Michel asked.

Sassy didn't respond but Michel could read the answer in her expression. He waited a moment before continuing.

"Sassy, I'll understand if you don't want to talk about it right now, but what happened between you and Carl?"

Something about the words "right now" caught Sassy's attention and she looked at Michel more intently, trying to read his expression.

"Are you asking me as a friend or a cop?" she asked.

Michel dropped his gaze for a beat, then looked back at her.

"Both," he said.

"What aren't you telling me?" Sassy asked, a look of anxiety clouding her face.

"I think we should go to the station," Michel said. "There's something you need to see."

Chapter 3

Sassy stared numbly at the three Polaroid photos on the table in front of her. From each, the eyes of a young girl stared back at her with terror. She was dizzy and felt like she might vomit. She closed her eyes and breathed deeply, trying to push the images from her mind for a moment and summon the professional detachment she'd developed over the years.

When she re-opened her eyes she felt calmer. She studied the photos more carefully. The three girls were seated on what appeared to be the same twin mattress with their backs against a vertical wood post. Their arms were stretched above their heads and held in place by handcuffs, the chain of which passed through a heavy steel eyehook imbedded in the post. Each was gagged by a white cloth. All three were blond and looked to be no more than 8 or 9 years old.

Her gaze stopped on the middle photo. It was blurred, but she knew with certainty who the girl had been. She'd seen her every night in her dreams.

"You found these at Carl's?" she asked without turning.

"They were on the floor in front of him," Al Ribodeau replied carefully.

Sassy turned around and leaned back against the table, her eyes fixed on the floor in front of her feet. Michel, Sgt. Al Ribodeau and Capt. Carl DeRoche looked at her expectantly, waiting for a reaction.

"Have you ID'ed any of them yet?" she asked without looking up.

"Not yet," DeRoche replied. "The codes on the back indicate the film was manufactured in 1979 so we're trying to gather missing persons reports from around that period."

Sassy nodded and brought her fingers to her eyes, rubbing them wearily. As she settled her hands on her thighs she looked directly at Michel.

"The middle one is Iris Lecher," she said without emotion. "I'd guess the other two are Missy Ann Macomber and Celia Crowe."

Michel had never heard any of the names before but he thought immediately of Stan Lecher, the chief investigator for the Orleans Parish Coroner's Office who had worked with Sassy and him on numerous cases. He gave Sassy a querying look and she nodded back, pursing her lips with resignation.

*****

Sassy settled in one of the green leather chairs in Carl DeRoche's office. Michel was seated to her left, both of them facing their boss across a battered metal desk. DeRoche had been Chief of Detectives for the 8th District for sixteen years, though he was only in his mid-50s. He was well respected by his squad and department and had a reputation as a thorough and tenacious investigator and a fair, though demanding, boss.

"It was the Lumley case, right?" DeRoche asked.

Although he'd been working in Lafayette at the time, he'd been aware of the case which made headlines throughout the state. He was also familiar with the files of all of his detectives and knew that Sassy had received a commendation for her work on the case during her first year on the force.

"What's the Lumley case?" Michel asked.

"You were just a kid back then," Sassy said kindly. "Two little girls were kidnapped in fall of '80. They were never found. A third one was kidnapped in spring of '81, my rookie year. I was assigned to the case to help with profiling suspects and interrogation because of my degree in criminal psych."

Michel nodded, encouraging her to continue.

"The third girl was Iris Lecher, Stan's daughter," Sassy said. "Stan was still a med student back then, raising Iris with his mother after his wife died during childbirth. Iris got taken from the grandmother's house."

Michel exhaled loudly. He'd always sensed that there was some special connection between Sassy and Lecher but he'd never understood what it was before.

"Carl was working for a man named Mose Lumley at the time," Sassy continued, "and I stopped by Lumley's one night to talk to him because I was worried about Carl. Lumley had been brought in for questioning at one point, but he had an alibi when Celia Crowe was kidnapped so he wasn't considered a suspect anymore. When I got there the door was open. I should have called for back-up but I wasn't thinking about the case at the time so I went in alone.

"When I got inside I thought I heard crying, so I began to search. When I got to the basement there was a door at the end of the hall. The crying was coming from the other side. There was a peephole in the door, so I looked through it and saw Iris. She was tied to a post but she was still alive. And then someone else was there."

She paused for a moment and took a sip of water from the coffee-stained mug she'd been cradling in her lap.

"It happened so quickly," she said, now lost in the memory. "I was looking at Iris and then I looked down for the door handle. Out of the corner of my eye I saw something move and when I looked back up I couldn't see Iris anymore. And then I was shot through the door. I fired back as I went down. I passed out and when I woke up Lumley had killed Iris and himself. I'd hit him but I didn't kill him.

"I was given a public commendation, but privately I was put on probation because I didn't follow procedures and it may have cost Iris her life. The department chose not to release the details. They told the press that Iris was already dead when I got there and that I killed Lumley. They thought it would be better PR if the public thought I was a hero," she finished.

She took another sip of water, moving it around in her mouth for a moment before swallowing, as if trying to wash away a bitter taste. Michel reached over and placed his hand on her left arm but she didn't seem to notice. For a full minute nobody spoke.

"Sassy," DeRoche asked finally, "does anyone else know exactly what happened?"

Sassy lifted her eyebrows in a shrug.

"I think everyone who knew about it is probably dead or retired by now. I never asked, but my sense was that the files were sealed...or worse."

"What about Stan?" DeRoche asked.

Sassy shook her head sadly.

"No," she said. "So far as he knows Iris was dead before I got there and I killed Lumley."

"There's a good chance he's going to hear about the photos through the grapevine," DeRoche said flatly.

Sassy nodded in agreement.

"I'd like to tell him before he does," she said.

"Are you sure about that?" Michel asked, his voice both surprised and concerned.

"Yeah," Sassy replied, giving him an appreciative smile and patting the back of his hand. "I owe it to him. I should have told him the truth years ago."

"Do you want me to go with you?"

"No," she replied, "but thank you."

"You can tell him about the photos, but that's all for now," DeRoche interrupted.

"What are you suggesting," Sassy asked. "That we just keep covering up what really happened?"

DeRoche sat back in his chair and gave her a measured look.

"Look," he said calmly, "I don't like cover-ups, but I'm also not so idealistic that I don't know that sometimes it's better to let sleeping dogs lie. Especially in this city. Before we make any decision about telling people what happened, I want to know that it's relevant. We'll do an internal investigation. I don't even want to bring in Internal Affairs yet. I want to handle it inside until we figure out the chain of events and determine if some evidence implicating Carl was missed because the department was busy trying to cover its own ass."

Sassy noted DeRoche's phrasing and appreciated that he wasn't singling her out.

"Did Carl have any family?" DeRoche asked.

"A brother, but I haven't heard from him in years," Sassy replied.

"If he shows up and wants to place an obituary in the paper that's fine, but I don't want anything else in the press," DeRoche said. "Let's keep this as quiet as possible for now. The less attention on it the better we'll be able to conduct our investigation without interference,"

Sassy and Michel nodded their agreement.

"One other thing," DeRoche said, looking directly at Sassy. "I need to put you on suspension until we clear this up."

"Why?" Sassy asked with dismay. "I'm the only one who was there. I'm the only one who can help put the pieces together."

DeRoche shook his head.

"Uh uh," he said. "You're a witness in this case and you had a personal relationship with the suspect. It's a clear conflict of interest. I want you home and available to help as needed."

Sassy gave him a baleful look but nodded.

"What about me?" Michel asked.

"Last time I checked you were on a leave-of-absence," DeRoche replied.

"I want to be re-instated," Michel said quickly.

"And you think you can be objective?" DeRoche asked.

Michel understood the implication of the final word. If Sassy had overlooked or disregarded evidence that pointed to Carl, he would have to be willing to expose the truth.

"Absolutely," he replied, levelly meeting DeRoche's gaze.

DeRoche regarded him for a moment and then spread his hands outward with the palms up in a gesture of acquiescence.

"Fine," he said. "You can start tomorrow. But you report directly to me. You can handle all the field work but I want to know exactly what you're doing every minute, and I want a report at the end of every day. Okay?"

Michel shrugged and managed a smile.

"You got it, Captain," he said.

Chapter 4

Sassy stood in the cool dim hallway outside the Orleans Parish Coroner's Office. She and Michel had left headquarters at 7 a.m. and she'd phoned Lecher from the car on the way to the building on Tulane Avenue, a mile northwest of the French Quarter. As she'd expected, he was already at work and had agreed to meet her. She'd been waiting in the hallway for him for nearly 10 minutes. With each passing minute her anxiety grew, yet on some level she hoped that he'd wait a while longer before appearing. At that moment the door opened and Lecher stepped into the hallway.

Though just shy of his 50th birthday, Lecher seemed much younger. It wasn't his actual appearance so much as the energy that radiated from him. He always seemed fully aware and engaged by his surroundings, observing and making mental notes. Even in the days following Iris' death, Sassy had never found him withdrawn or distant. He was reserved but fully present. He grieved openly and then seemed to take his grief and focus it, altering his career path from medical research to becoming an investigator for the coroner's office.

As always, his physical appearance was fastidious but never fussy. He was dressed in dark slacks and a lighter jacket, with a crisply pressed white dress shirt and striped tie. His light brown hair was short and neatly parted on the left side. Sassy noted that the silver at his temples had become more pronounced since she'd last seen him, yet his skin was still smooth. His features were unremarkable yet pleasant.

Sassy had always sensed that his neat, appropriate appearance wasn't so much a conscious choice as simply a manifestation of his orderly mind. She couldn't imagine him wasting time or energy thinking about his clothes or hair, nor ever trying to make a statement with them. She imagined that he'd had the same haircut since childhood and that his clothes were just newer versions of things he'd previously owned, probably originally bought by his late wife. His movements, too, seemed designed for efficiency. No energy was ever wasted. Everything was focused on the task at hand. Although he inhabited the physical world, he seemed to truly live in his mind. Everything else was merely a concession to the physical world.

Sassy knew that many people considered Lecher arrogant on first meeting him, but she believed the truth was that he was so fully engaged by whatever he was doing that he sometimes failed to observe common social etiquette. Although his intellect and powers of observation were far superior to most people, she never found him condescending. In fact he always seemed pleased when others operated on the same level that he did. Overall she found him to be a genuine and caring man who also possessed one of the slyest and darkest wits she'd ever encountered.

Although she felt the urge to hug him, Sassy knew that Lecher would find the action suspicious and later disingenuous. Instead she shook his hand perfunctorily and began walking in the direction of the stairwell.

"Let's go outside," she said.

*****

"So what's on your mind, Sassy?" Lecher asked.

Although she sensed that he was trying to put her at ease by affecting an easy tone, she could detect an underlaying anxiety in his voice. She turned to face him.

"Last night my ex-husband, Carl, was found dead. It looks like suicide," she said, trying to maintain a neutral tone.

"I'm sorry to hear..."

"Don't be," she said quickly, cutting him off. "They found pictures of three girls at the scene. Iris was one of them."

Lecher stared back at her without blinking. She could see that he was no longer actually seeing her.

"Stan," she said with more force than she'd intended, "it looks like Carl and Mose Lumley may have kidnapped Iris together."

Lecher's eyes regained their focus slowly.

"I'm sorry," he stammered.

"For what?" Sassy asked incredulously.

"Because I know this must be very hard for you."

Sassy tried to gauge his meaning: hard because of the death of her ex-husband?; hard because she had to tell him the news?; hard because she had failed to do her job correctly? She felt intuitively that he meant all of them.

"Stan, I don't know what to say," she stammered. "I'm so sorry. I'm sure the only solace you could have taken in Iris' death was that Lumley was stopped. And now that's gone. I failed you. I failed Iris."

She could feel tears welling and quickly wiped them away, not wanting to look like she was playing for Lecher's sympathy.

"Sassy, it wasn't your fault," he said gently, his voice calm and controlled. "You were a small part of the investigation. You more than did your part. And you killed the man who killed Iris."

Sassy felt a sudden surge of guilt but fought the impulse to blurt out the truth of how Lumley had died.

"I don't blame you and you shouldn't either," he continued. "You were in the hospital after, and when you came back you were walking a beat. If anyone is to blame it's the department for being so eager to close the case without fully investigating it."

Sassy was shocked by Lecher's words and reassuring tone.

"But he was my husband," she said, shaking her head. "I should have known."

Lecher reached out and gently grabbed her shoulders. Sassy couldn't bring herself to look at him.

"No," he said kindly, "you'd be the last person to know because you loved him."

Chapter 5

Michel got back to his house in the Faubourg Marigny at 7:20 a.m. The house was still and cool and he knew that Joel must still be asleep. He went to the kitchen and began quietly making coffee. Twenty minutes later as he sat at the counter reading the paper and smoking a cigarette, he heard the whisper of bare feet on the floor behind him.

"Good morning," he said, spinning on the stool to face Joel.

Joel stood in the doorway in only a white ribbed tank top and black-and-white polka dot boxer shorts. His longish, straight brown hair stuck up at odd angles, giving him the look of a cartoon character with his finger in an electrical socket. His boyish face was still slack with sleep and he looked at Michel through hooded eyes. He shuffled forward and leaned into Michel's body, giving him a quick kiss on the lips.

"Ewww, cigarette breath," he said, pulling back and making a sour face. "Let me have a drag."

He took the cigarette from Michel's hand and inhaled deeply, blowing the smoke back into the air with an exaggerated pucker of his lips.

"That's better," he said with a sly smile and leaned in to kiss Michel more deeply. "Now we both stink."

He pushed himself upright and shuffled to the coffee maker behind him.

"You need more?" he asked as he filled the mug Michel had put out for him.

"No, I'm good," Michel replied.

Joel walked back and settled himself on the stool to Michel's right, facing Michel with his toes wrapping the foot rail of Michel's stool.

"So what's up, chief?" he asked with a big yawn.

He looked at Michel and smiled. Even after six months, he was struck by Michel's face every time he looked at him. There was something almost pretty about Michel, yet he was entirely masculine at the same time. He had an angular face with high cheekbones and a strong jaw. His short black hair was slightly spiked in the front and his deep brown eyes were framed by thick lashes. Most striking of all, though, were his lips which were thick and expressive. They seemed to convey everything he was feeling at once. Joel studied those lips for a moment.

"You're going back, aren't you?" he asked after a moment.

It was more a statement than a question.

"I don't know," Michel replied honestly. "I need to do something for Sassy. After that I'm not sure."

Joel nodded without judgment. Their relationship was still too new and tentative for him to feel he had the right to express an opinion about Michel's life.

The pair had met six months earlier on the night Joel had arrived in New Orleans from Natchez, Mississippi. Their attraction had been powerful and immediate, but things had gone off-course and Joel had found himself spiralling downward into a life of drugs and prostitution. Events had culminated with Michel, Sassy and Joel's friend Chance rescuing him from a serial killer he'd thought was his friend.

Since then Joel had been trying to rebuild his life. He was living in a large house in the Marigny that had belonged to Lady Chanel, another friend who'd been a victim of the killer. Chanel had left the house to her best friend, Zelda, who'd lived there for a few months, but when Zelda was diagnosed with early-stage Alzheimer's she'd moved into a nursing home and had allowed Joel to live in the house for free in exchange for maintaining the property and looking after the two elderly tenants. Chance was back in Natchez. Joel had seen him only once, when he'd gone home for the funeral of Chance's father, though they spoke weekly. Chance had started a business but had been keeping the details secret.

Joel had been accepted at Tulane University for the coming fall semester where he planned to study criminal psychology. Although he wasn't yet sure how he wanted to apply his studies as a career, he knew he wanted to use his personal experience to help others. In the meantime he'd taken a job working at a nursery in Metairie, a few miles from the French Quarter. He enjoyed working outside and liked the balance it gave his life. Although he loved living in the city, he knew he was still a country boy at heart and the job gave him the chance to indulge both aspects of his nature. He'd also discovered that cultivating and nurturing the shrubs and flowers gave him a deep feeling of satisfaction and that he had a knack for it. In his spare time he'd added a rose arbor to the already-lush gardens at Lady Chanel's house and restored the neglected gardens at Michel's house.

Over time he and Michel had redeveloped a level of trust in their relationship, first as friends and finally as a couple. They'd been officially dating now for six weeks. Although technically he still lived at Lady Chanel's house, for all practical purposes he'd been living with Michel for most of that time. It was the first attempt at a serious relationship for both of them.

"Are you okay with that?" Michel asked, turning to face Joel and draping his arms over Joel's shoulders.

He noted that Joel looked even healthier than he had when he first moved to the city and that the exertions of his job had added some bulk and definition to his slim body.

"Of course," Joel said with a warm smile. "I just want you to be happy, and if being a cop makes you happy then I'm all for it."

Michel studied Joel's face carefully. He knew that Joel understood all too well the potential dangers of his job. Seeing no signs that Joel was holding back, he returned the smile and gave him a gentle kiss.

"I'm just jealous that I'm not going to have you all to myself anymore," Joel said with an exaggerated pout. "I've gotten spoiled having my lazy-ass man at my beck and call."

"Your 'beck and call'?" Michel repeated, chuckling at the antiquated expression. "Okay, grandpa. Is that what's been going on here? I've just been your convenient love slave?"

"You know it, baby," Joel replied, arching one eyebrow and wiggling the tip of his tongue between his teeth with comic lechery.

Michel pushed his right hand softly across Joel's face as if to wipe the expression away. He looked at Joel more seriously.

"We can make it work," he said. "Come fall you're going to be busy with classes, anyway, but I know we can make it work."

"I know we can, too," Joel replied, leaning forward and resting his forehead against Michel's as he wrapped his arms tightly around Michel's neck.

They both extended their lips for a soft kiss.

"Not that I want to encourage delinquent behavior, being as I'm a cop again and all, but what do you say you play hookey and we spend my last day of freedom together?" Michel asked softly.

"I was thinking the same thing," Joel replied with a smile.

*****

Stan Lecher leaned back in his office chair with his arms locked behind his head and stared at the single piece of paper on his desk. As soon as Sassy had left he'd gone to his office and called a friend at the Police Department, asking him to discreetly send over a copy of the Lumley file. The single sheet—dated May 8, 1980, six days after Iris died—had been the only contents of the file. Across the top of the page in large black letters the word CLOSED had been stamped. In addition to the dates and names of the officers on the scene, there were only two brief paragraphs.

Suspect Mose Lumley was shot and killed by Officer Alexandra Jones at approximately 9 p.m. Officer Jones was shot in abdomen by suspect and taken to Lindy Boggs Memorial for treatment. Kidnap victim Iris Lecher found dead at the scene from a knife wound to her throat.

Lumley also suspected in kidnappings and probable deaths of Missy Ann Macomber and Celia Crowe.

Lecher frowned, knowing there should have been hundreds of pages in the file. He sat forward and picked up the page, folding it neatly in thirds and placing it in the inside pocket of his jacket. He stood and pulled the bottom of his jacket to straighten it, then opened the door and walked casually to the stairs.

Let's see what we have, he thought, as he began to descend the stairs to the records room in the basement of the building.

*****

Sassy carefully descended the stairs from her attic carrying the large brown cardboard storage box. She placed it on the floor and folded up the stairs, then lifted the hatchway panel back into the ceiling.

She stared at the dusty box for a moment, wondering whether she truly wanted to open it. It had been a long time since she'd consciously chosen to revisit the memories it contained.

Chapter 6

A half hour later Stan Lecher returned to his office and closed the door. A stack of recent autopsy reports requiring his immediate attention had been placed in the center of his desk but he absently pushed them aside as he sat in his chair.

The autopsy files for Mose Lumley and Iris had been empty, save for a notation in each that the contents had been turned over to the New Orleans Police Department on May 12, 1980. The signature of the receiving officer was Patrolman Maxwell MacDonald. Lecher knew the name well: "Mac" MacDonald had been elected Sheriff of New Orleans four years ago. They were casual acquaintances and had worked together a few times over the years as MacDonald had risen through the ranks of the department.

Lecher closed his eyes and took several deep breaths, trying to clear his mind. His experience had taught him to examine the facts and construct a chain of logic before reaching any conclusions.

He knew only three facts: standard procedure for autopsy results in a criminal investigation dictated that only copies be sent to the police—all original documents and photos were to be kept by the Coroner's Office; neither the autopsy reports nor the full police reports were in the Lumley file at the police department; "cleaning" the records would have taken authorization by somebody with a lot of power.

The question was why anyone would want to clean the records? Had the police known that Lumley had an accomplice?

he wondered. That didn't make sense. Why would they have left a killer on the street? Even if they'd known it was Sassy's husband they would have arrested him, regardless of the fact that he was married to a cop. The department had always operated with a certain amount of corruption, but not to that level. Sassy had been a rookie. She would have been expendable.

Had Lumley been framed? Lecher could easily imagine the department pinning the kidnappings and killings on Lumley out of expediency, but only if they were certain that the actual killer was no longer a threat. Again there wasn't any logic to the conclusion. He couldn't imagine a circumstance where the actual killer would no longer pose a threat unless he were in custody or dead. In either case there'd be no reason for the police to cover up the truth.

The only conclusion that made any sense was that there had been a flaw in the investigation that would have caused embarrassment for the department. He tried hard not to draw a conclusion about what the consequences of that flaw might have been.

He opened his eyes. He knew he needed to be careful. He couldn't allow his emotions to cloud his judgment. He considered his options: the two most obvious leads he had were Sassy and MacDonald, and each had drawbacks.

Sassy was emotionally problematic for him. For twenty five years he'd been grateful to her for dispensing justice to his daughter's killer. Although it now seemed clear that her own husband had been involved, he couldn't imagine that she would have purposely covered up the information. She was too good a cop, too good a person. But if she had been involved in a cover-up he couldn't risk making her suspicious. If she hadn't, he couldn't risk hurting her.

Approaching MacDonald could be professionally dangerous. Although he seemed like an honest man and had done a lot to clean up corruption in the department since taking office, MacDonald was clearly well connected and a political animal with strong survival instincts. He couldn't have risen so quickly or gotten elected without them. And it would certainly be in his own best interests to protect the reputation of the department.

Lecher picked up the phone and began dialing the Sheriff's office. Perhaps MacDonald's instinct for self-preservation could work to his own advantage, he thought.

Chapter 7

Sassy sat on the edge of her bed with the contents of the box spread out on the floor in front of her. She'd already sorted and organized everything into rough piles representing different stages of her life. As she stared at them she was reminded uneasily of the photos that had been found with Carl's body.

She lowered herself onto the floor and picked up a small pile of black and white photos. They were images from her childhood in Butte La Rose, a small town in the St. Martin Parish in the Atchafalaya Basin. Her mother's people were Cajun. They'd worked a small farm on the edge of the bayou for over two centuries. They were a mix of Native American, French and African. Her father came from Indiana, though his family had originally been taken to Alabama from Africa.

Her parents had met at Louisiana State University where both worked. After marrying young, they'd moved to Butte La Rose to live with her grandmother. That's where Sassy had been born and lived until she was twelve, though no one who met her would have guessed at her rural Cajun background.

She picked out a photo of her grandmother and studied it carefully. Maybe there was some resemblance between them around the eyes, she thought.

As a girl she'd adored her grandmother, and as she'd grown she'd come to admire her as well. Despite a hard life working the farm and the loss of two husbands and three children, her grandmother had always maintained a fierce joy for life. It was a joy that Sassy herself had rarely experienced.

It was her grandmother who'd first started calling her "Sassy" when she was six. When she'd asked why, her grandmother had replied, "'Cuz maybe if you live with it long enough you'll grow into it." Sassy smiled at the memory. Maybe her grandmother had been a little right about that, she thought.

She pulled out another photo, this one of a group on the front porch of the family's house. Her grandmother was seated in the center with her children and their families around her. Her parents looked so young and happy. She guessed they couldn't have been more than 18 or 19 at the times: probably newlyweds. Her Uncle Robert and Aunt Emma were seated to the left with her cousin Devon and another baby in her aunt's arms. She guessed that was her cousin Mimi, which meant that she herself was still a year away from being born. And there, barely visible in the shadows behind everyone else, was her Uncle Jimmy. Sassy frowned and put the photos back down.

From the time that she was seven until she was ten, she'd endured repeated molestation from her mother's brother, who'd lived with the family. One day, shortly before her eleventh birthday, as she lay in the grass and felt him tracing a path up her inner thigh with his finger, she'd suddenly reached down and grabbed his hand. It wasn't something she'd planned or thought consciously to do. It just happened. She'd sat up and looked him in the eyes, and in a voice she hadn't recognized as her own she'd spoken a singe word: no.

Jimmy had frozen for a moment, then pulled his hand back as though it had been burned. He'd stumbled to his feet and stood over her, a mixture of fear and rage working his face. He'd begun to spew curses at her and then to ramble on about the trouble she'd be in if her parents ever found out what she'd been doing with him.

She'd begun to laugh hysterically then, in the true sense of the word, uncontrolled emotion roiling to the surface.

"You think I'ma be in trouble?" she'd managed. "Daddy gonna cut your thing off and feed it to the hogs. Then he gonna kill you."

She'd seen the shock in his face and it gave her a sense of power for the first time in her life. She'd grown suddenly calm.

"And if he don't," she'd continued in a low voice, "you can be sure I will. 'Cuz you know you gotta sleep sometime, and when you do, I'ma be there."

She'd gotten up then and walked away without another word. Jimmy never came looking for her again and a year later she and her parents had moved to Gentilly, just outside New Orleans. She'd never seen nor heard word of Uncle Jimmy again.

For the most part she'd been able to put what had happened out of her mind. She'd been too young when it had started to understand intellectually that she was a victim. She'd sensed it was wrong but had never felt shame of her own. She knew the shame belonged to Uncle Jimmy. By the time she became fully aware of what was happening she put a stop to it. She'd shifted the dynamic and taken control. That knowledge made her feel strong and capable.

Still, when the time came to declare a major in college she made her choice in large part because of her own experience. It wasn't a need to punish the phantom uncle of her memories. She simply wanted to understand what had motivated him. She received her undergraduate degree in psychology in May of 1977 and entered the Masters program in psychology and criminal justice that September.

Her professors had been shocked the following year when she announced her intention to join the police force. Sassy had been at the top of her class and they'd all assumed that she'd go on to a career in research or rehabilitative therapy. But research didn't interest her. She'd already gained the understanding she needed. The rest of her decision was a numbers game: where could she do the most good?

She knew that only a small percentage of pedophiles were ever "cured" and stopped sexually abusing children. Virtually none of them ever lost the impulse. On the other hand, one hundred percent of the sexual predators stopped molesting children while incarcerated. The choice seemed obvious. It wasn't motivated so much by a need for justice as the desire to protect other victims.

Next to the family photos lay her diplomas from Tulane, and next to those another stack of photos of her life with Carl. In the top photo a younger version of herself looked confidently back at her. She was dressed in a crisp blue police uniform and a smiling Carl had his arms wrapped around her. It had been the day she graduated from the academy. She was three weeks' pregnant at the time but didn't yet know it.

She'd met Carl in February of the previous year, her final year of school, during a night out at Tipitina's, a renowned music club in the Uptown section of the city. She'd gone with some classmates to hear the band Beausoleil, and by midnight they were all damp with sweat and more than a little drunk. As she'd moved through the crowd of dancers toward her table to rest, a handsome young man had materialized in front of her.

He was tall and slim, with a lean muscularity that was apparent even through the hideous shimmer of a bright chartreuse shirt.

"You're not leaving, are you?" he'd asked confidently. "We haven't even had a chance to dance yet."

Sassy looked around, unsure if he was speaking to her.

"We haven't even met yet," she'd replied, looking him up and down suspiciously.

There was a presumptuousness in his tone that she'd found both unsettling and intriguing.

"I'm sorry," he'd said, extending his hand. "I'm Carl...Adams."

She'd taken his hand firmly.

"Pleased to meet you, Carl...Adams. I'm Sassy...Jones," she'd said, mocking the stammer in his introduction.

He'd stared at her for a moment, seemingly unsure how to respond, and Sassy had studied him carefully. His skin was more tan than brown, but there was no mistaking his features as anything other than African, and he had large brown eyes and slightly sunken cheeks which gave him a hungry appearance. He was clean-shaven save for a thin black line of a mustache that wrapped his full lips, and his shiny hair had been combed back hard, the tendrils in the back glistening greasily.

Finally he'd broken into a warm smile.

"Okay, I see how it's gonna be," he'd said, nodding his head. "You're gonna make me work for it."

"It?" she'd asked archly, still gripping his hand tightly.

Carl had begun to sweat then, wanting to break contact with her and take a step backward, but unable because of the strong grip she had on his hand.

"Um...okay," he'd said, flicking his tongue nervously over his lips. "Maybe I should just be going."

Sassy had shrugged her shoulders in response but didn't release his hand.

"Or I could buy you a drink," she'd said matter-of-factly.

She was enjoying seeing him ill at ease after his initial show of bravado.

"Okay, Sassy Jones," he'd replied. "But can we go sit down now?"

The question indicated that he understood who was in control and Sassy had finally let go of his hand in response.

"Of course," she'd said, moving close to his body as she walked past him toward the table.

Over margaritas Carl had told her that he worked as a truck driver for a local seafood company, transporting shrimp and crawfish throughout the southeast. He'd told her it was just a temporary job until he found something steady in the area. Although he was vague about his past, she'd also learned that he'd grown up in Detroit and had come to New Orleans a year earlier to live with his older brother.

She'd chosen to be equally vague about her present, telling him only that she was studying psychology at Tulane, but not divulging her future plans. She knew that too many men were intimidated by the idea of a woman cop and also sensed that Carl might have spent some time on the wrong side of the law at some point in his life.

Sassy enjoyed talking with him and appreciated the fact that he mixed easily with her classmates. There was none of the confident posturing that she'd first seen and she sensed that he was still largely unsure of himself and had merely been affecting an attitude that he'd learned from watching TV and movies. He was sweet and attentive and she'd enjoyed his attention. He also had a sharp mind and an easy sense of humor.

As she watched him talking with the others at the table she'd begun to evaluate him—looks and personality: A+; job prospects: C; clothing and hair: well, I can fix those, she'd thought.

As the last words formed in her mind she'd been shocked into recognition of what she was doing. Never in her life could she recall looking at a man and assessing his suitability as a companion. It wasn't that she didn't like or was afraid of men. It was simply that she'd been so focused on studying and planning her own life that the thought of having a man in it had never occurred to her. She'd always felt already whole.

It frightened her how quickly this dormant instinct had revealed itself, like a snake striking forward suddenly from an unseen hole to snatch its prey. It was a quality in many of her female classmates that she'd always found repellent—a sort of constant, reflexive search and evaluation of husband material. Sassy had always considered it a "feminine trait" that she didn't share.

Still, she liked what she'd seen of Carl and the idea of opening her life to another person was exciting. She decided not to close herself to the possibility. She'd even allowed Carl to walk her to her car, despite her usual insistence on her own independence, and had given him a quick kiss along with her phone number.

The sound of her doorbell jarred Sassy out of her memories. She wondered how long she'd been sitting there on the floor. She quickly picked up the two stacks of photos and her diplomas and put then carefully back in the box. On top of them she placed a spiral-bound notebook. She put the lid back on the box and slid it across the carpet into the back left corner of her closet. She stood up and smoothed the front of her slacks, then headed to the front door.

Chapter 8

Although it had been over twenty years since she'd last seen the man at her door, Sassy knew him immediately. As always he was dressed in a simple black suit, crisp white shirt, yellow bow tie, and black shoes that had been buffed to a high gloss that matched the shine of his shaved head. His face was wide and pleasant and still largely unmarked by the passage of time.

Whereas Carl had been lean and angular, his older brother, Eldridge, had always been round, smooth and solid. His personality, too, was the inverse of his brother. Carl had been outwardly warm and friendly, with an easy charm and humor. Eldridge was outwardly more reserved but with a greater depth of compassion. Carl had drifted through most of his life before and after Sassy without purpose, unable to find his bearings and prone to making poor decisions in the heat of the moment. Eldridge had always seemed sure of his purpose. Even in his youth he'd possessed the earnestness and authority of a much older man. He'd always seemed wise and dependable.

"Eldridge," Sassy said with shock. "Good Lord, what are you...?"

She trailed off, realizing the foolishness of the question. Eldridge smiled warmly, acknowledging and forgiving her faux pas.

"Hey, Sassy," he said, stepping forward and briefly taking her hands in his as he kissed her on the right cheek. "It's good to see you. You look wonderful as always."

Although the same words spoken by anyone else would have

come across as an attempt at charm, from Eldridge they sounded like a simple observation.

"Please, come in," Sassy said, stepping aside.

"Thank you."

They walked down the hall to the living room and Eldridge took a seat on one of the chairs, leaving the sofa to Sassy.

"Did you just get into town?" she asked.

"No, early this morning," he replied. "Carl was supposed to meet me at the bus station, but when he didn't show up I took a cab to his place and saw the police tape. I went to the station and found out what happened."

"Oh my God, Eldridge," Sassy said, shaking her head. "I'm sorry you had to find out like that. I would have called you, but I didn't know how to reach you."

"That's okay," Eldridge said. "I don't suppose there's any good way to hear that kind of news."

They were both respectfully silent for a moment.

"Were you coming for a visit?" Sassy asked finally.

"Actually I'm moving back," Eldridge said with a sigh. "I decided it was time to spend more time with Carl. As I've gotten older I've started to realize the importance of family more. I was hoping we might be able to build some kind of real relationship again."

"I'm so sorry," Sassy said.

Eldridge nodded his thanks.

"Yes, it's a very difficult time," he said sadly. "It seemed like he was finally getting his life together, and now this."

It suddenly occurred to Sassy that she knew nothing about Carl's life. Other than his yearly phone calls, she'd had no contact with him and had long ago stopped keeping tabs on his life. They had no mutual friends and she'd last heard from Eldridge a few years after her divorce when he'd called to tell her he was leaving New Orleans to open a homeless mission in Mexico City.

"Was he?" she asked with honest curiosity.

"He certainly wasn't thriving," Eldridge replied, "but he was working steadily and he seemed to have left all that bad business behind him."

For the first few years after their divorce, Sassy had kept track of Carl through the police database. She knew that his address had changed every six months or so, moving into increasingly seedy neighborhoods. She also knew that he'd been arrested several times on suspicion of trafficking in stolen goods. Eventually she'd stopped. On some level she still loved Carl and it hurt too much to see his downward spiral. She'd assumed that one day he'd end up in jail or dead.

"What was he doing?" she asked.

"He'd gotten a job as a driver for a trucking company, doing regional routes," Eldridge replied. "I think that being on the road and away from here was good for him. It removed the temptations. Carl could be a weak man."

He shrugged matter-of-factly. Again his words would have sounded different coming from anyone else, but Sassy knew there was nothing condemnatory about them. It was simply an observation. Eldridge had spent his entire life trying to help others get their lives on track and she knew it was one of the great disappointments of his life that he'd been unable to do the same for his brother.

"And what about you?" she asked, hoping to change the subject away from Carl for a moment. "Last I heard you were opening a mission in Mexico."

Eldridge nodded. "That was long ago. I've opened four missions since then. I've been in the Houston area for the last few years."

Although he dressed like a minister in the Nation of Islam, Eldridge had no particular religious affiliation. His missions were secular, intended only to help the homeless get on their feet without proselytizing to them. Eldridge possessed the unquestioned belief in his calling of a preacher, however, and was capable of great passion and fire when soliciting support and donations from the local community. He'd originally come to New Orleans to start his first mission at the age of twenty six, though that mission had closed a few years after he left the city.

"That's great," Sassy said. "I'm very proud of you."

She realized it was an awkward thing to say and looked away for a moment.

"What's wrong?" Eldridge asked, leaning forward in his chair.

"El, I have something to tell," Sassy said, meeting his gaze again.

*****

Throughout the rest of the winter and into the spring, Sassy and Carl dated casually. He was frequently away because of his job and Sassy took advantage of the time to focus on finishing her degree. She also liked the way his absences forced their relationship to develop slowly. She graduated that May and looked forward to relaxing for a few months before entering the police academy in November.

She took a job that summer as a hostess at The Commander's Palace to make a little money and pass the time. Most of her former classmates had left the city after graduating and now that her parents had moved back to Butte La Rose she found herself truly alone for the first time in her life. She enjoyed the freedom, but also surprisingly found herself longing for Carl's companionship when he was away.

Whenever he was in town they spent all of their free time together and she quickly became intoxicated with being with him. Part of it was Carl himself, but she recognized that part of it was also the thrill of unfamiliar experience. Everything was new and exciting and frightening, but for all of her apprehension it seemed natural and right. In the few moments when she allowed herself to indulge in romantic fantasies she could even imagine how it might be to share her life with Carl.

But she knew that would never happen. In her gut she knew that Carl was just a trial relationship. She hated herself for it, but she knew it was true. Again she found herself exhibiting a way of thinking that she found reprehensible in other woman, but her logical mind knew that Carl was not the right one. He lacked the stability she knew she wanted in a man. He was fun and made her feel good about herself, but she would need more. She wanted someone steady who shared her goals and ambition. And that ambition itself presented a problem.

After a month of dating, Carl had confirmed what she'd suspected: he'd spent 2 years in a juvenile detention center as a teenager and had been convicted as an adult for breaking and entering and robbery in Detroit. He'd come to New Orleans after finishing a one-year sentence. Harsh as it was, she knew she could never achieve her ambitions within the police department with a husband who had a criminal record.

She knew that out of fairness to Carl she should just end the relationship before it got too serious, but the excitement and happiness it gave her were so powerful that she kept convincing herself to wait a while longer. Her life as a cop would be difficult. Cops saw all the worst of human nature on a daily basis. It might be years before she had the opportunity for another relationship. Selfishly she wanted the pleasure to last as long as possible.

*****

"I just don't believe he was a kidnapper and possibly a killer, El," she said after she finished telling Eldridge about the photos found with Carl's body. "He was a liar and a thief, but he couldn't intentionally harm anyone."

Eldridge was silent for moment, seemingly trying to absorb all that he'd heard.

"It is hard to believe," he replied finally, "but unfortunately I've learned that the heart harbors many dark secrets."

"Meaning?" Sassy asked.

"That we can never really know anybody completely," he replied. "We were raised in the same house, shared the same experiences, but they shaped us very differently. There was certainly a lot about his behavior I never understood."

"But El," Sassy said, "you've always been different...special. Not many people are willing to devote their lives to helping others."

"Am I different?" he asked. "Isn't that what you've done?"

Sassy considered the question for a minute. She wanted to respond that she hadn't had to sacrifice the way that Eldridge had, but she knew that wasn't true. Her life may have been more comfortable—she had a home and possessions and a few close friends—but she had made sacrifices as well.

"What really happened that night might come out," she said instead. "The department is going to investigate. They want to find out if there was any evidence linking Carl to the three girls that was missed back then."

Eldridge nodded slowly.

"And although no one said it," she continued, "I assume they'll try to find out if I knew anything and covered it up to protect Carl."

Her voice caught and tears began to well in her eyes. Eldridge stood and walked to the couch, kneeling low in front of her and looking up into her face.

"We both know you didn't," he said softly.

"I know," Sassy replied, wiping tears from her eyes, "but we also know why I was really at Lumley's. If I'd had my mind on the case where it should have been things would have turned out differently."

"You can't know that," Eldridge said soothingly. "And you stopped him that night."

"I didn't stop him," Sassy cried helplessly. "He killed himself."

Eldridge settled onto the couch beside her. He closed his eyes and took a deep breath before continuing.

"But if you hadn't been there," he said in measured tones, "if he didn't know he'd been caught, who knows how long he might have continued?"

Sassy stood suddenly and took a few steps away. She didn't want consolation or sympathy. She turned to face Eldridge and her expression had changed from sorrow to anger.

"How could I have been so stupid to think it would never come back?" she asked with a hard laugh. "I've worked so hard to build my career...to be a good cop...and it's all been built on quicksand."

They were both silent for a minute.

"Sassy," Eldridge said finally, "whatever happens, I'll be here for you. Even if it means trouble for me, I'll tell the truth."

"I don't know, El," she replied uncomfortably.

"Look, if it helps..." he trailed off, turning his palms upward in a gesture of giving.

He stood up and walked over to Sassy, taking her hands.

"Yes, mistakes were made," he said, "but you didn't know what was really happening. You were just trying to protect your husband because you loved him. "

Lecher had also absolved her from blame because of her love for Carl, and now Sassy wondered how much she had really loved him given what had ultimately happened.

"You know he still loved you," Eldridge said suddenly.

Sassy was shocked by his words and let out a harsh laugh.

"Oh yeah, that was real clear when he called me up every year to tell me what a cunt I was."

She gave Eldridge a hard look.

"I never said he was good at expressing his feelings," he replied with a shrug.

Sassy's body began to shake as she stared at Eldridge in disbelief. The shaking gained momentum, rising up from her stomach, and suddenly a laugh exploded from her lips. Tear began to roll from the corners of her eyes again as all the tension she'd been holding since she'd found out about Carl's death was released. She convulsed uncontrollably with laughter.

Finally after a minute she began to calm down and wiped her eyes with the back of her right hand. She let out a loud sigh.

"You know, I've missed you, El," she said, shaking her head appreciatively.

"I've missed you, too," he replied with a warm smile.

Chapter 9

Michel awoke at 5 a.m. and quietly slipped out of bed, trying not to wake Joel. He grabbed a pair of black sweat pants and a white t-shirt from the floor and walked into the hallway, closing the bedroom door silently behind him. After dressing he padded down the hallway to the kitchen and began the ritual of making coffee.

He was both excited and nervous to go back to work. For six months he'd been in a state of limbo, unsure whether he was truly suited to be a cop or what he wanted to do with his life. Actually, he had to admit that his uncertainty had been going on for longer than that. Since his mother had passed away almost a year ago he'd been drifting.

For his entire adult life until that point he'd always had certainty. Perhaps he'd never been happy, but he felt secure with the life he'd created. His existence was stable and safe and that suited him. Some might have found it funny that he considered being a homicide detective safe, but it was an environment in which he'd always felt comfortable. It had ritual and purpose and he thrived on unlocking the secrets of each case. Although the job brought him in contact with violence and tragedy, he felt safe because it was familiar.

He'd always considered his sexuality to be a small part of his identity. It wasn't that he was uncomfortable with being gay or that he'd ever tried to deny it to himself. It simply didn't play a large role in the life he'd chosen. New Orleans was, at its heart, a small town and he never wanted to cause discomfort for his mother by flaunting his sexuality. There were also the practical considerations of his career. He'd worked hard and didn't want to risk being ostracized for something that he considered insignificant.

He'd been content to dwell on the fringes of the city's gay scene, making discreet entrees into the bars whenever he'd felt lonely or in need of a night of companionship, but in the morning he'd always returned to his other life. Sex was something fleeting and clandestine. He'd had a few short-lived relationships, but had never really felt the need to have another person in his life.

But things had changed after his mother's passing. He'd found himself feeling empty and more lonely and had begun to frequent the bars, often during the day. He wasn't looking for sex. In fact he rarely engaged in conversation with anyone else. But being there gave him an odd sense of solace. He was able to find comfort in the company of strangers simply because they shared a common sexual inclination. It made him feel like he was a part of a larger community, that he belonged. And the alcohol had helped pass the time.

Then the killings had started and he'd met Joel: the two events that would lead him to question the life he'd built.

During that summer three men had been killed and Michel and Sassy had been assigned to the case. The first two victims had been visitors to the city and the third had recently moved there with his wife and children. The first victim had been gay. The second was straight and there'd been no evidence to suggest that he'd ever engaged in any gay activities. The third victim, though married, had a history of picking up men and taking them back to the hotel just outside the Quarter where his body had been found.

He'd met Joel at the Bourbon Pub the night after the first killing. Joel had just moved to the city to live with his friend Chance. Michel had recognized Chance and his other friends and knew that they were transvestite hustlers. He'd assumed the same about Joel but had taken him home that night anyway, against his better judgment.

In retrospect he knew that meeting Joel had been a turning point in his life. He'd started to fall in love with Joel that night and the following morning, and for the first time in his life he'd been able to imagine sharing his life with another man. It was the beginning of being able to see his sexuality as an important, integrated part of his identity. In the course of the investigation he'd even made the choice to reveal his sexuality to Capt. DeRoche, though it turned out to be anticlimactic since DeRoche had already known.

Eventually he and Sassy had stopped the killer, but they hadn't really solved the case. They'd gotten lucky. Michel had allowed his personal feelings to cloud his judgment and as a result Lady Chanel, a transvestite who'd been a venerated figure in the city, had been killed. It had made Michel question his ability to do his job.

He remembered sitting with Sassy on his front porch a few weeks later. She'd told him then that something similar had happened during her rookie year that had cost the life of a young girl. He knew now that the girl was Iris Lecher. But what personal issues had she let interfere with her work? What she'd described at the station yesterday morning was simply a procedural mistake, an error in judgment. What she'd told him on the porch suggested something more than that.

The woman he knew was pragmatic and professional. On occasion he'd had the sense that her need to bring justice was personal, but he'd never seen her allow her personal feelings to get in the way of the job. He tried to imagine what she'd had been like twenty five years earlier, and what in her personal life may have caused her to make a critical mistake. Although he tried to suppress the thought, he wondered whether she had ever suspected Carl's involvement. He knew at some point he might have to ask her.

First, though, he needed to study the details of the Lumley

investigation to determine whether there'd been any obvious gaps. Then he'd look for evidence of any cover-up beyond what was already known. He hoped that he wouldn't find any, both for Sassy's sake and his own.

He considered whether he would continue to be a cop when the investigation was over. He'd taken his leave of absence because of his doubts about his ability to separate personal feelings from the job, and those doubts still existed. Even now he was back only because Sassy was involved. He knew that he would be spending the day at home instead of working if Carl Adams had been anyone else. And although he'd assured DeRoche that he could be objective, he questioned what he would actually do if he found that Sassy had been involved in something more serious.

He pushed the question away. Despite his doubts, he realized he was excited to be going back. On some level he'd missed the job. It had always given him a sense of purpose. For the last six months he'd been more relaxed and—as his relationship with Joel developed—happier than he'd ever been, but that purpose had been missing. Whether it was as a cop or something else, he knew he needed to get it back.

Chapter 10

Lecher had asked Mac MacDonald to meet him for breakfast at the Sheraton on Canal Street at 8 a.m. He'd chosen the spot because he knew that most of the other patrons would be from out of town. He didn't want to be seen by anyone in the police department.

MacDonald had seemed surprised to hear from him, and even more surprised when he'd asked to meet privately for breakfast. MacDonald had asked—and then demanded—to know the purpose of the meeting, but Lecher had been vague, saying only that it concerned the reputation of the department. MacDonald had finally agreed, though not without making his irritation known.

MacDonald was already seated at a table when Lecher walked in five minutes early. As he approached the table he reflected that in many ways MacDonald looked like he'd come from central casting. If one were to imagine how a sheriff might look, an image would come to mind that was very much like the actual man.

Although he'd been born and raised just outside the Crescent City, MacDonald had adopted a style that was decidely Texan. He wore a brown leather vest over a blue and red plaid shirt, the neck of which was secured with a black leather bolo tie with a silver cinch. His pants were heavy brown cotton with wide straight legs to allow for his brown suede silver-toed boots. A large silver and turquoise belt buckle peeked out from under his ample stomach. On the table to his right a tan felt cowboy hat sat covering a plate, indicating that MacDonald was concerned enough by Lecher's call to want to ensure that no one sat next to them.

Although it was well publicized during his campaign that MacDonald had given up drinking 10 years earlier, his round face had retained a florid fleshiness. It was a look that one might expect to see in any dollar-a-shot bar in town at one in the afternoon. His face was framed by longish silver-black hair that was combed straight back, and thick sideburns. His most striking features were a graying handlebar mustache that he'd started wearing when he received his first command, and heavy, jet black eyebrows that seemed not so much to have grown as exploded from his brow, a clear indication that he'd never wasted any time reading articles on male grooming.

"Stan, good to see you" MacDonald said, standing and stepping forward to shake Lecher's hand as he reached the table.

MacDonald's voice and actions betrayed the practiced manner of a skilled politician.

"Please, sit down," he said, ushering Lecher toward a chair with a grand gesture.

"Thanks for seeing me," Lecher said as he settled into the chair.

"Not at all," MacDonald said, waving a finger to get the waitress' attention.

They were silent for a minute while the young woman poured coffee. Neither man ordered food.

"So what's this all about?" MacDonald asked when they were alone again.

"What can you tell me about the Lumley case?" Lecher asked without hesitation.

He'd decided to take a direct approach with MacDonald.

"The Lumley case? What about it?" MacDonald responded, clearly taken by surprise.

"The night before last, Sassy Jones' ex-husband, Carl Adams, was found dead. Apparently a suicide," Lecher said.

"Your people found photos of three girls there, including my daughter, Iris."

"Jesus Christ," MacDonald said, exhaling loudly. "I'm sorry, Stan."

"I checked the Lumley files at the department and at our office and they've both been emptied," Lecher continued without acknowledging MacDonald. "I want to know why."

MacDonald stared at him blankly for a moment, then his face began to work angrily.

"What the hell were you doing looking at police files?" he asked in a low voice.

"Why were the records cleaned?" Lecher asked more aggressively, ignoring the question.

"How the hell should I know?" MacDonald exclaimed. "That was over twenty years ago."

"You signed for the autopsy reports," Lecher said flatly, "and I guess somebody forgot to lose the receipt."

MacDonald tried hard not to react, but Lecher could see the shock in his eyes. He could also see MacDonald calculating his response.

"So what?" MacDonald asked finally, in a carefully composed voice.

"So I thought maybe you'd want to tell me what happened rather than explaining it to the press," Lecher said, trying to sell his bluff by underplaying it.

MacDonald stared at him for a moment, taking the measure of his adversary.

"Go ahead," he said calmly. "Go to the press. You have no evidence of wrongdoing. They're going to see you as a grieving father who never got over the loss of his daughter spouting some crazy conspiracy theory. I'll make sure of that."

"Maybe I can't prove it," Lecher replied with equal calm, "but I guarantee you that if I go to the press and tell them that Carl Adams was found with the photos of two missing girls and one who was kidnapped and killed, and that the police and coroner's records from those cases are missing, and that you personally took possession of the autopsy reports, you're going to be in for one hell of a shit storm."

"I should throw your ass in jail. This is attempted blackmail," MacDonald said, shaking his head with contempt.

"Yeah, but you won't," Lecher replied steadily. "How's it going to look if the sheriff who based his entire campaign on cleaning up corruption was part of a cover-up that allowed a killer to walk the streets for the past twenty five years? Do you think the voters will respond favorably to that? And how long before people start questioning how you managed to rise so quickly in the department?"

"You son of a bitch," MacDonald said, but it was clear from his expression that he'd already moved past anger to the practical process of negotiation. "So what do you want?"

"The truth," Lecher said simply. "The department was trying to cover something up. From what I can figure, that means there was a fuck-up in the investigation. What was it?"

MacDonald gave Lecher an appraising look.

"You sure you want to know?" he asked.

Lecher nodded, though he no longer felt so certain.

"It wasn't a fuck-up in the investigation," MacDonald said quietly, leaning closer and looking around to make sure no one was within listening distance. "It was what happened that night. Lumley had already been ruled out as a suspect, but Jones stopped by to ask him a follow-up question. It was spur-of-the-moment. She said she was on her way to the market with a friend and was passing his house. She stumbled into it."

He paused for a moment.

"Go ahead," Lecher said, his tone already resigned to what he would hear.

"Lumley shot her first. She got off a shot as she went down but didn't kill him. He killed your daughter and then himself while Jones was unconscious. Her friend heard the shots and called it in. When I got there Jones was almost dead, too."

Lecher closed his eyes and gripped the sides of the table tightly, fighting back nausea.

"And why the cover up?" he asked in a tight voice without opening his eyes. "To protect one of your own?"

"To protect everyone," MacDonald said. "Would it have made it easier for you if you'd known the truth?"

Lecher's eyes opened suddenly and he fixed MacDonald with an angry glare.

"You were trying to protect me?" he asked incredulously. "You thought it would be better for me if I didn't know that my daughter died unnecessarily because one of your cops fucked up? Bullshit. This was all about covering your own asses."

"It was also out of compassion for Jones," MacDonald said.

"For Jones? Why, because you didn't want to make her feel bad?" Lecher asked sarcastically. "Since when does the department practice positive reinforcement therapy?"

"Because she lost her baby." MacDonald replied solemnly.

"Baby?" Lecher asked, the sarcasm suddenly gone from his voice.

"She was ten weeks pregnant," MacDonald replied. "The bullet killed her baby."

Lecher felt his anger suddenly blunted by a surge of compassion. Whatever mistakes Sassy had made, she'd paid a price as steep as his own for them. He didn't know if he would ever forgive her, but he could empathize.

"Look," MacDonald said suddenly, "if you want to burn this whole thing down that's up to you, but so far as I know there was never any evidence to suggest that Carl Adams was involved. As for Jones, yeah, she fucked up, but she didn't know what she was getting into that night. Christ, she was just out of the academy. She didn't have experience in a situation like that. She was a victim, too."

He looked at Lecher expectantly.

"So what's it going to be, Stan? It's your move."

"I want the files," Lecher answered.

"For what?" MacDonald asked.

"I'm sorry, Mac, but I can't just take your word for everything. I need to know that Carl Adams was never a suspect. I need to know that there was no evidence that Lumley had a partner. I need to know that Lumley died the way you said. And I won't know those things until I see the reports, including the autopsy photos. Then I'll let it go."

"I'll see what I can do about the police files," MacDonald said with a deep sigh. "but the autopsy report and the photos are gone. I burned them myself on the way back to the station."

"Why?"

"Because that's what I was told to do," MacDonald replied. "You may think that I got where I am because I was willing to play dirty for the big guys, but that's not the way I saw it. Maybe I was naive, but I trusted them. If they told me something was necessary I believed them and did it. Later on when I quit drinking and started to realize the truth, I vowed to clean up the department. But I couldn't undo the past."

Lecher shook his head slowly.

"I never thought you were dirty," he said. "If I did I wouldn't have come to you in the first place. I just need your help."

Chapter 11

Sassy heard footsteps coming from the front porch of her house and leaned back in her chair to peer down the hall. Through the screen door she saw Lou Mitchell searching through his mailbag.

"Anything good today, Lou?" she called.

"Ed McMahon says you may have won a million dollars," he called back.

It was a joke she'd heard hundreds of times over the years but it still made her smile.

"Not like you to be home on a Friday morning, Miss Jones. You on vacation?" Mitchell asked without looking up.

"Something like that," she replied.

"Well you have a good one," Mitchell said as he placed her daily allotment of catalogs, letters and bills into the mailbox and headed on his way without waiting for a reply.

Sassy put the worn notebook she'd been leafing through on the coffee table and got up. Although she'd stayed in bed until almost nine that morning, a rare treat on a weekday, she'd slept fitfully and her body felt stiff. She rolled her head in a circular motion for a moment to loosen up her neck and shoulders, then walked down the hall to the front door. The early morning air had been cool but now she could feel the temperature rise with each step. Feels like summer's here a little early, she thought. She retrieved her mail and closed the front door against the heat, then walked into the kitchen.

Junk, junk and more junk, she thought as she stood over the

51

trash, sorting through the pile and dropping each offending piece into the open lid. When she'd finished she was left holding only her electric and VISA bills and a small white envelope with her address handwritten in black ink. There was no return address.

She placed the bills on the counter and took the envelope into the living room, running it through her fingers as she went. She could feel something small and hard inside. She examined the front and saw it had been postmarked in New Orleans on March 29, two days earlier. She turned it over and stared at the back but didn't move to open it. Mysterious letters had always made her nervous. They were like phone calls in the middle of the night: either bad news or from someone from whom you didn't want to hear. She held the envelope up to the sunlight coming through the back window and could make out the shape of a small key inside.

"Okay, this is silly," she said out loud. "If it's bad it ain't gonna get any better sitting in that envelope."

She pushed the nail of her right index finger under the flap and tore along the top seam. Inside was a single sheet of unlined white paper, folded in half with a brass key nestled in the crease. She carefully removed the key, holding the bottom of the stem between her right thumb and forefinger. It was tarnished and surprisingly heavy. One side of the round head was stamped with a fleur de lis with the letters B N O across the three petals. She recognized it as the logo of the Bank of New Orleans. The other side was engraved with the numbers 213 and the letters R.E.L. in a smaller size underneath. She took out the sheet of paper. It was blank.

"Is this where you put my million dollars, Ed?" she mused aloud to herself.

She placed the key back in the envelope and studied the address again. The handwriting looked familiar. She leaned forward and hooked her fingers into the cardboard box to her left, then pulled it between her feet. She reached inside and began sifting through the contents. After a minute she pulled out a faded red card. On the cover was a photo of Carl wearing a green-and-red striped stocking cap. He was seated on the lap of a department store Santa Claus. He'd given her the card on their first and only Christmas together. She opened it.

Sassy,
Having you in my life is the greatest gift I could ever have asked for.

Love,
Your devoted elf, Carl

She compared it to the envelope beside her. The handwriting was identical. She closed the card and put it back in the box, then got up and went to the kitchen. From a cabinet in the corner below the phone she took out a Yellow Pages directory and turned to the bank section. There were four branch office listings for the Bank of New Orleans: two in Metairie and two in New Orleans. None of them were close by. The two offices in Metairie were near Lake Pontchartrain in the Jefferson Parish. Carl had been living in the Warehouse District near Magazine Street, but the Magazine Street branch was several miles west beyond the lower Garden District. The other New Orleans branch was north, on Robert E. Lee Boulevard in the Spanish Fort area. Sassy thought of the letters on the key: R.E.L.

She picked up the phone and began dialing the number she knew too well.

"Detective Doucette," Michel answered on the first ring. "How may I help you?"

"How may I help you? I guess someone's excited to be back at work," Sassy said sarcastically. "Used to be I'd have to remind you that you were a public servant."

"Well, no one else was around," Michel replied in a small, embarrassed voice.

"It's okay," Sassy said. "So what are you doing for lunch?"

"Lunch? I've only been back at work for 3 hours."

"I need you to go to the bank with me," she replied.

"Why, are they giving away toasters again?" Michel asked.

"Toasters?" Sassy asked. "Damn, you're older than you look. No something much better. And don't forget to bring your rubber gloves."

*****

She picked Michel up at 12:15 pm and filled him in on the key as they headed north toward the Spanish Fort area. Fort St. John had been built by the French in the early 1700s to protect the city and the critical Bayou St. John trade route. It was rebuilt by the Spanish in 1779. In 1823 the fort was purchased by an American business man named Harvey Elkins who recognized the potential of the site as a lakeside resort and built a hotel. The area entered the height of its popularity in the late 1800s with the reconstruction of the Pontchartrain Hotel and the addition of a concert pavilion, casino, theater, restaurants and bathing piers, and the opening of a rail line from downtown New Orleans. In 1877 the site was purchased by Moses Schwartz who developed an amusement park. Dubbed the "Coney Island of the South," the park operated until the late 1920s. Like other areas of the city, the Spanish Fort had been in decline ever since. All that remained of the fort itself now was a brick wall across the street from a housing project.

They arrived at the Bank of New Orleans just before 12:30 and were ushered into the office of Mrs. Adell White, the branch manager. White was seated behind a large, intricately carved cherry desk. She was a small woman with a head of thick curly silver hair that contrasted sharply with her deep brown skin. She wore a pale blue jacket and a collared white blouse that was fastened at the neck with a cameo broach. They could only guess at what she wore below the waist since she made no attempt to stand to greet them. She simply peered at them over the top of her glasses and motioned them to the worn leather chairs in front of her desk.

"How may I help you?" she asked, though her tone suggested she considered their presence to be an annoyance.

"What can you tell us about this key?" Sassy asked, taking the key out of the envelope and holding it up by stem.

White pushed her glasses up and squinted at her without leaning forward.

"Give it here," she said, motioning brusquely.

"I'm sorry," Sassy replied evenly, "but I can't allow you to touch it."

White responded with a look of shock. It was clear that she was a woman accustomed to people doing as they were told.

"And why not?" she asked, sitting back in her chair and putting her hands on her tiny waist in a gesture of irritation.

"Because it's police evidence," Sassy replied. "I'm Detective Jones. This is Detective Doucette."

"And you have identification?" White asked with a tight smile.

"Of course," Michel said as he and Sassy placed their identification on the desk.

"Is it all right if I touch these?" White asked with more than a touch of sarcasm.

Michel and Sassy nodded as she leaned forward and picked up one wallet with each hand. It was obvious from the expression on her face that she was unhappy that they hadn't placed them within easy arms' reach. She held the two IDs up in front of her face and carefully studied them, looking over the tops at Michel and Sassy several times to confirm that they were, indeed, the people in the photos.

"Very well," she said finally, placing the wallets back on her desk so that Sassy and Michel had to stand to retrieve them.

It was clear she wanted to let them know who was in control in her bank.

"So can you *show* me this key then?" she asked.

"Certainly." Sassy said holding it up again.

When White made no motion to rise Sassy stood and walked slowly around the desk. Michel struggled not to laugh at the dour expression on her face.

Sassy held the key out and White reached up and grasped her wrist, pulling the key closer as she tilted her head up to see through the bottom of her bifocals. Sassy noted that for her age and diminutive size, White's grip was quite firm.

"Ah yes," White said. "That's one of our safe deposit keys."

She let go of Sassy's wrist and gave a slight nod of her head to indicate that Sassy was being dismissed. Sassy turned away and rolled her eyes at Michel as she walked past him on the way back to her chair.

"So it is from this branch then?" Michel asked.

"What else would the initials mean?" White responded smugly.

Sassy fought the urge to think of some obscene options.

"That was our assumption, Mrs. White," she replied instead. "We'd like to open the safety deposit box."

White fixed her with a stern expression.

"Do you have a warrant?" she asked.

"Look, lady," Sassy replied angrily, finally tired of the older woman's attempts to exert control, "The owner of that key is dead and this is a murder investigation. We don't need a warrant."

"Well why didn't you say that before?" White sniffed with exaggerated offense. "Come with me."

She rose quickly and walked out of the room without waiting for them. Sassy and Michel exchanged surprised looks and hurriedly followed.

"I half expected her to be wearing jack boots," Michel whispered as he nodded at the low-heeled black shoes White wore below her long pale blue skirt.

They caught up with her at the entrance to the safety deposit vault.

"Now I just need you to confirm the name on the account," White said as she opened a drawer in an old oak cabinet by the door and removed an index card.

She held it close to the end of her nose and quickly glanced at the information on it, then looked up expectantly at Sassy. This was something Sassy hadn't anticipated and she wondered if the surprise showed on her face. Until that moment she hadn't considered that the account might not be in Carl's name and suddenly regretted rushing to the bank. If she was wrong, White would undoubtedly call the department to report the incident and her suspension might become permanent.

"Well?" White prodded.

Sassy took a deep breath.

"Carl Adams," she said quickly.

"Very well," White replied, nodding toward the vault. "This way."

*****

Mrs. White and Sassy went to the room where the safe deposit boxes were housed while Michel waited in a private room in the vault. Without hesitating White walked directly to a spot two-thirds of the way down the left wall and pointed at the door for box 213. Sassy removed two surgical gloves from her left pocket and deftly pulled them on. She reached into her right pocket and removed the key while White turned away from her for a moment. When the woman turned back she was holding a similar key on a thin silver chain. Sassy wondered if White had turned away out of secrecy or modesty since it would have been necessary to unfasten the top of her blouse to remove the key from around her neck. She guessed the latter and it made her smile for a second.

They put their keys into adjacent locks on the small brass door and turned them simultaneously. The door swung open from the left. Sassy reached inside and removed a gray metal box approximately eight inches wide by six inches high by eighteen inches deep. She followed White down the hallway to the room where Michel waited.

"I'll be in my office when you're done," White said efficiently as she left Sassy standing outside the door.

Sassy watched the little woman walk to the vault entrance and turn left toward her office, then she opened the door to her left. Michel was leaning against the far wall pressing the gloved fingers of his right hand into the crooks between the gloved fingers of his left.

"These things are too tight," he said. "I need to get some larger ones."

Sassy let out a small barking laugh.

"Yeah right. If I had a dime for every guy who's told me that," she said, shaking her head.

Michel stared back at her open-mouthed. Even after all these years she could still shock him with her sudden lewd humor.

"If you weren't already on suspension I'd bring you up on charges of sexual harassment," he said with mock indignation.

"Whatever, little man," Sassy replied as she placed the safe deposit box on the scarred oak table in the center of the room. "You ready?"

"Are you ready?" Michel replied with a searching look.

"As I'm ever going to be," Sassy said.

*****

She and Carl finally became intimate on a typically sultry night that July in the small apartment she'd rented in the Bywater section of the city. Unlike her uncle, Carl had been a tender and giving lover who took the time to ensure that he pleased her, too. After, as she lay in his arms on top of the rumpled sheets of her narrow double bed, she thought how different this had been. She'd never truly understood how sex could be an expression of emotion.

She'd understood love, but not its connection to sex. Sex as she'd known it was painful. It was something to be taken from her and endured during the taking. Now she understood the difference between sex and making love.

As she lay in the darkness listening to Carl's breathing deepen into sleep, she felt exhilarated and powerful. Desire and the pleasures her body could experience had been unknown to her. Like relationships, they were things she'd never dwelled on. Carl had helped her discover those things.

She realized that she also felt guilty. It wasn't guilt about the act itself. She wasn't possessed of a puritan morality. It was simply that she felt she'd used Carl. It was clear that his passion had been a pure expression of love. She knew that she loved him, too, on some level, but it wasn't equal. For her their intimacy had also been selfish. It had been another new experience for her to collect.

She reaffirmed her intention to end the relationship soon. It was unfair to Carl to let it continue. He was kind and considerate and treated her as well as any man ever could. She couldn't fault him for any of the things he was or did. He didn't deserve to be led on when she knew the relationship couldn't continue. It was unfair, she knew, because he couldn't undo the things he'd done in his past and she truly believed that he was a changed man. Still, she couldn't allow his past to hurt her future.

*****

"I guess this was his final 'fuck you'," Sassy said sadly as she stared at the photos covering the top of the table.

The safety deposit box had contained thirty six Polaroid photos. Most had names written on the bottom in large block letters. She and Michel had arranged them in three neat rows of twelve in what seemed to be chronological order, based on the amount of wear and tear on each and the quality of the images. The photo in the bottom right corner was crisp and seemed to be carefully composed, as if the photographer had been developing his craft over the course of years. The photo in the upper left corner was blurred, as though it had been taken in a hurry or the photographer had been frenzied.

In each there was a single girl. They appeared to range in age from 11–15 years or so. Most were blond. As in the photos found at Carl's house, they were all seated on a twin mattress with their backs against a vertical wood post and their arms handcuffed over their heads. Each was also gagged by a white cloth. A few had cuts and bruises on their wrists, indicating they may have struggled to free themselves, but most appeared calm, as though they'd been drugged. They all had a resigned, almost weary look in their eyes.

Some of the photos looked to have been taken from the exact same position, suggesting the camera had been mounted to a fixed tripod, though all were nearly identical. There was a fetishistic repetition evident in the collection.

"Sas, I'm sorry," Michel said, gently putting his right arm over Sassy's shoulders.

"I'm responsible for this," she said quietly.

"No, you're not," he said firmly. "Carl was responsible."

"I know that," Sassy said, "but if I'd done my job correctly he wouldn't have had a chance to kidnap and probably kill thirty six more girls."

"Look at me," Michel said, turning her to face him. "You can't blame yourself. There was a whole department working on the investigation. No one found any evidence that Carl was involved."

Sassy was silent. In her heart she still felt she should have known because Carl was her husband, but she knew that if she said it Michel would respond as Lecher and Eldridge had.

"So what do you want to do?" Michel asked carefully.

"Take them to headquarters," Sassy replied dully. "You have thirty six more potential killings to investigate."

"Are you sure?" he asked.

Sassy nodded and gave him a brave smile.

"And how do I explain how they came into my possession exactly?" Michel asked. "My return to duty is going to be very short if DeRoche finds out I came out here with you knowing that there might be evidence in that box and didn't tell him."

"What's the choice?" Sassy asked, with a shrug. "You want to put them back and ask that nice Mrs. White to pretend that she never met us before when you come back with a search warrant?"

Michel was encouraged by her humor and pretended to weigh the options for a moment before responding.

"Okay," he replied, "but you're coming with me."

Chapter 12

"What part of 'suspended' didn"t you understand?" Capt. DeRoche demanded angrily as soon as they walked through the door of his office.

The few detectives at their desks nearby looked up, shocked by the uncharacteristic outburst. As DeRoche shifted his gaze toward them through the windows of his office they quickly dropped their heads and tried to look busy. Michel closed the door.

"How did you know?" Sassy asked, though she suspected the answer.

"I got a call from the bank manager, a very concerned woman named..."

"Mrs. White," Sassy finished.

"Yes," DeRoche said, glaring at her. "She called to confirm that two of my detectives had been sent to her bank to collect the contents of a safe deposit box from one her customers as part of a murder investigation."

"Fucking old witch," Sassy muttered under her breath.

"Excuse me?" DeRoche said, giving her a castigating look.

"Nothing," Sassy replied.

DeRoche looked at Michel.

"And you," he said. "You haven't even been back on the job for half a day and already you're making your own rules."

Michel thought better of correcting his boss by pointing out that he had, in fact, passed the halfway point of his first day.

"Let me explain, Captain," Sassy said, hoping to deflect the brunt of his anger away from Michel. "I asked him to come to the bank with me as a favor."

"Oh, I see," DeRoche said, feigning sudden enlightenment. "Because you asked him that makes him suddenly incapable of following orders."

Sassy stared at him for a moment without speaking. Michel could see the muscles of her jaw flexing.

"Look," she said, her anger barely controlled, "we can deal with all this later. I've already had enough shit from the little commandant at the bank."

DeRoche sat back in his chair and gave her a stunned look.

"I got an envelope in the mail this morning with a key in it," she continued. "There was no return address. I suspected it was from Carl but I didn't know for sure. For all I knew it could have been from my Aunt Audrey. But just in case I was right, I called Michel and asked him to come with me because he's the detective working the case. We went to the bank and got this."

She placed the box on DeRoche's desk.

"There are photos of thirty six more girls inside, all chained up and gagged like the three in the photos found at Carl's. We followed proper procedures so the evidence hasn't been tainted."

She took the envelope containing the key out of her inner jacket pocket and placed it on top of the box.

"Jesus Christ," DeRoche said slowly, staring at the box as if it contained the head of Medusa.

"Most have names written on them," Michel said, "so that should help us with identification, and we'll be able to narrow the search more using the serial numbers on the backs of the photos to find out when and where the film was sold."

"Jesus Christ," DeRoche repeated to himself, apparently not hearing.

Sassy looked questioningly at Michel and then at DeRoche. She realized that he was just beginning to comprehend the implications of the photos.

"Captain, are you all right?" she asked.

DeRoche looked up at her with a mixture of anger and bewilderment.

"Thirty six girls," he said.

"I know," she said calmly but deliberately.

"We may have the blood of thirty six girls on our hands," DeRoche said bitterly.

"Yes, we may," Sassy replied slowly, "but until we know for sure, there's no use wasting time with self-pity."

The words seemed to snap DeRoche out of his shock and he looked at her soberly. He thought about challenging her characterization of his feelings but realized she was probably describing her own initial reaction as much as his own.

"You're right," he said, looking into her eyes.

Sassy thought she detected a hint of compassion in the look.

"Was there a note in the box or the envelope?" he asked.

She shook her head.

"No, but the handwriting on the address looks like Carl's," she replied.

"Do you have a sample we can use for comparison?" DeRoche asked, his focus clearly back.

"I can send one over this afternoon," Sassy replied.

"Good," DeRoche said. "Is there anything in the photos to indicate where they were taken?"

Michel shook his head.

"Nothing obvious," he replied. "The setup is the same in all of them, but it's not even clear they were taken in the same place."

"Okay," DeRoche said, looking at him. "Log everything into evidence and get it dusted for prints. Also have the lab record the serial numbers for the film and contact the manufacturer to find out when and where the film was sold. I also want a team sent to Adams' place to search for other photos or items that might have belonged to any of the girls."

He looked at Sassy.

"You go home."

"Yes, sir," she replied.

"And just so you both know," DeRoche said, looking from Sassy to Michel and back, "at some point we will get back to your disregard for orders, not to mention the embarrassment you caused me with Mrs. White. She was ready to call the commissioner's office."

Sassy and Michel nodded, suddenly understanding that a large part of DeRoche's initial anger had been caused by having to deal with Adell White.

"Sorry, Captain," Sassy said.

He held up his hand, indicating the subject was closed for now. Michel picked up the box and started to follow Sassy to the door.

"Just a second, Michel," DeRoche said. "I want to talk to you for minute."

Michel and Sassy exchanged worried looks as she walked out the door and closed it behind her.

"Don't make me regret letting you work this case," DeRoche said as soon as Sassy was out of sight and Michel was seated. "You agreed to keep me in the loop on everything and then first chance you get you two run off chasing clues like the Hardy Boys. You're a great team and that's why I've never interfered with your work, but I need you to work with me this time. Until the investigation is over, Sassy is just another witness in a case you're working and you need to keep your priorities straight. If you're more concerned with being her friend then give me your badge now. You want to be a cop, then play by my rules."

Michel nodded. DeRoche stared at him for a minute, trying to gauge the sincerity of the response. Finally he nodded as well.

"We got the ballistics report," he said. "The bullet came from the gun in Adams' hand."

"Was that ever in question?" Michel asked with a surprised look.

"Everything is in question," DeRoche replied. "I don't want to take a chance on missing anything this time around."

Michel thought he detected a hint of reproach in DeRoche's words and wondered if DeRoche was referring to what had happened twenty five years ago or on his own last case. He pushed the question away.

"And the gun?" he asked.

"It was registered to Adams," DeRoche replied, "And his were the only prints on it."

"Okay, then I guess I'd better get to work," Michel said.

He started to stand but DeRoche motioned him back into his chair.

"I want you to focus on identifying the girls in the photos and connecting them back to Adams," DeRoche said.

Before Michel could protest DeRoche stopped him.

"Don't read anything into it. I'm not punishing you," he said.

"But why do we have to connect the girls back to Adams?" Michel asked. "Their photos were in his safe deposit box."

"Which means that all we know so far is that he was in possession of borderline child pornography," DeRoche replied. "We don't even know if the girls are dead or alive. You need to find out who they are, establish a connection to Adams, and find out what happened to them."

"But what about the Lumley case?" Michel asked.

DeRoche shook his head with frustration.

"We're stalled on it for now," he said. "When we got the file it was virtually empty. Just a summary page."

Michel gave him a concerned look.

"What does that mean?" he asked.

"It means that the department was trying to cover its track," DeRoche replied. "There may have been more going on than we initially thought."

Chapter 13

Lecher closed the last of the three manilla folders on his lap and took a long sip of 18-year-old Glenfiddich. It was nearly midnight and he'd been reading through the Lumley case files for four hours. The documentation had been thorough and detailed. There was no doubt that the police department had been working the case hard. There was also nothing to suggest that there had been any errors or gaps in the investigation.

Only three things had struck him as odd: one was a date that Sassy had asked Lumley about when he'd been interrogated, the second was the person whose name he'd given as an alibi, and the third was the fact that Lumley had been interrogated at all.

At one point during questioning, Sassy had asked Lumley where he'd been on the night of April 30, but Iris had been kidnapped the following evening. Lecher wondered if she'd been trying to establish that Lumley had staked out the kidnapping the night before. As an alibi Lumley had said that he was in a bar with Carl Adams that night, and a notation initialled S.J. said that Adams had confirmed that fact.

That Lumley had been brought in was more peculiar. Based on his police record and the report of a psychiatrist who'd examined him while he was in juvenile detention as a teenager, there was nothing to suggest that he was a strong suspect. He'd told the psychiatrist that he'd been sexually abused by his father as a child, but the psychiatrist had noted that he thought the claims were false and had been made to elicit sympathy in hopes of leniency. All of Lumley's arrests as both a teenager and adult had been for theft and fencing stolen property. He had no history of violence. Still, Lecher knew that his own knowledge of criminal pathology was rudimentary, and Sassy's instincts had apparently been correct.

Everything in the report seemed to corroborate what MacDonald had told him, including a copy of the coroner's report indicating that Lumley had died of a self-inflicted gunshot to the right temple. The report had been signed by Dr. Vincent A. Kahrs, the city's chief coroner for thirty five years until his death in 1992. Kahrs had hired Lecher and Lecher knew he'd been a competent, if unremarkable medical examiner.

The fact that the files contained no photos from the autopsy or crime scene bothered him, however. As an investigator he'd been trained to believe only what he could see for himself and there was no visual evidence to support either the police or coroner's reports.

He placed the folders on the small table next to his chair and drained the last of the scotch in his glass. He knew he didn't need another drink but he also knew he wouldn't be able to sleep easily. As he pushed himself up from the deep red leather chair his eyes focused on a large, grainy, black and white photograph on the far wall of his study. It was a rare photo of the back seat of the limousine in which John Kennedy was assassinated, taken by a bystander moments after the President's body had been removed. It had been a gift from his friend Lou Donnells, a forensic photographer who had worked with the Police Department for over thirty years.

Lecher had worked several cases with Donnells shortly after joining the Coroner's Office and they'd developed a close friendship based on their mutual interest in crime scene analysis. Although he was hired simply to shoot the scenes, Donnells had developed an uncanny ability to analyze what had happened based solely on the visual evidence. He and Lecher had spent hours together studying photographs of crime scenes that Donnells had collected and comparing their conclusions with the official verdicts. Donnells had been both a close friend and mentor.

Lecher wondered suddenly how much of his own work Donnells had kept in his collection. Although they'd never discussed it, he'd always assumed that Donnells had photographed the scene of Iris' murder. Donnells had passed away five years ago and had been a widower at the time, but Lecher remembered meeting his daughter at her father's funeral. Perhaps she might still have her father's collection.

He walked to his desk and turned on his computer, then quickly logged onto the Louisiana Registry of Vital Records.

*****

Michel gently lifted his arm from Joel's chest and quietly slipped out of bed. Joel had quickly drifted off to sleep after a typically energetic round of sex, but Michel had lain awake for the last hour, listening to Joel's breathing and the occasional sentence fragments he uttered from his dreams. Someday, he thought, he would have to ask Joel about Mrs. Melvoin and her dog, Dig Dig, who seemed to be recurring characters in his night time visions. He walked down the hall to the back of the house, pausing to grab his cigarettes and lighter, and let himself out onto the pation.

Like many in the Quarter and Marigny, Michel's house had been built in the "shotgun" style popular throughout the South in the 1800s and early 1900s. They were narrow and deep, usually consisting of only 3 or 4 rooms built in a row off a single corridor. The name was thought to have been derived from the fact that a shotgun could be fired from the front of the house to the back without hitting anything, though it may have had its origin in the African word To-Gan, meaning "meeting house."

A previous owner had bought the adjoining house and taken down the dividing wall to create a wide central kitchen and the bedroom and bathroom that Michel had used as a boy. There was also a large room that spanned the full width of both buildings at the back of the house that served as a living room and dining room. The patio was accessible through double French doors along the back of the room.

Also like many houses in the area, Michel's home hid a deep back garden that was surrounded by a high brick wall. For as long as he could remember, this had been his favorite part of the house, a place where he could escape and think.

Immediately outside the back door a narrow brick path lead under an arch of bougainvillea to a wide circular brick patio with a small fountain at its center. Around the edges of the patio thick patches of flowering bushes offered up their scents. The brick outer walls were nearly invisible, shrouded by dense tangles of clematis and wisteria. When he was in the garden Michel felt that the rest of the world ceased to exist. There was only his private garden with its sweet smells and the tranquil burble of the fountain. The only reminder of the rest of the world was the occasional airplane that left its mark across the sky above.

After his mother passed away, Michel had moved back to the house, spending two months renovating it by himself. While he was grateful for the comfort the familiar surroundings gave him, he felt that he had to make the home his own. He couldn't live in a museum dedicated to his mother's memory.

He'd refinished the scarred cypress floors and replaced the yellowing striped and flowered wallpaper with paint. He'd also updated the kitchen and bathroom counters and fixtures and installed new appliances. Finally he'd moved into his mother's bedroom and converted his old room into an office. The house was his now. He felt comfortable there.

He sat on the low brick wall surrounding the fountain and lit a cigarette. Already he could feel the weight of his job settling back onto him. It wasn't unpleasant or unwanted, but he'd forgotten the way the job stayed with him. His mind had shifted back into its former gear and he was unable to disengage it.

It wasn't identifying the girls in the photos that worried him. That was just a simple matter of searching databases and sending copies of the photos to other law enforcement agencies around the country. His mind was focused instead on what DeRoche had told him about the Lumley file. For five years his trust in Sassy had been absolute. Although he didn't want to admit it, the missing file and the events of twenty five years earlier had planted some doubt in his mind about her. It wasn't that he thought she was guilty of any real crime, but now he was forced to question her integrity. Was she actually the woman he'd thought she was?

A movement caught his eyes and he looked up to see a ghostly shape moving toward him under the shadowy arbor of Bougainvillea. As it moved into the full light of the moon it began to take more tangible form and he could see its untamed hair and sleek, naked body.

"Hey," he said.

"Hey, yourself," Joel said, walking across the patio and sitting next to him on the fountain wall. "Damn, this brick is cold."

"Maybe you should try wearing some clothes," Michel chided with a sarcastic smile.

"Why? You're just gonna rip 'em off me anyway, you big sex maniac," Joel replied, leaning over to kiss Michel on the cheek. "Besides, you're looking kind of naked yourself."

Michel laughed. He hadn't even been aware of his own nakedness.

"This is such a filthy habit," Joel said, deftly plucking the cigarette from Michel's hand and taking a deep drag on it. "You're really going to have to give it up one of these days."

Michel leaned back and gave Joel a deadpan look.

71

"Am I ever going to be able to finish a smoke on my own with you around?" he asked.

"Probably not," Joel replied around the cigarette firmly gripped in his lips, making it clear he'd claimed it as his own.

"Did I wake you?" Michel asked as he fished another cigarette out of the pack.

"No," Joel replied. "I woke up when I went to hug you and got an armful of pillow. I know you've been letting yourself go a little, but not that much."

Michel looked down at his flat stomach and then curled his upper lip as he shot Joel a sideways glance.

"You little fucker," he said.

"Darling, you can't be moaning 'oh you're so big' one minute and then be calling me a 'little fucker' an hour later," Joel said in his best Bette Davis voice as he took a dramatic drag on his cigarette. "It's just not consistent."

Although he knew he'd never spoken those words, Michel could feel himself blush.

"I should just drown you in the fountain now and save myself all the pain you're going to cause me," he muttered.

"Yes, but then you'd have to miss...the-e-e-e...dance," Joel replied.

Since he'd been working at the nursery, Joel had developed a fixation with the country music his co-workers favored and had begun working fragments of songs into his conversation. Michel guessed that this was one of those occasions and decided to let it go.

"I'm sorry," he said.

"For what?" Joel asked.

"For not being there when you woke up," Michel replied.

"Don't be," Joel said, leaning against Michel's shoulder. "This is actually how I always expected it to be, waking up in the middle of the night to find you gone on a case or brooding over the details in the darkness. I knew the last few months were Michel-lite."

Michel studied Joel's face, looking for hints of hurt or recrimination but could see none.

"And you're okay with that?" he asked.

Joel sat up and looked directly at Michel.

"Yeah, I am," he replied simply. "So long as you're with me when you can be, I'm okay with it."

He leaned forward and kissed Michel deeply, pushing his tongue past Michel's parted lips. Michel lifted his right hand and cupped it behind Joel's head as Joel slipped his left hand between Michel's thighs and began to stroke him.

"So," Joel said, barely pulling his lips away from Michel's, "you ever done any plowing in this garden?"

"You are such a dork sometimes," Michel replied softly.

Chapter 14

Deirdre Donnells lived on the first floor of a large Victorian, three blocks east of the campus of Loyola University where she taught undergraduate English. Lecher knew from her records that she'd owned the house for ten years. There were two other occupants listed at the address, both of them graduate students at Loyola.

The street was quiet and residential. Most of the homes were Victorian, though a few cottages dotted the block. It was a mature neighborhood, with tall oaks running along both sides of the street. The homes and yards were all well tended. As he drove past, Lecher noted the absence of toys or bicycles in the yards, suggesting that the residents were older; probably senior faculty members from Loyola and Tulane.

He'd called Donnells that morning and she'd agreed to meet at noon. As he pulled up in front of her house he saw a woman leaning into the open passenger door of an older silver Volvo parked in the driveway. She had a large, teal canvas bag imprinted with a white Loyola logo slung over her left shoulder and was gathering grocery bags into her arms.

"Oh, hey," Deirdre Donnells called as she stood and caught sight of Lecher. "Sorry but I'm running a little late. I ran into one of my students at the store and she wanted to talk."

"No problem," Lecher replied, walking toward her. "Do you need any help?"

"I think I've got it," Donnells replied, pushing the car door shut with her right hip, "but you could get the front door."

She jiggled the key ring dangling from the index finger of her right hand. Lecher took it and followed Donnells up onto the deep front porch of the house. Once they were inside she deposited her bundles on a cherry side table just inside the door and turned to face him.

"It's good to see you again," she said, leaning forward to give him a hug.

Although they'd met only once before, the gesture seemed natural and appropriate. Lou Donnells had adored his only child and Lecher felt as though he'd known her for years from hearing her father talk about her.

From her birth records, Lecher knew that Donnells was 57 years old, but she had a vibrant energy that made her seem much younger. It was similar to the energy her father had possessed. She had close-cropped silver hair and a wide, unlined face. Her eyes were large and startlingly pale blue, which made them appear even larger and gave her a look of pleasant astonishment. Although there was nothing particularly beautiful or even pretty about her features, Lecher thought that she was still quite attractive.

She was dressed in a loose, pale orange tunic blouse, cream linen pants, and old tan Birkenstock sandals. Her ears, neck and wrists were adorned by tastefully understated silver and turquoise jewelry. It was the look of a former hippie who'd achieved some measure of financial success without changing her basic style. Lecher had found it to be a common uniform of sorts among middle-aged academics, particularly those in the arts and literature.

The house, too, had an upscale bohemian feel. The living room was cluttered yet clean. The furniture was a mix of antique and contemporary, with oversized, comfortable couches and chairs nestled amongst beautifully crafted old wood tables and cabinets. Large colorful canvases, both modern and classical in style, covered most of the walls. As would be expected in the home of an English professor, thousands of books filled the shelves along one wall, with the overflow stacked in piles on the floor.

"Can I get you something to drink? Some iced tea?" Donnells asked, ushering Lecher into the room.

"No, thank you, I'm fine," he replied as he took a seat on one of the two facing red sofas that dominated the room.

Donnells settled onto the opposite sofa and kicked off her sandals.

"So I take it you haven't come a-courting," she said with a wry smile.

Lecher smiled back and shook his head.

"No, I'm afraid I haven't," he said. "I was hoping that you might be able to help me out with some of Lou's photos."

"Well I certainly have a lot of them," Donnells replied. "What are you looking for?"

"Some crime scene photos," Lecher replied.

"Oh God, those awful things," Donnells said. "For such a cheery man, I never could understand his fascination with those morbid pictures."

She gave an exaggerated shudder.

"Of course, I suppose it came with the job," she added quickly, remembering that Lecher shared her father's fascination.

"Yeah, I suppose so," Lecher said. "They're certainly not for everyone. So you got rid of them then?"

"Oh, no," Donnells replied, "I imagine they're out in the garage. I just put the boxes of all Dad's stuff out there after he died and I haven't gotten around to sorting them out yet."

For a moment she seemed lost in thought.

"I suppose that sounds terrible, doesn't it?" she said, looking back at Lecher. "Like I don't really care."

"Not at all," he replied with a kind smile. "It's not an easy thing to do. Our parents spend their entire lives accumulating the possessions that matter to them, and then we have to decide which of those possessions actually have some value to us. It's almost like having to pass judgment on their lives. Sometimes it's easier to just let it be. I imagine there are boxes that have been passed down from generation to generation that have never been opened."

Donnells looked at him with a mix of admiration and curiosity.

"That's somehow both comforting and really disturbing, Stan," she said with an amused laugh. "I suspect you have a unique perspective on death."

There was nothing judgmental in the words. It was simply an observation. Lecher shrugged in agreement.

"You won't mind going through the boxes on your own, will you? I've got to put away the groceries and...," she trailed off, leaving the thought incomplete.

"Not at all," he replied quickly, understanding the unspoken reason.

"Well, let me show you to the garage then."

*****

The eighteen boxes were unlabelled and the contents of each seemed to have been chosen at random. Lecher recognized many of the objects as he sorted through them and they brought back pleasant memories of the times he'd spent with his friend. After twenty minutes he'd finally found two boxes containing nine large leatherbound photo albums of crime scene photos and memorabilia, along with a loose assortment of larger photos. After another forty minutes of searching through the albums, Lecher had given up hope. None of Donnell's own work was included.

He placed the albums back in their boxes and stood up, arching his upper body backward to release the tension in his lower back, and let out a deep sigh. He knew he'd reached the end of his trail and although it went against his nature, he would have to accept the story Mac MacDonald had told him.

"Did you find what you were looking for?"

Lecher turned with a start to see Deirdre Donnell's standing in the doorway holding two glasses of iced tea.

"I'm afraid not," he replied, walking over to her.

"Well, what exactly was it?" she asked as she handed him a glass. "I might remember having seen something while I was packing up the boxes."

"Thank you," he said, tipping the glass to her before taking a long sip. "I'm looking for some photos Lou took of a crime scene 25 years ago."

Donnell's astonished eyes opened even wider.

"Oh, God, I'm sorry," she said. "I didn't realize you were looking for stuff that Dad shot. I've got his file cabinets down in the basement. I was planning to donate it all to the school at some point. I thought it might be useful for some of the criminology courses."

"I'm sure it would be," Lecher said. "Your father was very talented. I learned an awful lot from him."

"Thank you," Donnells said.

"So you think his case photos are down there?" Lecher asked hopefully.

"Every one of them," she replied with an enthusiastic nod. "Dad always said when you were working for the New Orleans Police Department you never knew when something might get conveniently lost."

"Smart man," Lecher said with a knowing smile.

*****

Ten minutes later Lecher was on his way back home. On the back seat of the car were the two boxes containing Lou Donnells' photo albums. Deirdre Donnells had insisted that he take them as a gift.

Although the unseasonably warm weather that had started the day before had blossomed into a full summer-like heat,

Lecher felt a chill as he looked at the yellow manilla envelope on the seat beside him. In Lou's Donnells' handwriting it had been inscribed with the words "Lumley — May 8, 1980." Lecher had looked in the envelope only long enough to confirm that it contained photographs.

Now as he neared the western edge of the French Quarter he wondered if he was truly ready to confront the details of his daughter's death. He knew he would never be satisfied about the events of that night until he could see the evidence for himself, but he also knew that the photos would make the way in which Iris died real in a way that he'd been able to avoid for over two decades.

He'd never allowed himself to think about her final moments and the fear and pain she'd endured. He'd been able to hold onto an image of her that was still alive and joyful. It was the way he'd chosen and wanted still to remember her, and he knew that he risked losing that image forever. Was that too high a price to pay to satisfy his own need for the truth, he wondered? But in his heart he already knew the answer.

Chapter 15

Michel looked up at the clock in the office that had been his childhood bedroom. It was nearly 3:45 pm. Joel would be home from work in another 15 minutes. He logged out of the missing persons database he'd been searching for the last four hours and collected the copies of the thirty Polaroid photos spread out on the floor beside him into a folder. He'd been able to identify six girls. The copies of their photos were now paperclipped to printouts of their information in a separate folder.

After finding only two of the girls by searching names, he'd expanded his criteria. As he'd feared, the actual first names of the other girls he'd identified had been different than those written on the photos, and all four were listed as probable runaways.

All six of the girls had disappeared within the last three years, two from northern Louisiana, one each from Mississippi and Florida, and two from along the Gulf Coast of Texas. So far he'd reviewed over 100 files. There were another 400 or so still to check: all of them girls under the age of 15 who'd gone missing in the last five years. So far he was limiting his search to the region stretching from Texas and Oklahoma east to North Carolina and south to Florida.

He placed the folders into the middle drawer of his desk and closed it. He'd made a conscious decision to try to keep his work separate from his life with Joel as much as possible. It wasn't that Joel had asked him, but that he wanted to maintain a balance in his life now. Work had always been his central focus, and in many ways he knew it always would be, but he no longer wanted it to be the only focus. Placing the files in the drawer was a symbolic gesture of that decision.

He logged onto his email and quickly began reading and deleting the slew of inter-departmental memos that had collected since morning. He'd often felt that the ease of communication brought about by computers had resulted in an increase in frequency and a sharp decline in quality and content. He consistently received emails on policies or investigations that had no relevance to him, most of them riddled with typos and grammatical errors.

The last email in the queue had been sent that morning by Earl Conroy from the department lab. It confirmed that Carl's fingerprints had been found on the photos and safe deposit box. There were other prints on the box, as well, but Michel guessed they belonged to either a previous renter or an employee of the bank. He knew that the formidable Adell White would never have granted access to anyone else. The email said the prints were being checked against the department's database. The lab had also identified traces of the powder used on surgical gloves on the photos.

He turned off the computer and went into the kitchen to make a sandwich for Joel. He felt tired and somewhat melancholy. He'd already contacted the trucking company to request copies of Carl's trip records and felt it would just be a matter of time before he could match the dates and route of one of those trips with the disappearance of one of the girls. The realization made him sad.

While he still had questions about her willingness to cover up what happened at Mose Lumley's house, he no longer questioned whether Sassy had known or suspected that Carl was responsible for the kidnappings. He'd seen the sadness and shock on her face when she saw the photos at the bank. Her reaction had been genuine and deep, and he knew that she would always blame herself on some level for whatever happened to those thirty six girls.

He wished for her sake that he could see some possibility that Carl had been innocent, but as he considered the evidence, that possibility seemed less and less likely.

*****

They continued dating throughout the summer and into the fall. Although she was unwilling or unable to end the relationship, Sassy was careful never to respond when Carl told her he loved her. She knew it wouldn't have been dishonest to tell him she loved him, too, but it wouldn't have been truthful either since she knew the love she felt for him was different. Her love was conditional and finite. She loved the person he was and the time they spent together, but she didn't love him enough to sacrifice her future to be with him.

It bothered her that she was treating Carl unfairly, but not enough to take action. In the back of her mind she hoped that the relationship would simply die on its own when she entered the academy. She knew that her free time then would be very limited and hoped that things would fade as they spent less time together. She hoped to avoid any final confrontation. Still, she kept her technicality intact, just in case: she'd never told Carl that she loved him.

When she finally entered the academy in November things did cool a bit. She was busy studying most nights and weekends and they were able to see one another only for brief periods once or twice a week. Carl remained constant, however. He called her daily, dropped off dinner on the nights he knew she was too busy to cook, and, when her birthday came, he sent three dozen roses to her house and offered to take her out for dinner. She declined but that didn't dampen his ardor.

Over the Christmas holiday she went back to Butte La Rose to visit her parents for a few days. When she returned she found a note from Carl under her door asking her to go out with him for New Year's Eve. She agreed. While she'd been grateful as some distance had developed in their relationship, she had to admit that she missed him. And maybe New Year's would also be a good time to officially transition their relationship into friendship, she reasoned.

*****

All day long a storm had been threatening the city, and when it finally hit a little after 7 pm its intensity was furious. As she stared out the window watching for Carl's car, Sassy could see the water already backing up out of the storm drains and creating pools in the street. As she looked down at her black silk Yves St. Laurent cocktail dress—a graduation gift she'd bought herself at a second-hand store with a large portion of her summer earnings—she regretted not owning an umbrella or boots for the first time in her life. They'd always seemed like such adult accessories to her and she'd never felt she had any clothing worth protecting before. She made a mental note to buy at least an umbrella that week.

Carl had been vague about their plans for the evening. All he'd told her was that she should "dress to impress" and be prepared to dine on the "finest cuisine the city has to offer." Now, as she watched her block begin to resemble Lake Pontchartrain she wished they were just staying in and ordering pizza.

She'd been excited and nervous all day. On the one hand she was looking forward to spending a whole evening with Carl. Even on their most mundane dates he made her feel special and she could only imagine what he had planned to celebrate the new year. On the other hand she knew that tonight would be the right opportunity to tell Carl the truth about her feelings for him and the future of their relationship. She was still unsure if she would take that opportunity.

She was startled by a knock at her door. She crossed the room and peered through the peephole. Sidney Poitier appeared to be melting in her hallway. She threw open the door to find Carl *standing in the doorway, a wicker picnic basket at his feet in the middle of a growing puddle. He was dressed in a black tuxedo, white wing-tipped shirt and black bow tie. He was clean-shaven and his hair had been cut very short.*

His effort at elegance had been undermined, however, by the rain that had soaked his clothes and hair and now dripped onto the floor from his nose and hands. The once squared shoulders of his jacket were rounded and slumped forward, forcing the sleeves almost to his fingertips. His pants bagged at the knees and the cuffs nearly hid shoes. His hair was matted and misshapen.

Sassy fought the impulse to laugh. The overall impression was truly comical but she could see the disappointment and humiliation in his face. He looked like a little boy who'd brought his mother flowers only to have her get stung by a bee that was hiding in them.

"Carl, are you all right?" she asked, gesturing him to come in.

"Just dandy," he replied with a sour smile.

He picked up the basket and walked slowly into the room. With each step Sassy could hear the squishing in his shoes and had to bite her lower lip to hold in the laughter.

"Let me get you a towel," she said, closing the door and hurrying to the bathroom.

She grabbed two large white towels and brought them into the living room. Carl just stood silently in the middle of the room, his body slightly trembling. Sassy didn't know if he was cold or crying and suddenly felt a strong desire to comfort him.

Carl turned his head and looked at her sadly for a moment.

"Surprise," he said in a small voice.

Sassy let out a loud snort. The laughter she'd been trying to contain suddenly burst forth. Carl stared at her with a look of dismay.

"You think this is funny?" he asked, turning to face her.

Sassy shook her head and tried to answer "no" but she was laughing too hard to speak. Carl appeared to be getting angry. He slowly and deliberately settled his arms across his chest. The air

84

trapped in the fabric of his jacket escaped with a loud, wet farting noise.

For a second Carl looked shocked. Then he began to chuckle. He looked down at his clothes and the chuckle began to grow into a full belly laugh. He doubled over, struggling to catch his breath.

"Oh, Lord," he managed to say, "I am so suave and sophisticated."

The words set Sassy off on a renewed jag of uncontrollable laughter and she had to wipe tears from her eyes.

"Stop, stop, stop," she said, waving her hand at Carl. "Don't say anything else."

They stood there just laughing for another three minutes. Each time one of them would start to calm down the other would make a noise that would get them going anew. Finally they began to calm down together.

"Okay," Sassy said finally. "You need to get out of those wet clothes before you kill me.

*****

While Carl dried himself, Sassy hung his clothes over the tub. She grabbed an orange silk robe from the back of the door and walked back into the living room. Carl was kneeling down in front of the picnic basket. It had been over a month since they'd last made love and the sight of his taught, naked body excited her. She imagined how it would feel to run her hands over that body. She pushed the thought away and handed him the robe.

"Thanks, baby," he said, standing and taking it from her.

He leaned in and gave her a lingering kiss. She fought the urge to reached down between his legs.

"You're welcome," she said, breaking the kiss and taking a step back.

She didn't know if she could trust herself to be so near Carl.

"So what's in the basket?" she asked quickly.

"Just what I promised you," Carl replied as he slipped the robe

over his shoulders and loosely tied it around his waist. "The best cuisine this city has to offer."

He knelt by the basket again and removed two large white bags. They were slightly damp but held together. He placed them on the floor and reached back into the basket. He pulled out a bottle of Dom Perignon and handed it to Sassy.

"My goodness," she said, "you've gone all out."

"Of course," Carl said with a courtly gesture. "Nothing but the best for my lady."

He grabbed the two bags and stood up.

"Sorry but I didn't have room for fine china and silverware," he said.

"That's okay," Sassy said. "Why don't you open this while I get some glasses and plates."

She handed him the champagne bottle and went to the kitchen. When she came back carrying the plates, glasses and utensils, Carl was placing a single red rose in a crystal vase on the table.

"Where did that come from?" she asked.

"From my magic basket," he replied.

"What else you got in there?" Sassy asked, arching her eyebrows provocatively.

"You'll have to wait to see," Carl replied with a devilish grin.

*****

An old friend of Carl's from Detroit who was now working as a line cook at Galatoire's, one of New Orlean's oldest and most esteemed restaurants, had provided him with a meal of fried oysters and bacon en brochette, veal chops in bearnaise sauce, and seafood-stuffed eggplant. Sassy decided not to ask exactly how the transaction had taken place. Although the food was slightly cold, it was truly some of the finest she'd ever tasted.

As they ate they filled one another in on the latest events in their lives. Carl told Sassy about some of the odder people he'd met during his travels and she told him about her latest courses at the academy. The evening was relaxed and the conversation was easy.

After they finished the main course Carl insisted that Sassy relax while he cleared the table and washed the dishes. He returned a few minutes later with one small plate and one spoon.

"What are those for?" Sassy asked.

Carl smiled enigmatically as he placed the plate and spoon on the table in front of Sassy and squatted down to his picnic basket with his back to her. When he stood up and turned back he was holding a small, white ceramic cup in his right hand and a miniature blue blow torch in his left.

"Voila!" he said.

"You planning to burn me up and put my ashes in that little cup?" Sassy asked, eyeing him curiously.

"Creme Brulee," he replied. "Leon told me I have to burn the top before I serve it."

He placed the cup on the plate and stood the blow torch on the edge of the table, then pulled a box of wooden matches from the right pocket of Sassy's robe. He removed a match and lit it with a flourish.

"Pretty slick," Sassy said admiringly.

Carl nodded and held the match in front of the copper nozzle of the torch as he slowly twisted the valve at the back. With a sudden whooshing sound the end began to glow with a blue flame.

"You're not gonna burn my house down, are you?" Sassy asked with a smirk.

Carl gave her a mock look of hurt.

"Oh ye of little faith," he said as he picked up the blow torch and began searing the top of the creme brulee.

After a few seconds he turned off the torch and placed it on the floor.

"I'm impressed, Mr. Adams," Sassy said.

"Thank you," Carl replied as he sat back at the table.

Sassy picked up a spoon and tapped the tip through the brown shell that had formed on the dessert. She scooped out a small mouthful and brought it to her lips.

"Oh my God," she said, closing her eyes as she savored the flavor, "this is amazing."

"That's what I hear," Carl said proudly.

"You aren't going to have any?"

Carl shook his head.

"It's just for you," he replied.

"Well, thank you," Sassy said. "This has been wonderful. You've outdone yourself tonight, Carl. I don't know how it could get any better."

She leaned over and kissed him on the left cheek. Carl beamed back at her, clearly pleased with himself.

"Well," he said. "I've actually got one more surprise for you."

He stood up and reached into the left pocket of Sassy's robe, then got down on one knee beside her. He held out a small, black velvet box in his left hand and flipped open the lid with his right.

"Will you marry me, Alexandra Jones?" he asked.

Chapter 16

Lecher had spent the afternoon finding ways to avoid confronting the contents of the envelope he'd gotten at Dierdre Donnells. Each time he'd gone to open it he'd thought of a chore that needed doing first. Now as he sat behind his desk with the envelope in front of him he knew he'd run out of excuses.

He closed his eyes and took several deep breaths as his left hand found the envelope. He opened the flap and reached inside with his right hand. He could feel the slick cold surface of the top photograph under his thumb. Slowly he pulled the photos out and placed them on the blotter in front of him, then brought his hands down over his stomach and clasped them tightly. He took another deep breath, trying to prepare himself for what he would see when he opened his eyes. His skin seemed to tingle and he could hear two sparrows playing in the bushes outside his window. All of his senses had become hyper-acute. He opened his eyes.

A close up image of the right side of Mose Lumley's head lay on the top of the pile. There was a dime-sized hole in his temple. The skin around the edges was raised and purplish black and there was a thin line of blood running from it to the back of his head. There was a larger circular pattern of first-degree burns around the wound. Lecher knew that meant Lumley had held the gun at a distance of a few inches from his head. If he'd held it directly against the skin the heat of the blast would have immediately cauterized the wound and the burn pattern would have been smaller.

Lecher stared at Lumley's profile. Although he'd long ago lost the naive notion that evil could be seen in the faces of killers, he was surprised by the softness of Lumley's face. Lumley's deep chocolate brown skin was smooth and his cheeks were full and rounded. With his long lashes he had an almost childlike look, save for his mustache and goatee. It looked like the photo of a man-boy caught peacefully napping. For the first time Lecher knew the face of his daughter's killer and it wasn't what he'd expected.

He took another deep breath and turned over the first photo. Underneath was a single sheet of plain white paper with a handwritten letter on it. Lecher recognized Lou Donnell's writing. It was dated September 18, 1999, a few months before Donnells had died. He'd already been diagnosed with lung cancer by then.

Lecher picked up the note and began reading.

Stan,

If you're reading this it probably means I'm gone. Hopefully I went peacefully and didn't end up the subject of some other photographer's work. If I did, I hope they lit me well.

I always knew that someday the truth about the Lumley case might come out and you'd find yourself looking at these pictures. You should know now that I've destroyed all of the photos and negatives of Iris. You'll have to trust me, Stan, there was nothing to be gained by you seeing them. Although it will be small comfort, you should know that she died quickly and she was never sexually abused.

I'm sorry that I never told you the truth. You need to believe that. It was a complicated situation and I just never saw any good coming from you knowing it.

When it happened we obviously didn't know one another. It was just another instance of the department taking the course that was most expedient and caused the least amount of scandal and I went along with it...as I did so many other times throughout the years. I'm not proud of that, but it was what I needed to do to survive. I'm not above admitting that sometimes I was a selfish man.

Later when we became friends, and I hope you will still think of me that way, I thought many times to tell you the truth, but I convinced myself that more bad than good would come from it. It would only take away any peace you'd managed to gain over the years. It would also cause problems for Detective Jones. I don't know whether she deserves sympathy for what happened that night or not, but I've watched her over the years and she's grown into a good cop. Maybe it's not my place to decide, but I feel like she's earned some peace.

Stan, I hope someday you'll be able to forgive me. I guess I'm just a sick old man trying to bargain his way into heaven now, but I truly believed that what I was doing was right. Maybe you'll see that some day.

Lou

Lecher put the letter down and sat back in his chair. He'd tried to prepare himself for anything he might find in the envelope, but he hadn't been prepared for what Donnells had written. He felt a mix of conflicting emotions: anger and relief, hurt and gratitude. On some level he felt betrayed, yet he also understood that Donnells had been protecting him as a true friend would. He tried to imagine himself in the same situation. He wanted to believe that he would do what was right, but as he'd learned over the years, sometimes there was a difference between what was technically right and morally right. He accepted intellectually that sometimes lies were right if they were told with compassionate intentions. In that moment he silently forgave Donnells.

He stood up and spread the photos out on his desk. There were ten in all. As he surveyed them he began shuffling them around until they formed a logical sequence, starting at the entrance to the room and ending with the close-ups of Lumley's body. He knew this was the way that Donnells would have shot them, from overview to detail. He began to study the sequence.

*****

Joel and Michel were clearing their dinner dishes when the phone rang. Michel crossed the kitchen and looked at the Caller ID: it showed Sassy's number. He hesitated, remembering DeRoche's admonishment not to blur the line between his friendship with Sassy and his professional responsibility. Joel gave him a questioning look and Michel mouthed Sassy's name in response.

"She can't hear you," Joel said in a loud voice, rolling his eyes.

Michel looked dumbfounded for a moment, then began laughing at his own ridiculousness. He picked up the phone.

"Mr. Chow's House of Egg Roll. You want the Cream of Sum Yung Guy?"

"I'm surprised there's any left," Sassy replied without missing a beat.

For the second time in less than ten seconds Michel found himself embarrassed. He could feel his face blushing.

"Hey, Sas," he stammered. "How are you doing?"

"I'm fine," she said. "How are you and the boy-toy?"

"Fine," Michel replied. "We just finished dinner."

Had anyone else referred to Joel as his "boy-toy" Michel would have been offended and angry, but he knew that Sassy liked and respected Joel.

"So what's up?" he asked.

"Don't worry, I'm not calling to ask you about the investigation," Sassy replied quickly. "I'm sure DeRoche gave you a royal reaming after I left yesterday...and not in the way you like so much."

"How do *you* know what I like?" Michel asked, playing along in hopes of finding a chance to embarrass Sassy back.

"I read it on the bathroom wall at the station," she replied matter-of-factly. "Who knew batons could be used for something other than subduing perps?"

Michel was silent for a moment, searching for a response to gain the upper hand. These games had always been a part of his relationship with Sassy.

"Well if anyone would know it would be you," he offered finally.

"That was weak," Sassy replied, "and you took too long."

Michel knew she was right. He'd lost the contest.

"It wasn't that weak," he protested mildly.

"Yeah, it was," Sassy replied. "If you'd just said, 'You' really quickly it would have been a good one."

"Fine," Michel said with exaggerated resignation. "So what's up?"

As soon as the words left his mouth he regretted giving Sassy another opportunity to embarrass him, but she was ready to move on.

"Carl is going to be cremated tomorrow," she replied. "I'm going to a memorial service at the funeral home with his brother, Eldridge. I was hoping you'd come, too."

Michel didn't need to ask why. The fact that Sassy had asked him to come told him everything he needed to know: she was suffering a rare moment of uncertainty.

"Sure," he replied. "What time?"

"At eleven. Bultman Funeral Home on St. Charles."

"I know the place," Michel said. "So are you doing okay?"

"Honestly I'm not sure," Sassy replied quietly. "I think it would have been strange going to his funeral anyway, but given the circumstances..."

"I understand," Michel said.

"I think it would be easier if the investigation were over," Sassy said.

There was nothing probing about the way she said it. Michel knew she wasn't fishing for information.

"Do you want me to pick you up?" he asked.

"No, thanks," Sassy replied. "Eldridge and I are driving over together."

"All right," Michel said.

"Oh, one more thing," Sassy said. "I haven't told Eldridge about the other photos yet. I wanted to wait until after the service. So please don't mention anything."

"I understand," Michel replied. "I'll see you in the morning. Try to get some sleep."

"Okay," Sassy said, though the tone of her voice made it clear she didn't expect to get much rest that night.

*****

Carl had been devastated by Sassy's rejection. He'd begun sobbing uncontrollably and begging her to reconsider. Sassy had known that she should make a clean break and tell him the truth about her feelings, but out of sympathy she'd told him she simply wasn't ready for marriage. Once again she'd found herself hoping it wouldn't be necessary to tell him the truth, that perhaps he would take her rejection as a sign that it was time to move on.

When she hadn't heard from him for two weeks she assumed that he'd decided he was better off without her. Her feelings about it were ambivalent. She missed Carl and was sorry for the pain she'd caused him, but she reasoned that ultimately it had worked out for the best and they had both gotten what they deserved: she was alone and he was free of her dishonesty.

In her heart, though, she knew she was rationalizing. Carl hadn't really gotten what he deserved. He deserved to be loved and appreciated for the man he was, not punished for a past he couldn't undo. She'd been selfish and she regretted that she hadn't been honest with him earlier. In fact, she'd never been honest with him at all. She'd gotten off easy. She'd gotten exactly what she'd wanted without having to expose herself to his anger, and all he'd gotten was hurt.

Throughout the rest of January and the first week of February she focused on her classes at the academy. She loved the course work and found the physical training both difficult and exhilarating. As with her first sexual experience with Carl, she was excited to discover unknown potential within her body. She quickly moved to the top of her class in marksmanship and more than held her own in combat training with her male classmates. She could feel her life going forward, closer to what she'd imagined, and with each passing week she thought of Carl less and less frequently.

The second Monday of February as she returned home from an evening class she was surprised to find Eldridge waiting in the hall outside her door.

"El, is everything all right?" she asked, suddenly frightened that something might have happened to Carl.

Eldridge nodded his large, smooth head.

"As well as could be expected," he replied. "May I come inside and talk to you for a moment?"

Sassy nodded curiously and unlocked the door, ushering Eldridge in before her. After turning on the lights in the living room she took a seat on the couch while Eldridge settled on the edge of the chair next to her.

"I generally make it a rule not to interfere in other folks' lives unless they ask me," he began right away, "but I'm concerned about my brother. Since you ended your relationship with him he's been drifting in a bad way. He's quit his job and I'm worried that he may be headed back to his old way of life."

Sassy stared at him for a moment, unsure how to respond. She was sorry to hear about Carl's situation, yet at the same time felt that Eldridge was unfairly trying to make it her responsibility. Carl was a grown man, after all.

"I never ended the relationship," she said, choosing to ignore the larger issue for the moment. "I just didn't accept his proposal. I never said I wanted to stop seeing him."

She knew that the words were technically true.

"But you haven't called," Eldridge said.

"I didn't think that would be appropriate," she explained. "I thought I should give him some time. I figured he would call me when he felt ready to talk."

Eldridge seemed to consider her words before responding.

"Do you miss him?" he asked finally.

"Of course I do," Sassy responded quickly, though those words were less true.

"But?" Eldridge asked, implying that she'd obviously left something unsaid.

Sassy studied him for moment. She'd met Eldridge only on a handful of occasions and had liked him. He'd seemed affable if slightly reserved. Now she sensed another side to him, a side that was more calculating. She couldn't put her finger on exactly how, but she felt that she was being artfully manipulated. She supposed that it was a skill Eldridge had developed to deal with people who often sabotaged their own lives. She wondered if he considered her one of those people. For some reason she felt compelled to answer him honestly.

"But it would never work out between us?" she answered.

"How do you know that?" Eldridge asked, leaning closer to her.

"Because I know me," Sassy answered, fighting the urge to sit back to create more space between them.

"And you don't think he could make you happy?"

Eldridge's voice was both concerned and probing. Sassy shook her head.

"It's not that. Of course he could make me happy. But I want more than that."

Finally she'd spoken the essential truth out loud and she felt an odd sense of relief. She looked at Eldridge for a reaction but he just nodded slowly.

"I see," he said. "You're worried that having a convicted felon as your husband is going to hurt your career."

Sassy tried to hide her astonishment. She wondered how he had interpreted the implication in her words so quickly.

"I'm sorry," she said automatically, though she wasn't sure if she *was apologizing for her actions or the fact that she had judged Carl unsuitable for her.*

Eldridge sat back a little and gave her a consoling smile.

"Sassy, don't be ashamed," he said. "Life is full of harsh realities. From what I know, you've worked very hard to get where you are, and it would be unfair to ask you to give up your dreams because of Carl's mistakes."

Sassy suddenly began to cry. It would have been easier for her if Eldridge had become angry and accused her of selfishness. His forgiveness was far more difficult to accept. She realized that she hadn't forgiven herself yet. She'd just moved on as she always did when things became emotionally difficult.

Eldridge reached over and took her right hand.

"Sassy, you need to do what's right for you," he said kindly. "Do what's right for you, so long as it doesn't hurt others. That's all we can ask of anyone."

Chapter 17

Things weren't right. He hadn't figured out exactly why yet, but Lecher knew instinctively that the story told by the photographs didn't match the one he'd been given by MacDonald.

He studied the fifth photograph which showed a close-up of Mose Lumley's chest. From the size of the wound it was clear that he'd been shot at close-range, no more than two or three feet. The wound was located about an inch to the right of his breast plate and was surrounded by what looked like large splinters poking through his tattered white shirt.

Lecher looked at the second photograph. It showed a marker where Sassy's body had been found, six feet outside the entrance to the room, indicating that she'd probably been shot while standing in front of the door and fallen back. Based on the splinters in Lumley's chest, Lecher guessed that they'd actually shot one another through the door.

He turned his gaze to the third photograph, taken from the doorway. Lumley was lying on his back, at least fifteen feet inside the room. He'd dragged himself from the spot where he was initially shot to his final location, stopping along the way to kill Iris. Lecher could see the pale, tiny toes of Iris' left foot extending into the left side of the photo, next to Lumley's body. He closed his eyes for a moment and took a deep breath to compose himself.

Where's the blood? he thought suddenly.

He opened his eyes again and looked at the floor leading

from the door to Lumley. There was no blood. If Lumley had dragged himself across the floor on his stomach there would have been a trail of blood across the floor. Instead there were only narrow scrape marks indicating that'd he'd dragged his heels behind him. But why didn't he use his legs to push himself along? The chest wound was high. If the bullet had hit his spine it wouldn't have paralyzed just his legs. And the efforts of pulling himself along on his back using just his arms would have caused blood to pump out of the chest wound.

Lecher looked back at the photo of Lumley's chest. The only blood on his shirt was a light spatter from the initial bullet impact. The wound hadn't bled after he was shot.

Lecher slumped back in his chair. He felt as though he'd been gut-punched and struggled to breath.

"How'd you miss that, Lou?" he whispered. "Lumley was already dead when Sassy shot him."

*****

A half hour later Lecher pulled to the curb two blocks from Mose Lumley's former home. It was just past 9 pm. He'd considered waiting until later but knew that the neighborhood was mostly deserted. Still he took the precaution of parking at a distance.

For the first two years after Iris' death he'd driven by the house every week. For two months there'd been no signs of activity, then one afternoon a For Sale sign had appeared on the narrow front lawn. For another nine months he'd watched anxiously to see if the property would be bought. He'd briefly considered burning it down. The thought of anyone moving into the house where his daughter had been murdered was too painful. But he'd waited, and one day the sign was gone. There'd been no indication that anyone had moved in.

After two years his visits grew less frequent. The high interest rates and economic problems that gripped the whole country were particularly hard felt in New Orleans. Lumley had lived in the Warehouse District, southwest of the French Quarter, and as shipping businesses began to close they abandoned their buildings in the area. Like many of the fringe neighborhoods of the city, Lumley's fell into sharp decline. Families moved away as indigents and drug addicts moved into the area to live in the abandoned warehouses. Lecher knew that no one would buy the house then.

Even after the 1984 World's Fair was held in the district in an attempt to revitalize the area, change had been slow. Lecher had driven by the house only a few times over the years since, when he'd been in the area for investigations. It had ceased to have any power over him and he no longer cared if it existed or not. He knew that Iris' soul didn't reside there.

In recent years the neighborhood had undergone a resurgence as the city's Arts District. Many of the warehouses had been converted to loft spaces and artists had begun to move into the area and open up galleries along the main roads near the museums that had been built. The small houses along the side streets remained largely vacant, however. After nightfall the areas away from Camp and Magazine Streets were quiet and empty save for the occasional gunshot or rantings of someone who'd consumed too much cheap liquor.

Lecher got out of the car and went to the trunk. He removed a large black canvas bag and walked quickly up the street to Lumley's house. There were no lights in any of the adjacent homes and the streetlight in front was burnt out.

He walked up the stairs to the front porch, stepping gingerly to test each board before putting his full weight on it. The wood creaked and buckled a bit in spots but didn't give way. He lowered the canvas bag onto the porch in front of the door and bent down to unzip it, then reached into his jacket pocket and took out a small flashlight. He twisted the end to turn it on and shone the narrow beam into the bag. From a mesh pouch along the right side he pulled a ring of master keys.

He stood and trained the light on the door lock. The screen door hung open to the left, attached only by the bottom hinge. The screen itself was missing. He began sorting through the keys. After two false tries, he found one that fit the cylinder and slipped it into the lock. For a moment the lock resisted, then the bolt gave way with a loud click like the cocking of a gun. He pushed the door open, picked up the bag and quickly stepped inside, looking back to see if anyone was watching before closing the door behind him.

The first thing he noticed was the smell. It was both sweet and fetid, like rotting apples. He inhaled slowly and deeply through his nose, testing it like a wine connoisseur rolling a sip of merlot over his tongue to discern the various notes of flavor. He could smell the rich, dank undertones of mildew, mixed with the softer, musky scent of decaying rodent. Floating over the top was the scent of wilted honeysuckle. Having lived his whole life in the city and worked in the coroner's office for over twenty years, he'd learned to distinguish the subtle nuances of all manner of decay.

He looked around, shining the high-intensity beam of the flashlight along the walls and ceiling. There were no signs of water damage. The house seemed to be structurally sound. With the city's rampant termite problems, however, he knew he would have to be careful.

He picked up his bag and began walking down the hall. A narrow staircase opened up to the right, opposite a wide doorway. He looked up to the window on the first landing. Two of its panes were missing and through the openings he could see the spindly branches of a honeysuckle tree. He turned to the doorway and shined the light into the room beyond. It was the living room. There were no personal possessions anymore, but a cluster of furniture remained. A couch, two chairs, and a floor lamp were arranged around a low coffee table in the center, all draped by a clear plastic tarp that was now nearly opaque with brown dust.

He continued down the hallway toward an open doorway at the back of the house where he knew he would find the kitchen. As he moved the beam of light over the appliances and cabinets he felt something like sympathy for the house. It had never asked to be the scene of a murder or to be in a neighborhood that had been blighted. It just wanted to be a home for someone who would love it and take care of it in return for shelter. It seemed to be waiting for that opportunity.

He shook his head sadly and turned to a door on the right, just outside the entrance to the kitchen. It was a simple oak door, stained a deep reddish brown like all of the woodwork in the house. It had single recessed panels on the top and bottom and a molded glass knob set in a tarnished brass plate on the right. There was nothing extraordinary about it, but Lecher felt his pulse quicken.

He turned the knob and pulled. The door opened with a high pitched whine and the smell of dampness washed over him. He shined the light through the opening, over cracked and yellowing plaster walls, then down onto the narrow wood landing. Holding onto the frame of the door with his right hand he extended his left foot and stamped it hard on the landing several times. It was solid. He stepped through the door and turned to the right.

He paused at the top of the stairs and aimed the light into his bag. He removed a larger flashlight with a wider beam and turned it on, then twisted the head of the smaller light to turn it off and put it in his jacket pocket.

The larger light fully illuminated the stairs and he began slowly descending, holding tightly to the railing on the left wall as he took each step. The right side of the stairs was open and as he moved down he could see a large empty concrete room than ran under the hallway and living room. It was surprisingly clean save for a five-foot-long inverted tear drop of mold growing down the wall in the front corner. The patch was mossy and nearly black in the center, turning green as it moved outward. It was ringed by delicate creeping tendrils of fuzzy white.

He reached the bottom of the stairs and stepped into the room. All of the walls were solid save for an opening under the stairs. He walked to it and shone the light into the space. It was empty. He moved back to the base of the stairs. Beyond the wall that ran down the left side was a hallway.

He hesitated for a minute. Although his senses had been heightened since he'd entered the house, now he could feel them kick into overdrive. He was acutely aware of the sound of his own breathing. It was quick and ragged. He tried to slow it by taking three quick breaths, holding the last for a few seconds below slowly exhaling. Now he felt ready.

He stepped into the hallway and turned left, knowing exactly what he would see. It was the first image from the photos Lou Donnells had taken. The hallway was about twelve feet long and four feet wide, with a plaster wall on the left and a concrete wall on the right. There was an open doorway at the end.

He lowered the flashlight and moved the beam slowly along the floor from his feet toward the door. Six feet from the door there was a light brownish stain on the floor, like the remnants of an old oil spill. He walked to it and knelt down. He placed the bag on the floor and took out a small whisk broom, then began sweeping the dust from the stain. He could see it more clearly now. It was nearly kidney-shaped, about three feet long by a foot wide. The borders were uneven, following the rough contours of the floor. At the top, in the direction of the door, were several pale streaks, disconnected from the larger stain.

He stood up. This was the spot where the marker for Sassy's body had been. In the photo the large stain had been dark red, almost black. He knew that it had been washed since, probably in an attempt to sell the house, but over time the stain had reappeared. Blood never went away and that's what he was counting on.

Donnell's photo had been cropped so the streaks hadn't been visible. Lecher knew now that Sassy had tried to crawl toward the door after she'd been shot. The streaks had been blood from her fingertips. The shape of the large stain told him that she'd finally collapsed in a fetal position.

He walked to the entrance of the back room and stood in the doorway. The room was about twenty feet deep and ran the full width of the house. As with the front room, there were no windows. Along the left wall stood a rusted furnace and water heater. In the back right corner was an open doorway leading to thick plank stairs that he knew would lead to a bulkhead door. Neither had been visible in Donnells' photos.

He looked at the floor directly in front of him and pictured Lumley's body lying there. Just to the left of the spot was a vertical wood beam which also hadn't been in the photos. He knew this was where Iris had been bound. He fought to keep the image from forming in his mind. This wasn't how he wanted to remember her. He turned away quickly and walked to his bag. He needed to remain focused on his work.

He knew from the photos that there'd been almost no visible blood leading from the door to Mose Lumley's body or around the body itself. He was looking for traces of blood that couldn't be seen. If he was right, that Lumley had already been dead when Sassy shot him, he needed to find blood that would tell him the story of what really happened.

He took an aerosol can and pair of infrared goggles out of the bag and walked back into the room. The door hung open to his right. He closed it. It was a wide door made of rough vertical oak planks held together by two horizontal cross pieces. There were three holes in it, all nearly vertically aligned. The top one was the size of a half dollar. It was smooth and perfectly round. It had clearly been routed as an eye hole. The other two holes were larger and rougher. One was at his chest height. The wood around the edges splintered inward toward him. The third hole was a foot lower, with the edges splintering out. He turned off the flashlight and fitted the goggles over his head. He could make out the basic shapes of the door but little more.

He raised the aerosol can and began to spray it around the edges of the middle hole. For a few second he could see a faint greenish-blue glow, then it quickly faded. He knew that if Lumley had been dead when Sassy shot him there would have been very little blood on the door from the impact of her bullet. Still, the test wasn't conclusive. After twenty five years, even the Luminol spray would be marginally effective, if at all.

Lecher considered Luminol to be the shotgun of blood detection methods: extremely effective and very damaging. The components in the spray reacted with the hemoglobin in blood to produce a brief luminosity. Even if the blood had been washed away, Luminol could still detect its traces. The downside was that the components of the spray could also destroy genetic material, making it difficult to use the blood evidence to identify suspects. Lecher wasn't concerned with identifying suspects, however.

Luminol was considered to be effective for detecting blood for several years after a crime had been committed. Lecher knew he was pushing it. Over time hemoglobin naturally deteriorated. His hope was that because the house had been vacant and closed up for over two decades the deterioration might have been lessened. The goggles were to ensure that he could see even the slightest glow.

He turned from the door and walked to the spot where Lumley had been found. He bent down and began spraying the floor in a back-and-forth pattern as he walked backwards. There was no reaction from the Luminol. He felt his butt bump against the door and turned sideways, completing the path of his spraying to the base of the door. For a half second he thought he saw a dim glow just inside the door.

He leaned forward and sprayed again. As the Luminol particles hit the floor he saw another faint glow, about the size of a dime, a foot to the right of the door jamb and two feet in from the wall. He took a step forward and sprayed again. Two more dime-sized spots, spaced about eighteen inches apart, briefly glowed. They were leading him along the wall away from the door.

He stood up and lifted the goggles onto his forehead, then switched on his flashlight, training it on the floor where he'd seen the last two spots. He could see them, very faint but still visible through the dust. He opened the door and went back into the hallway to retrieve the whisk broom, then walked back and began sweeping the floor along the wall. He uncovered two more small spots and finally a larger stain the size of a dinner plate eight feet from the door and close to the wall.

He moved the beam of light from the large spot to where Lumley's body had been found. There was no evidence of blood along the path. He moved back to the door and shone the light into the hallway. He could see more tiny spots, much lighter than the one that marked where Sassy had lain. They were washed while they were still fresh, he thought.

He turned off the flashlight and lowered the goggles, then crouched down and began to duckwalk down the hall, spraying the Luminol in front of him. Seven glowing dots lead him up the hall and around the corner to the foot of the stairs. He began to walk up. Three more dots appeared and quickly faded. He was now at the top of the stairs. He leaned through the doorway into the upstairs hall and released a heavy blast of Luminol close to the floor. There was no reaction.

He stepped into the hall and took a deep breath. The trail had stopped. He lifted the goggles again and turned on the flashlight. He no longer cared if the wide beam attracted outside attention.

He turned toward the kitchen. The floor was linoleum. He knew that if Lumley had been killed there he wouldn't find any evidence. The surface of the floor was too smooth. Most of the blood would have been washed away and the sunlight would have hastened the deterioration of the hemoglobin in any that was left.

He turned toward the front door and moved the beam of light across the hardwood floor. A two-foot-wide swath of wood in the center was slightly lighter than that closest to the walls. The swath ran from the basement door to the area between the base of the stairs and the entrance to the living room. Lecher walked to the end and directed the light down. The edges of the lighter area were soft but clearly squared. He knew there'd been a carpet runner in the hall at some point.

He walked into the living room and moved the beam of light over the walls. He noted that the tattered shades on the windows were down which may have helped preserve any hemoglobin in the room. He switched off the flashlight, lowered the goggles once again, and began spraying the floor just inside the entrance to the room. There were no traces of blood.

He moved closer to the center of the room, toward the plastic-covered furniture. The Luminol can began to sputter. He stopped spraying.

"Fuck," he said aloud, straightening up and pulling the goggles off in frustration.

He hadn't anticipated spraying such a large area and had brought only one can of the spray. He had another back at his house, but the thought of leaving and coming back was infuriating. He felt he was close to proving his theory. He just needed to find one blood stain large enough to have been caused by a gun shot to the head.

He knew he needed to think like a killer. He had to imagine how Lumley had been killed. He placed the flashlight, goggles and Luminol on the floor and began walking around the room.

The shot had been delivered at close range to make it look like suicide. If Lumley had been awake he would have struggled. It would have been very hard to shoot him directly in the side of the head. That meant he had probably been sitting or lying down with his eyes closed. Lecher thought about the rooms upstairs. What if Lumley had been in bed? That made sense, but then the killer would have had to drag him down two flights of stairs to the basement, and Lumley had looked large and heavy in the photos.

He looked at the furniture under its dusty tarp. Lumley could easily have been on the couch or one of the chairs, and if he had then the fabric may have been stained. The police might have missed it because they'd confined their investigation to the basement.

He reached down and grabbed the edge of the plastic sheet and began to pull it toward him. It made a sound like dry hands rubbing together as it whispered over the tops of the furniture. Even in the dim moonlight coming through the window on the stairs he could see clouds of dust rising into the air. He suppressed the urge to cough as the plastic came clear and floated onto the floor.

He picked up the flashlight, turned it on and walked to the couch. The fabric was a deep purple synthetic velvet. Fresh blood could easily have been overlooked on it, he thought. He got down on his knees and studied the cushions closely. There didn't appear to be any stains.

He pivoted on one knee toward the chairs and smiled. The one closest to the fireplace was a high-backed armchair with a wood frame and legs. The back and seat were fitted with clear vinyl slipcovers. It reminded him of the chairs in his grandmother's house that she'd always kept covered so they'd be clean for "special company," though he'd never seen any company special enough to warrant the covers' removal.

His heart began to race as he got up and retrieved the can of Luminol and infrared goggles and walked to the chair. He turned off the flashlight and placed in on the floor, then fitted the goggles back over his head. He felt something akin to giddiness rushing through his body. He shook the can of Luminol hard for a few seconds, then held it close to the back of the chair. He took a deep breath and held it as he depressed the nozzle.

The top right corner of the vinyl slip cover glowed a bright blue-green. The stain was about three inches wide by eight inches long, and diffuse. As the Luminol drifted down a more solid trail appeared a few inches farther down the back of the chair. It was wider at the top and narrowed as it approached the bottom. Below it was an almost circular stain, three inches wide, on the cover of the seat cushion.

Lecher could imagine how it had happened. Lumley had been sitting in the chair with his head tilted back. He'd probably been sleeping or drugged when the gun was fired from a few inches away. The impact had caused the diffuse spray pattern on the back of the chair. His body had been thrown sideways but as it hit the left arm of the chair it bounced back and his head snapped onto his right shoulder. The blood had dripped onto his shoulder and down his back. The wide part of the trail was where his shoulder blade had been pressed against the chair. As the blood flowed down it had formed a narrower trail and finally coalesced into droplets at the bottom of the chair back before falling onto the seat cushion.

He lifted the goggles and reached into the inside pocket of his jacket to remove a pen knife. He snapped it open and began cutting a four-inch square out of the seat cushion cover where he'd seen the glowing stain. Although the Luminol had probably destroyed the DNA, the blood type would still be identifiable. If it matched Mose Lumley's, he'd know with certainty he'd been right.

Chapter 18

I wonder how many people will show up for my memorial? Michel wondered, as he looked around the room at the handful of people who'd shown up to mourn Carl Adams' passing. Aside from Carl's brother, Sassy and him, there were only a half dozen men ranging in age from perhaps their early-30s to their late-60s. Though dressed in what he imagined were their best suits, it was clear that these men had had hard lives. It was etched in the lines on their faces and the slump of their shoulders.

They didn't appear to have come together so much to grieve as to express solidarity. Their demeanors and behavior had the feel of a well practiced ritual of paying respect to yet another fallen comrade. He thought it could have been expected among the older men who had probably already lost their parents and perhaps a wife or sibling, but the younger men, too, seemed too accustomed to loss. Michel wondered if it was just the result of a hard existence where loss was an everyday part of life or if it was something more specific to men who made a living driving trucks.

It was a rootless existence, he supposed. Friendships were made and left behind in a matter of days or hours, then picked up again on the next trip through town. Forming attachments would be hard and perhaps even foolish, and learning to deal with the transience of life would be a necessary survival skill. They were like battle-hardened warriors. Their grief was probably something they carried with them always but rarely expressed.

The behavior was familiar, he realized. It was the same way that veteran cops behaved when they lost one of their own. They came together for comfort and out of respect, but rarely expressed how they felt about the deceased beyond the usual proclamations that he or she had been a "good cop."

As the service ended everyone drifted outside and the men parted with just a few nods to one another. No one came up to speak with Sassy or Eldridge. The men probably didn't know who they were. Michel had the sense that they knew Carl, but were not close friends. They knew him but knew nothing about him other than the fact that he was one of them: a man who made his living on the road.

Sassy had been quiet since he'd arrived just before the start of the service. He'd found her already inside, standing in the front row with a large man wearing a black suit who she'd introduced as Carl's brother, Eldridge. After that she'd been silent. During the brief service Michel hadn't seen any tears in her eyes. Sassy was a battle-hardened warrior, too, he supposed. She'd dealt with a lot of loss, both professionally and personally. Given the circumstances, he could only imagine the mix of emotions she was feeling.

"Thank you for coming," Eldridge said as they stood in front of the funeral home.

It seemed an odd thing to say, Michel thought. He'd never met Carl and certainly hadn't come to grieve his death. He supposed that Eldridge still considered Sassy family and was thanking him for coming to support her.

"You're welcome," he replied.

"Do you have a cigarette, Michel?" Sassy asked.

He gave her a curious look but took the pack out of his jacket pocket and fished one out for her. He'd seen her smoke only on a few occasions in all the time he'd known her, and then only when she's had at least three drinks. He extended his lighter and flicked it under the end of the cigarette. He could see that her hand was trembling slightly as she held the cigarette to her lips and inhaled.

"Thank you," she said, gently touching the back of his hand for a second as he started to pull it away.

Michel noticed that her eyes were distant. He decided to give her some time to herself and turned to Eldridge.

"How long will you be staying in town?" he asked.

"For a while," Eldridge replied. "Seems to me that a lot of folks around here could use some help, so I'm re-opening my old mission."

Michel knew from the few stories Sassy had told him about her marriage that Eldridge had run a mission on N. Rampart Street, not far from Louis Armstrong Park, and had moved to Mexico to open another a few years after her divorce.

"It's too bad you had to come back under these circumstances," he said.

"Well, yes," Eldridge said, shaking his head sadly, "but I'd already been planning it. Carl was my only family and I was hoping we could spend more time together."

For a moment his gaze clouded over and Michel sensed that he was imagining lost opportunities. Then Eldridge's eyes cleared and he gave Michel a warm smile.

"But things happen for a reason, I suppose," he said, "And I think I'm meant to be back here. There are people here that need taking care of, too."

Michel nodded and looked at Sassy. She was still lost in her own thoughts, puffing absently on the cigarette. She seemed to sense him watching her and suddenly focused her eyes on him.

"I'm sorry," she said. "I'm just in a world of my own."

"That's understandable," he said, "I know you have a lot on your mind. I should be going anyway."

He leaned over and gave Sassy a hug.

"Thank you," she whispered in his ear.

He turned to Eldridge and extended his hand.

"It was nice to finally meet you," he said. "I'm just sorry it had to be now."

"Thank you," Eldridge said, taking the hand in his own right hand and wrapping his left over the top. "I appreciate you being here for Sassy."

Michel felt like a child suddenly. Eldridge's large brown hands seemed to swallow his own. He nodded quickly.

"You're welcome."

Eldridge released his hands and Michel began walking to his car.

*****

Sassy called Carl as soon as Eldridge left. She knew that if she let too much time pass she would lose her nerve. Carl agreed to meet her at his house the following evening at 7 pm.

When he opened the door Sassy was taken aback by his appearance. It wasn't so much his wrinkled clothes or heavily stubbled chin as the years that seemed to have accumulated on his face. He looked at least ten years older, and those years had apparently been hard ones. His skin had a grayish sheen, and his already gaunt cheeks had grown more sunken. It was his eyes, though, that she found most disturbing. They seemed to have receded back into his skull and the light she'd always seen in them was gone. They were flat and lifeless.

He stepped away from the door and walked listlessly to the couch without saying a word. Sassy stepped inside and shut the door behind her. The room smelled like a Bourbon Street bar in the early morning: all stale cigarette smoke, sweat and liquor. On the kitchen table she could see at least two dozen empty beer bottles. There were more on the floor amidst open boxes of half-eaten pizza, scattered newspapers and empty scotch bottles. She fought the urge to start cleaning and moved to the chair opposite Carl.

She sat down and looked at Carl. He wouldn't make eye contact with her.

"Carl," she said gently, "Are you all right?"

His head snapped up and he looked at her for the first time.

The light had returned to his eyes, but it was an angry glow. Instead of speaking he let out a short, bitter laugh.

"Carl, I'm sorry," she said.

"For what?" he asked, with a hint of challenge in his tone.

She was unsure how to respond.

"For what?" he repeated more angrily. "For not wanting to marry me or for stringing me along for the past year?"

Sassy sat back in her chair. She wondered how much Eldridge had told him.

"For everything," she said finally, purposefully ignoring the specifics of his question.

Carl shook his head and gave her a rueful smile.

"That's lame, Sassy. The least you can do is be honest with me now," he said, emphasizing the last word.

Sassy knew she was trapped. She would have to have the conversation she'd been hoping to avoid. She struggled to think of ways to express her feelings without admitting her own deceit or causing Carl more pain.

"Don't bother," Carl said, as though he'd been reading her thoughts. "I already know. Just tell me one thing. Can you honestly say that you don't love me?"

"No," she replied softly, looking down at her hands. "I can't."

"Then what the hell are you so scared of?" Carl asked, his tone more pleading than angry now.

"I'm not scared."

"Bullshit," he said flatly. "I've never met anyone so scared in my life. From the very first time I met you you've tried to keep me at a distance. You've been afraid of letting me get too close. Why?"

"That's not true," she replied defensively.

"It is, and it's not just me," he said with exasperation. "It's like you're afraid that if you let anyone too far inside you're going to lose control of your world. I may not have studied psychology, Sas, but I'm not stupid. I know people, and I see what you're doing even if you can't."

She was silent for a moment. She resented Carl's implication that she was too blind to apply what she'd studied to herself. She started to speak but he held up his right hand to stop her.

"If all you want to know is what you already know, then you're never going to know nothing else," was all he said.

She was dumbfounded by the simplicity and profundity of the words, and for the first time she realized how much she'd underestimated Carl's intelligence. She also realized that he was right.

She thought about the excitement and satisfaction she'd felt making love with Carl and during physical training at the academy. They were pleasures she hadn't known existed until she'd experienced them. What else had she missed out on because she'd been unwilling to open herself to new things or new people? For as long as she could remember she'd kept a protective distance around herself. She would let people close, but only on her terms and only for a while. She began to cry.

"Sassy," Carl said, kneeling in front of her and taking her hands, "I don't know what happened to you to make you the way you are, but I know you have a choice whether that's the way you want to be. I just think that world you're holding onto so hard is going to be a very lonely place if you don't let someone else in at some point."

He touched the fingertips of his right hand to her chin and lifted her head. He looked directly into her eyes without blinking.

"Please let me in," he said softly. "You'll never find a man who's going to love you as well as I will."

In that moment she found herself willing to take a leap of faith.

*****

For the next few weeks everything was new for her. She found herself thinking of Carl as much as, if not more than, herself. She discovered a capacity for taking care of someone else that she'd never known existed in her, and each time she was rewarded by an expression of Carl's love in return she felt stronger and more capable. In her more whimsical moments she imagined herself as the Grinch, standing above Whoville with the sleigh raised over his head after his heart had grown and grown to fill his chest.

By the end of February she and Carl were spending nearly every night together and they began looking for a larger apartment or small house for the two of them. It felt like the life she'd been planning had finally started. She had a man she loved, and she would join the police force at the beginning of April, two weeks after she graduated from the academy. Although Carl was having a hard time finding a new job that would keep him in the city, things were good. She could never remember being so satisfied or contented.

She graduated on March 15, 1980, at the top of her class. Her parents came down from Butte La Rose for the ceremony and she introduced them to Carl. They seemed to have an immediate and easy rapport. That night the four of them went out for a celebratory dinner at the famed Antoine's. Sassy tried to argue that it was too expensive but her parents insisted and she finally relented. She knew the extravagant gesture was their way of telling her they were proud. At the end of the meal when Carl tried to pick up the check her father managed to wrestle it away from him. Sassy was grateful for Carl's gesture but also grateful that her father had prevailed. She wondered if Carl had borrowed the money from Eldridge.

After, they went for a walk down by the river. The two men hung back, smoking and walking slowly, while Sassy and her mother walked ahead.

"He's a good man," her mother said after a while.

"Carl?" Sassy asked.

Her mother fixed her with a look of comic dismay.

"Who else would I be talking about, girl?" she asked.

Sassy laughed at herself. It was a warm, clear night and she was with all the people she loved.

"Yes, he is," she said.

"Do you love him?" her mother asked.

"Yes, I do," Sassy replied, nodding her head deeply.

"That's good," her mother said. "I've worried about you. I was afraid that maybe you were too easy on your own to let anyone else in."

Sassy thought about the word "easy." It was an expression her grandmother had frequently used and she knew that it had many subtle shades of meaning. It could mean comfortable or relaxed or simple, but also lazy or complacent. She considered what her mother had said and decided that she'd meant it both positively and negatively: she'd been comfortable being by herself, but also unwilling to risk change. She'd always envied her mother's ability to say a lot in very few words.

"Yes, I suppose that's true," she said.

They walked in silence for a while as Sassy debated whether to ask the question on her mind. She'd never openly sought her mother's approval before, but suddenly it was important to her.

"Do you like him?" she asked.

"Who?" her mother replied blithely, mocking Sassy's earlier obtuseness.

Sassy narrowed her eyes and gave her a sideways smirk.

"Doesn't really matter if I like him," her mother said, "but for what it's worth, yes, I do. And I think your daddy does, too. And don't you worry too much about him finding his feet. He's still a young man. He'll find 'em soon enough when he needs 'em."

"Thanks," Sassy said, reaching over and squeezing her mother's hand.

She continued to hold it for the rest of the walk.

*****

The next morning she was awakened just before dawn by a sudden intense nausea. She knew it wasn't a hangover. She'd had only two glasses of champagne during dinner and her head felt fine. While Carl slept she slipped into the bathroom and closed the door. Kneeling on the cold tile floor with her head over the toilet, she waited twenty minutes until the feeling passed, then got up and went to the kitchen to make coffee. She felt better but didn't have an appetite. Whatever it was, it had passed quickly.

When it happened again the following morning she knew she was pregnant. She didn't say anything to Carl about her suspicions, but she made an appointment with her doctor for that afternoon. When the results came back positive she was both elated and terrified.

As she drove home she thought about the changes that having a baby would bring to her life. Suddenly everything was entirely different from what she'd imagined. She'd been so focused on school and her career that's she'd never given the idea of having children much thought. It had just been a part of some possible distant future. She hadn't even been sure she wanted children.

She thought about Carl. Would he want the child? she wondered anxiously. It wasn't something they'd ever discussed, and they were both still so young and trying to make do for themselves. What would she do if he didn't want it or wasn't ready? And even if he did, how would they be able to take care of a baby? He didn't even have a job and they didn't have a place to live yet.

And what about her job? The question hung in her mind, and for a moment she allowed herself to consider the possibility of terminating the pregnancy. It would make life easier for now, she thought. Then she remembered her mother's words. Was that what she really wanted? "Easy"?

She knew then that she wanted the baby. Regardless of what sacrifices she might have to make, she wanted it.

*****

She'd decided to tell Carl about the baby after dinner, and as she picked at her food she was preoccupied with thoughts of how to approach the subject and how she would respond if he reacted negatively. At first Carl interpreted her silence as a bad mood and tried to engage her in light conversation a few times. When all she managed were single word responses he began to worry. Her sudden reticence made him uneasy and he wondered if she'd had second thoughts about their relationship. As the meal went on time seemed to slow for him and he could feel tension building across his shoulders and in his lower back as he braced himself for the words he was certain were coming.

When they finished eating they cleared the table, then went into Sassy's living room. Carl sat on the couch and when Sassy chose to sit on a chair rather than beside him his anxiety level jumped.

"Carl," Sassy said, "I need to tell you something."

His stomach clenched and nausea began to build. He was suddenly lightheaded and felt sweat pop out on his forehead and upper lip.

"This is really difficult," she said, then she was silent for a minute, just staring at the floor.

Carl's vision began to cloud and he felt like he was floating up from the couch.

"I'm pregnant," Sassy said abruptly.

As the tension in his body spiked Carl heaved forward and began to vomit on the carpet between his feet. His eyes rolled up into his head and his body lolled sideways as he lost consciousness.

*****

As he opened his eyes, Carl saw Sassy kneeling beside him. Her eyes were closed and she was crying. He looked around the room trying to get his bearing and struggled to remember what she'd been saying to him.

"Sassy," he said weakly.

Sassy started and opened her eyes.

"Carl, I'm so sorry," she said.

"For what?" he asked, still confused.

"About the baby," she said.

Her lower lip began to tremble and she let out a gasping sob. Suddenly Carl remembered what she'd been saying. He sat up quickly and had to grasp the back of the couch with his left arm to keep from falling backward again. He waited until his head began to clear, then reached out with his right hand and caressed Sassy's left cheek.

"Why are you sorry, baby?" he asked. "That's wonderful news."

Sassy blinked away her tears and stared at his with confusion.

"B-b-but you passed out," she stuttered. "I thought you didn't want the baby."

Carl twisted on the couch to face her and chuckled.

"It wasn't because of the baby," he said gently. "I thought you were going to dump my ass again."

Sassy gave him a startled look and wiped the tears with the back of her right hand. She began to laugh fitfully.

"You thought what?" she managed. "Carl...I'm done with that shit. I love you."

"And we're having a baby, for real?" he asked.

"For real," she replied, nodding.

Carl got down onto his knees beside her and wrapped his arms around her neck. He kissed her deeply.

"I'm so happy," he said, fighting to hold back his own tears. "Sassy Jones, will you marry me?"

Sassy smiled and nodded enthusiastically.

"Yes, I will, Carl Adams," she said. "Yes, I will."

Chapter 19

He'd expected to have trouble sleeping after the excitement of his discovery the night before, but Lecher had nearly collapsed onto his bed when he'd gotten home just before 10:30 pm. The tension of being in the house and his search had exhausted him. As he lay in bed now thinking about the night before it seemed like a fever dream. The images were vivid yet fragmented. They came to him in random bits and pieces.

Last night he'd been elated. Now he just felt tired and impassive. He rolled onto his side and looked at the digital display on the clock on his night table. It was 12:04 pm. He couldn't remember the last time he'd been in bed past 6 am. He swung his legs over the edge of the mattress and sat up with a groan. It felt like the night before had aged him ten years. He remained sitting on the edge of the bed and stared at the floor.

What had he really accomplished? he wondered. He may have come close to proving that Mose Lumley had been shot by someone else, but that didn't change the basic facts of what had happened that night twenty five years ago. Iris had died and Sassy had been shot and lost her baby.

If he was right, that someone killed Lumley and made it appear that Lumley had killed Iris and then shot himself, in all likelihood it was Carl Adams anyway. All he'd done was unravel another twist in the case. Nothing was clearer, nothing was changed.

He pushed himself up and nearly lost his balance. His whole body felt heavy and limp. He rolled his shoulders, trying to loosen the knot that had formed in his upper back during the night. The tension eased a bit and he took a few tentative steps. He felt more balanced.

He walked into the bathroom and turned on the shower, setting the water temperature a bit hotter than usual, then stepped out of his boxer shorts and under the spray. He stood there without moving and let the warm water run down his back. As the tightness began to ease in his muscles he could feel the lethargy fading. Suddenly his mind felt sharp again and the depression he'd felt just minutes earlier seemed like a distant memory. He'd never been one to dwell on the negative before and wondered what had caused his unnatural state of mind.

Maybe I inhaled too much Luminol, he thought with a small chuckle.

As he picked up the soap and began rubbing it over his chest he began to think about the implications of what he'd discovered. He knew three new facts with near certainty: someone, presumably Lumley, had been shot in the living room and moved to the basement; Lumley was already dead when Sassy shot him; someone else was at the house that night and staged things to look like Lumley killed Iris and shot himself.

He also knew that Carl Adams was the most likely suspect. But what was his motive? If he and Lumley had, in fact, been partners, perhaps he'd been afraid that the police were getting too close and decided to sacrifice Lumley to save himself. Or maybe Lumley hadn't been involved at all. Maybe he'd just been a convenient scapegoat. Had Adams known that Lumley was brought in for questioning in the case? It seemed logical that Sassy would have told him if the two men were friends. In any case it was a solid motive: Adams killed Lumley to protect himself.

So then the question was how much did Sassy know? Lumley had given Carl as an alibi on the night before Iris disappeared. Did Sassy suspect Carl, and if she did, had she tried to protect him? Was she part of the set up? It was odd that she just happened to be at Lumley's house that night, and the killer had seemed to know she'd be there.

It didn't make sense, he thought. She couldn't have known that the bullet wouldn't kill her, and she'd divorced Carl soon after. He also couldn't imagine her willingly sacrificing her baby to save her husband.

But maybe something had gone wrong, he thought. Maybe Adams was only supposed to shoot her in the arm or shoulder and miscalculated as he fired through the door. Or maybe he'd decided to tie up all the loose ends and kill her, too. Shooting her in the stomach seemed like a deliberate choice, an angry statement of some kind.

In either case he could understand Sassy filing for divorce as a result. She couldn't turn Adams in without implicating herself, but she could push him out of her life.

Lecher shook his head. Only someone with no conscience or sense of right and wrong could have willingly participated. Sassy wasn't that person. She had a core of steel but she wasn't without feelings or remorse. He'd seen that many times over the years. It was unfathomable to imagine her as a sociopath. He was sure of very little, but in his heart he felt certain of that. There was no question, however, that, wittingly or not, she was meant to be there that night.

He turned off the water and stepped out of the shower. As he dried himself he thought of his next step. He needed to confirm that the blood on the chair matched Lumley's blood type. After that, he really didn't know.

Chapter 20

It was late Sunday afternoon by the time Lecher arrived at the Coroner's Office. Because people had a tendency to die every day, he knew it wouldn't be empty. Half a dozen pathologists were at work in the autopsy suites and another two staff members were busy admitting new arrivals into the morgue. Only the offices and laboratories were quiet. It wasn't uncommon for him to come in on weekends so he knew his presence wouldn't attract any unwanted attention.

He went directly to one of the labs on the second floor and removed the swatch of vinyl he'd taken from Lumley's house from his briefcase. He took four test tubes and a flat-bladed scalpel from a cabinet and began scraping the surface of the vinyl, pushing the scrapings onto a sheet of sterile paper. After three minutes he had a small mound of yellowish flakes. He lifted the paper and bent the ends up to form a funnel, then poured roughly equal amounts of the flakes into each test tube.

He'd spent his first two years in the Coroner's Office working primarily as a serologist, determining blood types and analyzing DNA. The basic blood typing process was simple. Samples were mixed first with anti-serum antibodies for type A and type B blood. If samples coagulated only with the anti-A serum then the blood was Type A. If they coagulate only with the anti-B serum then it was Type B. Samples that coagulated with both indicated Type AB, and with neither Type O. After the type was determined, a similar procedure was done to determine if the blood was Rh positive or negative.

He would use two of the test tubes to test for reactions to the anti-serums and the other two to determine the Rh factor. Although there were twenty three additional antigen tests to ascertain more specific blood characteristics, he knew they wouldn't be necessary. Lumley had been in prison so his records would include his basic blood type, but it was unlikely that he would have been tested for any other antigens. The best he could hope for was that the basic blood types would match and that Lumley's blood type was rare enough that he could plausibly conclude that it was Lumley's blood on the chair.

He set the test tubes in a rack and walked to the refrigerator to get the anti-serums.

*****

That's a good start, he thought, as he studied the reactions in the first two test tubes. The sample mixed with the anti-B serum had coagulated, meaning the blood on the chair was Type B. That narrowed things down considerably. Less than ten percent of the population had Type B blood, and it was most common among those of African descent.

He picked up the bottle containing the Rh-positive anti-serum and added some to the third test tube, then repeated the process with the Rh-negative anti-serum in the fourth. He picked up both vials and swirled them gently, then placed them back in the rack and watched. The cloud of particles in the fourth tube began to come together into a mass.

Lecher smiled. He capped and labelled the four test tubes and placed them in his pocket, then put the bottles of anti-serums back into the refrigerator. After cleaning the work surface and putting the scalpel into the sterilizer, he turned off the lights and walked back upstairs to his office.

He was cautiously optimistic. Type B-negative was the second rarest blood type, found in only one in sixty seven people. If Lumley's blood matched, he could be nearly certain that it had been Lumley's blood on the chair. If not, then there was a whole new mystery.

He closed his office door and sat at his desk, then logged onto his computer and called up the New Orleans Criminal Database. He quickly entered Lumley's name and Lumley's face appeared on the screen almost immediately. The photo had been taken in 1973 when Lumley was 27 years old, seven years before Iris was murdered. He had been clean-shaven then, which only added to the childlike features Lecher thought he'd detected in Donnells' crime scene photos. His face was round and his eyes were set wide apart and had heavy top lids and long, thick lashes. They were almost doe-like. He looked terrified. Lecher wondered again if Lumley had been an innocent pawn in Carl Adams' game.

He pushed the thought away and began scrolling down the page. Lumley had had several arrests for petty larceny as a teenager and had spent three months in a juvenile detention center. It was during that time that he'd been evaluated by the psychiatrist who concluded that the boy's claim of having been sexually abused were probably false.

He was arrested again for breaking and entering and attempted larceny when he was 22 years old and had served six months in a work camp in upstate Louisiana. Then came the arrest in 1974 for trafficking in stolen property. He'd been sentenced to three years in the state penitentiary and had been paroled after 18 months. There were no more arrests after that. Lecher wondered again why Sassy had brought Lumley in for interrogation in the kidnappings.

He shrugged and continued scrolling down until he reached Lumley's medical records. On the third line he found his answer. Lumley was Type B-negative. His blood matched the blood on the chair.

Lecher sat back and locked his hands behind his head. He felt a sense of elation. The pieces of the puzzle fit together. He was certain that Lumley had been killed in the living room and dragged to the basement, and that someone, probably Adams, had set it up so the police would think Lumley was the kidnapper and that he'd killed himself after being discovered and shot by Sassy.

There were only three questions remaining: Had Lumley been involved with the kidnappings at all? Was Carl Adams the man behind it all? Had Sassy been willingly involved in a set up that ultimately cost her the life of her unborn child?

He knew that he would probably never have the answer to the first question. He could live with that. He didn't like the idea of an innocent man being wrongly accused, but ultimately the answer wouldn't matter. Lumley was long dead and exonerating him wouldn't change that.

He felt in his heart that he already knew the answer to the third question. He didn't believe that Sassy would willingly risk her own life and that of her baby to protect her husband. Unless he discovered something that changed his mind about that, that left only the second question.

He knew he'd have to trust the police to uncover the answer to that one. He didn't have the resources at his disposal. He wondered who was working the case and decided to call Mac MacDonald in the morning. He would tell MacDonald that he was satisfied with the story MacDonald had told him and then casually inquire about who was investigating the Adams case.

He was about to go home when he noticed the stack of autopsy reports on his desk. He reached for the one on top and opened it. It was the report on Carl Adams.

Chapter 21

The autopsy report was only two pages long. The examining pathologist had concluded that Carl Adams had died of a self-inflicted gunshot wound to the head. A blank line at the bottom of the second page awaited Lecher's signature. He turned the page over without signing. An eight by ten inch photo underneath showed the right side of Adams' head.

Lecher felt a chill run up his spine. The photo was almost identical to the one Lou Donnells had taken of Mose Lumley. He turned the report back over it and quickly scanned it. The pathologist hadn't performed toxin screens on Adams' blood or tested for gun powder residue on his hands. Lecher felt a surge of anger and shook his head, knowing that the pathologist had done only enough work to support the conclusion he'd expected to reach.

Lecher picked up the phone and dialed the morgue.

"City Morgue. This is Valdez," a voice answered after the second ring.

"Ricky, this is Stan," Lecher said. "You still have Carl Adams down there?"

"Let me check," Valdez replied.

Lecher could hear the sound of footsteps moving away from the phone and voices in the background. It sounded like a new body had just arrived. He heard the footsteps returning, then Valdez was back on the line.

"He was sent over to Bultman's last night," he said. "Why? Something wrong? He was really dead, wasn't he?"

Lecher was accustomed to the dark humor of the men and women who worked in the morgue.

"Yeah," he replied with a forced chuckle. "He was really dead. Thanks."

He hung up the phone and stared at it for a minute. If Adams' body was at the funeral home it was too late for testing. It had probably already been washed in preparation for a memorial service. He had only one hope: that the clothes Adams had been wearing hadn't been sent to the funeral home along with the body.

He got up and walked out of his office.

*****

As bodies were prepared for autopsies, the clothes and personal belongings were removed and bagged. The bags were kept in a storage locker or sent to the police if they were needed for evidence. Lecher knew it was unlikely that Adams' clothes would have been turned over to the police since his death had been considered a suicide from the beginning. Often times the morgue attendants were so busy that they neglected to pack the belongings with the bodies before sending them on for burial or cremation. He was hoping that had been the case with Adams.

He walked to the basement and let himself into the storage locker. Three walls of the narrow room were lined with metal shelves holding wire baskets. The baskets were arranged alphabetically, with the name of the person whose belongings it contained on the front of each. He turned to his left and began reading the names in the first row. The fifth basket from the top had a card with the name "Carl Adams" inserted into the nameplate.

He slid the basket forward and removed the bag inside. Through the clear plastic he could see green and blue plaid fabric. He unsealed the top of the bag and pulled the garment out. It was a long-sleeved cotton shirt. He held it up by the shoulders and looked at the sleeves. The fabric was unwrinkled. His luck seemed to be holding. Apparently Adams hadn't rolled up the sleeves. He quickly resealed the plastic bag and placed it back in its wire basket.

*****

As he spread the shirt out on a metal table in the lab where he'd tested the blood samples, he began considering the possible implications if Adams hadn't killed himself. Would it mean that he hadn't been responsible for kidnapping and killing the girls? No, he thought, Adams' murder wouldn't necessarily prove his innocence. Someone else may have discovered his crimes and killed him for them.

He took a gun powder test kit from a shelf and opened it on the table, then removed a test strip and deftly removed the backing to expose the adhesive side. He laid the strip on the right cuff of the shirt and pressed down for a few seconds, then smoothly peeled it up and laid it on the table, adhesive side up. He repeated the process five times on different parts of the cuff, then once on the right side of the collar. He took an aerosol can from the kit and began shaking it briskly.

But if someone discovered Adams' crimes why would they kill him rather than call the police? he wondered. Unless they were punishing him. He thought of Sassy. Would she have sought vengeance if she'd discovered the truth, if she'd found out that he shot her and killed her child? It was possible, but he couldn't imagine how the scenario would have played out. Assuming the gun belonged to Adams, how would she have gotten it, and how would she have gotten alongside of him and shot him in the head without a struggle? They would likely have been arguing.

He held the can a few inches above the test strips and depressed the nozzle. The strip taken from the collar began to turn pink. The others remained white. There were no nitrates on the cuffs. If Adams had shot himself the gun would have released powder on his right hand and wrist. If his sleeve had been buttoned, the nitrates would have been detectable on his cuff.

Lecher's instincts told him he was right—that Adams hadn't killed himself—but his training told him that he needed more evidence. Blood was routinely drawn at the start of autopsies to be used if the examination indicated death by mysterious circumstances. He'd need to run a toxin screen on Adams' blood.

He looked at his watch. It was almost 6 pm. It was going to be a long night.

Chapter 22

She could hear soft crying. She lifted her head from the cool hard floor and looked around in the darkness. Far off she could see a small circle of light. As she watched the light began to grow larger and brighter, taking on the shape of an open doorway. For a moment someone was standing in the doorway, but she couldn't make them out. There was just a heavy shadow, and then it was gone.

Now she could see Iris on the far side of the door. She was seated on the floor against a wood post, with her arms stretched above her head. Her wrists were held in place by a thick rope that encircled the post, and a dirty white cloth was tied around her mouth.

Even at a distance she could see Iris looking at her, imploring her for help with her eyes. She tried to push herself up to her feet. Pain exploded in her abdomen and she gasped, rolling onto her back. She put her right hand onto the small mound of her stomach and felt warm dampness. She lifted her hand and brought it close to her face. Even in the darkness she could make out the blackness of the blood on her fingertips. She felt her throat tighten and began to fight for air as a convulsive sob escaped her lips.

Something moved in the darkness beyond her hand and she tried to focus her eyes there. She could make out only a dark silhouette. Someone was standing there, watching her.

She tried to speak but the shape began moving quickly away from her, toward the door. She felt a sudden panic and rolled onto her stomach again. The shape was nearly to the door and she began clawing at the rough concrete floor, trying to pull herself forward. She could feel burning pain in her fingertips.

The shape was in the doorway now and seemed to turn back to face her. She couldn't make out any features, but something about it seemed familiar. She pulled harder at the floor but couldn't move forward. Her strength was fading and her vision was growing dark.

The doorway began to narrow. Now all she could see was Iris. The girl was no longer looking at her. She was focused on something in the room and her eyes grew suddenly wide. She began to thrash wildly back and forth, trying in vain to free her tiny arms from the rope that held them over her head. Then she was gone.

Sassy sat up in bed with a start, but didn't look at her hand. She reached for the phone and dialed Michel.

*****

"But, Sassy, it was just a dream," Michel said. "How can you be sure it was right?"

They were sitting in Sassy's living room drinking coffee just before dawn.

"I just am," she replied.

"Then why haven't you noticed it before?" he asked with frustration.

"She's always been tied," Sassy responded evenly. "I just never took note of it before because I didn't know about the handcuffs in the photo."

Michel gave her a skeptical look.

"Are you sure?"

"Michel, I've been having the same dream for 25 years," she replied. "The details are indelibly etched in my mind."

"But you said you've never seen anyone else in the dream before," he reasoned. "Now suddenly there's a shadowy figure who seems familiar. It's probably Carl. Your subconscious is changing the dream to mirror reality."

Sassy shook her head.

"There's always been someone else in the dream," she said, "but only when the door first opens. I think I've been waking myself up before I remember the rest. Besides, if my brain was changing the details to mirror reality, then she would have been in handcuffs, not the other way around."

Michel considered the logic of the argument and nodded grudgingly.

"So now what?" he asked.

"I want to go to the house and see if we can find the post where Iris and the first two girls were handcuffed. The photos showed a heavy eye bolt. We should still be able to find the hole at the least."

"And what if we can't? What will that prove?" Michel asked. "Maybe Carl and Lumley had another place where they kept the girls and they'd just moved Iris to Lumley's."

Sassy shot Michel an incredulous look.

"Carl barely had enough money to pay half our rent," she said. "You think he had another house somewhere else? And why would they take a chance on moving the girl when half the department was out looking for her? It's not like we were closing in on their secret hideout."

She realized too late that her tone was more disdainful than she'd intended. She saw the hurt in Michel's eyes.

"Look, I'm sorry," she said. "I know you're just trying to reign me in. Please, can we just go to the house and check it out? I need to be sure. Something doesn't feel right about this to me."

Michel gave her an appraising look. Something felt wrong to him as well.

"Okay," he said, "But I'm going alone. I can't take you with me."

For a moment Sassy felt a twinge of anger and bitterness,

but she pushed it back. She knew that Michel was trying to protect them both.

"All right," she said. "I understand."

Michel checked his watch. Before he left for Sassy's house he'd told Joel that he'd try to make it home for breakfast. He knew if he went to Lumley's house now he wouldn't make it before Joel left for work. He felt a small prick of resentment toward Sassy.

"Can I at least take a shower here before I go?" he asked.

*****

He waited until he was parked in front of Lumley's house before calling his house. He knew Joel would be awake by now. The machine answered after the third ring and he heard his own voice.

"Hey, it's me. Are you there?" he asked after the greeting had stopped. "Pick up."

He heard the receiver click, followed by Joel's voice.

"Hey, I'm here. Is everything all right?"

"Yeah, fine," Michel replied. "Did you just wake up?"

"No, I couldn't get back to sleep after you left," Joel said. "I've been watching your 'Buffy the Vampire Slayer' DVDs. Where are you? Are you on your way home?"

Michel felt a pang of guilt as he thought of Joel waiting for him for the last two hours.

"I'm sorry," he said. "I'm not going to make it back before work."

"Okay," was all Joel said in response.

Michel could hear the thinly disguised disappointment in his voice. They were both silent for a few seconds.

"So where are you?" Joel repeated finally.

"I'm at Mose Lumley's house," Michel replied. "Sassy had a dream and asked me to come check something out for her."

Even as he said it he realized how crazy it sounded.

"Joel, I'm really sorry," he said. "I know I promised I'd try to make it home for breakfast, but..."

"Don't worry about it," Joel interrupted. "It's okay. Seriously. I already told you I knew that work would have to come first sometimes."

"But I'm not even sure this is work," Michel replied helplessly. "It may just be some crazy errand Sassy has me on."

"Hey, she's been your partner and best friend for five years," Joel said reassuringly. "She's going through a tough time. If she needs you to do something crazy to make her feel better then you should do it...just so long as she doesn't start wanting to sleep in the bed with us."

"Not a problem," Michel laughed.

"Okay," Joel said. "I'll see you tonight."

"Hey, you know what?" Michel asked.

"What?"

"I love you."

"I love you, too," Joel replied.

As the line went dead Michel made a mental note to pick up flowers on his way home.

*****

The pale sun bathed the upper floors of the houses on the opposite side of the street, but the front of Lumley's house was still nestled in gray, early morning shadow. Michel grabbed the small flashlight from his glove compartment and slid it into his back pocket, then stepped out of the car. The air was still cool, but already he could detect a hint of humidity. He surveyed the buildings on both sides of the street. Seasons of neglect were obvious in the broken windows, faded paint, and overgrown bushes. The only signs of life he could see were a few sparrows who flitted nearby in a honeysuckle tree along the side of Lumley's house and a feral looking gray cat who paused in the middle of the street to stare at him before continuing on its way.

He closed the car door and walked to the foot of the stairs leading up to the front porch. Peering up into the darkness he could see the front door directly in front of him, its battered screen door hanging askew to its left, and a bay with three shaded windows farther to the left. The front and left edges of the porch were protected by a low wood railing. He took a last look around the deserted street and began climbing. His legs felt heavy and he wished he'd brought a cup of coffee with him.

As he'd anticipated, the porch was empty. He tried to imagine it in better days, when the dull, butterscotch-colored clapboards had been vibrant orange and the gray railing had been a gleaming white. He could picture window boxes filled with cheerful flowers resting on top of the wide railing cap, and a white wicker settee with green-and-white-striped cushions along the side rail. He could envision two large oak rockers in front of the windows, with a round, mosaic-topped table between them.

What the fuck am I doing? he thought. What is this, "CSI: Martha Stewart?" Martha comes in and reconstructs the decor of old crime scenes? He laughed softly and shook his head as he walked to the front door.

As he grasped the knob with his right hand it occurred to him for the first time that the house might be locked. He took a breath and twisted his hand hard. The knob didn't turn. He tried it again with the same result.

Great, he thought. I wish I'd known I was going to be committing breaking and entering when I left the house this morning. I might have brought some tools.

He took a step back and turned his left shoulder toward the door, then threw his weight hard against it. The impact made a dull thudding sound and he bounced off the solid wood.

"Ow, fuck!" he said aloud, as he grabbed his shoulder and began rubbing it. "I ain't trying that again."

He walked to the windows to his left and checked the locks, but they were all latched.

This is what happens when I agree to do things in my sleep, he thought mordantly, and he descended the steps and made his way around the right side of the house.

The concrete base of the house rose nearly four feet above the tangled grass. Although Lumley's neighborhood had been built on higher ground, the basements were only partially below ground because of the city's high water table. Michel looked up at the first floor windows and realized they were beyond his reach. He continued toward the back of the house.

The back yard was surrounded by the remains of a tall, wood stockade fence. Broken sections lay on the ground, nearly hidden in the tall grass, or hung inward between angled posts. Michel fought the urge to reconstruct how it might once have looked and turned to face the back of the house. A few feet to his right a rusted red bulkhead jutted out from the foundation.

Steel, he thought grimly. That's just perfect. Too bad I forgot my welding torch.

He walked to the doors and grabbed the handles without much hope, then pulled. To his amazement the doors gave a few inches. He let go and the doors dropped back into place with a loud metallic clang. He stepped up onto the concrete lip of the bulkhead, then squatted down and gripped the handles tightly. Using his legs, he began to pull upward. With a groan of protest the doors opened.

The sun was high enough to cast its light on the heavy wood stairs leading down into the house and onto the floor below. He could see rough concrete. He began to make his way carefully down the stairs.

As he reached the bottom he stopped in the doorway and looked around the large rectangular room. Even in the dim light coming through the bulkhead he could see the disturbed dust on the floor.

*****

He got back in his car and lit a cigarette. He'd been in the house for almost an hour. He sat back and inhaled the smoke deeply as he considered his next step.

The person who'd been in the house before him had been prepared and methodical. There were no signs of forced entry, which meant he'd brought a lock pick or set of master keys, and the even sweeping spray marks on the floors suggested an experienced investigator. Based on their locations relative to the large visible stains, it was clear he'd been searching for a blood trail, and from the missing square of vinyl seat cover it seemed he'd found it. From his footprint it was also clear that he wore smooth-soled shoes.

Before he'd left, Michel had remembered his original reason for coming to the house. There'd been only one exposed vertical wood beam in the basement. There were no holes in it to indicate that it had ever held an eyebolt. Sassy had been right. Iris Lecher had been tied when she'd found her. It also meant that Iris and the first two girls had been held somewhere else at some point.

He knew he should call Sassy and tell her what he'd found and then report it to DeRoche, but he decided to wait. Before he spoke to them he wanted to talk to the other person who'd been in the house.

Chapter 23

Lecher arrived at his office shortly before 9 am, an hour later than usual. Unlike the previous night when his investigation of Lumley's house had left him exhausted and he'd collapsed into deep sleep, last night he'd lain awake until well past 2 am, pondering the significance of that's day's discoveries. Adams' blood had contained nearly toxic levels of rhohypnol, the sedative commonly known as the "date rape" drug. Based on the amount in his system, Adams would have been completely incapacitated at the time of his shooting.

He knew that getting Adams to ingest the drug would have been easy since it had no odor, taste or color and could be hidden in food or liquid. While it was possible that Adams was drugged elsewhere and taken home, that seemed unlikely since that would have meant the risk of being seen dragging or carrying his body. More likely, the drugging had happened at home, which meant it was done by someone Adams trusted enough to leave alone for at least a brief while.

Again his thoughts had turned to Sassy, and this time he'd been unable to dismiss them. As much as he felt she was innocent, she was his only suspect. Whether she'd been a willing participant in Adams' plan twenty five years ago or not, she had a motive. If she had been a part of the setup and Adams had turned against her, she may have been seeking a long-awaited revenge. If she hadn't but had somehow uncovered the truth, she may have been seeking to rectify what she felt was her own mistake.

It was the possibility of an unknown party, though, that had occupied his thoughts most and kept him from sleep. What if someone else had kidnapped the three girls, and Lumley, Adams and Sassy had all been just victims? If that were the case, it would have to be someone who knew them all, and who bore a particular hatred for Sassy. Whoever it was would have used her and tried to kill her before, and now they were taunting her by making her believe that her ex-husband had been a kidnapper and killer.

Before he'd finally given in to sleep he'd made up his mind to follow his plan and call MacDonald in the morning to find out who was investigating the Adams' case. Then he would try to find the person who connected Sassy, Adams and Lumley.

*****

He waited until 10 am before placing the call. MacDonald picked up his private line on the second ring.

"Yeah?"

"Mac, it's Stan," Lecher said.

"Oh, hey, Stan," MacDonald replied in a voice that managed to be both warm and cautious. "What's going on?"

"I just wanted you to know I read the file this weekend, and I'm comfortable that things went down as you said," Lecher replied smoothly.

There was silence for a moment. Lecher guessed that MacDonald was trying to read the tone of his voice.

"Good," MacDonald said finally. "I know it was difficult for you, but I'm sure you feel better knowing the truth."

"I do," Lecher said.

"Good, good," MacDonald replied.

"I was just wondering if you know who's working the Adams' case now?" Lecher asked.

He tried to keep his tone neutral so the question would sound like a simple professional inquiry.

"Yeah, DeRoche is heading it up himself," MacDonald replied without hesitation, suggesting that he'd taken the question in the way Lecher had hoped, "but he's got Doucette working with him."

"Doucette?" Lecher asked with genuine surprise. "I thought he was on leave?"

"DeRoche said he asked to be reinstated so he could work the case," MacDonald replied.

Lecher knew he couldn't probe any more without raising suspicion.

"Well, he's a good cop," he said.

"No doubt," MacDonald said in a tone that indicated he was finished with the conversation.

A thought suddenly occurred to Lecher.

"Oh, one more thing," he said quickly before MacDonald could hang up. "Just out of curiosity. You told me that Jones was with a friend that night at Lumley's and that the friend called the cops. Do you remember who it was?"

MacDonald didn't respond for a few seconds and Lecher could hear him breathing through the phone. He wondered if he'd pushed too far and began regretting that he'd asked the question

"It was her brother-in-law," MacDonald said finally. "I think his name was Edgar, or Elmer. Something like that."

His voice was even and matter-of-fact. There was no indication that he'd become suspicious.

"Oh," Lecher replied with forced casualness. "Well, I appreciate your help. Thanks."

"Any time," MacDonald replied before hanging up, though his tone said he hoped not to hear from Lecher for a long time.

Well, that's two potential suspects, Lecher thought, as he placed the receiver in its cradle. The brother-in-law would have known at least Adams and Sassy.

He leaned back in his chair and looked up at the ceiling. He was both encouraged and concerned to hear that Michel was working the case. He had no doubt that Michel would be able to determine whether Adams had been the kidnapper or not, but wondered what he would do if it turned out that Sassy was somehow involved. Would Michel be able to put aside his personal feelings and turn her in?

Lecher knew he needed to find a way to keep close to the investigation without making it obvious. Michel was smart and would begin to question his motives if he showed too much interest, and that was something he didn't want.

He wanted Michel to stay focused on connecting the dots back to Adams. If it turned out that Adams was guilty, then that would be the end of it. He saw no reason to tell anyone what he'd discovered or to find Adams' killer. That was simply justice being served. The only question then would be whether Sassy had tried to protect her husband, and he didn't need to know the answer to that yet.

If Adams had been innocent, however, he wanted to find the true killer before the police did. He realized that now, though he wasn't sure what he would do when he did.

He knew he had an advantage. He was the only one who knew that Lumley and Adams had been killed. While the police investigated Adams, he'd be free to pursue other leads. Perhaps he could even use information from the investigation to help him. But he'd have to be careful. Michel would be quick to pick up on it if he did anything out of the ordinary.

The sharp ring of the phone broke his thoughts and he leaned forward and picked up the receiver.

"Lecher."

"Stan, it's Michel," the voice on the other end said. "I was wondering if you could meet me for lunch."

Lecher hesitated before replying. Although they'd worked together many times over the years, he and Michel had never gotten together socially.

"Yeah, sure," he replied finally. "Where?"

"The Quarter Scene. 12:30 okay with you?" Michel asked.

"Yeah, that's fine," Lecher replied. "I'll see you there."

He hung up the phone and considered the possible reasons for the meeting. The Quarter Scene was a small restaurant on Dauphine in the French Quarter. It was primarily frequented by local gay men and tourists. It was the sort of place they wouldn't be seen by other cops. Whatever Michel had on his mind, he apparently wanted to be discreet.

He shrugged. Maybe it'll be an opportunity, he thought.

*****

Michel was already seated in the raised back section of the room when Lecher arrived. He noted that the table was set away from any windows and there was no one else in the section.

"Hey, Michel," he said, walking up to the table and extending his right hand.

Michel stood and shook it, then they settled into their seats. A lanky waiter with short platinum blond hair appeared almost immediately.

"Hi, how are you today?" he asked energetically. "Do you know what you'd like or do you need some time to look at the menu?"

"I'll have an iced tea and a Creole omelette," Michel answered. "Wheat toast and a side of bacon."

Although he was nervous about confronting Lecher, he suddenly realized how hungry he was from missing breakfast.

"And you?" the waiter asked, turning his attention to Lecher.

"I'll have the same, I guess," he said. "No bacon."

He wasn't really hungry but wanted to appear cordial despite his curiosity.

"I've never been here before," he said, turning in his chair to look around the room before facing Michel again. "Nice place. How's the food?"

"Good," Michel replied with a noncommittal shrug.

They stared at one another for a few long seconds before Lecher decided to break the silence.

"So I take it you didn't ask me here for a date," he said.

Michel had assumed that Lecher knew he was gay, but he was surprised to hear it tacitly acknowledged. He didn't detect anything condescending in Lecher's tone and decided the remark was meant to be playful.

"No," he said with a small smile. "Definitely not a date. I was out at the Lumley house this morning."

He watched for a reaction but didn't see any.

"What were you doing out there?" Lecher asked in a controlled voice.

Michel had decided that if he wanted Lecher to be honest with him he'd have to share some information first to build trust.

"Sassy had a dream last night about the night she was shot," he replied. "Actually she dreams about it every night. But last night she noticed something and asked me to go to the house to confirm it for her."

Lecher leaned forward with genuine interest.

"What?"

"In her dreams, Iris is tied with a rope. In the photo we found at Adams' house she was handcuffed through an eyebolt imbedded in a wood beam," Michel said as gently as possible. "I went to the house to see if there were any signs of an eyebolt in any beams in Lumley's basement. There was only one beam and there were no holes in it."

Lecher exhaled loudly.

"So the photo wasn't taken at Lumley's house," he said.

"Which means if Carl Adams was one of the kidnappers, he may have had another house somewhere," Michel said.

Lecher gave him a curious look.

"What do you mean *if* he was one of the kidnappers? Is that in question?" he asked.

"You tell me, Stan. Is it?" Michel asked, looking directly into Lecher's eyes. "You were there. What did you find?"

Lecher was silent for a full minute. He knew it was useless to feign ignorance or try to bluff. Michel wouldn't have come to him if he hadn't already been certain that Lecher had been there. He wondered how much Michel had already figured out. Perhaps he could still work the situation to his advantage, he thought.

"Lumley didn't kill himself," he said finally. "In fact he was already dead when Sassy shot him."

The shock on Michel's face was obvious.

"After Sassy told me about Adams killing himself, I began to have questions about what really happened that night," Lecher began in response to Michel's unasked question. "I tried to get the investigation file through a connection in the department but it'd been cleaned."

Michel nodded, knowing that part of the story was true.

"Same thing with the autopsy report," Lecher continued. "Clearly there was some sort of cover-up and I wanted to know why, so I called Mac MacDonald. He was first on the scene at Lumley's house and he also signed for the autopsy report when the police took possession of it."

"Sheriff MacDonald?" Michel asked.

Lecher nodded.

"When I saw his name twice I got suspicious," he said. "The guy's had a stellar career and I began to wonder if his quick rise was connected to the cover-up."

"Did you accuse him?" Michel asked.

Lecher chuckled.

"More or less. Enough to scare him," he replied. "He told me that Sassy shot Lumley but she didn't kill him. He was still able to kill Iris and then he shot himself. He said the department covered it because it would have been bad PR because Sassy didn't follow procedures. And it was also out of sympathy for me and for Sassy because she lost her baby."

146

"Baby?" Michel exclaimed. "She was pregnant?"

Lecher gauged the reaction. It seemed genuine.

"She never told you," he said.

For a moment Michel wondered what else Sassy had never told him. He shook his head.

"Anyway, I was still skeptical so he agreed to get me a copy of the file," Lecher continued. "He said he'd burned the autopsy report on orders from the department."

"You have the investigation file?" Michel asked.

"Yeah, I'll get a copy to you," Lecher replied with a nod.

"So then what?" Michel asked. "How did you end up at Lumley's?"

"When I read the file I still wasn't convinced," Lecher replied. "It didn't make sense that Lumley was even brought in for questioning in the first place. He didn't seem like a solid suspect. And during the interrogation Sassy asked him about a date that didn't make sense."

Michel wanted to ask for more information about the date but decided to wait.

"Do you remember Lou Donnells?" Lecher asked.

Michel nodded.

"Lou and I were close friends," Lecher said. "We shared a common interest in crime scene analysis. He had a collection of old forensic photos and it occurred to me that he might have kept copies of his own photos as well. I visited his daughter and got the photos from the Lumley scene."

Michel gestured for him to continue.

"When I studied the photos they didn't fit the story. There was barely any blood around the wound in Lumley's chest, and none on the floor around him. If he'd been shot and dragged himself across the floor he would have been hemorrhaging badly. It didn't make sense. That's when I began to question whether he was already dead when Sassy shot him, so I went to the house to see if I could find a blood trail to prove it."

"And?"

"Lumley was killed in the living room and dragged downstairs," Lecher concluded as the waiter arrived with their food.

"But how can you be sure the blood belonged to Lumley?" Michel asked.

"I can't be absolutely sure," Lecher replied, "but Lumley's blood and the sample I took from the chair were both B-negative. That narrows the odds quite a bit."

Michel nodded, knowing the approximate prevalence of each blood type. He considered what Lecher had told him.

"So what's your conclusion then?" he asked.

"I think Adams set Lumley up to protect himself," Lecher said. "I don't know if Lumley was even involved in the kidnappings or if Adams just used him so the cops would think the case was solved, but it seems pretty clear Adams did it."

Michel nodded while he considered whether to tell Lecher about the photos he and Sassy had found at the bank. He decided it would just be a matter of time before Lecher found out on his own.

"And then he got smarter and started picking victims who weren't so close to home," he said.

Lecher gave him a blank look.

"What are you talking about?"

"Sassy got a key in the mail the other day," Michel said. "It was for a safe deposit box. When we opened it we found photos of 36 more girls, all like the ones of Iris and the other two girls."

For a moment Michel thought Lecher might begin to cry. His eyes clouded over and his body was wracked by a convulsive gasp that drew the attention of the waiter. Michel caught the man's eye and shook his head quickly to indicate he should stay away from the table.

"Stan, are you okay?" he asked, returning his attention to Lecher.

Lecher took a deep breath and nodded weakly at him.

"Yeah, I'll be fine," he said. "I just wasn't expecting that."

"I know" Michel said kindly. "I'm sorry to spring it on you like that."

"That's okay," Lecher said. "Did he kill them?"

"We don't know yet," Michel replied. "I identified six of them, but they're all still listed as missing."

"And they weren't local?" Lecher asked.

"No," Michel replied. "They were all from outside the area. Four of them were listed as runaways."

Lecher looked down at the table.

"So how did he find them, then?" he asked, looking back at Michel. "You think they came to New Orleans?"

"Adams was a truck driver," Michel replied, shaking his head. "He could have picked them up on the road. I've requested copies of his driving logs for the past few years and I'm going to cross-reference his routes to see if I can place him in the areas where any of the girls disappeared."

His expression turned suddenly troubled and he studied Lecher for a few seconds.

"One question, Stan," he said finally.

Lecher waited for what he knew was coming.

"Why didn't you come to us with your suspicions?"

It wasn't the question Lecher had anticipated.

"Would you have?" he asked in surprised response. "If you knew there'd been a cover-up, would you have come forward before you were sure of what really happened?"

"I suppose not," Michel replied, "but why not come to me unofficially? I wasn't part of the cover-up and you know me well enough to know I wouldn't be part of one now."

"No?" Lecher asked pointedly. "Even if it would protect Sassy?"

The waiter suddenly appeared and set their plates in front of them. Neither man reacted when he asked if they needed anything else. Michel could feel a flush in his cheeks.

"What are you talking about?" he asked angrily as soon as the waiter was out of earshot.

Lecher leaned forward, gazing at him evenly.

"I think that Sassy may have been involved with Adams' plan," he said. "She might have been helping protect him."

"You're out of your fucking mind," Michel hissed in a low voice.

"Think about it, Michel," Lecher said calmly. "Why was she at Lumley's that night? According to the report she was on her way to the market and stopped by to ask a question. She lived in the Marigny. Why would she be passing through the warehouse district on the way to the market? And Adams seemed to know she was going to be there. Everything was carefully planned out."

"You think she let herself get shot to save her husband?" Michel asked, shaking his head in bewilderment.

"Maybe not," Lecher replied. "Maybe Adams changed the plan and decided to tie up all the loose ends at once. She divorced him shortly after. That would make sense if he betrayed her. She couldn't turn him in without implicating herself, but she could divorce him."

Michel started to protest but stopped himself. He could see the logic of the argument, even though he found it hard to believe that Sassy would willingly participate in the plan.

"Okay," he said weakly, "suppose you're right. What do you suggest?"

Lecher felt almost gleeful but kept his expression neutral.

"How are things being handled in the department?" he asked.

"I'm working on IDing the girls and connecting them to Adams," Michel said.

"What more connection do you need?" Lecher asked with confusion. "The photos were in his safety deposit box. That seems like a pretty clear connection."

Michel nodded.

"True," he said, "but there's always the chance that something else was going on. It's possible Adams was working with a partner again, or maybe the photos belonged to someone else and he sent the key to Sassy because he was planning to turn that person in. DeRoche just wants to make sure we don't miss anything this time"

Lecher stared at his plate for a moment before responding.

"The second option doesn't jibe with his suicide," he said, shaking his head. "That wouldn't make sense."

"I know," Michel said, "but until we can connect him to the girls in the photos we have to consider it a possibility."

Lecher nodded thoughtfully.

"Anything else?" he asked.

"DeRoche is planning an internal investigation into the handling of the Lumley case and the cover-up, though without the files he didn't have much to work with," Michel replied.

"Why investigate the Lumley case?" Lecher asked with piqued interest.

"He wants to know if the department has 36 possible deaths on its hands because we were so busy covering our own asses that we let Adams get away," Michel replied.

Lecher was surprised by his candor.

"And you think he'll go public if it does?" he asked soberly.

Michel shrugged.

"If he can," he said.

Lecher understood the implications of the words. He believed DeRoche was an honest cop, but knew that political circumstances might keep him from disclosing the truth. Surprisingly he didn't feel any bitterness. He'd long ago accepted that practical realities sometimes took precedence over ideals such as truth.

"Stan, you never answered my original question," Michel said suddenly. "Is there any reason to suspect that Adams wasn't the kidnapper?"

It was the question Lecher had expected earlier. He knew Michel would return to it eventually. He shook his head and forced himself to look directly into Michel's eyes. He felt a slight tremor flutter his upper right eyelid but resisted the urge to blink.

"None that I know of," he said.

"I'd like a copy of his autopsy report," Michel said.

"Sure," Lecher replied. "I was looking at it just before you called this morning. I'll fax it over as soon as I get back to the office."

"I'd rather have you send over a hard copy," Michel said.

Lecher gave him a questioning look and Michel hesitated before answering. Lecher could see that he was debating how much information he wanted to share.

"Let's just say I'd prefer to know more before I share any information with DeRoche," Michel said.

Lecher guessed that Michel was being kept on a short leash and that he'd already wandered beyond the length of the chain at least once.

"Have you already told Sassy what you found at Lumley's?" he asked.

"No," Michel replied. "I've been dodging her calls all morning. I didn't want to say anything until you and I had a chance to meet."

"And now?"

"I'll tell her she was right about the ropes," Michel replied. "If I don't she'll go to Lumley's and check for herself. Unless she already knows she was right, in which case she'd know if I lied."

Lecher savored the final words. They meant that Michel had accepted the possibility that Sassy had tried to protect her husband.

*****

Lecher sat behind his desk and opened Carl Adams' autopsy file. His meeting with Michel had been more successful than he'd hoped. Now he would have access to whatever information the police uncovered in their investigation. More importantly, he'd kept his advantage of being the only one who knew that Adams was murdered, and gained another by planting doubt about Sassy in Michel's mind. That doubt would keep Michel from sharing information with her. He was encouraged, too, that Michel seemed determined to keep the information he'd learned about Lumley private for the time being. The less communication Michel had with Sassy and others, the greater the chance was of finding Iris' true kidnapper first if Adams turned out to be innocent.

He looked down at the autopsy report. The fact that no toxin screen had been run bothered him. Without it, Michel was sure to question the conclusion that Adams committed suicide. The examining pathologist had used a blue pen to make his notations. Lecher took a blue pen from the cup on his desk and put a check mark in the "Negative" box in the toxin screen section. He replaced the blue pen in the cup and picked up the black Mont Blanc pen beside his desk blotter. He signed his name at the bottom of the report to make it official. He knew he'd just crossed a line over which he might not be able to return.

*****

Michel took his time walking back to the station. He felt drained. His conversation with Lecher had left him strangely exhausted. He couldn't put his finger on why exactly, but it had felt like a game of cat-and-mouse and he'd been the mouse.

What Lecher had told him was all logical. If Carl had been the killer then he could have killed Lumley to cover his own trail. It pained him to think it, but even Sassy's possible involvement made sense. A week ago it was something he would have considered beyond the realm of possibility, but now he wasn't so sure.

Why hadn't she ever told him the truth about what had happened that night, or even about the baby she'd lost? Had it been shame, or was it something more? Had she liked her image of integrity too much?

That seemed too harsh a judgment. He thought back to the previous summer when he'd made the decision to come out in order to help the serial killer investigation. His fear then hadn't been based on losing an image he cherished. He'd simply been afraid that the perception of his abilities and accomplishments might be undermined by revealing his sexuality. Perhaps it had been the same for Sassy: she'd been afraid that her credibility with him would be damaged if he knew the truth. That motivation seemed more likely. Still, he knew he'd have to keep himself open to the possibility that she was involved and keep a professional distance from her.

He lit a cigarette and tried to push away his unease. Still, something told him he'd have to keep an eye on Lecher.

Chapter 24

The next week and a half were a blur as Sassy and Carl prepared for their life together. They rented a small house on the eastern edge of the Faubourg Marigny. It was a bit rundown, but there was enough room for the two of them and the baby, and the neighborhood was stable and relatively safe. The landlord had even mentioned the possibility of selling it to them when they'd saved up a down payment.

They spent their days cleaning and painting the new place and their evenings packing together at their old places. Sassy had suggested they make decisions about which belongings to take from each of their apartments before moving, and Carl had gone along with it, though he suspected that most of the items left behind would be his own. Much to his surprise, almost half of the final mix belonged to him. Sassy had made an obvious effort to ensure they would both feel like the new house was their home.

They were married by a Justice of the Peace on Sunday, March 30, 1980, eight days before Sassy was scheduled to start work on the force. Carl had accepted her decision to keep her last name without protest, though she thought she saw some hurt in his eyes when the Justice announced them as "Mr. Carl Adams and Mrs. Alexandra Jones." Eldridge served as witness and after he took them to the Court of Two Sisters for dinner to celebrate.

They postponed a honeymoon to finish working on the house and moved in at the end of the week. That night, as they lay exhausted on the mattress Eldridge had given them as a wedding present, Sassy realized how truly contented she felt. Her life had taken some unexpected turns, but the turns had led her to greater satisfaction than she'd ever imagined. She was excited about the life she and Carl were building together. She fell asleep wrapped in Carl's arms, imagining what possibilities life would hold for the two of them and the baby growing inside her.

That Monday Sassy reported for duty. She was assigned to a veteran street cop named Gilles Dupree as her partner. Dupree was a compact, unassuming man in his early-50s. Sassy guessed that he'd been the only one willing to take her on given that she was a woman. Dupree was nearing retirement and her first impression of him was that he was content to just pass his time without incident. At least he was friendly and willing to answer her many first-day questions about the practical application of her training.

As they spent their first week together patrolling the Marigny, however, Sassy began to see another side to her partner. He had a deep understanding of human dynamics and a gift for diffusing potentially dangerous conflicts. She watched the way he interacted with people and realized that he had a sure sense of himself and his position that others recognized and respected. He didn't feel the need to assert himself with aggressive words or actions, but at the same time his authority was unquestionable. Sassy likened his approach to that of a doctor: where possible help, but above all else do no harm. Though his arrest record may have been low, Sassy suspected that Dupree did more good for the city than most of his peers. She decided she could learn a lot from him.

She observed him carefully and began to incorporate his style into her own. She realized that her strong belief in right and wrong had translated into inflexibility in her dealings with other people in the past. She'd always been too willing to draw a line in the sand and had considered compromise a sign of weakness. Now she could see the usefulness of Dupree's approach. He never compromised the basic integrity of his beliefs, but he was willing to bend the letter of the law when it served a greater good.

She began to discover practical applications for the approach in other areas of her life, as well. She no longer cared if someone had sixteen items in their basket in the fifteen-item line at the grocery store, or if they waited until they were at the teller's window before filling out their deposit slip. She could let those minor infractions slip. And instead of pushing to get what she wanted she began to nudge. She found that people responded more positively to gentle encouragement and she felt less stressed.

When Eldridge found Carl a job working in the warehouse of a local produce company during the second week of April, everything seemed to fall into place. They had a good home, the baby was on the way, she was enjoying her work, and Carl had a steady job that wouldn't require him to travel. He was even able to pick up additional shifts at night to earn extra money. Everything was perfect.

Then on April 29, Sassy began to suspect that Carl was cheating on her, and two days later Iris Lecher was kidnapped.

*****

After her shift ended at five, Sassy went to the market and picked up some chicken and potato salad, then stopped at the bakery down the street from the house to get an apple pie. She got home just after six.

Carl had worked late the night before and three nights the previous week. He was working again that night and she'd decided to surprise him by bringing him dinner. She'd noticed that he seemed to be losing weight and wanted to bring him a special meal to show him how much she appreciated his efforts. She'd planned to make the potato salad and pie, as well, but she was tired so she settled for just frying the chicken. She made enough for Carl's supervisor, Mose Lumley, as well, since the two men had become close.

She left the house an hour later and drove through the Marigny and around the northern border of the Quarter, then down Canal Street to Magazine and zigzagged her way through side streets to the Bellini Brothers' Produce Company down by the river. The rolling chain link gate in front was closed and locked and the parking lot on the other side was empty. Aside from a dozen halogen lights around the perimeter of the fence, the only light she could see was a single bulb over a door on the loading dock of the squat brick building.

She got out of her car and walked to the fence. There was a green metal box to the left of the gate with a black button on it. She pressed the button but didn't hear any sound. She pressed it again and waited. She wondered what kind of work Carl was doing at night if no deliveries were coming in. She supposed they were packing produce for deliveries in the morning.

She was about to press the button again when the door on the loading dock opened halfway. A small brown head wearing a policeman-like cap slowly emerged around the side of the door. At first Sassy thought it was a young boy, but the white hair peeking out from under the cap and large glasses told her it was a very old man. The man didn't step forward. He didn't appear any too anxious to leave the safety of the building. She could see him adjusting his glasses and craning his neck forward to see her better.

"Can I help you?" he asked in a cracked gravel voice.

She suspected the tone was meant to be authoritative but it had been undercut by obvious nervousness. She guessed that the man had never had to face down a bad guy in his life, and now here he was confronted by the obvious threat of a pregnant woman armed with fried chicken. Sassy smiled to herself but didn't laugh. She didn't want to show disrespect for the old security guard.

"Hi," she said. "I'm here to see Carl Adams. I brought him dinner. I'm his wife."

The man adjusted his glasses again and stepped outside the door. She could see how frail he was. His pale blue uniform shirt looked to be three sizes too large and the collar hung loose around his tiny neck. He held up a bony hand and waved to her to indicate he'd be there in a minute. She watched as his stooped body slowly descended the stairs from the loading dock to the parking lot. He kept his left hand firmly on the metal railing, stepping down first with his left foot and then bringing his right beside it onto each stair before attempting the next. She wondered what would happen to the old man if a fire broke out.

After a full minute he reached the flat asphalt lot and began a bowlegged hobble toward her. When he was ten feet away he stopped and adjusted his glasses again to get a good look at her.

"What was that you were saying?" he asked, cupping his right hand behind his ear.

Sassy smiled at him.

"I said I'm here to see Carl Adams," she replied. "I'm his wife."

The old man looked at her suspiciously for a moment.

"Well, he's not here," he said, shaking his head. "Everyone's gone home. I'm the only one here."

As he said it he put his left hand on the flashlight in his belt, like a gun fighter preparing to draw in the event Sassy should get any funny ideas and try to get inside the fence now that she knew he was alone.

"Are you sure?" she asked. "He's supposed to be working the late shift."

The man took a few steps forward.

"Ma'am," he said kindly, "I've been working here for 55 years and there ain't never been a late shift."

Sassy felt her chest tighten and her heart began to race. The old man seemed to sense her anxiety and took a few more steps toward her.

"Now don't be worrying," he said, fluttering his right hand at her reassuringly. "A lot of the fellas here tell their women folk that they're working late when they're wanting to go out for a drink with the boys. I suspect that's all it is. I done it to my own missus more times than I care to remember back in the days when I was working the dock."

He pointed over his left shoulder at the four large steel bay doors that lined the top of the loading dock. Sassy was unable to respond. If this had been the first night Carl had told her he was working late she would have supposed the old man was right, but Carl had been gone for eight nights since he'd started the job. She turned away from the fence and started walking to her car.

"I'll tell your husband you were looking for him if he should stop by," the old man called after her.

"Don't bother," Sassy said under her breath as she opened the car door.

*****

As she sat in the darkened living room staring at the front door, Sassy realized how badly she wanted a drink and a cigarette. Her mind was racing and she needed to calm herself down before Carl got home. She tried arguing with herself that one glass of wine wouldn't harm the baby but lost.

She knew logically that her hormones were coloring her judgment. She had no proof that Carl was sleeping with another woman. In fact he'd been as attentive to her needs as ever. All she really knew was that he wasn't working nights at the produce company. Perhaps he'd taken a second job as a cashier at a mini mart and had been too embarrassed to tell her.

She tried to calm herself by imagining how Dupree would handle the situation. He wouldn't lash out. He'd confront Carl and get the facts before rushing to judgment. She wished for a moment that they'd been working together longer so she could seek his advice.

Then her anger flared again. Fuck that, she thought, I'm going to catch him at it. And when I do I'm going to snatch that bitch he's with bald.

She got up from the couch and walked to the stairs leading up to their bedroom. He's going to regret ever meeting me, she thought as she began to climb.

*****

By morning her emotions were under control. She'd decided to ask Carl what he'd been doing at night. As she prepared breakfast she reasoned with herself that it was the simplest approach and would bring the quickest resolution. Whatever she found out, she could deal with it. It was better to know.

She heard Carl's footsteps coming down the stairs and began spooning scrambled eggs onto the plates on the counter next to her.

"Good morning, baby." Carl said as he walked into the room.

He walked up behind her and wrapped his arms around her waist, then kissed her on the back of the neck.

"How'd you sleep?" he asked. "Did I wake you when I got home?"

"Nope. I slept fine," Sassy replied, pulling away from him and turning to hand him one of the plates.

He gave her a curious look, knowing that normally she would have turned to kiss him.

"Are you okay?" he asked.

"Yeah, I'm fine," she said with a shrug. "Just a little tired."

Carl took the plate and sat at the table while Sassy poured him a cup of coffee. She walked to the table and handed him the cup, then sat down on the opposite side of the table with her own plate.

"So how was work last night?" she asked casually.

She knew that she was playing games with him but wanted to see how he'd respond before she confronted him with what she'd learned.

"Busy," Carl replied, picking up a forkful of eggs. "We must have got in about ten truckloads of stuff. Bananas, tomatoes, vidalias. You name it we got it in. Had to unload it all and unpack it and then repack it to ship out to the stores this morning."

He smiled and put the eggs into his mouth.

Sassy felt a surge of anger. The elaborateness of Carl's lie offended her. Now she wanted him to dig himself in deeper.

"Was Mose working, too?" she asked.

Carl nodded as he took a sip of coffee.

"Mose, Skinny Watson, Shane Duval, me and Bo Archer," he said. "Normally there's just three of us, but Mose brought in some extra guys because there was so much coming in."

Sassy could feel the blood pounding in her temples. She looked down at her plate so that Carl couldn't read the expression on her face. She felt as though she might literally explode. She imagined the look on his face if she were to tell him she'd been at the warehouse looking for him last night. It would give her such satisfaction.

But now she wanted more. She would catch him in the act. That evening she'd be waiting outside the warehouse when Carl got off work and then she'd follow him.

*****

The day passed slowly. She'd tried to stay focused on her work but was preoccupied with her thoughts. Dupree had seemed to sense her reticence and left her alone, though she could see that he was concerned. As soon as they returned to the parking lot behind the station she said good night and hurried to the locker room to change.

She arrived at the produce warehouse at 5:50 pm and parked her silver Honda Civic a block down a side street where she wouldn't be noticed but could still keep an eye on the front gate. She could see Carl's car in the parking lot. She turned off the engine and watched. Four men were inside the large cargo bays sweeping up.

Ten minutes later the bay doors rumbled closed and a few men and women began making their way out through the door from which the security guard had come. She wondered what time he came on duty and hoped that he wouldn't see Carl and tell him that she'd been there.

A few minutes later, Carl and Mose Lumley walked out, followed by three other men. They all stood chatting in the parking lot for a while, then Carl and Lumley headed off together and got into Carl's car. Sassy turned the key and put the car into drive. Carl's car turned left out of the gate and then left at the corner, heading in the opposite direction on the street on which she was parked. She waited until they were a hundred yards ahead and then began to follow, keeping a steady distance from them.

Six blocks up Carl's car turned right onto Camp Street and she lost sight of it. She pressed down on the gas pedal. As she reached the intersection her heart jumped. Carl's car was parked four cars away on the near side of the street and the two men were getting out. If they began walking in her direction there was no way she could hide. She frantically tried to think of a plausible reason for being in the neighborhood.

As they began walking farther up the street she relaxed. She waited until they entered a door halfway up the block, then eased the car forward onto Camp. As she passed by she saw it was the entrance to a bar. She continued for a block then pulled to the curb.

*****

An hour passed. It was getting dark. Carl wouldn't notice her car now if he drove past it. She wondered if the security guard had been right, that Carl had just been out drinking every night. It didn't make sense that he would have lied to her about it, though. She'd never tried to keep him on a short leash. She might have objected to the frequency of his nights out, but she would have encouraged his friendship with Lumley.

But what if it wasn't just a friendship? What if Carl and Lumley were lovers? She laughed to herself. Now you're being crazy, she thought. She'd never seen any indication that Carl was anything but straight, and the bar they'd gone into certainly didn't look like a gay bar. It was a neighborhood bar in a rough neighborhood.

She saw the door of the bar open in her side view mirror and Carl and Lumley appeared on the sidewalk. She watched as they walked to Carl's car and got in, then saw the headlights come on. She started her car again. As Carl's car pulled away from the curb she slouched down low in her seat and waited for them to pass. When they'd gotten fifty yards ahead she began to follow.

They turned left onto Poydras Street and drove for a quarter mile to Interstate 10, then headed northeast on the highway for almost three miles. Traffic was moderate and Sassy was able to keep Carl's white Cutlass in view without staying directly behind.

Finally the Cutlass took a turn off just outside of Gentilly. Sassy slowed down and waited until Carl turned right before proceeding to the end of the exit ramp. She could see the white car turning left three blocks away. She turned right and sped up. As she neared the end of the street where Carl had turned she slowed down and turned on her blinker. She was about to turn when she saw brake lights. Carl had come to a stop on the right side of the street, twenty yards away. The lights went off and she saw Carl and Lumley getting out of the car. She turned off her blinker and drove another block, then pulled a u-turn and parked near the end of the street.

She got out of her car and crossed to the opposite side of the street on which Carl was parked. It looked to be an older residential neighborhood. The small houses were close together but built back from the street. Most had driveways and single-car garages. Though street lights lined the sidewalks, their glow was muted by the dense foliage of mature oaks that forms a canopy over the street.

Sassy kept to the shadows provided by the trees and walked toward Carl's car. It was parked in front of squat, white stucco bungalow. A high wood fence ran close to the right side of the house almost to the sidewalk, partially shielding it, but as she approached she could see the lights from an open garage door on the other side of the fence. There was a large truck parked in the driveway, its nose extending a foot into the street. She could make out the graphics on the driver's door: "Bellini Brothers" in gold type, arched above an illustration of a wicker basket of fruits and vegetables.

She looked around to see if anyone was watching her, then quickly crossed the street. She took another look around, then stepped into the neighboring yard and made her way carefully along the fence. The yard's house was dark and she hoped that they had no sensor lights or dogs.

As she got closer to the garage she could hear low voices. When she was nearly even with the back of the truck she crouched down and leaned close to the fence, peering through the slight gap between two pickets. The space between the truck and the garage was only a foot wide, but she could see two men loading boxing into the back of the truck. She recognized them from the parking lot of the warehouse earlier that night. She could hear Carl and two other men talking and supposed that one of them was Lumley. Though she couldn't make out what they were saying, their tone was relaxed and joking.

She focused on the boxes being loaded by the two men. Although she could see them only briefly before they were placed in the truck, she was able to recognize the Sony logo on several of them.

She felt a chill run up her spine and stood up. Carl wasn't cheating on her with another woman after all. He was running stolen merchandise. Tears began to well in her eyes and she swallowed hard to keep a sob from escaping. Not only was Carl breaking the law, he was endangering her career. If he were caught she would probably lose her job. At the very least her own competence and integrity would always be in question.

She was startled by the loud rumble of the truck's cargo door rolling shut and leaned close to the fence again. Lumley appeared in the opening between the garage and the truck. His back was to her and he was saying something to someone in the garage. He had keys in his right hand.

Sassy stood up and began running back toward her car.

*****

When she got back to the house she went immediately upstairs to their bedroom and began to undress quickly in the dark. She knew that Carl would be arriving momentarily and wanted to appear to be asleep when he got there. As she slipped into the bed and pulled the sheet up over her naked body she heard keys in the door downstairs. She closed her eyes and listened.

She could hear Carl walk into the kitchen and open the refrigerator, then the sounds of plates and utensils being set out. She knew he wouldn't be coming to bed for a while and tried to relax as she thought about what she'd seen.

After the truck left the house she'd followed it onto Route 610 heading northwest, then onto Interstate 10 west. They'd driven for a little over 20 miles to the town of Belle Place. There she'd followed Carl and Lumley for another mile into the center of town.

The main street of Belle Place had been two lanes wide and lined with two- and three-story brick buildings on both sides. Aside from a few cars parked in front of a building two blocks up on the right, the street had been empty. From the neon glow in its windows, Sassy had guessed the building was a bar. She'd pulled to the side of the road just outside the town proper and turned the car's lights off so that she wouldn't be noticed.

The truck had driven to the first intersection, then turned right and immediately left into an alley behind a row of shops. She'd gotten out of the car and jogged to the entrance of the alley. The truck had been parked a half block up. Lumley had been standing behind it talking with another man while Carl opened up the back.

She'd slipped into the alley, staying in the shadows along the backs of the shops, and moved to a dumpster fifteen feet from the three men. The stranger had handed Lumley an envelope which he'd folded and placed into his shirt pocket. Then Lumley and Carl had walked off, heading farther up the alley. She'd guessed they were heading to the bar.

The man had gone into a doorway just behind the truck for a minute, then returned with three other men. They'd spent twenty minutes unloading the truck and moving the contents inside the adjacent building. She'd counted 62 boxes. When the truck was empty, one of the men had lowered the cargo door and all four had gone inside the building, closing the door behind them.

A few minutes later Carl and Lumley had reappeared and she'd followed them back to the house outside Gentilly. They'd parked the *truck on the street there and switched into Carl's car, then driven to N. Rampart street in the seedier section of the French Quarter and parked near a row of clubs not far from Eldridge's mission. The club they'd gone into was called Exotique. From the name and the silhouettes of large-breasted women painted in black on the windowless exterior, she'd known it was a strip bar.*

She'd parked nearby and settled in to wait. An hour and a half later Carl and Lumley had emerged with a young blond woman wearing a skintight black mini skirt and silver lame halter top. Lumley's uneven gate had suggested that he was drunk. He'd leaned heavily on the woman who laughed and tried to steady him, though she'd had trouble keeping her own balance on a pair of black six-inch stiletto heels.

They'd gotten into Carl's car, the woman sitting in the back alone, and driven to a house on Poeyferre Street in the Warehouse District, not far from the produce warehouse. All three had gone inside. Sassy had parked a few cars behind Carl's car, with a van in between them to conceal her.

She'd wondered if Carl was guilty of both trafficking in stolen property and cheating on her and questioned which would be harder to forgive. When the door to the house opened three minutes later and Carl had walked onto the porch, she'd realized that—at least for tonight—he was innocent of the latter offense.

As Carl walked to his car she'd felt a sudden panic. She was parked behind him. If he drove directly home he'd arrive before she did. She'd wracked her brain trying to think of a shortcut but couldn't think of any. Anxiously she'd begun to follow Carl. They'd been nearing Elysian Fields when Carl had pulled to the side of the street in front of a small market. She'd waited until he was inside and then speeded past and headed home, arriving just after 12:30 am.

Now she could hear Carl cleaning up in the kitchen. She rolled onto her side so that her back would be facing him when he got into bed. She wondered if she snored when she was sleeping, but settled into a relaxed rhythm of deep breathing instead.

She heard Carl come up the stairs and into the room, then undressing behind her. As he got into bed he leaned forward and gently kissed her left shoulder before lying back. A few minutes later his breathing slowed and thickened, matching the sound of her own.

She opened her eyes and let her breathing return to normal. She was confused by the conflicting emotions she felt. She was angry and hurt that Carl had betrayed her, yet she felt a powerful urge to turn and hold him tight. She wondered how she could feel such tenderness for him under the circumstances and realized it was because she knew why he'd done what he'd done: he was trying to provide a better life for her and their baby in the way he knew best.

She felt tears forming in her eyes and quietly got out of bed and walked down to the living room. She sat on the sofa and began to cry. More than anger, she felt sorrow. The life she'd imagined for them was about to be gone. As much sadness as she felt for herself, she felt more for Carl. He wasn't a bad man. He'd just made stupid decisions. She knew that no matter what happened she and the baby would be okay, but Carl's life might be ruined.

She dropped her head into her hands and wished that the whole night had been a dream, that when she woke in the morning everything would be back to normal. The thought stuck in her mind and she wondered if it was possible in a way. Could she make what had happened disappear?

She considered what would be necessary and realized that first she would have to be able to forgive Carl completely. If she couldn't let go of blame it would fester, eventually turning to resentment. She would never be able to trust him. She knew it would be a difficult thing to do, but she felt it was possible. She loved Carl enough. So long as he stopped now she felt that she could truly put what had happened behind her.

But could Carl, she wondered? Would he be able to go on as before, knowing that she'd caught him lying? Would he feel too much shame, or that the balance of the relationship had shifted in a way that made him her inferior? She could imagine the struggles *he'd face. No matter what reassurances she gave him he might always doubt whether she would trust him again, and that doubt might be like a slow-acting poison.*

No, she thought. She couldn't risk that. She had to find a way to stop things without Carl ever knowing what she knew. She thought about Mose Lumley. Lumley was a problem no matter what else happened. Even if Carl stopped, there was the chance that Lumley and the other men might be caught and implicate Carl. She realized that to make everything that had happened truly disappear she would have to stop Lumley, as well, and she'd have to make sure he and the other men could never hurt Carl.

Chapter 25

Michel received the package from Lecher late that afternoon while reviewing the information on the six missing girls he'd identified with DeRoche. The thick manilla envelope had no return address but he knew immediately what was in it. Anticipating that DeRoche would question him about the package, he made a show of opening the flap and leafing through the contents.

"Adams' driving logs for the last few years," he lied. "I'm going to take them home and review them tonight."

He closed the flap and casually placed the envelope on the edge of his desk. He'd received the actual driving logs just after his meeting with Lecher and they were safely tucked away in his bag.

"Good," DeRoche replied, apparently satisfied with the explanation. "I wouldn't spend too much time on them, though. We already know he was driving from New Orleans to Houston, and if the girls were runaways he could have picked them up anywhere along that route. Just check the dates to see if Adams was on the road within a two-week period around the times the girls were reported missing."

He looked up and saw Michel staring at him blankly.

"I didn't need to tell you that, did I?" he asked.

"Um, no," Michel replied, shaking his head and smiling slyly.

"I'm sorry," DeRoche said, with a chuckle. "I haven't run an investigation in a while, and the cops I was working with back in those days weren't that bright. They required a bit more spoonfeeding."

"That's okay," Michel said. "I'm a little rusty, too, so it helps to know we're on the same page."

DeRoche's expression turned serious.

"Have you spoken to Sassy recently?" he asked.

"I saw her at Adams' memorial service yesterday," Michel replied. "She's called me a few times today but I haven't returned her calls yet."

He knew the answer was technically truthful, though incomplete. He hadn't told DeRoche the reason he hadn't returned the calls or that he'd been at Sassy's house at 4 o'clock that morning.

"How's she doing?" DeRoche asked with genuine concern.

"I'm not sure," Michel replied. "We only spoke briefly after the service and her brother-in-law was with her so I couldn't really talk with her. She asked me for a cigarette, though, if that gives you any indication of her state of mind."

DeRoche nodded thoughtfully.

"Well, hopefully this will all be over soon and she'll be able to come back to work," he said.

"Any progress with the Lumley case?" Michel asked.

He saw the warning look in DeRoche's eyes and held up his hands defensively.

"I'm not asking for details," he added quickly.

"No," DeRoche replied with a resigned sigh. "Without the files we're up shit's creek. The only other cop we know was there that night was Mac MacDonald, and we can't question him without tipping that we're investigating it."

Michel thought about the envelope resting beside him and wondered if there was a way he could get a copy of the report to DeRoche without raising more questions. Could he plant it somewhere it was sure to be found?

"So then Sassy is your only witness," he said.

"Yeah," DeRoche said, "And I think she's already told us

everything she knows. Or at least anything she wants us to know."

Michel gave him an appraising look.

"You don't really think she's trying to hide anything, do you?" he asked.

He hadn't lied when he told DeRoche it was helpful to know if they were on the same page. He wanted to know if his boss had any doubts or suspicions about Sassy.

DeRoche considered the question for a minute before answering.

"Personally, no," he replied finally, "but professionally I have to consider it a possibility, and every possibility needs to be investigated."

Michel nodded. DeRoche had echoed his own feelings exactly. Although he had more reasons to doubt Sassy, he still felt in his heart that she was innocent. Still he had to be sure. He couldn't allow his personal feelings to get in the way of finding the truth. He felt a small sense of vindication for the attitude he'd adopted.

"So, any luck identifying the other girls?" DeRoche asked, breaking the thoughtful silence they'd both fallen into.

"I wanted to talk to you about that," Michel replied. "If it's all right with you, I'd like to focus all my time on trying to connect Adams to the six we already know and let someone else handle IDing the others. I've already established some search parameters I can give them. I just think I'll be able to contribute more in that capacity."

DeRoche considered the request for a moment, then nodded.

"Yeah, you're probably right," he said. "It's a waste of your skills spending all day looking at photos. And the sooner we can establish a connection with Adams the better. Just be available to help out if whoever gets stuck with the job has any questions."

Michel smiled.

"Any thoughts on who it will be?" he asked.

"No, but the day isn't over yet," DeRoche replied dryly. "I'm sure someone will piss me off before it is."

*****

Michel spent the rest of the afternoon fighting the urge to look at the report he'd received from Lecher. The final hour seemed to stretch out for days. Each time he looked at the clock expecting to see that it was time to leave the minute hand had moved only a few increments forward. Sassy called his cell phone again at 4:45 pm and he let the call go into his voice mail. He imagined her sitting at home cursing at the phone and knew she was going to be pissed when he finally spoke to her.

At five exactly he packed the envelope into his bag and left the squad room. As he was pulling out of the parking garage he realized he hadn't made any plans for dinner yet and dialed his house on his cell phone. To his surprise, Joel answered on the second ring.

"Getting pretty comfortable there, I see," Michel said.

"I saw your number on the caller ID," Joel replied a bit defensively. "Besides, if anyone asked who I was I'd tell them I was your houseboy. Your *naked* houseboy."

"Well I hope the Jehovah's Witnesses call then," Michel replied. "Listen, I was tied up all afternoon and didn't have a chance to think about dinner. I don't think there's much in the fridge so I was thinking we'd order out."

"Fine with me," Joel said. "You in the mood for anything particular?"

"No, it doesn't matter," Michel replied. "Something quick. I'm going to have to do a few hours of work tonight."

"You want me to stay at my place tonight so you can concentrate?" Joel asked.

"No," Michel replied. "I want you there when I finish so I can have my way with you."

"Oh, I see how you are," Joel said with a chuckle. "Just keep me in the corner until you're ready for your fun."

"Nobody puts Baby in the corner," Michel replied dramatically, then began to laugh.

Joel was silent.

"Hello?" Michel said.

"I don't get it," Joel replied flatly.

"Oh my God," Michel said. "I *so* have to introduce you to the classic cinema of the 80s. That's from 'Dirty Dancing.' Damn, you must have grown up in Mississippi or something."

Joel began laughing hard.

"I still got the straw in my britches to prove it," he said.

"That explains that rash I got," Michel replied. "Anyway, I'll be home soon so go ahead and order whatever you feel like."

"Ten-four, big buddy," Joel replied. "See you soon."

Then he hung up.

*****

After they finished their pizza Michel went to his office to review the files from Lecher while Joel went onto the patio to read. Michel knew he'd been distracted thinking about the files all during dinner and made a mental note to give Joel his full attention when he was done. Although Joel hadn't said anything about it, Michel was aware that he'd been focusing very little of his energy on him since he'd gone back to work. The balance he'd hoped to maintain between his personal and professional lives had clearly tipped toward the latter.

He removed the manilla envelope from his bag and slid the contents onto his desk. Carl Adams' autopsy report was on top. He opened it and reviewed the findings. From the photos it was clear that Adams had died from a gunshot to the right temple, but no tests had been done for nitrates on his hands to confirm that the wound had been self-inflicted. He looked at the name of the examining pathologist: Lee Catlin. He knew Catlin casually and liked him, but found him to be professionally lazy. He was surprised that Lecher hadn't flagged the omission.

The toxin screen section had been marked negative, but there were no additional notes on the tests performed. Again he was surprised that Lecher hadn't sent the report back for additional detail. He decided to call Catlin in the morning to get the information.

He closed the folder and put it aside, then opened the Lumley investigation file and began to read.

Iris Lecher was kidnapped on Friday, May 2, 1980, between 8 and 9 pm from her paternal grandmother's house on Prytannia Street in the Garden District. Her grandmother, Delores Lecher, called the police just after nine when she went to check on her granddaughter and found her bed empty and a window in the first floor bedroom open.

During questioning by the police Mrs. Lecher said that two nights earlier she'd heard noises outside the house around 8 pm, but when she went outside she didn't find anything. The next morning she'd found a cigarette butt in the garden along the side of the house near Iris' window, but had assumed one of the gardeners had dropped it. She'd planned to speak to them about it the following week when they came to mow the lawn.

The two gardeners, Leon and Jesus DeSistis, were questioned but both were at a birthday party for their mother at the time of the kidnapping.

Mrs. Lecher's son, Stan, was attending class at Tulane when his daughter disappeared, a fact confirmed by his professor and several other students in the class.

There was no forensic evidence found in the bedroom or outside the house and no sign of a struggle. The police suspected that Iris had either slept through the kidnapping or more likely been drugged.

Sassy was added to the investigation team on Saturday, May 3, to develop a psychological profile of the kidnapper and help identify suspects from criminal records. On the first day she compiled a list of ten suspects, including Mose Lumley. Lumley was brought in for questioning on Sunday at 11:00 am.

During the interrogation, which Sassy conducted, she asked Lumley his whereabouts on the nights of Sept. 22 and Nov. 4, 1979, and April 30 and 31 and May 2, 1980. Lumley had been unable to recall his whereabouts on the first date, but said he'd been on vacation in Barbados on the second, the night that Celia Crowe was kidnapped. He said he'd been out drinking on the other three nights and as a witness gave the name of Carl Adams.

Notations in the records indicated that the department had confirmed the trip to Barbados and Sassy confirmed the alibi with Carl, though no notes were made about her relationship to him and Lumley gave no indication that he knew who she was during questioning.

Michel perused the interviews with the other nine suspects. None had been detained and notes indicated they all either had alibis or were considered low-probability. Another fifty or so pages were devoted to interviews with Mrs. Lecher's neighbors and others connected to the family. The investigation appeared to be aggressive and thorough, though no further suspects were identified.

The final few pages were reports from Mac MacDonald and the other officers who'd responded to the scene at Lumley's house. The call came in at 9:03 pm. MacDonald arrived on the scene first at 9:08 pm. A second unit arrived five minutes later and a third two minutes after that. Michel didn't recognize the names of any of the other officers. They were no doubt long retired.

According to MacDonald's report, the call was placed by Eldridge Adams. Eldridge said he and Sassy were on their way to the market when she asked if she could stop at Lumley's house. He waited in the car while she went inside. A few minutes later he heard gunshots and went into the house to call the police, then began to search for Sassy. He found her unconscious in the basement. Lumley and Iris were already dead.

Michel closed the folder and thought about Lumley's house. If someone else had been in the basement that night they could easily have gone out through the bulkhead without Eldridge seeing them. Still, he wondered if Eldridge had seen something without realizing it. At the very least Eldridge might be able to give him some useful insight into Sassy's and Carl's marriage. He decided to stop by the old mission on N. Rampart during lunch the next day to see if he could find Eldridge.

He heard the phone ring in the kitchen and started to get up, but then heard Joel pick it up and start speaking. He really is becoming comfortable here, he thought with a smile. He looked at his watch and saw that it was 8:40 pm. He'd been absorbed in his reading for almost two hours. He stood up and stretched, then walked into the hall. Joel was coming toward him with the phone. He had a concerned look on his face.

"It's Sassy," he said quietly, holding his hand over the mouthpiece. "She sounds pissed."

"I'll bet," Michel replied, grimacing as he took the phone.

"Hey," he said.

"Don't you fucking 'hey' me," Sassy lit into him. "Where have you been? I called you six fucking times."

"I'm sorry," Michel replied. "I was with DeRoche from the time I got into the office until I left. I just got home a little while ago and needed to have something to eat first. I swear I was going to call you in a few minutes."

He looked up and saw Joel staring at him, then turned and walked back into his office, closing the door behind him.

"Look, I really am sorry," he said.

"Fine," Sassy replied, grudgingly accepting his apology. "So did you go to Lumley's?"

"Yeah," Michel said, "as soon as I left your place."

"And?" Sassy asked with obvious frustration.

"And you were right," Michel replied. "There was only one

wood beam in the basement and there were no signs of an eyebolt in it. The photos of Iris and the other two girls weren't taken at Lumley's."

Sassy was quiet for a minute.

"What about the attic?" she asked finally.

"I couldn't risk going up there alone," Michel replied. "No way of knowing how safe the stairs are. Besides, the beam in the photos was too thick for an attic."

"That's true," Sassy said.

They were both quiet for a while.

"So is there anything else I should know?" Sassy asked, breaking the silence.

"No, I don't think so," Michel replied with forced casualness.

"So does that mean there's nothing, or nothing you think I should know?" Sassy asked pointedly.

Michel hesitated. He didn't want to get into a verbal sparring match.

"Look, Sas," he said. "I need to go. It's been a long day and I'm beat. Let's talk about this tomorrow, okay?"

"Should I wait for your call?" Sassy asked with obvious sarcasm.

"Good night," Michel said and hung up.

He stood in his office for a minute trying to sort out his feelings. He knew that Sassy's anger was justified. He should have called her as soon as he left Lumley's house. Avoiding her had been unfair and cowardly. At the same time he felt some resentment toward her. Six months earlier she'd called him on the carpet when he let his personal feelings for Lady Chanel interfere with the way he ran the serial killer investigation, and now she seemed to expect him to share details of the current investigation because of their friendship. It was hypocritical, and worse it showed a lack of respect for his professionalism.

There was a light knock on the door.

"Yeah?" he said.

Joel opened the door and took a step into the room.

"Are you all right?" he asked.

"Yeah, I'm fine," Michel replied with a sad smile.

"So what was that all about?" Joel asked. "Why did you tell Sassy you just got home?"

"It's a long story," Michel sighed with a dismissive wave of his hand.

"That's okay, I've got time," Joel said.

His tone made it clear that he didn't intend to be put off so easily. Michel gave him a curious look. This sudden resoluteness was a side to Joel he hadn't seen before.

"Okay," Michel said. "Let's go get a couple of glasses and some ice and I'll tell you and Jack Daniels all about it."

*****

Sassy wished she had it in her to scream or break something. There were times when her self-control got in the way of being able to vent her anger and frustration. This was one of those times. She imagined that physically releasing her feelings would be very cathartic. Maybe I should have taken those scream therapy classes in college after all, she thought wryly.

"And six months later I'd have been squatting over a mirror introducing myself to my vagina," she said aloud, shaking her head.

She'd always had a wary contempt for what she saw as the "pseudo-psychological, self-help crap" that had attracted so many of her peers in school.

She walked to the refrigerator and took out an open bottle of chardonnay. There were less than two inches of wine in the bottom so she opted not to use a glass and carried the bottle into the living room. She sat on the couch and lifted the bottle to her lips. This is a much healthier form of therapy, she thought, as she took a long swig. She placed the bottle on the coffee table and pulled her legs up beside her on the couch.

She knew she had a right to be angry with Michel, but she also understood he was in a difficult position. It had been unfair of her to question him about the case or imply that he was keeping information from her. She had a connection to a case he was investigating. He had to treat her the way he would a stranger under the same circumstances. If the situation were reversed she knew that she'd do the same thing.

She realized that her frustration had less to do with Michel's behavior than the fact that she had no control. She was used to being in control of her life and work, but now she was forced to sit on the sidelines without knowing what was going on. She felt helpless. Suddenly she could empathize with all the people she'd met over the years whose lives had been inadvertently touched by criminal investigations. She vowed to be more compassionate in the future.

Most of all, she realized, she was bothered by the fact that the distance between Michel and her had seemed to grow greater in the last few days than it had during the six months that he'd been on leave. During that time they'd been able to maintain their emotional connection, though they didn't see one another that often. Now that connection seemed to be breaking. She felt isolated. Michel had been her partner and best friend for the past five years, but now she felt cut off from him and it hurt.

She picked up the bottle and drained it, then got up and went to the kitchen to open another.

*****

"You don't really think Sassy had anything to do with what happened, do you?" Joel asked incredulously when Michel finished talking.

"Personally, no, but professionally I have to consider it a possibility," Michel replied evenly, using DeRoche's words.

"So in the meantime you're willing to treat her like shit just in case?" Joel asked, shaking his head. "Isn't that sort of like administering punishment before you've established guilt?"

"I'm not punishing her," Michel replied with an angry edge to his voice. "I'm trying to maintain a professional distance. Sassy knows she's involved in the case. She knows I can't talk to her about it."

"I'm sure that's a great comfort to her," Joel said sarcastically.

Michel felt a surge of anger. He began speaking before he could stop himself. Even as the words were leaving his mouth he regretted them, but it was too late.

"So tell me," he said, "with your vast experience and superior judgment, what do you think I should do?"

Joel looked as though he'd been slapped. His face registered both shock and hurt. He stared open-mouthed at Michel for a moment and then his expression turned dark and he stood up.

"I think you should learn how to use your right hand again," he said slowly and deliberately, then turned and walked out of the room.

Chapter 26

Lecher sat down with his first cup of coffee for the day and turned on the computer in his study. Around the closed window blinds he could see the pale orange glow of the rising sun. He logged into the Criminal Records database and entered Mose Lumley's name. Scrolling past the sections he'd already read, he went to Lumley's parole information. According to the file, Lumley had been hired at the Bellini Brothers' Produce Company a month after his release from prison in 1975. He'd maintained the job at least throughout the duration of his three-year probation.

Lecher returned to the database home page and entered the name Carl Adams. A single page appeared. Adams had been picked up and questioned for suspicion of trafficking in stolen goods five times between 1981 and 1985 but hadn't been arrested. There was no other information except an address in uptown. Lecher knew that neighborhood had been torn down at least fifteen years ago to make way for a Walmart. He logged off and took a sip of coffee.

Bellini Brothers' was still in operation. The green trucks were as familiar to anyone living the city as those of the Postal Service. The warehouse was located a few blocks from Lumley's house. Lecher wondered if anyone working there now would have known Lumley. It seemed possible. The shipping and warehouse industry often offered the only job opportunities for people without many prospects. They were havens for those with criminal records or difficult pasts who just wanted to make an honest living without being hassled. Generally the people who worked there weren't ambitious. They stayed on, happy for a steady paycheck and a familiar, comfortable routine.

He checked his watch. It was just after 5:15 am. He knew the warehouse would be open by now, sending out early deliveries to local markets and restaurants. If he showered quickly he could stop by and still make it to the office on time.

*****

The first wave of trucks had already left by the time he arrived an hour later, and most of the workers were sitting on the edge of the loading dock drinking coffee and smoking while they waited for the arrival of fresh produce to unload. A few looked old enough to have known Lumley but their sullen, suspicious gazes made him think better of approaching them. He knew that his look and manner would have immediately told them that he was somehow connected to the police. A few younger men and women were slowly walking around in the parking lot, engaged in lazy conversation.

He walked up the stairs to the loading dock and entered the green metal door at the top. There were a half dozen men standing together having a lively debate about something to his left. As soon as they noticed him they all stopped talking and turned to look at him, then after a few seconds looked away and picked up their conversation where they'd left off. He'd seen the same behavior when visiting prisons to investigate killings. As he was paraded through by the guards, groups of prisoners would stop to look at him, each man trying to assess whether this stranger would mean trouble for them personally. Then there would be a collective shrug as they all decided at the same moment that he was harmless and they'd return to whatever they'd been doing.

He was about to ask the group who was in charge when he saw someone moving quickly up the hallway to their left. It was a woman. She appeared to be in her sixties though he thought that she could have been ten years older or younger. Her ruddy face was weathered and wrinkled, but her body was slim and surprisingly muscled. She had straight, steel-gray hair that was pulled back into a loose ponytail and wore green work pants and a green t-shirt with the company logo over the left breast. Her stride was purposeful and—unlike everyone else he'd seen who seemed content to move only as quickly as necessary—fast. She turned left at the end of the hall and went through an open doorway.

Lecher walked past the group of men to the door. The word OFFICE was stencilled neatly on its glass. The woman was standing behind a desk sorting through papers with practiced efficiency.

"What can I do for you?" she said without looking up.

Her voice had the deep, fractured huskiness of a seasoned smoker.

"Me?" Lecher asked, taken by surprise.

The woman stopped her sorting just long enough to give him a look that was both amused and chiding.

"I know what everyone else is doing here," she said with a small laugh, returning to her work.

"I'm sorry," Lecher said. "I didn't realize you'd seen me."

"Guy in black dress pants, a gray sports jacket and striped tie shows up around here you tend to notice it," she said.

She looked up again and studied him for a moment.

"Sorry. Dark brown pants," she said. "So again, what can I do for you?"

Lecher decided he liked the woman. There was nothing unkind in her tone but she clearly didn't like to waste time. He decided to get right to the point.

"I'm not sure you can," he said, "but I was hoping I might be able to talk to someone who was working here 25 years ago."

"Go ahead," the woman responded.

For a moment Lecher wasn't sure how to interpret her

words, but as she gestured impatiently for him to continue he realized that she was inviting him to talk to her.

"Did you know a man named Mose Lumley who worked here?" he asked.

"Sure," the woman replied with a wary look. "He hired me in '79. He was the foreman here. Why are you asking about him? You're not a cop."

"What makes you say that?" Lecher asked.

"You didn't come in here swinging your dick around," the woman replied. "When cops come in here they have a tendency to do that. They think its funny because they know most of our people have done time and they like to fuck with their heads."

Lecher knew she was telling the truth. He'd seen too many cops try to intimidate former felons just for fun over the years. He decided he liked the woman more because she'd referred to the workers as "our people."

"You're right," he said. "My name is Kyle Smith. I'm with the Coroner's Office."

"Effa Bingham," the woman said, looking at him curiously. "I'm the dispatcher here."

"Nice to meet you, Ms. Bingham," Lecher replied.

"Call me Effa," she said, gesturing for him to take a seat in one of the two chairs in front of her desk.

She sat behind her desk and lit a cigarette.

"So what does the Coroner's Office want with Mose Lumley?" she asked through a thick curl of smoke. "He's been dead for a long time."

Lecher considered how to respond. Effa Bingham didn't strike him as the sort of woman who would go out of her way to confirm anything he told her. She'd probably put him out of her mind as soon as he left and get on with her life. At the same time he didn't want to lie to her any more than necessary.

"I'm afraid it's classified," he said, opting for the simplest approach.

Effa Bingham sat back in her chair and blew out smoke

with a sharp rasp. She began to chuckle, a sound that was more like a low-pitched cackle. She shook her head and sat forward, fixing Lecher with her clear green eyes.

"I wouldn't have believe whatever you told me, anyway, Mr. Smith," she said, "but I was curious what you'd come up with."

Lecher felt himself blush.

"Well, I..." he began to stammer.

Bingham held up her hand to stop him.

"I'm sure you have your reasons," she said. "I don't need to know 'em. I don't suppose you can do Mose any harm now anyway. Go ahead and ask your questions."

Lecher took a breath and tried to regain his composure. He wasn't used to having other people get the upper hand on him. He felt an increased admiration for the older woman, both because she'd seen through him and because of her willingness to still talk with him.

"Did Lumley have any close friends here?" he asked.

"Oh sure," Bingham replied. "He was tight with a group. There was Shane Duval, and Bo Archer, and Bill Watson. But he was probably closest to Carl Adams. They seemed to hang out a lot together after work."

Lecher was stunned, realizing how little he knew.

"Carl Adams worked here?" he asked.

"For a little while," Bingham said, nodding her head. "He started about a month before the unfortunate incident with Mose and then stayed on for a few months after. I'm not sure what happened to him after that. Do you know him?"

Lecher nodded distractedly before realizing what he'd been asked.

"No," he replied. "I've just heard his name before."

"In other words, none of my bee's wax," Bingham said with a knowing nod.

"I'm sorry, it's not that," Lecher replied. "I knew Lumley and Adams were friends. I just didn't know Adams had worked here. So they were close?"

Bingham nodded.

"Like two peas in a pod," she said. "Mose hired him as a favor to the brother, I think, but then they just hit it off."

Lecher felt the hairs on his neck stand up.

"What do you mean?" he asked anxiously. "Whose brother?"

"Carl's," Bingham said. "Eldridge, I think his name was. Mose used to volunteer over at the mission he ran on N. Rampart. I had the sense that the brother asked Mose to hire Carl."

Lecher sat silent, staring blankly at a spot a few inches in front of Effa Bingham's face.

"Are you okay?" she asked. "You look a little flushed."

"I'm fine," he replied, shaking away the thoughts that had begun to crowd his mind.

He stood up.

"I appreciate your time, Effa," he said, automatically extending his right hand.

The woman stared at it for a second before taking it into her sandpapery grasp. It was clear that handshakes were as foreign in her world as well-intentioned men in suits.

Lecher left her office and began walking quickly to his car. He felt both elated and nervous. He'd found a new suspect. Eldridge Adams was Carl's brother and Sassy's brother-in-law. He'd also known Mose Lumley and had been at Lumley's house the night Iris was killed.

As he got into his car he wondered what else he could learn about Eldridge Adams.

Chapter 27

The buzzing seemed to have been going on forever. Still caught in the limbo between deep sleep and waking, Michel tried to figure out where it was coming from. He was floating on inky black water and knew that he could drift peacefully away if not for the annoying sound that seemed to anchor him in place. The buzzing was growing louder and he struggled to open his eyes. A faint glow filtered through his lashes. Summoning all his discipline, he forced his eyes to open the rest of the way. He was staring up at the familiar pendant light in the center of his bedroom ceiling. He rolled to his side and slapped his right hand across the top of the alarm clock on his nightstand. It was 7:27 am. The alarm had been buzzing for almost a half hour.

He'd been awake most of the night, reliving his confrontation with Joel and imagining all the things he should have said and done differently. He'd finally given in to exhaustion and fallen asleep just before 6 am. Now his head felt like it had been stuffed with cotton candy while he slept. It felt heavy and thick and his thoughts were slow, as though pushing their way through sticky, pink clouds.

He dragged himself closer to the edge of the bed, then extended his lower legs out from under the sheet and pushed himself up into a sitting position. He focused his thoughts on the coffee maker in the kitchen and willed it to turn itself on.

I'm such an asshole, he thought. Why didn't I think before I spoke?

He got up and walked unsteadily to the bathroom. As he stood over the toilet emptying his bladder he rubbed his fingers gently against his temples, then began tugging at handfuls of his hair, trying to revive sensation in his head. As the sound of his stream hitting the water diminished he looked down and saw that his unguided effort had badly splattered the rim of the porcelain bowl. He shook his head and decided to leave the clean-up until later.

After splashing his face with cold water he headed to the kitchen. The still-dormant coffee maker on the counter silently mocked him. Fucker, he thought, as he poked the button sharply to turn it on.

He moved to the living room and picked up his cigarettes, then took a seat at the kitchen counter and lit one. The events of the night before began to play again in his head.

He knew what he'd said to Joel was cruel. In essence he'd said that he didn't consider Joel his equal, and he'd done it by mocking the two areas about which Joel would be most insecure: his maturity and his judgment. He wondered whether he actually considered Joel to be his equal.

Certainly in terms of life experience they weren't equal, he thought. Joel was still figuring out who he was and what he wanted to do with his life. Although he realized that he'd been questioning the same things for the past six month and was still uncertain what he would do after the Adams case was closed, he decided their situations were different. His experiences had led him to question what he was already doing, whereas Joel was still finding his direction. He was going through the stage of defining himself that was natural for his age.

Emotionally, too, they were unequal. He admired Joel's openness and ability to express his feelings, and the fact that he had been able to accept his sexuality as an integrated part of life at such an early age. He also appreciated Joel's enthusiasm. It was a trait that he'd aspired to regain for himself. At the same time he realized that he often felt that Joel still saw the world as a child did; he didn't yet have an understanding of emotional complexity and tended to see things as black or white.

Thinking back on the months that they'd known one another, he realized that as often as he'd been astounded by Joel's insights and emotional maturity, he'd just as often found himself listening indulgently and thinking patronizingly that Joel's viewpoint would change as he got older.

The burbling of the coffee maker broke his thoughts and he got up and poured himself a cup. As he sat back at the counter he lit another cigarette.

His thoughts turned to the question of judgment. Seven months earlier Joel had viewed the boys who lived at Zelda's house as his friends, as a "family" to which he wanted to belong. His desperation to be a part of them had been so strong that he'd begun smoking crystal meth and had allowed himself to be drawn—actually chosen to be drawn—into hustling so that he'd fit in.

They'd discussed it many times over the months since and Joel had explained how his desire to belong had been so overwhelming that he'd allowed himself to ignore his conscience. Michel had never criticized him for it, but at the same time he'd always felt that Joel's desperation and poor judgment had been a sign of immaturity.

As he stubbed out his cigarette and immediately lit another Michel realized that he was trying too hard to answer his own question. In his heart he already knew the answer. He loved and appreciated Joel, but in many ways he still considered him a kid. Just by virtue of the fact that he was a decade younger, Joel would always have less life experience than he did and they would always be at different points in their lives.

He wondered whether that meant he would never see Joel as his true equal. He knew he could respect Joel, but would he ever lose the feeling that the gap in their maturity made them different? He decided that until he was sure of the answer it would be unfair to Joel to try to mend the rift between them.

Chapter 28

Michel waited until DeRoche left for an 11 am meeting before calling Lee Catlin. Catlin picked up on the third ring.

"Lee, it's Michel Doucette," Michel said.

"Hey, Michel," Catlin responded around a mouthful of bagel. "How've you been? I heard you were on sabbatical or something."

"Just a break for a few months," Michel replied, "but I'm back now."

"Great. So what can I do for you?" Catlin asked quickly, already sounding bored with the conversation.

"I just had a question on the autopsy you did on Carl Adams," Michel replied.

"Which one was that?" Catlin mumbled as he took another bite of bagel.

"Suicide. Black male, mid-50s. He was brought in last Thursday," Michel replied, rolling his eyes.

"Oh yeah," Catlin replied. "I remember. What about him?"

"I was just curious what toxins you screened him for. There were no notations on the report," Michel replied.

There was silence for a moment. Michel wondered if Catlin was checking his records or finishing his breakfast.

"Uh, that would be because I didn't run any," Catlin replied finally.

"You didn't?" Michel asked.

"No, he was a suicide," Catlin responded patronizingly. "Why would I run a tox screen?"

Michel briefly fought the impulse to light into Catlin for his lackadaisical approach to his job. He was more concerned, however, by the suspicion that had crept into his mind and wanted to end the call quickly.

"Oh yeah," he said. "Sorry, I thought there was a check mark on the report. I can see now it's just a smudge."

"Cool," Catlin replied, clearly too disinterested to ask any questions. "I'll be seeing you around."

Michel hung up and stared at the phone for a moment. He'd left the report at home, but knew he'd clearly seen a check mark in the Negative box in the tox screen section. That meant that the report had been altered after Catlin turned it in. He'd been surprised that Lecher hadn't flagged the report for being incomplete, but it made sense if Lecher had altered the report himself. The question was why he'd do it.

Michel thought back to his conversation with Lecher. At the time he'd thought nothing of it, but when he'd asked if Lecher had any reason to believe that Carl wasn't guilty, Lecher's right eyelid had twitched before he responded. He realized now it had been a tell, the kind of involuntary tick that most people displayed when they lied.

But why would Lecher keep his doubts secret, and why would he want the police to believe Carl killed himself? he wondered. It didn't make sense. So long as the police believed Carl killed himself, the investigation would stay focused on Carl because his apparent suicide lent credence to the assumption that he was guilty. Other potential suspects might be overlooked.

Michel felt a chill run up his spine as the realization hit him: Lecher was purposefully misdirecting the investigation because he didn't want the police to look at other options. If the investigation stayed focused on Carl, Lecher would be able to gain an advantage looking for other suspects on his own. He was planning to find Iris' real killer first if they determined Carl was innocent.

Michel knew he couldn't let that happen. He doubted whether Lecher was capable of killing another man, but didn't want to have to find out. He thought briefly of simply telling Lecher that he'd found proof of Carl's guilt, but knew Lecher would want to see the proof for himself. No, for now it was better to play along and let Lecher believe they were working together.

Keep your friends close and your enemies closer, he thought.

He knew he had to act quickly. The longer it took him to determine if Carl was guilty, the greater the lead Lecher might gain toward finding another suspect. First he would go ahead with his plan to talk to Eldridge. While he didn't expect Eldridge to know anything about any of the girls in the photos, he might be able to provide missing information on what happened that night at Lumley's house, or give some insight into his brother. Then he would work on connecting Carl directly to one or more of the missing girls.

He knew he had an advantage for the moment because Lecher didn't know he knew Carl's autopsy report had been altered. He also felt that Lecher had a weakness: a belief in his own intellectual superiority. That might give him a chance to gain some ground because Lecher wouldn't expect him to figure out what was really happening so quickly. He wondered for a second if he shared the same weakness, but decided he didn't believe he was smarter. He was simply more experienced in criminal investigation. He hoped that would be enough.

The only question that remained was whether he should tell DeRoche what he'd found out. If he did it was possible that DeRoche would remove him from the investigation, if not the force entirely. He'd broken direct orders by not divulging what he was doing. He may have gone too far to turn back. He knew if he went any further he would certainly be risking his career.

He picked up his jacket and cigarettes and headed for the stairwell. I guess that's a risk I'm willing to take, he thought.

*****

As Michel arrived at the building on N. Rampart Street he saw a silver canteen truck parked in front. To his surprise, a dozen men in hardhats were lined up by the side, waiting patiently to buy their lunch.

Damn, Eldridge moves fast, he thought.

He studied the workers as he walked up to the front of the building. A few had the look of professionals. They were dressed in steel-toed boots and had heavy leather tool belts fastened around their waists. They also had the thick muscularity of men who did hard labor on a daily basis.

The others appeared to be day-laborers. From 7–9 on any weekday morning, groups of these men would gather on specific corners throughout the city, hoping to be hired for a day's work. Some days they might be helping out a construction crew, hauling materials and cleaning. Other days they might find work landscaping or hauling trash. This was the underclass of workers who kept the city going by doing the work no one else wanted, often for less than minimum wage. Many of them were illegal immigrants or paroled felons with no other employment opportunities, and local companies exploited that fact.

The group in front of the mission ranged in age from early-20s to mid-40s. All were black or Latin or some blend of both. As he approached they subtly lowered their heads and shifted their bodies away from him.

"Hey, is Eldridge Adams around?" he asked one of the men who appeared to be a professional worker.

"In the back, down the hall to the right," the man replied tersely.

Michel entered the building through the open double doors. The room inside was large, at least fifty feet wide by forty deep. There were no windows along the sides or back, but the wall facing the street had four large, paned windows that allowed the light in. The floor was thick with dust but appeared to be wide planks of cypress. The cracked and peeling ceiling was at least twelve feet high and was edged by ornate crown molding. Michel guessed that at one point the building might have been a hotel and this room was the lobby. He saw a swinging double door in the center of the back wall and an open doorway in the back right corner. He walked to the corner.

The doorway opened into a twenty-foot-long corridor. There were two doors along the right side, one marked "MEN" and the other "WOMEN." At the end was a dark wood door with a pebbled glass panel in the upper half. He walked to that door and knocked.

"Come in," Eldridge replied.

Michel opened the door and found Eldridge seated behind a massive steel desk. As he saw Michel he smiled and stood.

"Officer Doucette," he said, moving out from behind the desk and extending his right hand.

"Please, call me Michel," Michel said, taking Eldridge's large hand and shaking it briefly.

"Welcome, Michel," Eldridge said warmly. "What brings you down here? Is this an official visit or did you just want to check the place out?"

"More official, I'm afraid," Michel replied. "You sure didn't waste any time getting to work, though, did you?"

Eldridge laughed appreciatively.

"No, I guess not," he said. "Being busy keeps my mind off of less pleasant things, I suppose."

Michel nodded sympathetically.

"So how did you get the lease and permits and line up your crew so quickly?" he asked with genuine amazement. "It usually takes a year just to replace a pane of glass in this city."

"Well, I still have a few friends around here," Eldridge replied with a chuckle. "Plus I've been planning to come back for a few months now. As I mentioned at the service, I'd been hoping to spend more time with my brother, so I already had everything in the works."

"I see," Michel said, nodding. "So I'm curious. Was this building ever a hotel?"

"The Congo Square Inn," Eldridge replied. "Built in 1826 and operated until 1865. After that it was a restaurant for a few years, then a casino. When I took it over the first time it had been vacant for seventy-some years."

"It looks to be in pretty good shape," Michel said.

"They built them solid back in those days," Eldridge replied. "All we need to do is clean it up, update the wiring and plumbing, and do some painting. I plan to open within the month."

"That's great," Michel said, wondering how to transition the conversation to his purpose for coming.

"So what can I do for you?" Eldridge asked, as if reading his mind.

"I wanted to talk to you about the night that Sassy was shot," Michel replied.

Eldridge gave him a surprised look.

"Of course," he said. "Shall we sit?"

He gestured toward two brown leather chairs by the window of the room and they sat down.

"I understand you were waiting in the car while Sassy went in the house to talk to Lumley," Michel began immediately. "Is that correct?"

Eldridge nodded.

"We were on our way to the market and she said she had to ask Lumley a question. I waited outside while she went in," he replied.

"Why were you in the Warehouse District?" Michel asked. "Why wouldn't you go to a market in the Marigny, closer to Sassy's and Carl's house?"

Eldridge looked perplexed for a moment, as though the question had never occurred to him before.

"I'm not sure," he replied, shrugging. "We finished dinner and Sassy asked me to go to the market with her. I never thought to ask why she drove to the Warehouse District. I guess maybe she planned to speak to Lumley all along."

Michel knew Eldridge hadn't anticipated the question and his response had seemed genuine, so he decided to move on.

"So then what happened?" he asked.

"She'd been inside for about five minutes when I heard what sounded like two muffled gunshots," Eldridge said. "I had the car windows closed so I couldn't be sure where they'd come from or even if they were gunshots, but I got worried so I went to the front door and started ringing the bell. After a minute when no one answered I tried the door and it was unlocked. I went into the hallway and started calling Sassy's name, but she didn't respond, so I called the police."

"Then what?" Michel asked.

"The door to the basement was open so I went downstairs. I found Sassy lying in the hallway. She was unconscious but still breathing at the time. I started to roll her onto her back but then I saw the bullet wound to her stomach and became worried the bullet might be near her spine and she'd be paralyzed if I moved her. So I took my jacket off and held it against the wound until the police arrived."

"Did you see Lumley or Iris Lecher?" Michel asked.

"No," Eldridge replied. "The door to the back room was closed. I could see the light coming through the holes in it but I couldn't see inside from where I was."

"Did you hear any noises from the back room?"

Eldridge shook his head.

"How much time would you say passed from the time you heard the shots until you found Sassy?" Michel asked, leaning forward in his chair.

"No more than two minutes, I'd guess," Eldridge replied, shrugging. "Why?"

"I think that your brother may have been there that night,

too," Michel replied. "There's a bulkhead that leads from the back room into the yard. He could have gotten out that way. I was hoping you might remember seeing or hearing something to support that theory."

Eldridge looked at Michel coldly for a moment.

"Are you suggesting I knew Carl was there?" he asked, leaning forward to match Michel's position.

"Not at all," Michel replied quickly. "But given the circumstances, it's possible you saw or heard something without even realizing it. I just wanted to see if you could remember anything."

Eldridge seemed satisfied with the answer and relaxed back into his chair a bit.

"I'm afraid not," he said. "In fact I remember the quiet. It was unnerving."

Michel gave him a curious look.

"What about Sassy? She wasn't making any noise?"

Eldridge shook his head quickly and a shiver seemed to run up his spine at the memory.

"After a minute or two her breathing stopped," he said. "When the first officer arrived he checked her pulse and said she was dead. The paramedics revived her."

"How long before they arrived?" Michel asked.

"About five minutes," Eldridge replied. "Maybe a little longer. I'm not really sure."

Michel imagined Eldridge as a younger man and the fear he must have felt that night.

"I'm sorry to have to put you through this," he said, "especially given all you've been through the last few days."

"I understand," Eldridge replied with a forgiving smile.

Michel knew he should leave, but he still wanted to get some sense of Sassy's and Carl's relationship.

"Sassy never told me much about her marriage," he said suddenly, "I'm curious what kind of a relationship she and Carl had."

Eldridge studied him for a moment before responding. Michel couldn't read his expression.

"That's kind of an odd thing to be wondering about," Eldridge said. "Does it have some bearing on your investigation?"

"Possibly," Michel replied carefully. "Part of my job is trying to get inside the heads of suspects so I can understand what motivates them. I guess I'm just trying to get into your brother's head. I don't know much about him, but it seems that his relationship with Sassy was an important part of his life. It wasn't something he just forgot about. He called her every year on their anniversary."

Eldridge nodded to indicate that he knew about the calls. He looked like he was going to ask a question, but then stopped himself. Instead he pursed his lips and looked at the floor, his brows furrowed in contemplation.

"I thought that Carl and Sassy were meant for one another," he said finally. "I know that sounds awfully romantic, but I did. They complemented one another. Sassy helped ground Carl and give him a sense of purpose. For the first time I felt he had a desire to accomplish something with his life. He wanted to make her proud of him and provide a good home for her and the baby.

"And Carl seemed to awaken a side of Sassy that I didn't see when I first met her. I always liked her because she was smart and self-directed, but there was also something distant about her. I felt she didn't want to need other people."

Michel nodded to himself, knowing that side of Sassy well.

"With Carl that changed," Eldridge continued. "She became more open...generous of spirit, I guess I'd call it. I think they were very much in love and appreciated one another."

"So there weren't any problems that you knew of?" Michel asked.

"Nothing that suggested imminent divorce," Eldridge replied.

"I imagine the loss of the baby may have been a catalyst," Michel said. "From my experience that kind of trauma either makes couples much stronger or drives them apart."

"That's true," Eldridge said, nodding thoughtfully, "but I thought it would bring Carl and Sassy closer together. Their relationship seemed strong enough to weather it. Obviously I was wrong. I know Carl didn't want it to end, but Sassy's feelings changed. It was like her heart was wounded, and when it healed it had closed up again."

"Do you think Carl hated her because of it?" Michel asked.

Eldridge seemed to consider the question seriously before replying.

"On some level, I suppose," he said. "It certainly made him bitter, and I think he started to blame her for his own failures afterward. But I also don't think he ever really stopped loving her."

The answer felt honest and Michel nodded in acknowledgment.

"What kind of a man was Carl?" he asked.

"That's a hard question to answer," Eldridge replied. "How do you summarize a person in a few words?"

Michel knew the question was rhetorical and waited for Eldridge to continue.

"I guess the best way to put it is that he was very different than he appeared," Eldridge said. "If you were to meet him on the street, both as a boy and a man, you'd think he was sweet but not particularly ambitious. He had an easy-going charm, and came across as someone who was contented with his lot in life and didn't feel the need to rock the boat or draw attention to himself. In reality, though, he had a lot of ambition, and he was smart enough to understand that he could get away with more if no one was paying attention to him."

"Meaning?" Michel asked.

"He was...deceptive," Eldridge replied. "Not in a purposeful way, mind you, but practically speaking. He may have seemed contented or even lazy, but most of the time his mind was calculating. He was always on the lookout for an opportunity. I'd say that he was a natural schemer, but unfortunately not much of a planner. He could identify an opportunity, but not figure out the best way to capitalize on it. All of the time he spent in jail was because of poor planning. He was simply not an instinctively good criminal."

Michel tried to form a picture of Carl in his mind.

"Let me give you an example," Eldridge said. "One summer our folks sent us to our uncle's tobacco farm in Virginia. Carl was about eleven at the time. They just wanted us to get away from the city for a while and enjoy the fresh air. After we'd been there about a week, though, our uncle offered us a dollar an hour to pick tobacco. He probably didn't expect us to do more than a few hours of work a week. Just enough to earn some money for candy and what-not.

"Well, I decided that if my aunt and uncle were going to put me up for the summer then I ought to earn my keep, so I started going out in the fields at sunrise and working til sunset along with everyone else. And much to my surprise, a few days later Carl did, too. In fact, Carl probably worked harder than anyone else.

"Now by this point I was old enough to know that Carl was up to something. It wasn't that he'd ever been afraid of work, but I knew that if there was an easier way to do something, or an angle to profit more, he'd find it. So I kept an eye on him, but I could never figure out his plan."

Michel imagined Eldridge as a boy keeping a watchful eye on his scheming younger brother.

"So the end of August arrived and our folks came to pick us up," Eldridge continued. "We'd each come with one suitcase full of clothes and I took mine out to the car and noticed that all Carl's clothes were already in the trunk in two paper bags. I went back in the house and asked him where his suitcase was. He got a panicky look on his face and said it was too heavy for him to carry. So our father went into our room and saw the suitcase laying on its side on the floor. He grabbed the handle and tried to lift it and the bottom ripped off, leaving about eighty pounds of tobacco leaves on the floor.

"Carl had gotten it into his head that he could sell the tobacco on his own back home, so he'd been hiding a few leaves under his shirt every day and putting them in his suitcase. What he hadn't taken into account was the fact that the leaves needed to be dried. Instead they'd just sat in that suitcase and as he added more the ones on the bottom started to compost and the dampness rotted the fabric of the suitcase.

"That was the essence of Carl. He was a lot more clever than other people suspected, but a lot less clever than he himself believed."

Michel didn't sense any judgment in Eldridge's tone and smiled at both the story and Eldridge's assessment of his brother.

"What do you think motivated him?" he asked.

"Insecurity, I suspect, and I think I'm to blame for that." Eldridge said matter-of-factly. "I know this will sound egotistical, but it's really just an old man reflecting on himself as a child. From a very young age I had a sense of purpose for my life. I was always active in our church and community, and did as much as I could to help folks out. I gained a reputation for doing good works. Because Carl was my brother, people expected the same of him and I think that was very difficult for him. He felt like he was living in my shadow. After a while when people's expectations for him diminished, I think he sensed it and wanted to prove that he could be successful in his own right."

Michel wondered how this aspect of Carl might manifest itself.

"Did he ever express anger or resentment toward you?" he asked.

Eldridge shook his head and smiled.

"No," he said. "In fact I rarely saw Carl get angry at anyone. He was one of the gentlest people I've ever known. I can remember only a handful of instances when he even raised his voice."

Eldridge seemed to struggle with what he wanted to say next.

"I know this may sound odd after what I've told you," he said after a moment, "but I think my brother was basically a good man. He was just a victim of his own weaknesses. Up until Sassy came along there was never any sense that he planned his life. He just took whatever opportunities presented themselves without thinking of the long term consequences, and as a result he made a lot of mistakes. I've come across thousands of men who were no different in my work, and I imagine you have as well."

Michel nodded. Although he knew he could argue that most of those men had been guilty of no more than petty larceny, he decided to let it go.

"Well, I appreciate your time, Eldridge" he said, pushing himself up from his chair. "This has been very helpful."

"Not at all," Eldridge replied, rising as well and walking Michel to the door of his office.

"By the way," Michel asked, "where are you staying in case I need to talk to you again and you're not here?"

"At Carl's," Eldridge replied. "I have to say it's been quite a job putting it back together after your people finished ransacking it. I haven't even had a chance to move my own things out of his storage locker in the basement yet."

Michel decided that the choice of the word "ransacking" had been intended humorously but felt compelled to apologize anyway.

"I'm sorry about that," he said. "We had to be certain we didn't miss any evidence that might link your brother to one of the girls."

Eldridge gave him a confused look.

"But he was found with their photos," he said. "What more evidence would you need?"

"I meant the other girls," Michel replied.

Eldridge's eyes began to blink quickly.

"What are you talking about?" he asked, his voice suddenly anxious. "What other girls?"

Michel realized with a sick feeling that Eldridge didn't know about the photos in the safe deposit box. He'd assumed Sassy would have told him by now.

"Eldridge," he said gently, "we found the photos of thirty six more girls in Carl's safe deposit box."

The color drained from Eldridge's face and for a moment his upper body seemed to sway in a small circle. Then he began to fall toward Michel.

*****

All the next day Sassy was preoccupied thinking about how best to enact her plan. She was still convinced that Mose Lumley was the key, but wasn't sure what kind of approach to take with him. If she went to him as Carl's wife and asked him to leave Carl alone he might be sympathetic, but there was also the chance that he would tell Carl about her visit. There also would be no guarantee he'd stop what he was doing, and the longer he continued, the greater the chance that he'd get caught and possibly implicate Carl.

Confronting him as a cop seemed safer and more likely to be effective. She'd never met him and doubted that Carl had ever told him that her real name was Alexandra, and since she'd kept her maiden name it was unlikely he'd make the connection. The question was how she could justify approaching him officially. The police weren't in the habit of issuing warnings for felonies. Lumley would become suspicious if she didn't arrest him.

She wished that she had a sense of him, of whether he would respond better to reason or threats. She considered going to Eldridge for help since he knew Lumley, but decided against it for the moment. She knew that Eldridge wouldn't approve of her plan and would insist she confront Carl directly.

On some level she knew that he would be right. Even if she succeeded in ending the current situation there was no guarantee Carl wouldn't begin again with someone else or on his own. She might just be postponing the inevitable. She knew that if she ever saw any evidence that Carl had started up again she'd have to confront him. For now, though, she was willing to try her approach first. She wanted to protect Carl and give him the chance to change on his own.

That morning Carl had told her he was working late again that night. She'd tried to talk him out of it, telling him that she was planning a special evening for them, but he'd told her he had no choice. As she drifted off to sleep late that night she prayed that he wouldn't get caught for another night.

When the phone woke her at seven the next morning she felt a rush of panic. Carl wasn't beside her and his side of the bed was undisturbed. She picked up the phone after the second ring.

"Hello?" she asked anxiously.

"Officer Jones?" a male voice responded.

"Yes?"

"This is Lt. Maddox of the Louisiana State Police," the voice said. "I'm sorry to disturb you so early on a Saturday, but I need you to meet me at your station house as soon as possible."

"What's the matter?" Sassy asked as she began imagining all of the things that might have happened to Carl.

"There was a kidnapping last night," Maddox said. "A little girl in the Garden District. I'm heading up the investigation, working with NOPD. Your commander tells me you have a degree in criminal psych and we'd like your help putting together a profile of the kidnapper."

"Oh," Sassy said, sudden relief flooding her body. "I can get there in about an hour, if that's all right."

"The sooner the better," Maddox replied. "The first 48 hours are always critical."

Sassy hung up and walked downstairs. Carl was asleep on the couch, the TV still on with the volume turned low. She leaned down and nudged his shoulder gently.

"Carl, honey," she said softly. "Honey, wake up."

She nudged him again and his eyes slowly opened. He looked up at her in confusion.

"Hey, baby," he said. "What's going on? Is something wrong? Is the baby all right?"

"Everything's fine," she replied, "but I have to go into the station."

Carl sat up and rubbed his face.

"What for?" he asked. "It's Saturday."

"Another little girl was kidnapped last night," she replied. "The State Police want me help them develop a profile of the kidnapper."

"How can someone do something like that?" Carl asked, shaking his head sadly. "That's just not right."

"I know," Sassy said, touching the side of his face with her left hand. "Hopefully I'll be able to help find whoever did it so it doesn't happen again."

Carl put his hand over hers and held it against his cheek.

"You're a good woman, Sassy Jones," he said.

While she showered and dressed Carl made coffee and toasted her an English muffin. She was anxious to get to the station but he insisted she eat something for the baby's sake and she relented.

She arrived at the station at 7:53 am and went immediately to the Detective Division. It was the first time she'd been there. At least two dozen plainclothed men were seated at desks around the large room, intently reading through stacks of files or talking on the phone. Another dozen in uniform were busy bringing more files to the already-overloaded desks. No one seemed rushed or excited, but she could feel a focused energy in the air.

When her presence had gone unnoticed for a full minute she approached the desk closest to her. A beefy, red-faced man was just hanging up his phone. He sensed her presence and looked up. The look on his face told her that he wasn't excited to see her.

"*Can I help you, sister?*" *he asked impatiently.*

Both his tone and use of the word "sister" set her teeth on edge but she kept her expression neutral. Although it seemed like a foolish thing to have to think about when a girl's life was at stake, she understood intuitively that she needed to make the right first impression if she hoped to be taken seriously in this new environment. She suspected that the man already knew who she was but was playing a game with her. She looked down quickly and saw a black acrylic nameplate engraved O'HALLORAN on his desk.

"*Yes, Detective O'Halloran,*" *she replied confidently,* "*I'm looking for Lt. Maddox of the State Police.*"

The man sat back in his chair and gave her a wolfish smile. She could practically read the words "uppity nigger" in his eyes and knew he would try to take her down a peg.

"*What makes you think I'm O'Halloran?*" *he asked in a loud voice clearly intended to draw attention.*

Sassy could sense people stopping what they were doing and turning to look at them, but she kept her gaze focused on the man. He was clearly relishing the temporary power he wielded over her. She imagined that he had already prepared several remarks to make her look foolish in anticipation of how she might respond.

She gave him a sweet smile.

"*Well how many fat fuck Irishmen do you have around here?*" *she asked.*

The room was silent for a moment as the man's face turned redder and his mouth began to work angrily. Then the room erupted with laughter. Sassy wondered for a moment if O'Halloran would charge her, but the laughter was suddenly cut short by a penetrating voice from across the room.

"*Are you Jones?*"

She turned and saw a man with a silver crewcut and pale blue eyes staring at her from a doorway at the back of the room. He looked to be in his late-50s but appeared still taught and muscular under his dark blue suit. He had the bearing of a military man.

207

Sassy nodded.

"If you please," the man said, gesturing her toward him.

Without looking back at O'Halloran she began crossing the room. She was aware of the buzz of voices starting up again and decided she'd passed her first test.

The doorway led to a small office and she walked in. The silver-haired man was standing behind a desk near the back of the room, flanked by two other men she didn't recognize.

"Officer Jones, I'm Lt. Maddox," he said immediately.

"Nice to meet you," Sassy replied, though she felt odd saying it under the circumstances.

"This is Capt. Giraux and Lt. Sinclair of the NOPD," Maddox said, nodding first to the man on his right and then the one on his left.

To Sassy the two men looked like twins. Even their rumpled brown suits were nearly identical. They both appeared to be in their mid-40s and had pale round faces with nondescript features. Their seemingly immovable helmets of dull brown hair with flecks of gray at the temples were short and parted neatly on the right sides. Sassy thought they could easily have passed as the weekend weathermen on a local TV station. She nodded to each of them.

"I'm sorry about that," she said, pointing over her shoulder toward the main room.

"Don't worry about it," Maddox replied curtly. "If they thought they could shit on you you'd never earn their respect. Take a seat."

Sassy sat in the only chair on her side of the desk while Maddox took the chair behind it. Giraux and Sinclair perched themselves on opposite edges of the desk with their arms folded across their chests, creating the impression of bookends. Sassy realized that the important conversation would take place in the space between them.

"I know from your file that you've only been on the job for about a month," Maddox began, "but you were top of your class at the academy and your partner seems to think very highly of you. He thinks you're very smart."

"That's very kind of him," Sassy said reflexively, wondering to whom Dupree had expressed his opinion.

"I've spoken to your commander and he's agreed to let you work with us until we solve this case," Maddox said, studying her. "Do you think you're ready for this?"

Sassy's initial thought was to be humble, but she recognized that she was being given an opportunity to distinguish herself that might not come along again.

"Yes, sir," she said.

Maddox studied her for a moment longer, then nodded.

"Good," he said. "Let's get started."

*****

Maddox reviewed the facts of the case for her, with Giraux and Sinclair chiming in occasionally to provide secondary information. Maddox seemed resigned to tolerating their presence, though his manner made it clear who was running the investigation.

Sassy knew that the majority of kidnappings were committed by a close family member, usually in response to a fight for custody, but Maddox told her that Iris' father and grandmother had already been cleared and that there were no other relatives in the area. With the immediate family ruled out, Sassy assumed the investigation would focus primarily on friends and acquaintances, the group next most likely to have committed the crime.

She waited until Maddox had finished his briefing before speaking.

"Have you found any connections between the Lechers and the families of the first two girls who were kidnapped?" she asked.

Maddox shook his head.

"We never found a connection between the Crowes and the Macombers, so I doubt we'll find anything that connects all three," he said.

"So you don't really think it's someone who was close to the family?" Sassy asked, though it was more of a statement.

"Officially, I can't say" Maddox replied, "but off the record I'd say no."

Sassy decided she liked his directness.

"So far we don't have any physical evidence that even confirms that the kidnappings are related," Maddox continued, "but it seems pretty clear they are. All three girls were about the same age, they were all blond, and they were all taken from their homes at night."

Sassy nodded.

"So you want me to create a profile for the wild card," she said.

"Exactly," Maddox said. "We still have to interview anyone who knew the girl or her family, but I'm betting we won't find anything. I want to start looking at other options."

"Do you have the case files for the first two girls for me?" Sassy asked.

Maddox nodded.

"We've set up an office for you down the hall," he said.

"Why not here?" Sassy asked, concerned that she was being isolated from the rest of the investigation.

Maddox looked at Giraux and Sinclair before responding.

"Officer Jones," he said, meeting her gaze, "there were never any ransom demands for the first two girls. We have to assume that they're dead, and that Iris Lecher will be, too, if we don't find the kidnapper first. While I appreciate your desire to be a part of the team, every moment you have to spend making your bones by putting some redneck cop in his place is a moment we lose finding the girl. It will be much less of a distraction for everyone if you work alone."

Though it bothered her philosophically, Sassy knew that Maddox was right. She thought about Dupree's approach to the job and realized that she could do the most good by accepting the situation.

"Okay," she said. "Just point me in the right direction."

Maddox smiled at her.

"We're hoping that's what you're going to do for us," he said.

Chapter 29

God bless the internet and parents who give their children uncommon names, Lecher thought, as he sat back in his office chair and listened to the printer chugging away behind him. In less than an hour he'd been able to piece together a chronology of Eldridge Adams' life for the past twenty five years.

His search had yielded three news articles. The first had appeared in the Chicago Tribune in June of 1995 when Eldridge received an award from a community service group for his efforts helping the city's homeless. The article said that Eldridge had been operating his mission on the South Side since 1992, after opening missions in New Orleans in 1977, Mexico City in 1982, and Los Angeles in 1986.

The second article was from the New York Post from August of 1998. Eldridge was quoted in an article about a series of violent attacks against homeless men in Harlem. The story identified him as an advocate for the homeless who ran a shelter in the Tribeca area of Manhattan.

The final piece was an editorial in the Houston Chronicle from May of 2000, in support of a proposed shelter in the city's Greater Fifth Ward. The paper cited Eldridge's successess helping the homeless in other major U.S. cities as the primary reason for its support.

The printer went silent and Lecher picked up the printouts and put them in his briefcase. From what he'd read, Adams had devoted his adult life to helping people. He knew that fact should have eased his suspicions, but something bothered him.

Michel had told him that four of the girls he'd identified were listed as runaways. One of the things that linked the five U.S. cities where Adams had opened his missions was that they were all meccas for teenage runaways. He supposed the same was true for Mexico City. They were among the handful of cities that seemed to offer almost-magical promise to unhappy teenagers with dreams of a better life. He imagined that many of them found their way to homeless shelters when their money ran out.

There was something else that bothered him, as well. Missy Macomber, Celia Crowe and Iris had all been taken from their homes. At least four of the girls in the photos were runaways. If any of the others had been reported as kidnapped, Michel would have been able to identify them by now. That meant they were most likely runaways, as well, or had no family to report them missing. Why the change in pattern? he wondered. Were the first three kidnappings done by Carl Adams or Lumley and the rest by Eldridge?

He realized he was getting ahead of himself. His evidence against Eldridge was circumstantial at best. While the cities where he'd opened his missions were popular destinations for runaways, they also had higher than average poverty levels and homeless populations. They were logical locations for shelters. Until one of the missing girls could actually be linked to one of the missions, any further speculation was essentially useless.

He looked at his watch and saw that it was nearly 2 pm. He wanted to call Michel to find out if any progress had been made identifying more girls or linking any of them to Carl but decided to wait. He didn't want to appear too anxious. He would let Michel call him.

*****

Twenty minutes later Michel left the mission. Eldridge had never lost consciousness, but he'd clearly gone into shock.

Michel had almost called an ambulance, but then Eldridge's eyes had begun to clear and he'd started to respond to Michel's voice. After a few more minutes he seemed back to normal, though badly shaken. When he was convinced the worst was over, Michel had left, but not before suggesting that Eldridge visit a doctor that afternoon.

He walked up a block and turned left on Ursuline Street, then paused to light a cigarette. He took out his cell phone and dialed Sassy's number. She picked up on the first ring.

"It's about time," she said.

"Look, Sas, I just left Eldridge," Michel said. "He's in pretty bad shape."

"What happened?" she asked, her voice full of concern.

"Why didn't you tell him about the other photos?" Michel asked.

"Oh, shit," Sassy said. "I didn't know how to bring it up. I guess I was putting it off as long as I could. Did you tell him?"

"Not on purpose," Michel replied with frustration. "I assumed he already knew and mentioned them."

"I'm sorry, Michel," Sassy replied. "It didn't occur to me that you might talk to him. I thought I had some time."

"Well, you might want to give him a call," Michel said, ignoring her apology. "I suggested he go to a doctor to get checked out, but I don't know if he will."

"A doctor?" Sassy asked with surprise.

"Yeah," Michel replied. "It hit him hard. He was in shock for a few minutes."

"I really am sorry, Michel," Sassy said.

"I know," Michel replied.

They were both quiet for a few seconds. Michel knew that he had to acknowledge the previous night's conversation even though he wasn't ready to discuss it yet.

"Listen, about last night...," he said finally.

"Don't," Sassy interrupted. "I was out of line. I had no business saying what I did or prying for information. It was unfair to you as a friend and disrespectful professionally. I'm sorry."

Michel felt a surge of affection for Sassy and smiled to himself.

"Thank you," he said, his voice catching for a second. "That means a lot to me."

"Okay, okay," Sassy replied with mock brusqueness. "Don't be getting all Hallmark on me."

Michel began laughing.

"All right," he said, "but I'm going right home to watch a Lifetime movie."

"And that would be different from every other day how?" Sassy asked, laughing as well.

They enjoyed the comfort of one another's humor for a few moments before Sassy spoke again.

"Listen," she said, her voice suddenly serious, "thanks for telling me about El. I appreciate it. I'll give him a call now."

"Okay, "Michel said. "I'll talk to you soon."

He hung up and began walking back to the station. He felt better for the moment, but wondered how long it would last.

Chapter 30

When he got back to the station Michel found a folder on his desk containing the results of the inquiry to the manufacturer about the film used to take the photos of the girls. He picked up the folder and headed down the hall to the Evidence Room to cross-reference the information with the actual photos.

His conversation with Eldridge had raised his doubts about Carl's guilt. It was common for family members to insist on the innocence of suspects, usually with an element of hysterical denial as if they couldn't allow themselves to consider the possibility of guilt, regardless of the evidence. There'd been none of that with Eldridge. He'd never tried to argue for Carl's innocence at all, yet he'd succeeded in doing so nonetheless. He'd been clear-headed and reasonable, and his equanimity had made his words all the more credible. The man he'd described was flawed, but didn't sound capable of kidnapping and potentially killing anyone.

Michel signed for the photos and took them into a viewing room. Each photo had been catalogued with a number in the lower right hand corner and he began laying them out on the room's metal table in numerical order. It occurred to him that this would be the first time he saw all thirty nine photos together. Previously he'd viewed them only in the groupings in which they'd been found.

When he finished laying them all out he was surprised to see that there were two photos before those of Missy Ann

Macomber, Celia Crowe and Iris Lecher. He picked up the folder and opened it. The number of each photo was listed on the sheet inside, followed by the serial number, date of manufacture, and the destination to which the film had been shipped. He noted with disappointment that all of the destinations had been regional distribution warehouses for chain stores, with no exact store locations listed. The photos had been numbered based on the date of the film's manufacture. There was a note at the bottom of the page indicating that the film was considered viable only for about three years after that date.

The film used to take the first two photos had been manufactured and shipped in July of 1977, over a year before that used to take the photo of Missy Ann, Celia and Iris. The film for both had been shipped to a Rite Aid warehouse outside New Orleans.

He looked down the rest of the list. There were eleven different serial numbers, all manufactured between July 1977 and December 2004. The first three lots had been shipped to the Rite Aid warehouse, the second two and last three to a Walmart warehouse in Arizona, the next one to a Chicago distribution center for CVS Pharmacies, and the next two to a Walgreen's warehouse in New Jersey. He saw that the film used to photograph the six girls he'd already identified had been shipped to Arizona, beginning in February of 2000.

He shook his head, knowing that the shipping information would be useless. Each of the retailers probably had only a handful of distribution centers in the country, with each shipping products to hundreds or thousands of individual stores

He looked at the photos and wondered who the first two girls were and why their names hadn't been uncovered during the Lumley investigation. Something didn't feel right.

He closed his eyes for a moment, trying to clear his mind, then opened them, hoping to see the photos in a new way. At first glance they were all essentially identical, but his instincts told him that the photos of Missy Ann, Celia and Iris didn't belong with the others. He moved them away from the rest of the group and studied them all again that way. The differences were more apparent now.

Missy Ann, Celia and Iris were younger than the other girls by several years. They also had expressions of genuine terror in their eyes while the others appeared dazed or possibly even bored—certainly not in fear for their lives. They were all probably drugged, he thought, but perhaps it had been necessary to keep the older girls sedated because their greater strength made them harder to handle, or perhaps they'd simply been photographed before the effects of the drugs had worn off. The inconsistency of the latter idea bothered him.

He studied the photos more carefully. The girls in the photos found in the safety deposit box had a maturity that went beyond the fact that they were a few years older. They possessed an obvious sexuality that was missing in the younger girls. There was something carnal, Lolita-esque, in their appearances and expressions. Missy Ann, Celia and Iris were still clearly little girls, while the others looked like young women, despite their actual years.

Michel furrowed his brow. Because there was no evidence to suggest the kidnappings had been committed for revenge or financial gain, they were most likely done to satisfy some craving in the kidnapper. If he was a pedophile, he would have chosen victims who met specific physical characteristics that excited him. The fact that they were prepubescent and displayed no sexual awareness should have excluded the three younger girls from his criteria. They were also the only girls known to have been taken from their homes.

Michel thought about Carl and Lumley. Was it possible that they were both kidnapping girls, but separately? No, the similarity of the photographs had to be more than coincidence, he thought. There must have been some connection.

Perhaps they were both responsible for kidnapping the first two girls, but then Lumley kidnapped Missy Ann, Celia and Iris on his own, he thought. The possibility was intriguing. He knew that there was a perverse sense of morality among criminals. Murderers and rapists viewed pedophiles as morally repugnant and felt justified in torturing and killing them in prison. Perhaps Carl felt that Lumley had crossed a moral boundary by kidnapping girls who were too young and killed him for the crime.

It was an interesting hypothesis that explained the differences in the ages and appearances of the girls. It also explained the reason for Lumley's murder. There was one problem, however: Iris was still alive when Sassy arrived at Lumley's house, which meant Carl would have had to kill her on his own since Lumley was already dead. That didn't make sense if he considered her kidnapping alone reprehensible.

Perhaps he'd intended for the police to find Iris still alive but Sassy's unexpected arrival caused him to panic. Maybe he'd planned to leave Lumley in the basement hallway but when he heard noises upstairs he dragged him into the back room and Iris saw his face. Carl would have been forced to kill her to protect himself then.

Michel nodded to himself. He liked the scenario. It seemed plausible, and even if someone other than Carl had been involved it explained the evidence. Best of all it seemed to confirm that Sassy had no prior knowledge of what was happening. She simply stumbled into the situation.

Michel considered his next steps. He wished suddenly that he'd gone to DeRoche right after his conversation with Lecher and told him everything. Now it was too late. He would certainly be suspended or worse if he disclosed what he'd been doing. While he was willing to make that sacrifice in the end, he couldn't make it now. DeRoche simply wasn't an option.

Still, he realized that he was working in a vacuum and it made him uncomfortable. He needed someone to test his ideas on, to see if they made sense to anyone other than himself. That was what he'd always relied on Sassy to do. She helped him find the flaws in his logic and reigned him in when his enthusiasm or feelings got in the way of his judgment. She made him a much better cop.

He began to reach for his cell phone but stopped himself. What if the scenario he'd imagined was wrong? What if he was willing it to make sense only because it exonerated Sassy? If she had been involved in Carl's plan she would only reinforce what he wanted to believe in order to protect herself. He felt in his heart that she wasn't involved and that she would never hurt him like that, but accepted sadly that he couldn't risk taking the chance.

His thoughts turned to Lecher. Lecher was certainly a clear-minded and logical investigator, and may even have found evidence in the basement to support or debunk his theory about Lumley and Carl. Under normal circumstances he wouldn't have hesitated to seek his help, but he knew he couldn't trust Lecher in this case. Lecher had a personal stake in the investigation and seemed intent on pursuing his own agenda. Any information he shared might give Lecher an advantage if Carl was found to be innocent.

Michel realized with frustration that he'd backed himself into a corner. He couldn't turn to any of his usual allies for help, and had succeeded in alienating Joel, his primary source of emotional support.

I'm doing an excellent job of managing my life and career, he thought sarcastically, shaking his head.

Suddenly he remembered Sassy's comment to DeRoche: "There's no use wasting time with self-pity." Although the context was entirely different, he realized she was still right. He had put himself into a difficult situation, but he still had himself to rely on. He could still move forward.

Putting aside all of the speculation about what might have happened, he still needed to find out conclusively if Carl had any connection to the girls he'd identified. He could work backwards from there.

In the meantime DeRoche might still be able to help if he had a copy of the Lumley file. Michel decided to pick it up from his house after work and make a copy, then leave it anonymously on DeRoche's desk early in the morning. Although he knew DeRoche would question its miraculous appearance, he suspected his boss wouldn't spend much time trying to find the source until later. *And my career may be over by then anyway*, he thought.

After he dropped off the files he'd hit the road. He'd gotten a copy of Carl's route for the last few years from the trucking company and hoped that he might be able to find a truck stop or diner along the way that Carl had frequented. Maybe someone had seen him there with one of more of the girls. It was probably a long shot if Carl intended to kidnap them, but it was the best option he could see for now.

*****

Eldridge arrived at Sassy's house promptly at 7 pm. When she opened the door she was shocked by his appearance. It wasn't that he was unkempt or dressed less fastidiously than usual, but that the life seemed to have been drained out of him. His eyes were listless and glassy and he appeared to have gotten smaller. His neck had disappeared, seemingly crushed by the weight of his head, and his broad shoulders were slumped forward like those of a very old man. The sudden transformation frightened her.

"El, come on in," she said quickly.

"Thanks," he replied with an empty, reflexive smile. "I appreciate you inviting me over."

As he walked ahead of her toward the living room Sassy noticed that even Eldridge's walk had changed. His usual purposeful stride had devolved into a slow amble.

"Please, sit down," she said as they reached the living room. "Can I get you something to drink?"

"Some scotch, if you have it," Eldridge replied flatly.

Sassy was surprised. She'd seen Eldridge drink wine with dinner on occasion, and champagne when she and Carl were married, but hard liquor only once before. She poured them each a drink.

"I'm sorry I didn't tell you myself," she said as she placed a glass on the table in front of Eldridge and took a seat in the chair closest to him.

"It's okay," Eldridge said without looking at her.

He picked up the glass but just held it in both hands on his lap.

"I just didn't know how to bring it up," Sassy said weakly. "I wanted to, but I kept putting it off. I should have realized Michel would want to talk to you. I'm sorry."

Eldridge's eyes lifted and slowly shifted to look at her.

"Please don't blame yourself," he said.

The imploring tone of his voice indicated that they weren't just empty words and Sassy felt suddenly anxious.

"Eldridge, are you all right?" she asked, looking at him seriously to convey that her question also wasn't empty.

Eldridge looked down at the floor and lifted the glass to his lips. He took a long sip, his face registering no reaction to the taste.

"I will be," he said without emotion as he lowered the glass back to his lap. "I will be."

Sassy sensed that there was more meaning to his words than the obvious and felt her anxiety increase.

"What are you saying, El?" she asked cautiously.

Something in her tone seemed to strike a chord with Eldridge and he looked up at her suddenly. His eyes were clear and focused.

"How did you find the photos in the safe deposit box?" he asked.

Sassy was taken aback by the change in his demeanor. Before her eyes he was becoming himself again.

"Uh...Carl sent me the key," she said, confused by what was happening. "It arrived in the mail on Friday."

Eldridge nodded thoughtfully.

"Was there a note?" he asked.

"No," Sassy said, shaking her head.

She still felt flustered by Eldridge's sudden shift.

"El, what's going on?" she asked.

Eldridge smiled at her warmly.

"Nothing to worry about," he said. "I just needed some time to come to grips with things, I guess."

Sassy tried to decipher a deeper meaning in the words but couldn't find any. She nodded slowly.

"Well, I should be going," Eldridge said, placing the half-full glass of scotch on the table and standing up. "I've got a busy day tomorrow."

"Um, okay," Sassy said.

She walked him to the door, noticing how complete the transformation in his appearance and comportment had become.

"Thank you," Eldridge said at the door, taking her hand and kissing her on the cheek.

"For what?" she asked.

Eldridge shrugged and smiled.

"Just for being here," he said.

Then he quickly left. Sassy stood in the doorway for a moment staring after him until he disappeared into the gathering darkness.

"What the hell just happened?" she asked herself helplessly.

Chapter 31

Sassy finished reviewing the investigation files for Missy Ann Macomber and Celia Crowe, as well as the information that had been gathered so far about Iris Lecher's kidnapping. She'd been surprised by the volume of paperwork and the number of interviews that had been conducted for each. Becoming a detective had been the goal of virtually every member of her class at the academy, but most had viewed it as a reward for time on the beat that would allow them to earn a higher salary without working too hard. She understood firsthand now that that wasn't the case at all, and felt a profound respect for the men working down the hall from her cloistered office.

As she'd expected, the investigations had focused primarily on relatives, friends, and acquaintances of the girls' families. When Celia Crowe disappeared there was also a concerted effort to find a connection between the Macombers and Crowes. It was clear from notes in the files, though, that the department and the state police hadn't been sure that the cases were actually related. With the kidnapping of Iris Lecher that had obviously changed: the disappearances of three young girls, all taken from their homes at approximately the same time of night, had to be more than a coincidence.

Her job was clear. She was being asked to create a profile of the kidnapper that would help the police to identify likely suspects with no connections to the families. She opened the spiral bound notebook she'd been given and began jotting down thoughts:

- *Sexual predator/pedophile—absence of ransom notes or any connections between families of three girls suggests kidnapper is acting out of a compulsion to satisfy own needs*
- *Male, 17–45 years of age—virtually all non-custodial kidnappings committed by men; 71% of all pedophiles are white men between the ages of 17–45.*
- *Given higher-than-average percentage of blacks in city, suggest also including in search*
- *Higher than average intelligence—kidnappings were planned and well executed; no evidence left behind*
- *Compelled to act, but not impulsive*
- *Smoker—cigarette butts found outside Lecher house*
- *Lives alone or with invalid parent(s) in house—needs a place to take victims without fear of detection; probably secluded or has attic/basement*
- *May work with children or have job that brings in contact with children—has to be able to find victims without attracting attention (school, restaurant, arcade, mall, playground, bus driver, police)*
- *Probable repeat offender—rate of recidivism among sexual offenders among highest of all crimes; pedophiles can learn to control impulses but not be cured*
- *Probable history of sexual abuse—majority of sex offenders were abused as children*

She put down her pen and stared at the list. She knew it was general, but she had no evidence that would allow her to narrow the parameters or add characteristics that were more unique.

Although searching criminal databases would only uncover suspects who had already been arrested or convicted of other crimes, she felt it would be a smart first step given the high rate of repeat offenders. There really wasn't much choice anyway: the chance of identifying an unknown offender quickly was very small given the scant evidence, and she suspected Iris Lecher didn't have long to live if she wasn't dead already.

She met with Maddox, Giraux and Sinclair just before noon to review the profile she'd developed. Maddox seemed pleased and suggested she take a lunch break because she'd be working late that night and might not have a chance to eat again until she got home. As she made her way toward the squad room door and O'Halloran's desk she could sense people looking up in anticipation of another confrontation. Instead the big redhead only glared at her momentarily. *Chalk one up for the uppity nigger,* she thought to herself as she walked into the hall.

When she got back to her office a half hour later she found a small stack of files on her desk. There was a note from Maddox on top:

"Take a look at these and see if any of them are worth questioning. More to come."

She spent the afternoon reviewing the criminal records that had been pulled based on the profile. Each time she got near the bottom of a pile another would be brought in by a uniformed officer. At first she was enthusiastic, but by the time she was halfway through the third batch her enthusiasm had turned to frustration.

Did anyone even read the profile? she wondered. *Half these guys are too old, most of them were arrested for robbery, and some of them were in jail when the first kidnappings occurred.*

She was able to weed out most of the files automatically based on the absence of sex-related offenses. Others she discarded because of the circumstances of the offenders' previous arrests. She knew that anyone who used his own car for a daylight getaway or left his wallet at the crime scene didn't possess the intellect or attention to detail necessary to plan and execute the kidnappings.

Just before 4 pm she had a break and called Carl. She realized that she hadn't thought of him all day.

"Hey, it's me," she said.

"Hey, baby," Carl replied. "How's it going?"

"It's going," she said. "I've probably looked at the records of half the criminals in this city."

"Anyone I know?" Carl asked with a laugh.

"Not so far," Sassy replied flatly, unable to share the humor.

She wished suddenly that she hadn't called. The work had allowed her to keep her mind off Carl's situation for a few hours, but now it all came flooding back on her.

"Listen," she said, "I probably won't be getting home until ten or eleven. Go ahead and eat without me."

"You want me to save you a plate?" Carl asked.

"No, I'll probably just catch a sandwich or something here," she replied.

"Make sure you do," Carl said seriously. "You have to take care of yourself and our baby."

Despite her darkening mood, Sassy managed a smile at the thought of the baby.

"Okay, papa. I will," she replied.

"You think you're going to be in there again tomorrow?" Carl asked.

"Probably, unless we find the kidnapper tonight," she replied. "Why?"

"No special reason," Carl replied. "I was just hoping we could spend the day together. With all the extra hours I've been working it seems like we never see one another anymore. But maybe I'll call Mose and see what he's up to if you think you're going to be busy."

Sassy felt a swell of bitterness rise up from her stomach.

"Yeah, why don't you do that," she said, trying to keep her tone neutral.

"Okay, baby," Carl replied. "I'll see you when you get home. I love you."

"I love you, too," Sassy said without hesitating.

*****

By 9 pm she'd identified eight men she thought were worth bringing in for questioning and was almost finished reviewing the final group of files. She felt tired, but also satisfied. She'd dreamed of being a cop for so many years and now she had the opportunity to prove that she could make a valuable contribution to the force.

As she opened the third to last file she felt a jolt of adrenaline. Although the picture inside was several years old, she recognized the man immediately. It was Mose Lumley. Reflexively she looked around to make sure no one was watching her through the windows of her glass cubicle, then began quickly reading through Lumley's arrest record.

It was clear from the nature of his crimes that Lumley wasn't a viable suspect. All of his crimes had been larceny-related, and although he had claimed to have been sexually abused as a child, the examining psychologist had considered the claims false. Disappointed, she put the folder on top of the stack to her left and reviewed the remaining two files.

When she was done she sat back in her chair and stared at the pile on her desk. She knew she should call to have it picked up and returned to the records room but hesitated. She realized that this was the opportunity she'd needed. She'd wanted to meet Lumley to get a sense of him, but hadn't been able to think of a way to justify approaching him officially. Now she could have him brought in without raising his suspicions.

She considered the potential drawbacks. She was still comfortable that Lumley wouldn't recognize her name and make the connection to Carl, but it was possible he might mention being questioned. No, she decided, given the nature of the crime being investigated it was unlikely he'd tell anyone. It would raise too many questions about why he'd been brought in and he'd have to reveal his probably fictitious history of sexual abuse.

The other potential drawback was far more serious. While the police were busy interrogating Lumley they might miss the opportunity to catch the real kidnapper, and any time wasted increased the odds that Iris Lecher wouldn't be found alive. Sassy closed her eyes and wondered if she would be able to live with herself if Iris was killed, knowing that her own actions may have contributed to the girl's death. Her thought turned to the baby in her womb and how she would feel if her own child were kidnapped, and she realized she couldn't do anything that would potentially jeopardize Iris' life.

Still, maybe there was an option, she thought. If she told Maddox that she considered Lumley only a marginal suspect, perhaps he'd let her interrogate Lumley on her own. No man-hours would be wasted and the experienced members of the team would still be free to question the other suspects she'd identified. She recognized that she was rationalizing, but it was a compromise she could accept.

She reached across the desk and pulled Lumley's file from the stack.

*****

Mose Lumley was brought into the interrogation room just before eleven the next morning. Sassy and Maddox stood behind the observation window watching him. Lumley appeared nervous, Sassy thought, but probably no more than would be expected for someone who had been awakened and taken to the police station for questioning on a Sunday morning. Although he seemed to be making an effort to keep still, she noticed that his left leg erupted occasionally into a jittery bounce and his light pink tongue darted repeatedly over his full lips.

"Are you sure you want to do this alone?" Maddox asked.

Sassy looked at him. Although he was unshaven and his clothes were wrinkled, his eyes still had a focused intensity. She wondered if he'd slept at all since Iris Lecher was reported missing.

"Yeah, I'm sure," she replied. "As I said, I don't think he's really a very strong suspect. Probably not worth wasting anyone else's time on. I just want to cover all my bases."

Maddox studied her for a moment, then nodded.

"Okay," he said. "Just hit the red button on your side of the table to activate the recorder. Hit the black one to stop it when you're done. I'll be next door questioning one of the other suspects,"

he said, "but there'll be an officer right outside the door if you need him. Good luck."

"Thanks," Sassy replied. "Oh, one other thing. Would it be all right if I identified myself as Detective Jones? It might give me more credibility."

"Fine," Maddox replied, "but don't get too used to it yet."

He gave her a teasing smile and she decided that she liked him immensely.

"Mr. Lumley, I'm Detective Jones," Sassy said as she entered the room and walked to the chair on the far side of the table from him.

Lumley noticeably relaxed when he saw her and she felt a momentary touch of resentment, assuming that it was because she was a woman. She sat in her chair and hit the button to start recording, then deliberately took her time arranging her notebook and pretending to read through his file.

"I'm sorry to bring you in here so early on a Sunday," she said, not looking up at him, "but I have a few questions to ask you."

She chose her words carefully to give the impression that he was there solely at her behest.

"I'm assuming you read the paper?" she asked, finally looking up and giving him an expectant smile.

"Uh, yeah, sure," Lumley replied, giving her a confused look.

She noticed that his voice was soft and lilting. It seemed consistent with his open, childlike features.

"Then you probably read about the little girl who was kidnapped Friday night?" she asked.

Lumley's expression changed from confusion to worry.

"Yeah, I read about it. That's a terrible thing," he replied.

Sassy nodded mechanically.

"Can you tell me where you were on the night of September 22, 1979?" she asked.

"September 22?" Lumley repeated.

"Yes," Sassy replied, giving him a look that suggested any normal person would be able to recall their exact whereabouts on a given night seven months earlier.

"I don't know," Lumley replied, with a defensive shrug. "That was a long time ago. I'm not sure where I was last week."

"And what about November 4, 1979?" Sassy continued, ignoring his attempt at humor.

Lumley's face scrunched almost comically, as though he were a child imitating how an adult would look deep in thought.

"I know the answer to this one. Just a second," he said.

His expression suddenly changed and he beamed at Sassy as though he'd just figured out the answer to a particularly difficult math problem in school.

"I was in Barbados," he said proudly. "I knew that date sounded familiar. I flew down November 2 and I stayed for a week."

"And you can provide us with your passport to confirm that?" Sassy asked.

Lumley nodded in response.

"And what about last Wednesday, the 30th?" she asked.

Lumley fixed his eyes on the ceiling for a moment and Sassy imagined him turning back cartoon calendar pages in his mind.

"I was out with a buddy that night," he replied finally. "We hit a couple of bars on Magazine and N. Rampart."

"And your buddy's name?" Sassy asked.

"Carl Adams," Lumley replied.

"Carl Adams," Sassy said aloud as she made a show of writing the name in her notebook. "And do you have a number for Mr. Adams?"

As Lumley recited her own phone number to her she realized that he'd be forced to tell Carl he'd been questioned now, and would probably mention her name. She had to think of a way to ensure his silence.

"And what about the night of the 31st?" she asked, already knowing what the answer would be, but stalling for time as she tried to think of a solution to her dilemma.

"I was out with Carl," Lumley replied, nodding to himself.

"And Friday night? May 2nd?"

"*Same thing,*" *Lumley replied with a shrug.*

"*Okay, Mr. Lumley,*" *Sassy said, looking up from her notebook.* "*If I have any other questions I'll be in touch.*"

"*That's it?*" *Lumley asked with a look of surprise.*

"*Unless you have anything else you'd like to tell me,*" *Sassy replied, arching her eyebrows expectantly.*

"*No, nothing,*" *Lumley said quickly.*

"*Okay, then we're all done for now,*" *Sassy replied.* "*I'll arrange to have an officer take you home and you can show him your passport.*"

Lumley nodded, though his expression indicated he wasn't thrilled by the idea. As he began to stand, Sassy realized she had to act now if she wanted to keep him from mentioning her name to Carl. Casually she reached down and hit the black button to turn off the tape recorder, hoping that no one was watching her from the observation room.

"*Oh, one more thing,*" *she said.*

Lumley froze in mid-motion and gave her a nervous look, making it clear that he'd spent enough time on the wrong side of the law to know that a casual "one more thing" usually meant trouble.

"*Because of the sensitive nature of this case we'd appreciate it if you wouldn't mention that you were questioned,*" *Sassy said earnestly.* "*We don't want the kidnapper to know any details about how we're running the investigation. You understand, don't you?*"

Sassy could see the sudden relief in Lumley's eyes and he began nodding enthusiastically.

"*Good. And when I call your friend...Mr. Adams,*" *she said, deliberately consulting her notes for his name,* "*I'll be very discreet. He won't know what my call is in reference to...and it will be in your best interest if it stays that way.*"

"*No problem,*" *Lumley said, his eager tone making it clear that he'd recognized the implied threat.* "*I promise I won't mention it to anyone.*"

*****

Maddox was still interrogating one of the men she'd identified as a potential suspect, so Sassy went to her office to think while she waited for him. Her conversation with Lumley had left her confused about how to proceed.

On the one hand she knew that scaring Lumley off wouldn't be a problem. He seemed to have a natural fear of the police that she could exploit. She suspected he'd never even question her reasons if she told him to leave town. The problem was that she doubted that getting rid of Lumley would stop the stolen goods operation. He'd struck her as a good soldier who could be counted on to follow orders, but not someone capable of conceiving and planning anything so elaborate. Unless he was far more clever than she perceived, his thinking was too childlike.

Her thoughts were interrupted by a knock on her door and she turned to see Maddox standing in the open doorway.

"So how did it go?" he asked.

Sassy shrugged ambivalently.

"Pretty much as I'd expected," she replied. "He's not a good suspect. He was in Barbados when Celia Crowe was taken and had alibis on April 29 and Friday night."

Maddox nodded.

"Out with a Mr. Carl Adams," he said.

Sassy tried to hide her surprise as she realized that Maddox had already listened to the tape of her session with Lumley.

"Yeah, that's right," she said.

"Of course, we'll have to check that out," Maddox said matter-of-factly.

"Actually, I already did," Sassy replied, hoping that she hadn't said it too quickly. "I called him right after Lumley left and he confirmed they were together on the three nights Lumley said."

"I was wondering about that," Maddox said. "Why did you ask him about the 31st?"

Sassy hesitated for just a second before replying.

232

"Well, Mrs. Lecher said that she went outside when she heard the noise on the 30th," she said evenly. "I figured the kidnapper may have just been staking the place out that night and she scared him off before he finished, so he may have come back the next night."

Maddox seemed to consider the logic for a moment before responding.

"Yeah, it's possible," he said, nodding his head, "but if he was there long enough to smoke a cigarette he probably had enough time to finish his planning, too. In any case, I was just curious."

"You're probably right," Sassy replied. "So did you have any luck?"

Maddox shook his head.

"Nothing solid," he said.

"I'm sorry," Sassy said, looking down at the floor.

"For what?" Maddox asked sharply. "Did you think we expected you to come in and miraculously identify the kidnapper all by yourself? I'm not sure if you're naive or egotistical, but that's not the way it happens. No matter how good a profile is, it still takes a lot of hard work by a lot of people to solve a crime."

Sassy felt both encouraged and chastened by Maddox's words and fought the urge to apologize again. Instead she looked up and gave him a contrite smile.

"Listen, Jones," Maddox said, his tone softer, "I know there wasn't much to it, but you did a nice job in there. You asserted yourself appropriately and took control of the interview. That's not an easy thing and it takes most cops years to learn how to do it."

"Thank you," Sassy replied. "I appreciate you saying that."

"Would you mind a little advice?" Maddox asked. "From an old cop to a young one?"

"Of course not," Sassy replied, though she wondered if she really wanted to hear what he had to say.

"Be patient," Maddox said. "This assignment may be the worst thing that could happen to you right now because it's going to whet your appetite for bigger things. Trust me, you're not ready for them *yet. There's a hell of a lot more to being a good cop than being smart, and you're going to have to learn those things through experience. Don't let your ambition get in the way of taking time to grow into the job."*

"Am I that obvious?" Sassy asked, smiling with embarrassment.

Maddox laughed, a short barking sound that seemed to escape from deep within his chest.

"Ambition isn't a bad thing," he said. "Very few people succeed without it. But you need to keep it in check. Let's face it, you've got two strikes on you already: you're educated and you're a woman. Around here that's going to make people uneasy right off the bat. If you're too outwardly ambitious, as well, you're going to be in for a rough ride."

"Just two strikes?" Sassy asked, holding her hands up and turning the backs toward Maddox.

Maddox stared at her hands without comprehending for a moment, then he began to chuckle as he realized what she was saying. Sassy thought the reaction seemed genuine and decided that Maddox didn't think of people in terms of color.

"Well, I didn't want you to think you were out before the game even began," he replied with another barking laugh.

"So what do you suggest?" Sassy asked seriously,

She felt suddenly anxious. Maddox seemed to sense her anxiety and gave her a comforting smile.

"You can't separate yourself too far from the rest of the crowd," he replied. "It's natural to want recognition for your accomplishments, but you can never give the appearance you think you're superior."

"I'm not sure exactly what you mean," Sassy replied.

Maddox hesitated before responding. Sassy could tell he was weighing his words carefully.

"As an example," he said finally, "just because you're smarter than 95% of the guys you'll ever work with doesn't mean you have to show it all the time. A little well timed humility, false or not, can be a very effective tool for softening people's attitudes."

"So you want me to dumb it down so I'm not threatening?" Sassy asked with a derisive snort. "In other words, you want me to act like a girl."

Maddox closed his eyes and sighed.

"There's not a one of us who hasn't let someone think they were smarter than us, or kissed some prudent ass occasionally," he replied, opening his eyes and looking at her empathetically. "It's all part of the game."

Sassy pursed her lips and studied her shoes for a moment. Philosophically she found the idea abhorrent, but she knew that in practical terms it would be useful.

"Okay, I can see your point," she said, nodding slowly. "What else?"

"You'll need to reach out to people for help sometimes, whether you need it or not," Maddox replied. "I know I stuck you in this isolation tank, but my gut tells me you'd rather do things on your own, anyway. If you want to make it as a cop you're going to have to learn to work as part of a team instead. By asking for help you show respect for your peers, and in turn they'll begin to respect you for it."

"That makes sense," Sassy said thoughtfully. "I guess I've always had a tendency to separate myself from other people, but I can see why that's not a good thing for a cop."

"Good," Maddox replied.

"Dare I ask if there's anything else?" Sassy asked with a comic grimace.

"Make amends with O'Halloran," Maddox replied flatly.

Sassy started to protest but he held up his hand to stop her.

"I understand why you did what you did," he said in a placating tone, "and your instinct about how to play the situation was absolutely correct, but now you've backed him into a corner. If he doesn't retaliate he risks losing respect with the rest of the squad. If he does retaliate, it could make things very unpleasant for you. I don't want to see that happen."

"So how do I handle it?" Sassy asked.

"Make some gesture of conciliation to him," Maddox replied. "A peace offering, if you will. If you demonstrate respect for him, he saves face and you prove to everyone that you're a team player."

Sassy considered the suggestion for a moment.

"Okay," she replied. "Just so long as I don't have to fuck him or stand on his front lawn holding a lantern."

*****

Before she headed home Sassy stopped in the building commissary to buy an apple. As she rode the elevator back up to the eighth floor Detective Division she nervously polished it against the front of her plum suit jacket. Her mouth felt dry and her heart was racing.

The elevator doors opened and she could see O'Halloran standing in the middle of the squad room talking with two other men. She took a calming breath and began walking toward him. As she approached she could hear conversation dying in the room. She prayed silently that she'd judged him correctly.

When she was seven feet away, O'Halloran turned his head and saw her, his face immediately clouding with anger. She walked up to him and stopped. Without a word she held the apple out on the palm of her right hand. O'Halloran's expression changed immediately to confusion.

"Why the hell are you giving me an apple?" he sputtered loudly.

Sassy knew she had to play this right.

"Because they were all out of watermelons?" she said, with an exaggerated shrug.

O'Halloran's face began to redden, but then Sassy gave him a mischievous grin that clearly took him by surprise. He stared at her in bewilderment for a moment, then began to laugh.

"Son of a bitch," he said, shaking his head. "Son of a bitch. Okay, you got me."

Everyone else in the room, who had all been anxiously awaiting his reaction, joined in the laughter.

"*I'm sorry about yesterday,*" *Sassy said, taking advantage of the noise to make her apology private.*

O'Halloran smiled and nodded at her.

"*You're okay, Jones,*" *he said.*

*****

As she drove home Sassy was pleased with the way things had gone. She'd guessed correctly that O'Halloran had a sense of humor that would transcend any prejudices he held. The idea of groveling for forgiveness or allowing him to feel he had bested her had been incomprehensible, but the shared joke had given them both a chance to maintain their dignity. It was a win-win situation. She'd been able to admit her mistake and show respect, while still making a point about O'Halloran's racism, whether he realized it or not. She felt that things would be easier now.

Her thoughts turned to Mose Lumley. If she was right that he wasn't the person running the stolen merchandise operation, then approaching him could create larger problems. Lumley would certainly go to whoever was in charge and that person would try to find out more about her. Inevitably Carl would find out that she knew about his activities.

Her goal was to protect Carl, including his pride, and she knew he could never find out what she knew without risking that. If he lost his pride their lives might never be what they had been before. She thought about the parallel to her situation with O'Halloran and wished she could solve this problem with an apple, too.

She knew that she needed advice. Approaching Dupree wasn't an option. As much as she liked and admired him she couldn't be sure that he wouldn't report what she told him. She needed to talk to someone she could trust who would understand her situation. She decided it was time to tell Eldridge what was happening.

She looked at the clock on the dashboard and saw that it was 7:36 pm. Hopefully he'll still be there, she thought as she turned left and started driving toward the mission.

Chapter 32

Michel pulled into Fat Ernie's just after 11 am. Like the other ten diners he'd visited that morning, its dirt parking lot was large enough to accommodate big rig trucks. A few were parked in the shade of the cypress trees that ran around the perimeter. He'd been on the road since 4:30 am, after stopping at the station to leave a copy of the Lumley file on DeRoche's desk, and was now a few miles outside Beaumont, TX, on Interstate 10. Depending on how many more stops he had to make, he figured it would take another two or three hours to reach Houston.

Fat Ernie's was the first place he'd stopped that looked like it had been built on the spot, rather than brought in on a trailer. It was a wide, low building with a nearly flat corrugated tin roof. The exterior walls were vertical wood planks, stained a faded blood red. Except for the two large picture windows that looked like they'd been added more recently, it resembled a roadhouse bar more than a diner.

He parked to the left of the front door and stepped out of his car. A cloud of tan dust hung low in the hot, still air. Rolling his head, he was rewarded with several tiny pops from the back of his neck. It always amazed him how much the simple act of sitting in a car for a few hours took out of his body.

He wondered whether he should put on his suit jacket but decided against it. No reason to look even more like a cop, he thought, as he closed the car door and walked to the diner entrance. Through a small glass window in the door he could see three men sitting at the counter directly in front of him. They looked like truckers.

He walked in and immediately began scanning for the restroom. He'd had two cups of coffee before he left the house that morning and at least part of each cup he'd bought at his other ten stops.

"Can I help you, darling?" a voice called out from his right.

He turned and saw a large man in a stained white t-shirt and a chef's hat standing behind the counter. He had a round face and thick reddish-brown beard and mustache. From the girth stretching the front and sides of his shirt, Michel guessed he was Fat Ernie.

"Yeah," he replied. "The restroom?"

"The restroom is only for paying customers," the man replied, not unkindly.

Michel smiled.

"I'm a paying customer," he said reassuringly.

"Down the end," the man replied, pointing a stout finger toward a doorway at the left end of the counter.

Michel walked quickly to the doorway. Beyond it were two doors, both marked MEN. He opened the one on the left and stepped up to a urinal. Even in his hurry he noticed that the small room was surprisingly clean, and thought he even detected a hint of lavender in the air. It occurred to him suddenly that the man had called him "darling" and wondered if it had been an intentional comment on his appearance or was simply the man's stock greeting for everyone. It struck him as odd either way, as did the apparent absence of a ladies' room.

He finished emptying his bladder and washed his hands, then walked back to the counter, taking a seat along the side just outside the bathroom. The three men further down didn't appear to take any notice of him.

The large man appeared from a break in the back wall carrying three plates of food which he set down in front of the truckers.

"You boys need anything else right now?" he asked.

"No thanks, Ernie," they replied in near-perfect unison.

"Okay," Ernie said, thumping his chubby right fist once on the counter. "You know where to find me if you do."

He turned his attention to Michel and sauntered slowly up to him. His expression seemed purposefully neutral.

"Coffee, darling?" he asked as he reached under the counter and pulled out silverware, a red-and-white-checked cotton placemat and a matching napkin and began deftly laying them out in front of Michel.

"No, I think I've had enough for one day," Michel replied with a smile. "You still serving breakfast?"

"So long as the chickens ain't gone home yet," Ernie replied chuckling. "What can I get you?"

Michel noticed that his voice had the musical drawl of a Cajun rather than the flat twang of a Texan.

"A couple of scrambled eggs, home fries, white toast, a side of ham, and some orange juice" Michel replied.

"Well, you must have worked yourself up quite an appetite this morning," Ernie said with a mischievous smile. "You up from New Orleans?"

Michel gave him a surprised look.

"Yeah, how'd you know?" he asked.

"I saw your plates when you pulled in," Ernie replied, "plus I recognized the accent. I spent a lot of time down that way before I come out here. I grew up in the Basin."

"I thought you sounded more Cajun than Texan," Michel replied, "but I always heard there was a heavy Cajun influence around here."

"That's true," Ernie replied with a warm smile. "Well, I best get in the kitchen. Your breakfast ain't likely to cook itself now, is it?"

As Ernie walked away and disappeared into the break in the back wall Michel sensed that the big man had been reluctant to end their conversation. He wondered how Fat Ernie had ended up opening a diner on the outskirts of Beaumont. He didn't seem to belong in the area for some reason.

Michel looked around the room. It was unlike any diner he'd ever seen before. It had the requisite red leatherette stools and banquettes with formica-topped counter and tables, but the overall look was far more pulled-together and homey. The walls were painted a pale yellow and were accented by gleaming white trim. Instead of linoleum, the floor was wood that had been buffed to a high polish. Valances that matched the placemats and napkins were hung above the large windows, and small vases of fresh daisies were placed along the top of the counter and on each table.

Did I stumble into the only gay diner in Texas? he wondered, laughing to himself.

A few minutes later Ernie reappeared carrying Michel's breakfast, just as the three truckers were getting up to leave.

"Thanks a lot, Ernie," one of them said. "The money's on the counter. I'll see you next week."

"Okay, darling," Ernie replied warmly. "You boys drive careful now."

He set the plates in front of Michel as the men walked out, leaving just the two of them in the diner.

"Nice fellas," Ernie said as he poured Michel's juice from a pitcher that had been resting in an ice tray on the back counter.

"And they don't mind you calling them 'darling'?" Michel asked curiously.

Ernie began laughing wheezily.

"Not that anyone's ever said," he replied. "Just so long as Ernie takes good care of 'em I don't suppose they care one way or t'other what I call 'em."

Michel nodded and smiled.

"Well, I'll leave you in peace," Ernie said, and again Michel thought he detected a reluctance to leave in the man's voice.

Michel wasn't sure if it was just because his hunger had been building for hours or not, but the meal was one of the best he could remember having in a long while. He was glad that Ernie wasn't there to watch him as he set into it like a starving dog on a pork chop. He was just finishing when Ernie appeared again.

"Looks like that agreed with you," he said with a broad grin.

"That was delicious," Michel replied. "Did you add something to the eggs? They were great."

"If I told ya I'd have to kill ya," Ernie replied with a wink.

Michel smiled at the joke he imagined Ernie had told hundreds of times over the years. Ernie made him feel comfortable and he decided to ask the question that he'd been wondering about.

"Can I ask you something?" he asked.

"Well, I figured that's what you were doing here," Ernie replied.

Michel cocked his head and gave him a puzzled look.

"You're a cop, ain't ya?" Ernie asked.

"Well, yeah," Michel replied, embarrassed that he was so easily spotted, "but this isn't a police question."

Ernie arched his pale orange eyebrows in surprise.

"Okay," he said.

Michel leaned closer and spoke in a low voice, even though there was no one else there to hear him.

"Is this a gay diner?"

"What would make you ask that?" Ernie asked with a serious look. "The flowers or the matching table linens and curtains?"

He began laughing hard, leaning forward and holding onto the edge of the counter. Michel suspected that if it weren't for his ample stomach he would be doubled over. The wheezing laughter continued for almost a minute and Michel began to worry that the big man might have a heart attack, but finally it subsided and Ernie straightened up and wiped tears from the corners of his eyes.

"Ooh, boy," he said, suppressing a residual chuckle. "That was a good one. Sometimes I just crack myself up."

"Are you okay?" Michel asked.

"Oh yeah, I'm fine," Ernie replied. "I just haven't had a laugh like that in a while."

He shook his head appreciatively.

"To answer your question," he said, "I don't know that anyone who comes here thinks of it as a 'gay diner,' but I suppose they know that if they get a little lonely and decide to spend a little more time parked around back than they should I'm not likely to call the cops on 'em."

Michel smiled at the discreet phrasing.

"So it's a cruising area out there?" he asked.

"You asking as a cop or for personal reasons?" Ernie asked with a knowing smile.

Michel felt himself blush at being so easily spotted for the second time.

"Well, I don't have any jurisdiction here," he said with a comic shrug.

Ernie chuckled.

"Let's just say when it gets a little darker it's not uncommon for some of the local boys to come around," he replied.

"Well, you've got yourself a nice place here," Michel said, deciding he should let the subject drop.

"Thanks," Ernie replied.

His tone suggested he understood they were moving on.

"So what brings you out this way?" he asked. "You don't look like you're dressed for vacation."

"No," Michel replied with a small smile. "I'm trying to find information on some missing girls. The man we suspect took them drove a truck along this route and I'm hoping that someone might have seen him with one of them."

Ernie's expression turned suddenly serious.

"Good lord," he said. "That's a terrible thing."

Michel nodded.

"Did a man named Carl Adams ever come in here?" he asked.

"I don't know," Ernie replied. "I only know most of the truckers on a first name basis. What does he look like?"

Michel started to reach inside his jacket but realized he'd left it in the car. He excused himself and went to retrieve it. As he was closing the car door he saw a faded green Camaro pull into the lot and park along the left edge. He wondered if it was one of the 'local boys.' The idea was oddly exciting but he pushed it away and walked back into the diner.

"Here you go," he said, placing a copy of one of Carl's autopsy photos on the counter.

"Jesus," Ernie said, recoiling at the sight of the lifeless face. "Carl's dead?"

"So you knew him?" Michel asked.

"Yeah," Ernie said, pushing the photo back toward Michel with distaste. "Carl was a regular. Been coming in a few times a week for the last three or four years, I'd guess. And you think he may have taken some girls?"

"Seems that way," Michel replied. "We found some photos in a safety deposit box after he killed himself."

"He seemed like such a gentle man," Ernie said, shaking his head.

Michel almost replied that Jeffrey Dahmer's neighbors had probably felt the same way, but thought better of it. He liked Fat Ernie too much to say something unkind.

"Did you ever see him in here with any younger girls?" he asked instead. "Teenagers?"

"Sure," Ernie replied. "He came in here with all sorts of people he picked up on the road. Men, women, boys, girls. Most of the truckers won't pick up hitchhikers because they'll lose their job if they get caught, but Carl didn't care. He was always picking up strays. He'd bring them in and buy 'em a meal, too."

"And you didn't think it was odd that he was with teenage girls?" Michel asked.

Ernie shrugged.

"No more than anyone else he brought in," he said. "I never got the sense there was anything funny going on. He just seemed to be doing a good turn."

Michel felt the response was truthful.

"Would you mind taking a look at photos of a few of the girls to see if you recognize any of them?" he asked.

Ernie gave him a squeamish look.

"They're not dead, are they?" he asked.

"Not in the pictures," Michel replied obliquely.

Ernie nodded hesitantly and Michel laid the photos of the six girl's he'd already identified on the counter. Rather than the photos found in the safety deposit box, he'd chosen to bring copies of the missing persons reports that showed the girls' faces more clearly. Ernie moved closer and looked down cautiously. When he saw the photos he visibly relaxed and began studying them carefully.

Suddenly the front door opened and he and Michel looked up. A pale slim woman with short hair that had been bleached a few shades too light for her complexion stood in the doorway. She was wearing a waitress' uniform in the now-familiar red-and-white-check pattern. Michel guessed she was in her early-twenties, though the hard lines around her mouth betrayed that they hadn't been easy years. She looked at them both nervously.

"Loreen, where you been?" Ernie asked gruffly. "How do you expect me to handle this morning rush by myself?"

He gave Michel a conspiratorial smile and winked.

"Sorry, Ernie," Loreen replied, looking down at the floor. "Daryl had himself a big night last night and wrecked his truck. I had to drive him to work."

"He didn't get rough with you, did he?" Ernie asked protectively.

"No, nothing like that," she replied. "He just come home and passed out on the kitchen floor again."

"Well, stow your gear and come over here. I want you to take a look at something," Ernie said kindly.

He looked up at Michel and shook his head.

"I wish that husband of hers would go missing," he whispered.

Loreen walked behind the counter and put her pocketbook on a shelf on the back wall. She walked toward them, keeping her eyes on the ground.

"Loreen, this is...actually I don't know your name," Ernie said, looking at Michel.

"I'm sorry. Detective Doucette," Michel said, extending his hand first to Ernie and then to Loreen.

"Detective Doucette is trying to track down some girls that went missing," Ernie said. "You know Carl? Black fella, brings in a lot of hitchhikers?"

Loreen nodded but still kept her eyes down.

"Seems like he might have something to do with it," Ernie continued. "The detective brought in pictures of some of the girls. Why don't you take a look and see if you recognize any of 'em."

For the first time Loreen looked directly at Michel. Her wary eyes were a milky green. He imagined that she would have been quite pretty if her life had gone a different way. Slowly she walked up to the counter and looked down at the pictures.

Ernie began studying them again, as well. After a minute he nodded his head and tapped one of the pages with his stubby right index finger.

"She was definitely here with Carl," he said confidently.

"And maybe this one, too, though her hair was different," he said, tapping another photo. "What do you think, Loreen? They look familiar to you?"

He looked up at her expectantly. Loreen stared at the pictures for a moment, then gave a slight nod. Michel thought he saw a glimmer of fear in her expression for a second, then it was gone.

"I think so," she said quietly.

"Any of the others look familiar?" Michel asked.

Loreen shook her head quickly and took a step back. She didn't look up at him.

"I better go out back and get set up for lunch," she said, then turned and walked into the kitchen.

"Don't mind her," Ernie said with a paternal smile. "She's just a bit skittish around strangers."

Michel smiled back, though he suspected there was more to Loreen's nervousness around him.

"I appreciate your help, Ernie," he said. "If it's all right with you, I'll have someone from the local police give you a call so they can arrange to take your statement. Loreen, too."

"Sure enough," Ernie replied. "Happy to help out."

"And if you think of anything else that might be helpful, I'd appreciate it if you gave me a call," Michel said, taking his wallet out and removing a business card from it.

He placed the card on the counter and wrote his cell phone number on the back. As an afterthought he took out a second card and repeated the process.

"Just in case Loreen thinks of anything," he said casually, sliding the cards toward Ernie.

Ernie nodded.

"You be sure to stop by again if you're ever in the area," he said, "and tell your friends about us. We're always happy to have new customers."

Michel paid his check and headed back outside to his car. Loreen's reaction made him curious, but unless she called with some surprising information he was at the end of the road. He had witnesses connecting Carl to one, and possibly two, of the missing girls. He wondered why he didn't feel more satisfied.

Chapter 33

Sassy parked opposite the mission and turned off the headlights. She was about to open the door when she saw someone step out onto the sidewalk across the street. Even in the semi-darkness she recognized Mose Lumley and slouched down into her seat.

Lumley stood on the sidewalk and took a cigarette out of the pack in his shirt pocket. By his fast, erratic movements Sassy thought he seemed agitated, and as he lit a match she caught a brief glimpse of anger in his face. It was an expression she hadn't thought him capable of and wondered what had upset him. Lumley looked up and down the street and then began walking in the direction of the distant lights of the strip club where Sassy had seen him with Carl four nights earlier.

Sassy waited until he was two blocks away, then stepped out of her car and quickly crossed the street. The door to the mission was unlocked and she let herself in. A few men and women were gathered on the floor watching an old television. They looked up at her with disinterest and then returned their attention to the sitcom they were watching. Sassy crossed the room to the back corner and walked down the hall to Eldridge's office. The door was closed.

"Come in," Eldridge replied to her knock.

Sassy opened the door and saw Eldridge seated behind his desk. For the first time she could remember he had no suit jacket on, and his bow tie hung undone. He looked tired.

"Sassy," he said, his expression brightening. "This is a pleasant surprise."

He stood up and walked around the desk to kiss her cheek.

"I wish it were," Sassy replied.

Eldridge gave her a curious look.

"Pleasant, I mean," she said. "But maybe we should talk another time. You seem to have other things on your mind right now."

Eldridge's expression changed to concern.

"No, not at all," he said, gesturing for her to take a seat in one of the leather chairs by the window. "What's on your mind?"

"I just saw Mose Lumley outside," Sassy said as she sat down. "He seemed upset. Is everything all right?"

Eldridge sat in the other chair and let out a weary sigh.

"Nothing to worry about," he said. "Sometimes Mose just gets frustrated when the realities of running a place like this conflict with the ideals. He'll be fine after he has a few drinks."

Sassy felt that Eldridge wasn't being completely honest. Lumley's demeanor had suggested more than frustration.

"And that's all it was?" she asked.

Eldridge smiled indulgently at her.

"I didn't realize you knew Mose," he said.

Sassy knew he was being evasive but let it go.

"Actually that's why I came to see you," she said.

"Oh?" Eldridge replied, arching his eyebrows in surprise.

Sassy nodded.

"I have something to tell you," she said.

*****

Eldridge listened quietly while Sassy told him what she'd learned and described her dilemma. When she finished he stood and walked to his desk. He opened the bottom drawer and took out two shot glasses and a bottle of scotch.

"Drink?" he asked, holding up one of the shot glasses.

"I better not," Sassy replied, patting her stomach and eyeing him cautiously.

"Of course," Eldridge said with a small smile. "Do you mind?"

"No," Sassy replied as he walked back to his chair carrying the bottle and one glass, *"but I have to say I'm a bit surprised. I've never seen you drink hard liquor before. Are you okay?"*

Eldridge sat down and placed the glass on the table between them, then poured a shot. He downed it quickly and refilled the glass, but left it on the table and put the bottle beside it.

"I'm afraid I have something to tell you, too," he said finally. *"Mose works for me."*

"Works for you how?" Sassy asked nervously.

"You're right that he's just a 'soldier'," Eldridge replied. *"It was my idea and I planned everything."*

"Jesus Christ, El," Sassy said angrily, standing up and walking to the middle of the room. *"Why?"*

"How do you think I keep this place open?" Eldridge asked in a quiet, measured voice. *"Donations? The only time people care about the homeless is when they start moving into their neighborhoods."*

Sassy spun around to face him.

"But El, stealing for noble purposes is still stealing," she said, trying to regain her composure. *"It doesn't make it okay."*

Eldridge nodded.

"I know that," he said softly. *"I suppose I'm guilty of practicing situational ethics."*

"Don't bullshit me, Eldridge," Sassy said, *"and don't bullshit yourself. You're guilty of a lot more than 'practicing situational ethics.' Aside from the fact that you're committing a felony, you've also gotten Carl involved. Do you have any idea what would happen to him if he got caught, given his record? For God's sake, he's your brother."*

"Mose did that on his own," Eldridge replied. *"I introduced them because Carl needed a job. I had no idea Mose would involve him. In fact he tried to keep it from me. When I found out he agreed to push Carl out once the baby is born."*

"Assuming he's not already in jail by then," Sassy replied bitterly. *"No, it's going to stop right now."*

Eldridge stared at her for a moment. He seemed to be grappling with whether to say something else, but then he nodded.

"Okay," he said.

Sassy sighed with relief.

"Does Carl know you're involved?" she asked.

"No, Mose is the only one who knows," Eldridge replied, shaking his head. "The others think he's in charge."

"So if he stops the whole operation will stop?" Sassy asked hopefully.

Eldridge nodded.

"Good," Sassy said. "I want you to call him in the morning and tell him it's over."

Eldridge picked up the shot glass and studied it for a few seconds before draining it.

"I'm not sure that will work," he said, looking up at Sassy.

"Why not?" she asked. "What aren't you telling me?"

"Mose and I had a falling out," Eldridge replied. "That's why he was angry. I'm not sure he'll listen to me now, and he knows enough about the operation to keep it going on his own."

"Shit, Eldridge," Sassy said, slowly shaking her head. "Now what the fuck do we do?"

"I think if you go to him and tell him to leave town he'll listen," Eldridge replied.

"And what if he asks why I'm not arresting him?" Sassy asked.

"Tell him you have personal reasons that are none of his business," Eldridge replied. "He may bluster a bit, but if you scare him enough he'll back down. You saw for yourself, he's like a child pretending to be a man."

Sassy let the scenario play out in her mind. She knew that the fact she'd already interrogated Lumley for the kidnappings would help her intimidate him. If necessary, she could imply that she had evidence linking him to the case as well.

"Okay," she said finally, "but I want you with me in case there's any trouble. You can wait in the car."

Eldridge nodded.

"It looked like he was heading down the street to the clubs when he left," Sassy said, "so he probably won't be home until too late tonight. Is there anything planned for tomorrow night?"

"No," Eldridge said. "The next shipment of merchandise isn't due until Wednesday."

"Good," Sassy replied. "Then we'll go to his house tomorrow night. I'll tell Carl you're coming over for dinner. Afterward we'll come up with an excuse to go for a ride and I'll confront Lumley. Hopefully that'll be the end of it."

Chapter 34

Michel made the trip back to New Orleans in just over four hours, arriving at the station at 4:12 pm. As he parked behind the building he tried to decide how much he should tell DeRoche. The fact that Carl had been seen with at least one of the girls meant they had solid evidence to conclude that he was responsible for kidnapping the girls in the photos. They still needed to identify the other girls and find out what had happened to them, but essentially the case could be closed so far as anyone in the department knew.

He knew differently, however. The questions of who killed Carl and Mose Lumley and why still remained. The problem was that no one else was even aware their deaths weren't suicides. He realized he'd made a tactical mistake by keeping the information Lecher had given him secret, and wondered if Lecher had maneuvered him into it. The only way out he could see now was to come clean and accept the consequences.

That option didn't seem very appealing. While he knew that his time on the force was likely coming to an end anyway, he wasn't ready to go just yet. Looking at the case objectively, Sassy would be the obvious suspect in Carl's murder, and the revelation that Lumley was murdered would raise suspicions about her involvement in that, too. While he was confident she would eventually be exonerated in both cases, the damage that might be caused to her career could be irreparable. He wasn't willing to hurt her like that and knew he had to stay on the case until he could solve it.

During his drive back he'd tried to think of a scenario that both fit the facts and ended with Sassy killing Carl. The only one he could imagine seemed far too convoluted: Lumley was responsible for kidnapping and killing Missy Ann Macomber, Celia Crowe, and Iris Lecher; Carl found out and killed him, but Sassy stumbled into it and Carl shot her; Carl then kidnapped the other 36 girls; after twenty five years he decided to confess what he'd done and sent Sassy the key to the safety deposit box to ensure he couldn't change his mind; that night he called her and told her what he'd done; she went to his house and killed him. It seemed plausible only in that Sassy may have gone into a killing rage if she'd found out that Carl was responsible for shooting her and killing their baby. The rest seemed like the plot of a bad dime store novel or soap opera.

There were also two major problems with the scenario. The first was the question of why Carl would have kept the photos of Missy Ann, Celia and Iris. There was no sensible reason. The second was why Sassy would have called when she received the key to the safety deposit box. If she'd gone to the bank alone and destroyed the evidence no one would ever have known about the other girls and the investigation would likely be over by now. She was too smart a cop to purposely introduce evidence that would prolong the case and potentially lead to her crime being discovered.

Logic dictated that Sassy was innocent of killing Carl, and while he knew he still had to consider her a suspect until he could figure out who was responsible, he wasn't willing to expose her to unnecessary scrutiny by the department. For now, he decided, he would just tell DeRoche that he had witnesses who'd seen Carl with one of the girls.

His thoughts turned to Lecher. He wondered how much more Lecher had uncovered since they'd last spoken. It was possible that Lecher already knew who'd really killed Carl and was just waiting to find out if Carl had, in fact, been responsible for the missing girls and Iris' death.

His instincts told him it was time to lay his cards on the table. He would arrange to meet Lecher after he spoke to DeRoche, and tell him everything he knew, including his belief that Lecher had lied to him about Carl's suicide. Even if he couldn't convince Lecher that Carl was guilty, he might be able to scare him into stopping his own investigation.

Chapter 35

"I expected to hear from you before this," Lecher said as he settled into the chair opposite Michel in his study, a glass of bourbon in his hand.

"Stan, I know what's going on," Michel said immediately.

"Meaning?" Lecher asked, his tone casual.

"I know that Carl Adams was murdered," Michel replied, "and I know you think his killer may have been responsible for killing Iris."

Michel thought he saw a flicker of shock register in Lecher's eyes.

"What makes you think that?" Lecher asked, his tone still controlled.

"Does it matter?" Michel replied. "It's true, isn't it?"

Lecher regarded him thoughtfully for a moment, then nodded.

"Yes," he said softly, with a hint of resignation. "I guess I underestimated you."

Michel was surprised that Lecher had conceded so quickly and it made him uneasy.

"I also think you were planning to go after whoever was responsible yourself if Carl turned out to be innocent," he said.

Lecher blinked but didn't respond.

"Look, Stan, I don't want to play games with you anymore," Michel said with frustration. "I'm willing to tell you everything I know, but you need to do the same."

Lecher stared at him blankly for a moment then nodded.

"Okay," he said without emotion.

Michel tried to gauge the sincerity of the response. Though it wasn't the resounding declaration of solidarity he'd hoped for, he decided to continue.

"First of all, I don't think Iris, Missy Ann and Celia were taken by the same person who took the other girls," he said. "They were younger, and the circumstances of their abductions were different. So far as we've been able to find, they were the only girls taken from their houses."

When Lecher didn't question his assertion Michel realized that Lecher had already reached the same conclusion. He wondered apprehensively what else Lecher already knew.

"I think Lumley and Carl were working together," he continued, "but Lumley kidnapped the younger girls on his own. When Carl found out he killed Lumley because he found it morally offensive. Lumley crossed the line by picking girls who were too young. And I also think that Carl planned for Iris to be found alive, but when Sassy showed up he had to improvise, and in the course of it Iris saw him. He killed her to protect himself."

Lecher was silent for a moment, considering the logic. He knew enough about the criminal code of relative morality that he didn't doubt that part of it was plausible.

"And you're sure Sassy just 'showed up'?" he asked finally.

"Think about it," Michel replied. "If she had been involved she would have been relieved to have it all end with Carl's apparent suicide. She wouldn't have called me when she got the key for Carl's safe deposit box. I don't think she was involved that night and I don't think she killed Carl."

"Then who did?" Lecher asked.

Michel studied him curiously.

"I was hoping you might be able to tell me," he replied. "I'm sure you haven't been sitting around just waiting for me to come up with the answer."

Lecher smiled slightly and shook his head.

"No, I haven't," he admitted, "but I haven't had any luck either. I agree that it wouldn't make sense for Sassy to lead you to the photos if she was guilty, but so far she's the only likely suspect."

Michel sighed wearily, knowing it was true.

"And you're sure Carl didn't kill himself?" he asked hopefully.

"It's possible," Lecher replied, "but he had so much rhohypnol in his system when he died that I don't think he could have lifted the gun. There also wasn't any powder residue on his right cuff."

"So you did falsify his autopsy report?" Michel asked.

Although he'd already suspected it, he was still mildly shocked when Lecher nodded.

"I felt it was necessary at the time," Lecher said. "I wasn't sure I could trust your people."

"And now?" Michel asked.

"I think I can trust you...or have to, at any rate," Lecher replied with a shrug. "Let's face it, we've both been operating outside the bounds of accepted practice."

Michel smiled at the understatement. Though he still didn't trust Lecher, he knew that they were bound together now.

"I found witnesses linking Carl to two of the girls in the photos," he said.

Lecher blinked at him again before responding.

"And they're certain?" he asked.

"Positive ID on one of them, probable on the other," Michel replied. "I only showed them the photos of the six girls I'd already identified. We'll ask the police in Beaumont to show them the rest when they come in to give their statements."

"Beaumont?" Lecher asked, his interest obviously piqued. "Texas?"

Michel nodded.

"What were you doing in Beaumont?" Lecher asked.

"I drove Carl's route this morning," Michel replied. "I

figured someone might have seen him with one of the girls somewhere along the way. Assuming they were runaways and he picked them up on the road, it seemed logical."

"That makes sense," Lecher replied, though he seemed suddenly distracted.

"He was a regular at a place called Fat Ernie's," Michel said. "Ernie and a waitress there recognized one of the girls. Ernie thought another one was familiar, as well. He said that Carl brought hitch hikers in all the time so no one thought anything of it."

"So he was on his way to Houston?" Lecher asked a little too quickly.

"Yeah, why?" Michel asked pointedly.

He felt unsettled by the tone of the question and Lecher's sudden interest in geography.

"Just curious," Lecher responded, with a shrug. "I figured it was probably Houston or San Antonio if he was driving Interstate 10."

Michel knew that Lecher was being evasive but realized he couldn't ask more questions without making his skepticism obvious. He tried to read Lecher's eyes, but Lecher was intently studying his drink.

"So the case will be closed," Lecher said suddenly.

"Unless I tell DeRoche otherwise," Michel replied.

"And what about the investigation into the Lumley cover up?" Lecher asked.

"I discreetly left a copy of the case file you gave me on DeRoche's desk this morning," Michel replied. "I don't think they'll be able to come up with any proof that the cover up was anything more than what we already know, so it'll be dropped."

"So it's all over then?" Lecher asked, though it was more a statement than a question.

Michel stared at him incredulously.

"Not exactly," he replied. "We still need to find out who killed Carl."

"Why?" Lecher asked calmly. "He killed my daughter, and probably thirty six other girls. He deserved to die."

Michel was shocked, though he wasn't sure if it was because of the moral certainty of the statement or the fact that it had been made so coolly.

"You can't be serious," he said.

"No?" Lecher replied. "I just wish I'd gotten there first."

Until that moment Michel had questioned whether Lecher would actually be capable of killing the person responsible for Iris' death. Now he believed he could, and his suspicion that Lecher was keeping something from him made him nervous.

"Stan, I'm not going to stop looking," he said, hoping that Lecher would understand the implied warning.

"Do what you have to do," Lecher replied flatly, "So long as you're certain that Adams killed Iris, though, justice has been served as far as I'm concerned."

He gave Michel a look that was part question and part challenge.

"I'm certain," Michel replied with as much authority as he could.

Lecher nodded.

"Then I'm done," he said quietly.

*****

Michel got in his car and drove around the block, parking again far enough up the street where he wouldn't be easily seen from a window but could still keep an eye on Lecher's front door. He couldn't shake the feeling that something bad was about to happen.

Three things about his conversation with Lecher bothered him. The first was the feeling that Lecher wasn't telling him everything he knew, the second was Lecher's interest in Carl's driving route, and the third was Lecher's apparent willingness to let Carl's killer remain free. On their own he might have been willing to overlook the first two, but the third was thoroughly inconsistent with Lecher's character.

Of course seeking vengeance is also out-of-character, Michel mused darkly. Perhaps when it's personal, belief systems no longer apply.

He looked up the street. The lights inside and on the front porch of Lecher's house were still on. He decided to wait until Lecher went to bed, then he'd go home. He hoped that nothing would happen before then.

Chapter 36

Michel had been watching Lecher's house for just over a half hour when his cell phone rang. He didn't recognize the phone number or the 512 area code.

"Doucette," he answered.

"Detective Doucette?" a woman replied.

Her voice was rushed and nervous, and Michel thought he detected a slight Texas accent. He sat up in his seat, his senses suddenly alert.

"Yes," he replied.

"Detective Doucette," the voice repeated, "my sister Loreen gave me your number."

"Okay," Michel replied, picturing the young waitress at Fat Ernie's who'd seemed so anxious around him. "How can I help you?"

"She said you were at the diner where she works and you were showing pictures of some girls?" the woman replied, her voice dropping almost to a whisper.

"That's right," Michel replied. "Do you know something about them?"

There was a long silence and Michel began to worry that the woman had hung up.

"One of them was me," she said finally.

"Excuse me?" Michel replied, thinking he'd misheard her.

"One of the girls in the photos was me," the woman replied quickly, her voice still hushed. "Loreen said that one of them was me."

Michel tasted copper as his adrenaline surged. His mind began to race and he breathed deeply to calm himself.

"Ma'am, what's your name?" he asked.

"I can't say," the woman replied.

"I already have your phone number and know where your sister works," Michel said. "I promise you won't get into any trouble."

"If my husband finds out he's going to leave me and take my babies," the woman replied, her voice breaking.

"If he finds out what?" Michel asked. "That you were kidnapped."

Michel heard the woman taking short, labored breaths. He imagined she was on the verge of crying.

"It's going to be okay," he said soothingly. "Just tell me what happened."

"I wasn't kidnapped," the woman replied, her voice full of despair. "I posed for that picture."

The words hit Michel like a sucker punch, as all of his assumptions were suddenly knocked sideways.

"Ma'am, I don't understand," he said urgently. "Do you mean you posed for that picture for Carl Adams?"

"No," the woman replied, gasping for breath, "for his brother."

Michel felt like he'd been dropped into a maze.

"Eldridge Adams?" he asked, trying to make sense of what he was hearing.

"Yes," the woman replied, openly sobbing now.

"But how did you get to him?" Michel asked, his mind frantically searching for a way out of his confusion.

The woman didn't respond for a moment and Michel could hear her breathing hard.

"Four years ago," she said finally, her voice more controlled, "when I was 14, I ran away from home. Carl Adams picked me up and gave me a ride. He told me that his brother ran a mission and would help me."

"I understand," Michel replied encouragingly.

"He took me there," the woman said. "After I'd been there for a few days one of the other girls told me that Eldridge would give me money if I let him take my picture. She said he wouldn't touch me...and so I let him."

As she said the final words she broke into deep sobbing again. Michel waited patiently until it subsided.

"And what happened?" he asked then.

"Nothing," she replied weakly. "He took my picture and gave me some money, and a few days later I left."

Michel thought about Eldridge's reaction when he'd told him about the photos in Carl's safety deposit box. Eldridge hadn't fainted because he thought Carl had killed all those girls. It had been because the photos belonged to him. He wondered suddenly if Eldridge had killed Carl to prevent Carl from turning him in.

But then who had taken the photos of Missy Ann Macomber, Celia Crowe and Iris Lecher? he wondered. Carl, Eldridge or someone else? He pushed the questions away and focused his attention back on the woman. Something still didn't make sense to him.

"Ma'am," he said, "how did Carl get you to Mexico?"

"Mexico?" she asked, clearly confused.

"To Eldridge's mission," Michel replied.

"The mission wasn't in Mexico," the woman replied. "It was in Houston."

*****

Michel sprinted up the street to Lecher's house and began hitting the doorbell repeatedly. There was no sound from inside. Looking through the narrow window to the left of the front door he could see up the hallway to the kitchen. Lecher was no where in sight.

"Fuck," he said aloud, banging the door with his right fist.

As soon as the woman said the word "Houston" he'd known that Lecher would be gone. In that moment he'd realized that Lecher had already known that Eldridge had been running a mission in Houston and was just waiting for evidence connecting Eldridge to one of the girls in the photos. He'd given Lecher that evidence. Unfortunately, Lecher was about to punish Eldridge for the wrong crime.

Maybe he could still stop him, he thought, scanning the street to confirm that Lecher's car was there. He knew that Lecher wouldn't have risked calling a taxi from his house because it would leave a trail of evidence, so he'd probably taken a side street up to St. Charles to flag one down. Even if he'd gotten one right away, it would still be a 10-minute drive from the Garden District to the mission. Depending on when Lecher had sneaked out of the house, there might still be time.

Michel jogged back to his car and called the dispatcher on his radio.

"This is Detective Doucette," he said. "Is Al Ribodeau on duty tonight?"

"Yes, detective," the dispatcher replied.

"Can you patch me through to him?" he asked.

"Just a moment, please," the woman replied.

Michel waited while his call was redirected. After a minute Ribodeau's voice came over the speaker.

"This is Ridodeau."

"Al, it's Michel," Michel said quickly. "Where are you?"

"Down at the French Market," Ribodeau replied. "Why?"

"I think that Stan Lecher is planning to kill Carl Adams' brother, Eldridge," Michel replied. "I want you to get up to the old homeless mission on N. Rampart and keep an eye out for him. I'll meet you there as soon as I can."

"Jesus," Ribodeau said. "Shouldn't you call it in?"

"I'd rather not," Michel replied. "I'll explain it to you later. I don't think he'd hurt anyone else, so just try to keep him there if you see him. Tell him I'm on my way."

There was a moment of silence and Michel knew that Ribodeau was debating what to do.

"All right," Ribodeau responded finally, "but I'm not happy about this."

"I know," Michel replied. "I'll buy you a beignet. Just hurry."

Michel got into his car and started the engine. He hoped he wouldn't be too late.

*****

As he got close, Michel could see three squad cars blocking the street in front of the mission. A crowd had gathered on the periphery of their flashing blue lights, making the scene look like an outdoor rave party. He slowly drove up onto the curb and parked on the far side of the street. He could see Al Ribodeau standing outside the door to the mission watching him, and quickly got out of his car.

"Sorry," Ribodeau said as Michel approached. "As soon as I got here I heard a gunshot inside. I had to call for back up."

"That's okay," Michel said, shaking Ribodeau's hand. "Adams?"

"He's dead," Ribodeau replied grimly. "Shot in the head."

"And Stan?" Michel asked, afraid of the answer.

"He's inside," Ribodeau replied, jerking his head to indicate the door to the mission. "He's pretty shaken up."

"Did he do it?" Michel asked.

"Hard to say," Ribodeau replied. "There's an unfinished letter on Adams' desk that looks like a suicide note, and I found Stan performing CPR on him. He told me to call an ambulance."

As if on cue, Michel could hear the distant siren of an ambulance cutting through the humid night air.

"CPR?" he asked. "Did he say what happened?"

Ribodeau shook his head.

"He said he'd only talk to you," he replied.

"Then I better get in there," Michel said.

He squeezed Ribodeau's left shoulder, then walked into the mission.

Although crime scenes were flurries of well choreographed activity, they were usually hushed. Voices were kept low out of respect for the victims. Still, Michel was struck by the quiet in the room. There was no conversation at all, and Michel realized that this time it was out of respect for the suspect, who was one of their own.

He saw Lecher seated on the floor against the back wall. His knees were pulled up close to his chest with his arms encircling them, his bloody hands clasped in front of them. Michel slowly crossed the room and squatted down beside him. Lecher kept his eyes on the floor in front of him. His face was expressionless.

"Stan," Michel said, in a voice that was both quiet and forceful, "are you okay?"

Lecher looked up at him and nodded, his blank expression turning suddenly remorseful. Michel felt a pang of pity, something he'd never expected he would ever feel toward Lecher.

"I was wrong," Lecher said in a voice that seemed to have aged years over the last hour.

"I know," Michel replied. "I got a call a little while ago from the sister of the waitress at the diner where Carl was seen. She told me she was one of the girls in the photos I showed. She said Eldridge paid her to pose for him."

Lecher nodded.

"He told me," he said.

"Then why did you kill him?" Michel asked.

Lecher gave him a stunned look.

"I didn't," he said. "He shot himself."

Michel knew they would have to perform comprehensive forensic tests to prove it, but his instinct told him Lecher was telling the truth.

"But you came here to kill him?" he asked more quietly.

"I don't honestly know," Lecher replied. "Originally that was what I thought I wanted, but I think more than anything I just needed to hear him confess what he'd done to Iris."

"Then why didn't you tell me what was happening?" Michel asked. "Why did you come here alone?"

Even before Lecher responded Michel knew the answer. He realized that in Lecher's situation he would have done the same thing. He would have wanted to keep his options open.

"Because I wasn't sure what I would do," Lecher replied, shrugging weakly.

Michel heard the ambulance pull up outside. He knew that any more questioning would have to take place at the station, and that more likely than not his career was about to come to an end. He placed his left hand gently on Lecher's shoulder.

"Come on, Stan," he said. "I've got to take you in."

Chapter 37

"Jesus Christ, Michel," DeRoche said, not for the first time that night.

It was nearing midnight and they'd been in the interrogation room for just over two hours. Michel lit a cigarette and stared at the table while DeRoche paced in front of him.

"You had to know this wasn't going to end well for you," DeRoche said, sighing with frustration. "This is going to mean your badge."

"I know," Michel replied. "I've known that for a while."

"Then why the fuck didn't you tell me what was going on?" DeRoche yelled, slamming both hands down on the table and leaning across it toward Michel.

Michel didn't even make an attempt to look contrite. Although he liked and sympathized with DeRoche, he was too tired to make the effort. Beyond that, he didn't see the point. Before the night was over he knew he'd no longer be a cop.

"I'm sorry I've put you in this position," he said wearily, "but at the time I thought I was making the right decision."

"Then you're not the cop I thought you were," DeRoche replied bitterly.

Michel felt a catch in his throat. While he'd been willing to accept the consequences of his actions, the fact that he'd also lost DeRoche's respect hurt deeply.

"There's a sad irony in all this," DeRoche said, shaking his head. "We started out investigating a cover-up, yet you've covered up more information at every step of the investigation. And now someone is dead as a result. If Lecher killed Eldridge Adams, then his death is on your hands."

"He didn't kill him," Michel said flatly.

"I hope for your sake he didn't," DeRoche replied.

Despite DeRoche's anger, Michel thought he heard a note of genuine concern in his voice. He realized DeRoche probably felt emotionally conflicted, like a father who'd discovered his son had committed a terrible crime. He was torn between righteous anger at the crime and his instinctive desire to protect his child.

"What's going to happen to Stan?" Michel asked.

DeRoche stared at him for a moment and his anger seemed to subside a bit.

"I don't know," he said. "Assuming he didn't kill Adams, he'll probably be let go. I don't think the department is going to want to go through a public trial to get him on obstruction of justice. But his career will be over."

Michel nodded. He imagined that the same would be true for him, that no charges would be filed because of the bad publicity it would generate for the department. DeRoche was right about the irony of the situation, he realized.

"What about the note Eldridge left?" he asked.

"What about it?" DeRoche replied.

"Can I see it?" Michel asked.

DeRoche stared at him in disbelief.

"Are you shitting me?" he exclaimed. "In case you haven't realized it yet, you're no longer working this case."

"I know that," Michel replied, "but I was hoping you'd show it to me as a courtesy."

"A courtesy?" DeRoche replied with a mirthless laugh. "I think you've already been extended enough courtesies. If you'd been anyone else you'd be in a holding cell right now."

Michel knew it was true and looked back down at the table. He knew the end was getting close.

"Does Sassy know what happened?" he asked, looking up again.

"Not yet," DeRoche replied. "I didn't want to call her until we know exactly what happened. Once we get the forensics reports I'll give her a call."

"If you don't mind, I'd like to be the one to call her," Michel replied. "As my last official act."

DeRoche shook his head.

"Call her if you like," he said, "but you've already performed your last official act. All I need now are your badge, gun and car keys."

*****

Michel walked out of the station as the sun was beginning to cast its light across the rooftops of the Quarter. Below, the streets were still in shadow, and he flipped up the collar of his jacket against the chill air. Al Ribodeau had offered him a ride home, but he'd declined. He felt like walking. He lit a cigarette and started toward the Marigny.

Chapter 38

Sassy was just pouring her first cup of coffee when she thought she heard a soft knock at her front door. Curious, she walked down the hall and peered through the peephole. Michel was standing on her porch, staring blankly at the ground.

"Jesus, you look like shit," she said, as she opened the door.

"Thanks a lot," Michel replied with an exhausted smile. "Can I come in?"

"Come on," Sassy replied, waving him in. "You look like you need some coffee."

Michel followed her to the kitchen and took a seat on the counter.

"I can't believe it," he said with exaggerated surprise while Sassy poured his coffee.

"What's that?" Sassy asked, eyeing him suspiciously.

"I thought you actually slept in a suit," Michel replied with a mischievous grin. "Who knew you owned pajamas?"

Sassy gave him a sour look.

"Anyone who has ever had the privilege of spending an evening in my boudoir," she replied with mock hauteur.

"So basically no one, then," Michel replied, breaking into a fit of laughter.

Sassy stared at him with a deadpan expression.

"You know, they sell coffee at the corner store," she said.

"I'm sorry," Michel replied, trying unsuccessfully to calm himself, "but I've literally never seen you in anything other than work clothes before."

"And you never will again," Sassy replied, shaking her head like a tolerant mother. "Come on, Giggles, let's go sit on the back porch."

As they walked to the back of the house Michel managed to regain his composure. He knew his laughter had been inappropriate given what he had to tell Sassy and regretted it, but realized it had been an hysterical outburst caused by tension and lack of sleep. They sat at the black wrought iron table on the veranda that hugged the back of the house and Sassy handed Michel his coffee. The smell of lavender permeated the still-cool air.

"So why are you intruding on me so early in the morning and why do you look like you haven't slept all night?" Sassy asked, giving Michel a concerned look.

Michel fought the urge to light a cigarette.

"Eldridge is dead," he said as gently as possible.

Sassy blinked at him uncomprehendingly for a moment, then the meaning of the words hit her and she slumped back in her chair. She closed her eyes and took a deep breath, exhaling loudly.

"What happened?" she asked softly.

"It was probably suicide," Michel replied.

"What does that mean?" Sassy asked, opening her eyes. "What else might it have been?"

Michel stared at her for a long moment before replying, wondering if their friendship would ever be the same once he'd finished telling her everything he had to say.

"Stan may have killed him," he said finally.

*****

"Why didn't you tell me any of this was going on?" Sassy asked when Michel finished talking.

"Because I didn't know how involved you were," Michel replied.

273

"What do you mean, how involved I was?" Sassy asked, narrowing her eyes at him.

Michel let out a sigh.

"I had to consider the possibility that you were trying to protect Carl," he said.

"Protect him how?" Sassy replied more aggressively.

"That night at Lumley's," Michel replied, looking down at his hands. "It seemed possible that you and Carl set Lumley up so that Carl wouldn't get caught."

Sassy shook her head in disbelief.

"You think I let Carl shoot me to protect him?" she asked with a derisive snort.

"No," Michel replied. "I thought that maybe he changed the plan so he could tie up all the loose ends."

Sassy stared at him for a moment. He couldn't read her expression.

"I gotta tell you, Michel," she said, "I'm really feeling the love now."

"I know," Michel replied, shaking his head sadly. "I'm sorry. It was just that the way things went down that night was odd. It seemed like too much of a coincidence that you showed up when you did. I never really believed you were involved, but after what happened with Chanel I vowed not to let my personal feelings get in the way of doing a thorough investigation."

Sassy regarded him thoughtfully for a moment.

"I realize that," she said in a forgiving tone. "I've realized that all along. It didn't make it any less painful being shut out, but I realized it. I just can't believe that you thought I was helping Carl."

"Then I don't suppose you'll be any too thrilled to know that I also questioned whether you shot him," Michel replied with a defensive smile.

"You what?" Sassy exclaimed with an incredulous laugh. "I am so going to kick your ass one of these days."

"Try to look at it objectively," Michel replied. "Suppose you'd found out that Carl shot you?"

"I wouldn't have killed him," Sassy replied firmly. "I would much rather have seen his ass rot in jail."

She pursed her lips and looked at the table for a moment, then began nodding her head.

"But I can see why you had to consider the possibility," she said in a conciliatory tone.

"I really am sorry," Michel said. "I made a lot of mistakes on this one. I allowed myself to get in a position where I was working in a vacuum. I realize now that that was Stan's plan. He was trying to plant doubt in my mind about you to keep us apart. I don't think he ever actually believed you were involved either, but he wanted me to question it so we wouldn't talk."

"He's a smart man," Sassy replied with a shrug.

"Yeah," Michel replied. "Smarter than I gave him credit."

"Don't be too hard on yourself, Michel," Sassy said. "You did fuck up royally, but at least...actually there is no at least. You just fucked up royally."

"Now who's feeling the love?" Michel asked with a pained laugh.

Sassy's smiled for a moment, then her expression turned serious.

"I need to explain why I was really at Lumley's house that night," she said.

Michel gave her a questioning look.

"Am I going to need a cigarette for this?" he asked.

"I think we both will," Sassy replied.

Michel slid the pack and lighter across the table and Sassy took out a cigarette and lit it. She passed the pack back to Michel and he did the same.

"Okay," he said, "I'm ready."

"A few days before Iris Lecher was kidnapped, Carl was working the late shift so I decided to bring him dinner at the produce company where he worked," Sassy began. "Only when

I got there I found out there was no late shift. Being pregnant and hormonal at the time, I immediately assumed he was cheating on me, so I decided to catch him in the act.

"The next night I waited for him outside the produce company and followed him. He and Mose Lumley drove to a house in Metairie where they picked up a truck and drove it to Belle Place. I figured out they were moving stolen merchandise."

"Okay," Michel said uncertainly, trying to figure out where the story was headed.

"I knew I had to stop him," Sassy said. "Not just because I was a cop, but because I loved Carl. I didn't want to see him get hurt and I didn't want our baby to grow up with a father in jail. The problem was that I didn't want to confront him. I was afraid that if he knew that I knew about what he was doing, it would change the dynamic of our relationship. He'd always be worried that I didn't trust him, or that I looked down on him, and he wouldn't feel like we were in an equal partnership. I didn't want to put him in that position. Does that make sense?"

Michel thought immediately of the parallels to his relationship with Joel. For the first time he truly understood Joel's perspective.

"Unfortunately, it does," he said.

"So I decided that my best bet was to try to scare off Lumley," Sassy said, "but I wasn't sure how to do it. I'd never met him so I didn't know what kind of approach would work with him.

"Then Iris was kidnapped and I was brought onto the case to do the profiling. One of the names that turned up was Lumley. He wasn't a good suspect, but I figured if I interrogated him it would give me a chance to figure him out, so I had him brought in."

"Jesus," Michel said, realizing the implications.

"I know," Sassy said. "A little girl was missing and I was fucking around trying to save my marriage."

"I don't know what to say," Michel replied.

"You don't have to say anything," Sassy said. "I'm not looking for you to tell me it was forgiveable given the circumstances. It wasn't, and I've had to learn to live with that."

Michel nodded. He was beginning to understand the events that had shaped Sassy.

"That night I went to Eldridge for advice," Sassy said. "He admitted that Lumley was working for him."

"Wait a second," Michel interrupted. "Eldridge was behind the stolen goods operation?"

Sassy nodded.

"So Carl was working for his brother?" Michel asked.

"He didn't know he was," Sassy replied. "Lumley never told Carl about Eldridge."

"But why did Eldridge need the money?" Michel asked. "He didn't strike me as someone with much interest in material goods."

"To fund the mission," Sassy replied. "He told me that no one wanted to donate money for homeless people so he had to find other ways to support his cause."

"I would have said that seemed out-of-character for him," Michel said, "but I didn't peg him for taking dirty pictures of teenage girls either."

He seemed lost in thought for a moment, then shrugged.

"So how did you end up at Lumley's?" he asked.

"El and Lumley had had a falling out." Sassy replied. "El was afraid that if he tried to pull the plug Lumley would just continue on his own. But he thought that if I went to Lumley and told him I knew what was going on I might be able to scare him into leaving town."

"But wouldn't Carl find out you were involved then?" Michel asked.

Sassy shook her head.

"Lumley didn't know I was Carl's wife," she replied. "He only knew me as Detective Alexandra Jones."

"And you think it would have worked?" Michel asked.

"Lumley wasn't the sharpest tack in the box," Sassy replied, "and he had a healthy fear of cops. He wasn't likely to question my motives if I told him to leave town."

"So that's why you went to his house?" Michel asked in amazement. "Just to scare him away?"

"That's it," Sassy replied. "Eldridge came with me in case there was any trouble. He waited in the car."

There was a thoughtful silence as Michel reflected on everything Sassy had told him.

"So you could never tell the department what really happened," he said finally. "Carl and Eldridge would have gone to jail and you would have been booted off the force."

"Or gone to jail, too," Sassy replied. "Aside from my professional misconduct, I was trying to cover up Carl's and El's crimes."

"Shit, Sas," Michel said. "I wouldn't mind having you join me at the unemployment office, but I don't want to have to visit you in prison. They took away my car. I'd have to take the bus."

"Your concern is touching," Sassy replied sarcastically, though she appreciated Michel's attempt to lighten the situation. "Seriously, though, I don't know what to do. I know what I did was wrong, but on some level I feel like I've already paid my debt. Maybe I'm just rationalizing, but I think the public has been better served by me being a good cop than they would have if I'd gone to jail. At the same time, I'm tired of keeping the secret."

"I can't tell you what to do," Michel replied quietly. "You have to do what's right for your conscience and accept the consequences. As far as I'm concerned, though, what you told me stays here. I don't see that you caused Iris' death."

"But if I'd been more focused on the case we might have found her before she was killed," Sassy replied.

"How?" Michel asked. "You said it yourself: Lumley didn't fit the profile. And neither did Carl. Do you think you could have done a better job on the profile if you hadn't been distracted by what was happening with Carl?"

"Not with the information we had," Sassy replied.

"Then I don't see that you're responsible for Iris' death," Michel said matter-of-factly. "You're only guilty of misjudgment and trying to cover up crimes that took place twenty five years ago. The statute of limitations on those ran out a long time ago. If you tell DeRoche everything now all you're going to accomplish is ending your career."

Sassy was quiet for a moment, considering the logic of Michel's assessment.

"What do you think really happened?" she asked finally. "Did Carl kill Lumley?"

"I don't know," Michel replied with a shrug. "I suspect we'll never know until Carl's killer is found. Unfortunately, that's out of my hands now."

"Just like that? You're just going to let it go?" Sassy asked, looking at him skeptically.

"You know I'd never do anything that might get me in trouble with the law," Michel replied with a sly smile.

Chapter 39

Michel got home just after 10 am and climbed immediately into bed. Despite his physical exhaustion, he was unable to rest, managing only to doze fitfully for a few minutes at a time. Each time deeper sleep seemed about to overtake him, his thoughts would turn to Joel or Carl and he'd come awake again. Although he knew he should be thinking about his future instead, that was too big an issue for his tired mind to contemplate. He also suspected that until he'd settled the past he wouldn't be able to move forward with any conviction or enthusiasm.

At 1 pm he finally gave up and went to the kitchen to make some coffee. As it brewed he perched on a stool at the counter and lit a cigarette. He felt an overwhelming urge to call Joel.

But why bother? he thought dejectedly. I'm no closer now than I was three days ago to knowing what I want to do. If anything, it's worse.

Although he knew that he loved Joel and that they had a strong connection, the insight Sassy had inadvertently given him into Joel's feelings made him wonder if he should even try to salvage their relationship. Had he already done too much damage? he wondered. Would Joel ever be able to feel like an equal partner now, regardless of what he might do or say to convince him?

It also worried him that the relationship itself didn't seem equal. On some level he'd always felt that he benefitted more from it than Joel. Joel had opened his mind and helped bring balance and as much serenity as he'd ever felt to his life. What had he provided in return? Without him Joel would have ended up at the same place. It may have taken longer, but he had no doubt that Joel would have gotten there anyway. What did he really bring to the table that was of any value to Joel?

Maybe he should just let Joel go, he thought. Given his own doubts, perhaps it was the right thing to do for Joel's sake. Then Joel could get on with his life.

Suddenly he realized what he was doing and the realization made him sit up straight. He was trying to make a decision for Joel that he had no right to make. The decision of whether to end the relationship belonged to both of them, yet he had presumed to make it on Joel's behalf.

"What an egotistical prick I am," he said aloud.

If Joel were ever going to feel that they were equals, he have to let Joel to make his own decision about whether he wanted to be in the relationship. All he could do was decide for himself if it was what he wanted, and then be honest with Joel about his feelings. Then it was up to Joel.

His mind felt suddenly much clearer. The only person he had to think for was himself. After that it was out of his hands. He was startled by the simplicity of the idea and wondered how much unnecessary anxiety he'd caused himself over the years trying to make decisions for others.

So the only question he had to answer was whether he wanted to be in a relationship with Joel. He already knew the answer. Putting aside all the doubts and questions of whether it was the right thing for both of them, his feelings were clear: he wanted to be with Joel.

He looked at the clock on the stove. Joel would be at work for another two hours. He decided to call and leave a message. He picked up the phone and dialed.

"Hi, this is Joel," Joel's voice came on after the third ring. "You know what to do...and if you don't, you should probably be raising a barn somewhere in Pennsylvania right now."

Michel smiled, wondering how many callers actually got the Amish reference.

"Hey, it's me," he said, making an effort to keep his tone light without sounding like he was pretending nothing had happened. "I'd really love to talk to you. I'll be at home if you want to give me a call."

He hung up and crossed the room to the coffee maker. He felt good suddenly and knew he'd made the right decision by calling. Things might not work out as he hoped, but at least he'd taken the first step. Now it was Joel's decision whether he wanted to call back or not. He poured his coffee and headed for the garden, grabbing the phone and his cigarettes and lighter on the way.

The air in the garden was warm and moist, and bright sunlight still bathed most of the patio. He put his things on the ground and dragged a chaise lounge into the narrow band of shade along the right wall. This will do, he thought, as he lay down. Two minutes later he was asleep.

Chapter 40

The shrill ring of the phone startled Michel awake, and for a moment he wasn't sure where he was. As he studied his surroundings with bleary eyes he realized he must have fallen asleep on the chaisse lounge and wondered how long he'd been there. The shadows had reached halfway up the far wall and he guessed it was nearly 5 pm. That meant he'd been asleep for almost four hours.

He stumbled off the chaisse and snatched the phone off the ground. Suddenly he remembered the message he'd left for Joel and his heart began to beat faster. He quickly punched the "talk" button.

"Hello?"

"Michel, it's Stan," Lecher's voice replied.

Michel felt a mix of disappointment and curiosity.

"Oh, hey Stan," he replied. "Where are you?"

"I'm home," Lecher replied. "They released me about three hours ago when the results of the forensic tests came back."

"So I guess that means you didn't kill Eldridge," Michel replied with a small laugh.

"No," Lecher replied, "but I think you already knew that."

"To be honest, I wasn't sure at first," Michel answered, "but yeah, after I talked to you I did."

There was silence for a moment.

"Listen, Michel, I'm really sorry," Lecher said finally. "I was so focused on my own agenda that I didn't consider the consequences for you."

"Sure you did, Stan," Michel replied without judgment, "but I made my own decision to follow you over the cliff. I'm not blaming you. I'm pretty sure I'd have done the same thing in your situation."

"I appreciate you saying that," Lecher replied, "but I really am sorry."

"Let's face it, we were trying to play one another," Michel replied. "We're both at fault. If we'd actually been working together we'd probably know who killed Carl by now."

"That's why I'm calling," Lecher replied. "When I told you I didn't care who killed him I was lying. I was just trying to get rid of you so I could go after Eldridge."

"I sort of figured that out after the fact," Michel deadpanned, "but thanks for pointing it out."

"I already told you I'm sorry," Lecher said, chuckling softly.

"I know," Michel replied. "So what's on your mind?"

"Before Eldridge shot himself he talked to me," Lecher replied. "He was pretty incoherent, but he said some things that were curious. I was hoping we could get together to see if any of it makes sense to you."

"Did you tell DeRoche about it?" Michel asked, unsure what response he wanted to hear.

"Yeah," Lecher replied with a sigh of resignation.

"Then shouldn't we leave it to the cops to figure things out from here?" Michel asked.

When Lecher didn't respond Michel began to wonder if they'd lost their connection.

"Stan?" he asked. "You still there?"

"Yeah, I'm still here," Lecher replied dryly. "I've just been waiting for you to say 'April Fools'."

"What do you mean?" Michel asked.

"You don't expect me to believe you're just washing your hands of everything because you're off the force, do you?" Lecher replied.

"Why not?" Michel asked.

"Because I know you," Lecher replied. "You could no more let it go than I could."

Michel debated how to respond. He knew it was true, yet it bothered him that Lecher believed he knew him so well. A part of him wanted to be contrary just to prove Lecher wrong. The rest of him, however, was intrigued to hear what Eldridge had said.

"Okay," he said finally. "Why don't you come by in a half hour. I need to take a quick shower."

"Great, I'll see you then," Lecher replied and hung up.

*****

Lecher arrived just after 5:30 pm. He was dressed in jeans, a white t-shirt, and white sneakers. Michel was surprised not only by his clothes, but also by the obvious tautness of his body. It had never occurred to him that Lecher might work out.

"Who the fuck are you?" Michel asked as he pushed open the screen door.

"Look who's talking," Lecher replied, taking in Michel's cargo shorts and tight black t-shirt. "I said I wanted to talk, not go to the Bourbon Pub."

"Funny man," Michel replied quickly, aware that he was beginning to blush. "Come on in."

Michel lead Lecher down the hall to the back of the house and out into the garden. He'd already set up two glasses and a pitcher of iced tea on a cocktail table between two cushioned wrought iron chairs. He gestured for Lecher to take one of the chairs and sat in the other.

"This is beautiful," Lecher said, looking around. "No wonder you wanted to quit your job and spend more time at home."

Michel gave him a fake smile as he poured the iced tea.

"Cute," he said. "What's your excuse?"

Lecher laughed appreciatively at the quick response.

"So tell me about what Eldridge said," Michel said as he handed one of the glasses to Lecher.

"Let me show you something first," Lecher said, putting down the glass and leaning forward to pull something out of his right back pocket.

He handed a folded sheet of paper to Michel.

"What's this?" Michel asked, eyeing the paper curiously.

"Eldridge's suicide note," Lecher replied nonchalantly.

"How the hell did you get it?" Michel asked with a look of amazement.

He began quickly unfolding the paper.

"I memorized it," Lecher replied. "After Ribodeau arrived I had a few minutes alone in Eldridge's office."

"And you memorized it?" Michel asked, shaking his head. "Are you sure it's accurate?"

"Yeah," Lecher replied. "Maybe you haven't noticed but I have sort of a photographic memory."

"Yeah, I've noticed that," Michel replied, remembering all the times he'd been surprised by the level of detail that Lecher had immediately absorbed at crime scenes.

He turned his attention to the page in his hand. There were only three paragraphs. The jagged, uneven, cursive handwriting conveyed a state of emotional turmoil. He began reading.

There are things inside us all from which we can't hide. Destinies are shaped in an instant by callous cruelty, and the beast takes root and begins to grow. Try as we may to outrun or control it, the beast is always within, waiting to emerge again.

I'm responsible for the beast within my brother, and therefore all that he did. I should have been his keeper, but I didn't protect him. I know that everything he did was because of me, because I failed him. I've spent my whole life trying to atone for that mistake, but I know now it couldn't be undone. I may not have pulled the trigger, but I killed my brother. For that alone I deserve to be punished.

I've also done things on my own for which I'm truly sorry. I knew it was wrong and tried to stop, but the beast was too powerful, as it must have been for Carl, both shaped by our common experience. The person responsible has already been punished. I don't expect forgiveness, but it needs to be said for my own peace of mind. I'm so tired of running. I'm too much of a coward to face the consequences of what I've done, but I can't run any more. Living with what I've done is too painful.

"This is really what he wrote?" Michel asked when he finished. "The beginning reads like a demented sermon."

Lecher nodded.

"I know," he said. "The whole thing has a biblical, Cain-and-Abel-meet-the-devil sort of feeling to it."

"Which is odd," Michel replied, "because I remember Sassy telling me once that his missions were nonsectarian. She said he was very active in the church as a boy, but didn't use his work to proselytize."

Lecher stared up into the sky for a moment, seemingly counting the stars.

"Maybe his reference to 'the beast' is psychological rather than religious," he replied, looking back at Michel. "The language reflects his religious upbringing, but the concept also makes sense in a psychological context. He could be talking about the root trauma that motivated both their behaviors."

Michel considered the explanation and began nodding.

"That makes sense," he said. "Their crimes had some common elements. Carl just took things to a greater extreme. The most obvious trauma would be sexual abuse."

"And Eldridge was probably abused first," Lecher replied. "It would explain the part about feeling responsible for the beast in Carl. Eldridge must have felt that he should have protected Carl from suffering the same abuse he did."

Michel picked up his iced tea and took a long sip as he thought through the merits of their supposition.

"It would explain a lot," he said finally. "Unfortunately it doesn't give us any clues about who killed Carl."

"No," Lecher replied, "but what he told me might."

"Which was?" Michel asked, leaning forward attentively.

Lecher closed his eyes and took a sip of his iced tea before responding. Michel didn't sense that he was stalling, but rather trying to return to the previous night in his mind.

"When I got there he was in his office, sitting at his desk writing the letter," Lecher said after a moment, his eyes still closed. "There was a bottle of scotch next to him and he seemed drunk. He didn't see me at first, so I just watched him for a minute until he noticed me standing in the doorway."

"What was his reaction?" Michel asked.

"It was almost as if he was expecting me," Lecher replied, furrowing his brow as though unsure he'd used the right word.

"But you'd never met him, had you?" Michel asked.

"No," Lecher replied, "but he didn't seem at all surprised to see someone standing there with a gun pointing at him."

"Do you think he was in trouble?" Michel asked. "Loan sharks or someone?"

"Maybe," Lecher replied.

His voice had grown flat, as though he were in a trance.

"So then what?" Michel asked.

"I told him who I was," Lecher replied. "I could see that he made the connection to Iris right away when I said my name."

"Did he seem afraid then?" Michel asked.

"No, he was calm," Lecher replied. "In retrospect I think he was already resigned to dying and didn't care if I killed him or he killed himself."

Though Lecher's eyes were still closed, Michel nodded for him to continue and Lecher seemed to sense the gesture.

"Last night I told you that I wasn't even sure if I wanted to kill him when I went there, that more than anything I just wanted to hear him confess," Lecher said, "but when I saw him I didn't even want that anymore."

Michel gave him a questioning look that again Lecher seemed to sense.

"There was something about the look on his face that made me feel sorry for him," Lecher said with a slight shrug. "I could see that he was emotionally broken and it took away my desire to see him punished."

"So what did you do?" Michel asked.

"I talked to him," Lecher replied.

"Talked to him? About what?"

Lecher's eyes closed tighter as he concentrated harder.

"He apologized to me for what Carl did to Iris," Lecher replied, his voice cracking slightly as he said the last word. "He said that he didn't realize what was happening because he was preoccupied with his own problems. I asked him what kind of problems, whether he meant the girls in the photos, and he began crying. He said he hadn't hurt the girls. He knew what he did was wrong, but he swore he didn't hurt them.

"Then I asked him where the girls were now and he said he didn't know, that after he took the pictures he paid them and eventually they left. I asked him if he touched them and he said no, that he'd never do that. He just liked to look at them."

Lecher twisted his head slightly, as though listening to a distant voice.

"I said that he'd mentioned that he had problems and asked what kind of problems," he continued. "He said, 'The money. I had to keep paying him more money so he wouldn't tell what he saw'. I asked him who, but he didn't answer that. He said, 'Finally I got tired of running. I decided to come back and face him and I told him I wouldn't pay him anymore. And after Carl died he agreed, just like that time before. But that time he found me and told me I had to pay again. I kept moving and he kept finding me. But it's over now'."

Michel felt a chill as he realized that Lecher's voice had taken on the cadence and tone of Eldridge's voice as he recounted Eldridge's part of their conversation. It was as though he were channeling Eldridge's spirit, or playing back half of a tape recording.

"I asked if he killed the person," Lecher continued, "and he said, 'No, but he agreed, and if he changes his mind again I won't be here.' I asked him again who made him pay and he said, 'Shhhh...it's a secret.' So I told him he had to tell me and he said, 'I can't. I've caused too much pain already.'

"Then I told him that the person may have killed Carl and I could see that it didn't register in his eyes. He just shook his head and said, 'No, I killed Carl'."

Lecher opened his eyes and looked at Michel. He seemed dazed, as though just waking from a dream.

"That's when he pulled the gun out of a drawer," he said. "I tried to get to him but he pulled the trigger before I could stop him."

"Jesus, Stan," Michel said, exhaling loudly. "That was kind of creepy. You didn't do your seance routine for DeRoche, did you?"

Lecher gave him a small smile.

"No, I didn't want to spend thirty days under observation," he replied with a chuckle.

Michel's expression turned more serious.

"So he was being blackmailed," he said.

"Sure sounded like it," Lecher replied. "Seems like someone knew about the pictures, or something else we don't know about, and made him pay in exchange for silence."

"Carl?" Michel asked. "Maybe when El told him he wouldn't pay anymore he decided to turn him in and sent Sassy the photos?"

"No," Lecher replied. "He said the person agreed to stop blackmailing him after Carl died."

Michel nodded thoughtfully, trying to mask his embarrassment at overlooking that obvious fact.

"But it must be someone here," he said, "because he said he decided to come back and face the person."

"I agree," Lecher replied. "So whoever it is must have found him in Houston and was extorting money again."

"So they were in contact," Michel said, continuing the train of thought, "which means there might be phone records."

"Exactly," Lecher replied with a self-satisfied smile.

Michel stared at him with exasperation.

"You know, if you already knew that you could have just told me instead of weirding me out with your freaky mystic routine," he said.

"Like you wouldn't have asked me a thousand questions? Besides, I know how much you gays like a good show," Lecher replied with a mischievous grin.

"Seems to me you were the one being the drama queen," Michel replied with mock umbrage.

"Okay, maybe a little," Lecher replied, smiling warmly. "So getting phone records is a little outside my sphere of expertise. What do we do?"

"Normally I'd put an official request in to the phone company," Michel replied, "but I don't think that option's open to me anymore. We'll have to search his phone bills."

"You don't think the cops have impounded all of his things by now?" Lecher asked.

Michel stared blankly at him for a moment and Lecher could see the wheels turning in his head.

"Everything they know about," Michel said suddenly with a victorious smile.

"What does that mean?" Lecher responded, looking at him quizzically.

"When I went to visit El at the mission the other day he mentioned what a mess the cops made searching Carl's apartment," Michel replied. "He said he'd just finished cleaning it up and hadn't even had a chance to move in his own stuff from the storage locker in the basement. I'd be willing to bet he never did."

Lecher grinned back at him.

"See, I knew you weren't going to be totally useless," he said.

*****

They arrived at Carl's apartment building on Gaienne Street in the Warehouse District at 6:15 pm. Unlike those around it which were all former or current warehouses, Carl's building was clearly designed for residential purposes. It was four stories high, with a gray stucco exterior and large plate glass windows. It was the sort of nondescript, early 1970s architecture one might expect to see in any lower-middle-income city neighborhood in the country.

Michel and Lecher let themselves into the small vestibule. There were mail boxes on the left wall and a buzzer panel on the right. Through the glass door leading into the building interior they could see stairs and a hallway with three doors on each side of it. Michel tried the door. It was locked.

"I think it's a little too soon to use this," he said, shaking his right arm to indicate the crowbar he'd hidden in the sleeve of his jacket.

"Yeah," Lecher replied. "Let's see if someone will let us in."

He turned to the buzzer panel and pressed a button for an apartment on the fourth floor. There was no response. He tried a second with the same result. On the third try the speaker crackled to life.

"Yes?" a voice said through heavy static.

It sounded like the voice of an old woman.

"Mrs. Mitchell?" Lecher replied, reading the name on the panel.

"Yes?" the voice said again.

"I'm here from building maintenance," Lecher replied smoothly. "We got a report there's a problem with the buzzer but I can't find anything wrong. Would you mind hitting the button to open the door for me so I can see if it's working?"

292

There was silence for a moment and Michel and Lecher exchanged curious looks. Then the speaker crackled again.

"That buzzer hasn't worked in five years," the woman said, "and it's no wonder if you can't find anything wrong with it. Tell me, can you find your own ass with both hands?"

Lecher stared at the speaker with a stunned looked.

"Uh, yes I can," he sputtered.

"Good," the woman replied. "Then why don't you use the key under the mat to let yourself in, find your ass, and get it up here so you can fix the toilet I've been calling about for two weeks."

"Yes, ma'am," Lecher replied quickly. "I'll be right up."

He lifted the bottom left corner of the rubber mat, grabbed the key and unlocked the door. He and Michel started down the hallway.

"By the time the old bat makes her way down from the fourth floor to look for us we'll be gone," he said with a chuckle.

The door to the basement was at the end of the hall on the left side. They opened it and walked down a short flight of stairs. The smell of sewage hit them immediately.

"You gotta love these builders who put in basements in a flood plain," Michel said, wrinkling his nose in disgust.

The basement ran the length and width of the entire building. It was concrete with a low ceiling. The stains from past flooding were apparent on the walls and floor. The room was divided into narrow cubicles by rotting plywood panels along the left and right walls. Each cubicle had a door made of wire mesh tacked to a wood frame. The overall effect was of a kennel for very tall dogs.

They began walking up the center of the room, looking into each space. Most were empty and unlocked, the residents having no doubt realized they were better off storing anything of value in their apartments. There were only two rusted bicycles in one and an old floor lamp in another. Near the end on the right they finally found one that was secured by a combination lock. Through the mesh door they could see a stack of boxes, a cushioned chair and a few small tables.

"My intuition tells me this is the one," Lecher said dryly.

Michel looked at him, shaking his head tolerantly.

"You think?" he asked.

He reached into his jacket with his left hand and pulled the crowbar out of his right sleeve, then wedged the curved end under the metal hasp on the door and jerked down quickly on the other end. The metal loop holding the lock popped easily out of the wood frame and the door swung open.

"Let's get to work," Michel said.

Chapter 41

It was dark and quiet. There was no pain, just coolness against her right cheek. She felt a squeezing sensation in her left hand and opened her eyes. Eldridge was kneeling beside her, staring at her with a look of fear and concern.

"Hold on, Sassy," he said. "Help is coming."

She tried to smile but wasn't sure if anything happened. She returned to the darkness.

She was aware of the distant sounds of footsteps and then voices. She couldn't hear them clearly and started struggling toward them. It felt as though she were waist deep in tar and she wanted to rest, but knew she had to keep pushing forward.

"She's dead," a man's voice said.

She felt her arm move and then her left hand was resting against the coolness, too.

"Where's the goddamn ambulance?" Eldridge asked angrily.

"It's on its way," the other voice replied impatiently, "but it doesn't matter. They're all dead."

She recognized the voice now. It was Mac MacDonald.

A vision of being buried alive came into her mind and she felt a rush of terror. She tried to call out to let them know she wasn't dead but her mouth wouldn't open. She began silently screaming.

Suddenly the tar began to suck her downward and she thrashed her arms and legs frantically to keep her head above the surface. The harder she struggled, though, the faster she sank. She stopped moving and her descent slowed. She took fast shallow breaths to calm herself and tried to focus on the sounds around her.

"How am I going to tell Carl?" she heard Eldridge ask, his voice choked with tears.

"You need to pull yourself together," MacDonald replied coldly. "We've got business to discuss."

"Business?" Eldridge replied incredulously. "Fuck business."

"No, fuck you," MacDonald replied. "This is going to bring a lot of heat that neither of us wants. I know Lumley was your front man. You better hope he didn't leave any clues lying around."

"Who gives a shit about that?" Eldridge cried. "My sister-in-law and a little girl are dead."

"And nothing we do is going to change that," MacDonald replied, adopting a reasonable tone, "so we may as well protect ourselves. What were you doing here?"

The only response was the sound of Eldridge softly crying.

"Eldridge, we need to work together here," MacDonald said smoothly. "Tell me what you were doing here."

"Sassy found out about the stolen goods," Eldridge managed between gasping breaths. "She was going to try to scare Lumley out of town."

"Why?" MacDonald asked. "Why wouldn't she just turn him in?"

"She was trying to protect my brother," Eldridge replied, his voice more controlled. "She was hoping that if Lumley was gone Carl would stop stealing."

"So your brother knows she was coming here?" MacDonald asked, his tone suddenly alarmed.

"No," Eldridge replied. "He doesn't even know that she knew what was going on. She didn't want him to know."

There was silence for a moment and Sassy felt the tar slip over the top of her upper lip. She took a deep breath and held it.

"That's good," MacDonald replied finally. "We can still get out of this if you play it smart."

"What do you mean?" Eldridge replied.

"The cops are going to want to know why you were here," MacDonald responded. "Lumley was brought in for questioning.

Tell them that you and your sister-in-law were on your way somewhere and she wanted to ask him a follow-up question."

"No one is going to believe that," Eldridge replied skeptically.

"Sure they will," MacDonald replied. "He was found with the girl's body. They'll believe anything."

"Okay," Eldridge replied quietly, after a moment.

"Oh, one more thing," MacDonald said quickly over the sound of an approaching siren. "So far as anyone else is concerned, we've never met before."

"Okay," Eldridge replied again.

"And for now, our arrangement is done," MacDonald said.

Sassy woke with a start, staring up at her living room ceiling. She could still hear the echoes of the words from her dream.

"Our arrangement is done," she repeated aloud.

"That has a familiar ring to it," a voice to her left said.

She turned her head quickly, a jolt of adrenaline shooting through her body. Mac MacDonald sat in one of the chairs on the far side of the coffee table smiling at her, a gun in his hand.

*****

"Lucky this guy traveled light," Michel said as he placed the last of the seven boxes on the floor outside Carl's storage bin.

"I guess you develop the habit when you have to move every three to five years," Lecher responded.

He kneeled beside a box and pulled a Swiss Army knife from his back pocket. He flipped it open and deftly slit the tape sealing the top of the box, then passed the knife to Michel who did the same with another box. They both began searching through the contents.

"Stan, have you thought about what you want to do if we figure out who it is?" Michel asked after a minute.

"You mean, am I going to try to go all cowboy again?" Lecher asked, looking up at him.

"Something like that," Michel replied, standing up and brushing dust from his bare knees.

He picked up the pocket knife and moved to another box.

"No," Lecher replied thoughtfully. "Justice needs to be done, but I don't have to take it into my own hands. I realized that when I was with Eldridge."

"Good," Michel replied simply as he ran the knife across the top of the box.

He lifted the cardboard flaps and looked inside.

"Bingo," he said.

"What is it?" Lecher asked, standing up.

"Bills," Michel replied, reaching into the box and pulling out a handful of envelopes.

Lecher walked over to him and stared down into the box.

"You want to take them back to your place?" he asked.

"No way," Michel replied. "This is official evidence. I don't want it in my house."

"But you're okay illegally searching through it?" Lecher replied, arching his left eyebrow.

"We all have our lines we won't cross," Michel replied breezily as he began sorting through the envelopes in his hand. "Besides, this place smells like ass and I don't want that ass smell getting all over my house."

"Since when?" Lecher replied with a chuckle.

"You know, being gay isn't just some great big butt sex fest," Michel said playfully. "Unless I'm just doing it wrong."

"Well, I don't want to know if you start doing it right," Lecher replied quickly.

"Hey, I'm not the one who brought it up," Michel replied with an impish grin.

He finished going through the stack of envelopes and set them on top of another box.

"You planning to help with this or are you just going to watch me do all the work?" he asked, looking at Lecher and gesturing to the box.

"You want me to get ass smell on my hands?" Lecher asked with a mock grimace.

"Maybe if you buy me dinner first," Michel replied winking.

Lecher rolled his eyes at him.

"I don't know how Sassy put up with you all these years," he said.

He kneeled beside the box and pulled out a stack of envelope. Michel did the same and they began looking through them in silence.

"Here we go," Lecher said excitedly after a minute. "Phone bills for the last few months."

He picked four envelopes from the middle of his pile and placed the rest on the floor.

"Cross your fingers," he said, pulling two folded sheets of paper from the first envelope.

He set aside the summary page and began scanning the list of calls.

"There are a few local calls here," he said, running his finger down the page. "Most look like business numbers. Probably contractors he hired to work on the mission."

He paused for a moment near the bottom of the page, then quickly turned it over and checked the numbers on the back. After a few seconds he handed it to Michel, then opened the second envelope and began reading.

"He must have decided to come back in mid-February," he said after a few seconds. "That's when all the calls to New Orleans started. Prior to that there's only one and it keeps showing up. I'd bet that's Carl's number."

Michel looked up from the first bill.

"You know, it's possible he waited until he got back before he contacted whoever was blackmailing him," he said. "If I were being blackmailed and was going to try to put a stop to it, I think I'd want to do it in person. I'd want to gauge the blackmailer's reaction."

Lecher nodded thoughtfully.

"So do you think we're wasting our time here, then?" he asked.

"Not necessarily," Michel replied, "but we may be looking in the wrong place. Maybe we should be looking at bank records or for money wiring receipts."

Lecher looked at the unopened boxes and an expression of distaste crossed his face.

"In other words, you think we need to check them all," he said.

"Or we put them back and in the morning I call DeRoche and tell him I remembered Eldridge mentioning a storage space in the basement," Michel replied.

Lecher gave him a querying look.

"A change of heart?" he asked.

"More like an acceptance of our limitations," Michel replied with a resigned sigh. "I'd love to figure this out on our own, but realistically we just don't have the resources. It would take us a few days to go through this stuff thoroughly. The department can do it in a few hours, and they can also get a subpoena for Eldridge's incoming call records. Even though they booted my ass, I guess I still feel an obligation to make sure the case is solved as quickly as possible."

"What about the broken lock?" Lecher asked. "Won't DeRoche wonder about that?"

Michel looked at the frame of the narrow opening.

"I think I can fix it," he replied.

Lecher shrugged.

"All right, then I vote for option two," he said without hesitation.

Michel removed a small black notebook and a pen from his back pocket.

"What are you doing?" Lecher asked. "Leaving a note?"

"I just want to see if Sassy recognizes any of the numbers," Michel replied.

He quickly copied five phone numbers from the bill onto a page of the notebook.

"Okay," he said, as he slipped the notebook and pen back in his pocket. "We should probably cut the tape on all the boxes so it doesn't look suspicious."

"You know, sometimes you think just like a cop," Lecher said with a smile.

Chapter 42

"I hope you don't mind me letting myself in," MacDonald said in an amiable tone. "Your back door was open and you looked so peaceful napping on the couch that I didn't want to disturb you."

Sassy sat up slowly, sending the Vanity Fair magazine resting on her chest sliding to the floor. She turned to face him.

"What are you doing here?" she asked.

"I think you already know the answer to that, based on what you said when you woke up," MacDonald replied with a wolfish smile.

Sassy stared at him for a moment before responding. She wondered if she could reach the pistol she kept under the couch before he shot her, but decided it was too risky to attempt for now.

"You were blackmailing Eldridge," she said finally.

MacDonald nodded for her to go on, but she just shrugged her shoulders.

"Sorry, Sheriff, I haven't had a chance to figure the rest of it out yet," she said. "I just remembered the part about the blackmail."

MacDonald studied her, trying to decide if she was telling the truth.

"Well then, I guess my timing was impeccable," he said. "It would have been unfortunate if you'd had a chance to tell anyone else about that."

"Yeah, unfortunate," Sassy replied mockingly.

"You've got a pretty smart mouth for someone in your position," MacDonald drawled, his face losing all traces of humor.

Sassy wondered what exactly he'd meant by her "position." While there was the obvious fact that he had a gun aimed at her, she suspected from his tone that it was more than that. He seemed to be judging her as his inferior.

"What have I got to lose?" she asked, smiling defiantly.

"True," MacDonald replied without emotion.

They silently watched one another for a moment.

"So why did you kill Carl?" Sassy asked suddenly.

"What makes you think I did?" MacDonald replied.

"You wouldn't be here with your little gun if you were just worried about the blackmail," Sassy replied.

"Sure I would," MacDonald responded casually, "but you're right, I did kill him."

"Why?" Sassy asked.

"Because your ex-husband found some receipts for money that his brother wired to me," MacDonald replied.

"He figured out you were blackmailing El?" Sassy asked with mild surprise.

"Not entirely," MacDonald replied. "He hadn't made the connection with the photos he found yet, but he was curious enough to contact me."

"And you went to his house and killed him," Sassy concluded bitterly.

"No, actually we met at a bar," MacDonald replied. "He was smart enough to insist that we meet in a public place. He showed me one of the receipts and asked me what it was for."

"What did you tell him?" Sassy asked, her curiosity genuinely piqued.

"That it was repayment for a loan that I'd given Eldridge to start his first mission," MacDonald replied.

"And he bought that?" Sassy asked.

"Apparently," MacDonald replied, nodding.

"Then why the fuck did you kill him?" Sassy asked angrily.

"To tie up lose ends," MacDonald replied. "I couldn't risk him asking Eldridge about the receipts. So I put a little something in his drink while he was in the bathroom. Not enough to incapacitate him, but enough to make it appear he was very drunk. He left in a cab and I followed him home."

"How did you get into his place?" Sassy asked. "There were no signs of forced entry."

"I knocked on his door," MacDonald replied, laughing to himself. "He was in a very sociable mood by then and let me right in. That's when he told me about the photos that he'd sent you. He also told me it was your anniversary and all about how you'd ruined his life. I probably shouldn't tell you this, but I think he still loved you."

"Fuck you," Sassy replied in a low, threatening voice.

"So anyway, I managed to slip a little more rhohypnol into his drink while we were chatting," MacDonald continued as though he hadn't heard her, "and once he was unconscious I took care of business. I found the rest of the receipts for the money Eldridge wired and took them with me."

He gave Sassy a self-satisfied smile.

"Wait a second. What about the photos of the three girls?" Sassy asked warily, suddenly realizing the implications of MacDonald's story. "Where did those come from?"

"They were mine, of course," MacDonald replied with a look of exasperation. "You're really not as bright as I thought you were."

Sassy felt her heart pounding. She breathed deeply to calm herself.

"So you killed the three girls," she said.

"And many more since," MacDonald replied, smiling. "But thanks to what I learned from watching Eldridge, no one is looking for them...or at least not their bodies."

"What do you mean, 'from watching Eldridge'?" Sassy asked.

"I was on patrol one night and saw this pretty young thing come out of the mission and walk into the alley next to it," MacDonald replied. "I was debating whether to follow her when Eldridge came out and went down the alley, too. I waited a few minutes and then I followed.

"There was an old slaves' quarters back there. I found a gap in the boards covering one of the windows and saw Eldridge and the girl inside. She was chained to a post and he was putting a gag in her mouth. She wasn't struggling or trying to get away, so I just watched. He took her picture and uncuffed her, then she got dressed and left. He stayed and masturbated looking at the photo."

"You're a sick fuck," Sassy said.

"Me?" MacDonald replied. "Your brother-in-law was the one taking the picture."

"And who took the pictures of Iris, Celia and Missy Ann?" Sassy asked in an accusatory tone.

"I did," MacDonald admitted, "but that was just for protection. I figured if things got too hairy I could kill Eldridge and plant the photos on him. The cops would find his other photos, too, and pin the kidnappings on him."

"So that's what you learned from Eldridge?" Sassy asked derisively. "How to chain girls up and take their pictures?"

"No," MacDonald replied patiently. "After all the heat that came down when I kidnapped the last girl I figured I'd have to change the way I was doing things. I thought about Eldridge and realized that runaways were the way to go. Unless their bodies turn up, no one worries too much about them."

Sassy felt a surge of anger that made her momentarily dizzy. She closed her eyes and waited for the feeling to pass.

"So then you started blackmailing Eldridge," she said after a moment, opening her eyes.

"About a week later," MacDonald replied nonchalantly. "I staked out the mission until I saw him go back there with another girl and then I took their picture."

Sassy pretended to look at her hands. In her peripheral vision she could see that MacDonald had let the barrel of his gun drift away from her toward the left wall. She realized that the longer she kept him talking, the more relaxed he would become and the greater her chance would be of taking him by surprise and escaping. She also knew this might be her only chance to get the full story of what had happened.

"How did Lumley fit into all this?" she asked, looking up.

"Lumley figured out what was going on," MacDonald replied, seemingly pleased that she'd asked. "After a while he wanted to know why Eldridge needed so much money for the mission and Eldridge told him the truth."

Sassy remembered the night she'd seen Lumley angrily leaving the mission. The pieces were all falling into place.

"Lumley confronted me about it," MacDonald continued. "I was afraid that if he went to the cops they'd search my house and find Iris in the barn, so I agreed to pay him off and told him I'd bring the money to his house that afternoon."

"And instead you killed him and framed him for the kidnappings," Sassy said.

"I didn't have any choice about killing him," MacDonald replied, "but the inspiration to frame him came when he asked me if I knew you and said that you'd brought him in for questioning. That was just a stroke of luck."

Sassy felt a wave of nausea at the words but ignored it.

"And me?" she asked.

"You were just in the wrong place at the wrong time," MacDonald replied with a look that seemed almost sympathetic. "After I killed Lumley I went to my place and got the girl. You showed up before I had a chance to kill her."

"So you shot me?" Sassy asked.

She could feel her blood pulsing hard in her temples.

"It certainly wasn't the girl," MacDonald replied, shrugging.

"Iris," Sassy said in a tight voice.

MacDonald stared at her blankly.

"Iris," she repeated. "Her name was Iris."

"Her name doesn't matter," MacDonald said, his composure breaking a bit for the first time.

"Then why don't you say it?" Sassy challenged.

MacDonald stared at her for a moment, his eyes flashing angrily under the prominent bush of his brow. Then he started to smile again.

"That was very good," he said, nodding slowly. "Trying to make me angry in hopes I'd make a mistake."

Sassy leaned forward, her hands dangling between her knees near the edge of the coffee table. Her heartbeat began to quicken.

"Can't fault me for trying," she said.

"No, I suppose I can't," MacDonald said with a humorless laugh. "Not that it's going to do you any good."

Sassy saw the barrel of his gun moving back toward her and braced her feet. With an adrenaline-fueled quickness that surprised even her, she hooked her fingers under the edge of the table and stood, simultaneously heaving upward with her shoulders. The heavy glass table top lifted onto its side and began falling toward MacDonald. Sassy could see him trying to move to his right out its path, but the edge struck his left shoulder, driving him back hard into the chair.

Sassy dropped to the floor. She could see her gun directly beside her under the couch and reached for it with her right hand as the sound of shattering glass filled the room. Her hand closed on the grip and she pulled the gun toward her. As it cleared the edge of the couch, she pushed herself onto her knees and twisted her body to her left, swinging the gun upward.

Suddenly she felt a blow behind her left ear and was knocked forward onto her right elbow. Pain exploded up her arm but she kept her hold on the gun. She tried to roll to her left, but MacDonald's foot came down hard on her right shoulder blade, the thick heel of his boot driving her body flat against the floor.

"You fucking cunt," she heard him hiss, then everything went dark.

Chapter 43

Michel bought a fresh pack of American Spirit Lights at the market where Lecher had dropped him on Kerlerec Street, then stepped out on the sidewalk. The streetlights were just buzzing to life, their light intensifying against the encroaching darkness. As he opened the pack and lit a cigarette he looked at his watch. It was just after 7:30 pm. Though Sassy's house was only a few blocks away, he began walking in the other direction. One unannounced visit per day is enough, he thought. Two would be pushing it.

He turned left on Chartres Street and walked two blocks to the Friendly Bar. As usual, the door to the small neighborhood hangout was open. Two older men and a middle-aged woman occupied stools at the bar, engaged in easy conversation. They all looked up and nodded to him in greeting as he walked up to the bar.

They sure named this place right, he thought, as he waited for Robey, the bartender, to make his way to him.

"Hey, Detective, what can I get you?" the stout older man asked with a welcoming smile.

"A Jack on the rocks and some quarters for the phone, please," Michel replied, wincing a bit at the no-longer-accurate greeting Robey had used.

He wondered how long it would be before news of the change in his career status filtered through the area.

"Local call?" Robey asked.

Michel nodded.

"Just use that one," Robey said, indicating an old black rotary-dial phone mounted to the wall to his right behind the bar.

"You don't mind?" Michel asked.

"Naw," the bartender replied with a cheerful laugh. "It's not like we have to keep the line open for reservations."

As he stepped away to pour Michel's drink, Michel walked around the end of the bar and picked up the receiver of the phone. He was surprised at its weight and wondered how long it had been since he'd used a rotary dial. He began dialing Sassy, waiting impatiently as the rotary spun back after each number.

He dialed the last number and waited. After three rings Sassy's answering machine picked up. As he listened to her greeting, Robey placed his drink on the bar and Michel smiled in acknowledgment.

"Hey, it's me," he said after the tone. "I'm at the Friendly Bar. I'm going to have a drink here and then head over. I just wanted to give you some warning so you wouldnt be doing anything perverted. Hopefully you'll be home when I get there. Otherwise I'll wait for you out back."

He hung up and walked around to the front of the bar, taking the stool closest to his drink. He pulled out his wallet and laid down a ten-dollar bill.

There could be worse ways to spend a warm spring evening, he thought.

*****

As he drove past the midway point of the Crescent City Bridge, Lecher turned to look at the lights of the Quarter far below to his left. He realized it might be the last time he saw them. He was leaving the city that had been his only home, not knowing if he'd return. In the distance he heard the mournful bellow of a ship's horn and imagined it was the city saying goodbye.

His initial impulse when he'd seen MacDonald's private number on Eldridge's phone bill had been to tell Michel and turn the information over to the police. MacDonald's crimes were so heinous that the district attorney would be forced to prosecute. Even in a city renowned for its history of corruption, a cover up wouldn't be possible.

As he'd considered the consequences, however, it occurred to him that it might be better for everyone if MacDonald never stood trial. MacDonald had made a mockery of the police department, rising to its highest office while kidnapping, killing and blackmailing. If his crimes were made public, the damage to the department's credibility would be immeasurable.

There also wasn't any certainty that MacDonald would be convicted or punished if he went to trial. MacDonald had been playing the political game for a long time. He was well connected and had undoubtedly amassed an arsenal of dirty secrets he could leverage against prosecutors and judges. If it were anyone else, he'd thought, he would have been content to let the courts do their job, but MacDonald was too dangerous. He had to be dealt with in a way that guaranteed he wouldn't be set free.

For a while he'd entertained the idea of doing to MacDonald what MacDonald had done to Mose Lumley and Carl Adams and staging a suicide. There was a poetic justice to the idea that he'd found appealing, but as he'd thought it through he'd realized that it would create too many complications. The police would be suspicious in light of what they'd recently learned about Lumley's and Carl's deaths and MacDonald's connection to the case. They'd launch a full investigation, and even with his knowledge of forensics he'd feared that he wouldn't be able to completely cover his tracks.

The solution came to him as he drove Michel back to the Marigny. If MacDonald appeared to die of accidental or natural causes, all of the potential downsides would be gone. Aside from the fact that no criminal investigation would be warranted, MacDonald's death would provide the police with an excuse not to go public when they uncovered his crimes. With no one to prosecute and no living victims, the details could be swept under the rug. It could even be justified as an act of compassion for the families of Celia Crowe and Missy Ann Macomber, who believed that their childrens' killer had been dead for twenty five years. For once the corruption in the system would be an asset. Justice would be served, there would be no scandal or additional suffering for the other victims' families, and the public's confidence in the police would be preserved, whether that confidence was deserved or not.

After dropping Michel at a market a few blocks from Sassy's house, he'd driven by MacDonald's house on Royal Street in the Quarter. As he'd expected, the building was dark and the gated driveway empty. Although the house was MacDonald's official residence, it was well known that he used it primarily for entertaining or occasional overnight stays. His real home was a farm in the town of Boutte, twenty three miles outside the city, on the other side of the Mississippi. Lecher had been there once for a barbecue MacDonald had hosted for senior law enforcement officials right after he was elected Sheriff.

As he'd driven home, Lecher had pondered the best way to kill MacDonald. Staging an accident was too difficult, he'd decided. It would require thorough planning, and sedating or restraining MacDonald, both of which would leave evidence. While a sudden death from natural causes might raise a few eyebrows, it would be easier to stage and the evidence harder to detect.

The two most obvious ways to induce death were to inject air into MacDonald's blood stream to cause an aneurysm or inject potassium chloride or ethanol into his heart to induce a heart attack. Both methods could be accomplished while MacDonald slept, but both carried risks.

Injecting air into MacDonald's blood stream might only result in a stroke. The prick of the needle also would probably wake him, giving MacDonald a chance to retaliate or call the police before the air reached his brain. It would also be necessary to inject the air directly into a vein, which would be problematic in the dark and would leave a detectable mark.

On the other hand, injecting potassium chloride or ethanol into the heart would leave a much less noticeable mark, particularly if MacDonald had chest hair, and would have an immediate effect. Even if MacDonald awoke he'd be incapacitated by the pain. The risk, however, was that the potassium chloride or ethanol could be detected if a pathologist were looking for them.

Still, inducing a heart attack seemed like the best choice, he'd decided. MacDonald was a prime candidate for a coronary. He was overweight and smoked, and had been a heavy drinker until ten years ago. He was also undoubtedly hypertensive, based on his florid complexion. A heart attack wouldn't seem unlikely, particularly if it appeared that he'd begun drinking again. It would also leave open the option of suffocation if the attack itself wasn't fatal. While the signs of asphyxiation might be unusual, they would be dismissed so long as MacDonald's heart showed appropriate damage and his troponine and creatine kinase enzyme levels were elevated.

Before going home he'd stopped at a liquor store and bought a pint of grain alcohol, paying for it with cash. While the commercial ethanol used at the coroner's office to preserve tissue samples was more concentrated, it also contained denaturing chemicals which would make it more easily detectable. The grain alcohol had fewer contaminents and would still deliver a dose of 50% ethanol, which he believed would be sufficient to induce cardiac arrest.

When he got home he'd quickly changed into a black, long sleeved shirt, then began examining the shoes in his closet, looking for the pair with the least distinctive sole pattern. He'd finally settled on some old brown Topsiders whose soles had been worn nearly smooth and slipped them on. From the top of the closet he'd grabbed a dark blue, nylon duffel bag and headed to the garage.

Six few years before he'd begun designing and building furniture as a way to relax, and had set up a workshop in the garage. Eventually, he'd developed enough skill that he'd approached a shop owner in the Quarter who'd begun selling his pieces. It had developed into a lucrative sideline that he often imagined pursuing full time when he left the Coroner's Office.

As his work had become more refined, he'd begun finding innovative ways to apply the tools of his other trade to his furniture-making. Among the innovations had been the use of cardiac syringes, whose long, thick needles were perfect for delivering glue into deep, narrow joints. Because the glue dried quickly, however, each syringe was good only for a single session, so he'd begun buying them in bulk from the manufacturer who supplied the Coronor's Office.

He'd taken two unopened syringes and needles from his supply cabinet and put them in the duffel bag, then gone into the house and added the bottle of grain alcohol and a pair of rubber cleaning gloves. Finally he'd been ready. As he'd walked through the house for possibly the last time, he'd turned off the lights as he went.

Now, as he exited the bridge on the far side of the river, he wondered if he would be able to carry out his plan. While he believed MacDonald deserved to be punished, and felt that his reasons for handling things the way he'd chosen were strong, he questioned whether he would be able to follow through when the time came. He'd devoted his life to bringing criminals to justice, but now he was on the verge of committing the most serious crime of all himself. The thought made him slightly queasy and he knew in his heart that if he succeeded his life would never be the same again. He would always be haunted by his act of vengeance.

He punched a button on the radio and turned the volume up loud, hoping to drown out his thoughts. The impassioned voices of a gospel choir filled the car.

Abel's blood for vengeance
Pleaded to the skies
But the blood of Jesus
For our pardon cries.

He looked at the radio and grimaced. I hope that will be enough, he thought.

Chapter 44

After finishing his drink, Michel considered calling Sassy again but decided against it. *She'll either be there or she won't,* he reasoned, *and I've already given her fair warning that I'm coming so she better not be naked.*

The air had cooled a bit and it felt good against his bare arms and legs as he stepped outside the bar. Though he knew he had no reason, he realized that he felt remarkably optimistic. He was actually looking forward to starting over again, though he had no idea what he would do. As he started up Chartres Street he began to muse about possible career directions.

When he arrived at Sassy's house five minutes later, convinced that he would make an excellent flight attendant, the light on the front porch was off, though he could see light coming through the transom over the door. He rang the doorbell once and waited. There were no sounds from inside the house. He hit the doorbell twice more, but there was still no response.

"Where are you, my nubian queen?" he asked aloud, as he stepped from the porch and walked to the right front corner of the house.

Unlike nearly everyone else in the city, Sassy always left her side gate unlocked. She reasoned that the chances of anyone just happening to try the latch were minimal, and if someone really wanted to get inside a lock wouldn't deter them anyway. She also kept an arsenal of guns hidden around the house in case anyone was foolish enough to try.

Michel let himself into the narrow alley between Sassy's house and the brick wall that separated her property from her neighbor's and walked to the back yard. Through the railing of the porch, the living room lights cast long shadows like the bars of a jail cell over the garden, making it look like the flowers and shrubs had been locked down for the night.

"Don't worry, you'll get out in the morning," Michel said to them as he passed by.

He climbed the three stairs onto the porch and looked through the back door. The only light inside the house came from the domed fixture on the living room ceiling. That's odd, he thought absently. Why didn't she leave the outside and hall lights on?

As he settled in at the wrought iron table and lit a cigarette he hoped that Sassy wouldn't be long. The drink he'd had at the Friendly Bar had made a quick trip through his system and he didn't think he'd be able to hold it in for very long.

*****

Lecher drove a quarter mile past the mailbox and pulled off the road, stopping under a low hanging willow twenty feet from the pavement. He turned off the headlights and cut the engine. The lights of MacDonald's house were visible in the distance across a field of high grass.

He reached into the duffel bag on the passenger seat and took out the bottle of grain alcohol and the syringe. He opened the bottle and set it between his legs, then uncapped the syringe, dipped the needle into the bottle, and drew out 100 cc's of alcohol.

That should do it, he thought.

He put the plastic sheath back on the syringe, recapped the bottle and put it back in the bag, then opened the door and stepped out of the car. A warm wind had begun to blow and he searched the sky for signs of rain. Only the moon and a few early stars were visible against the expanse of deep purple.

He slid the syringe into his back right pocket and checked his watch. It was 8:22 pm. He started walking back toward MacDonald's driveway.

*****

She was back floating in the thick inky tar, only this time she didn't have to struggle to stay afloat. Something was holding her wrists from above, keeping her from slipping below the surface. She was aware of a dull ache in her shoulders and numbness in her hands and lifted her head to look at them. A sharp burst of pain exploded at the base of her skull and Sassy snapped back to consciousness, her body rocking forward.

"Oh, fuck." she gasped as she felt a burning sensation in her wrists and her body was jerked back as if on a leash.

She opened her eyes and stared into the darkness around her. Each beat of her racing heart caused the pain in her head to flare, and she forced herself to take slow, even breaths to relax. Finally, after a full minute, the pain had subsided enough for her to focus on her surroundings.

The room was bathed in a dim blue glow. Though its far corners were hidden in shadow, she could see that it was large and rectangular. She closed her eyes and listened for any movement. All she could hear was the steady buzzing of cicadas that seemed to come from all directions.

She opened her eyes again and looked at the area immediately around her. She was seated on what appeared to be a small mattress, its fabric marked by large dark stains. Suddenly she remembered MacDonald and knew where she was: he'd taken her to his barn.

A snorting sound to her right startled her and she turned her head quickly, causing the pain to surge again. She closed her eyes tightly for a moment and waited for it to pass. When she opened them again she could see a row of stalls along the right wall of the room. She peered into the blackness beyond their doors, searching for movement, but didn't see anything.

The snorting sound came again, farther to her right, and she carefully twisted her head to look over her shoulder. Floating above the door of the last stall she could see a ghostly white diamond. It hovered motionlessly for a few seconds, then lifted and she heard the sound again. In the darkness she could just make out the silhouette of ears and a large narrow head.

"Hey horsey," she said in a weak voice. "You wouldn't happen to have any aspirin would you?"

The horse stared at her silently for a moment, then seemed to lose interest and pulled back into the shadows of its stall, its ghostly diamond marking growing dimmer and then disappearing all together.

"Thanks a lot," she said sarcastically.

Slowly she turned her head to study the rest of the room. The far wall was too dark to make out any detail, but she could see a wide vertical support column twenty feet directly in front of her. She guessed that she was bound to a similar column and an image of Iris Lecher flashed briefly in her mind.

She turned to her left. In the back corner the wheels of a tractor peaked out from under a gray canvas tarp. Further forward, a collection of scythes, rakes, pitchforks and shovels lined the wall. Carefully she tilted her head back and looked up. A loft ran the full width of the room and extended a few feet in front of her. She couldn't angle her head enough see her hands, but the burning in her wrists told her they were probably held by handcuffs.

Behind her she heard soft footsteps, then a door opening. Suddenly the room was filled with bright light, forcing her to close her eyes. The footsteps moved toward her across the packed dirt floor.

"You awake?" MacDonald asked, stepping in front of her.

"What do you think?" Sassy replied, squinting up at him with sullen anger.

"Always the smart mouth," MacDonald said, shaking his head. "It only makes me want to hurt you more before I kill you."

"You should have killed me at my place while you had the chance," Sassy replied.

"That would have raised too many questions," MacDonald replied.

"As opposed to a lot of broken glass and the fact that I'm missing?" Sassy replied derisively.

MacDonald studied her with cold intensity for a moment.

"You know, I was planning to kill you when I visited you at the hospital after I shot you," he said, "but when you didn't seem to remember anything I decided to let it go. I guess that was a mistake."

"Yeah, I guess so," Sassy replied mockingly. "So what's your plan, genius? Shoot me and bury me in the yard?"

MacDonald shook his head and laughed at her.

"No need for that." he said. "I'm just going to dump you in the bayou and let the gators take care of you. But first I'm going to hurt you real bad to make sure there's lots of blood to attract them."

"You never watched Batman, did you?" Sassy asked, smirking.

"What?" MacDonald replied with a perplexed look.

"You know, Batman, the TV show?" Sassy replied. "Every week the bad guys made the same mistake. They'd go on and on about how brilliant they were and unveil their whole plan, then they'd come up with some elaborate way to kill Batman instead of just shooting him and getting it over with. Then inevitably Batman would escape and foil the plan."

"I don't think you'll be getting out of this one, Batman," MacDonald replied.

"Maybe not," Sassy replied, unsuccessfully attempting a shrug, "but Robin and Commissioner Gordon will catch your ass one way or another."

MacDonald looked at her curiously, wondering if she was delirious from the kick he'd delivered to the back of her head.

"Michel Doucette and Stan Lecher already know that Lumley and Carl were murdered," Sassy replied, as though explaining to a child. "DeRoche knows now, too."

"Oh, that," MacDonald replied matter-of-factly. "Yeah, that's unfortunate, but they'll never trace it back to me. The only evidence connecting me to anything were the receipts for the money Eldridge wired and your memories. The receipts are already gone and pretty soon you will be, too."

"I think you're underestimating the competition," Sassy replied.

"Doucette is off the force and Lecher will be fired as soon as the Coroner's Office holds its kangaroo court," MacDonald said. "They won't be a problem anymore."

"Like I said, I think you're underestimating the competition," Sassy replied. "If you think that's going to stop them you're deluding yourself. And my sudden disappearance is only going to make them search harder."

"Are you trying to scare me into turning myself in, detective?" MacDonald asked with comic disbelief. "Because if you are, you're wasting your time. If Doucette and Lecher become a problem I'll just take care of them. My enemies have a way of disappearing. You're not the first person to go for a ride in the bayou, and I'm sure you won't be the last."

"I guess we'll just have to wait and see about that," Sassy replied with a defiant smile.

"I guess we will," MacDonald replied, smiling back, "though I'm afraid you won't be around to find out one way or the other. Now if you'll excuse me, my dinner's probably about ready. I'll be back for you a little later when it's darker and the gators come out to feed."

*****

The pain in his bladder had finally become unbearable and Michel jumped to his feet and walked to top of the porch stairs. He searched the shadowed periphery of Sassy's yard for a place to relieve himself.

This is humiliating, he thought, as he clenched his inner thigh muscles.

He spotted an azalea along the back wall and quickly descended the stairs and headed for it. He was nearly across the patio when he noticed a grouping of decorative clay pots in the right corner and remembered Sassy once telling him that she kept a spare key hidden there. He changed course, praying that she hadn't changed her hiding spot.

Once he'd made up his mind to pee behind the bush the pain had intensified, as though his body knew it was nearing relief and had entered a final countdown. He frantically lifted each of the pots, breathing hard and keeping his knees locked together. Under the largest of the pots he found the key and snatched it up.

He took one last look at the azalea. Breaking and entering or peeing in her bushes? he wondered. I've got to think she'd rather have me go in the house, he decided, and began a jerky power walk toward the door.

*****

After he'd taken care of his business, Michel walked into the kitchen and turned on the light. Well, I've already broken the law and violated her privacy, so I may as well make myself at home and do something useful, he reasoned, as he opened the refrigerator and took out a bottle of Dixie beer. He crossed the room and grabbed Sassy's phone from the counter, then walked to the living room.

That's odd, he thought, noticing that the coffee table was missing. I wonder if she's redecorating?

He sat on the couch and placed the beer on the floor by his

left foot, then pulled out his wallet. While he'd been waiting outside it had occurred to him that he didn't need the phone company to trace the numbers on Eldridge's phone bill. He could simply call them himself.

He took out the ATM slip and began dialing.

*****

The first two numbers had reached the answering machines of a general contractor and a plumber, and the third had been Carl's house. It was the first time Michel had heard Carl's voice and he'd been surprised by how different he'd sounded from Eldridge. Whereas Eldridge had had a precise, authoritative tone, Carl had a slow, soft musicality. He sounded like a natural southerner. Michel imagined that he could have been quite charming and pictured a young Sassy falling under the spell of that voice.

As he waited for the fourth number to connect he reached for his beer and noticed something on the floor against the edge of the carpet. He picked it up and held it up to the light. It was a chunk of glass, roughly a quarter-inch square.

"Hey, baby" a woman's voice said in his ear.

"Excuse me," Michel mumbled, taken by surprise.

He placed the piece of glass on the floor next to his beer.

"Who is this?" the woman asked accusatorially.

"Who's this?" Michel replied, unsure how to proceed.

He got up and walked back to the kitchen, wondering if Sassy had anything to eat.

"I asked you first," the woman replied in a cautious tone that indicated she had no intention of revealing her identity to a stranger.

"Okay," Michel said, as he began looking in cabinets. "My name is Carl Adams."

"So, why are you calling this number, Carl Adams?" the woman asked.

"My brother recently died and I'm trying to call all of his friends," Michel replied, hoping that it sounded plausible, "and I found this number on his phone bill. Did you know him? His name was Eldridge Adams."

There was silence for a moment. When the woman spoke again she sounded frightened.

"I'm sorry, Mr. Adams," she said. "I thought you were my boyfriend. I didn't know anyone else would be calling this number at this hour. I don't want any trouble."

Michel closed the last cabinet and stared down at the counter with a perplexed look.

"I'm sorry, miss," he said, "but you've got me a bit confused. Is this your number?"

"Please, sir, I could lose my job," the woman pleaded.

Michel was only half listening. He'd been distracted by Sassy's pocketbook and keys resting on the counter near the wall. He picked up the pocketbook and looked inside. Sassy's wallet was there.

"Hello?" the woman said when he didn't reply immediately.

"I'm sorry," Michel said, putting the pocketbook down. "Where am I calling?"

"Please don't get me in trouble," the woman said.

Michel felt a sense of dread growing in his stomach.

"Look, I'm not going to get you in any trouble," he said sharply. "I just want to know where the hell I'm calling."

"The Sheriff's Office," the woman replied tearfully.

"The Sheriff's Office?" Michel repeated. "You're a cop?"

"No," the women replied, "I'm the cleaning lady."

"Then why didn't an officer answer the phone?" Michel asked impatiently, his mind racing.

"This is his private line," the woman replied, her voice choked with sobs.

"Whose private line?" Michel asked urgently, though he already knew what the answer would be.

"Sheriff MacDonald," the woman replied.

Chapter 45

Lecher lay in the high grass at the edge of the driveway, watching MacDonald pour the steaming contents of a large pot into a colander in his kitchen sink. While he knew he should use the opportunity to slip into the house and find a place to hide until MacDonald went to bed, his curiosity had been piqued.

He'd been nearing the house, sticking to the shadows of the dense trees that lined the driveway, when the barn door had opened and MacDonald had stepped out. MacDonald had looked around for a moment, then padlocked the door and gone into the house. It had struck Lecher as odd that a man who left his front door open would bother locking his barn. He'd decided to see what—or who—MacDonald was keeping locked up.

He pushed himself up into a crouch, then began crab-walking through the tall grass toward the barn. He kept his eyes on the kitchen window and front door of the house until he reached the curve of driveway that ran back toward the road, then sprinted across the narrow open space. The sound of his feet against the dirt and gravel seemed deafening in his ears.

When he reached the cover of trees on the far side of the driveway he dropped to the ground and looked back at the house. His heart was beating much harder than he knew it should after such a short run and he tried to slow his breathing. After a minute, when he'd seen no movement near the house, he rolled under the lowest rail of the high, white fence that enclosed a small field next to the barn, then stood up and walked quickly to the side of the building.

*****

Michel finished searching the house and walked back into the kitchen, trying to decide what to do. He knew that the evidence indicating something had happened to Sassy was circumstantial at best: her wallet, keys, and pocketbook in the kitchen; her car in the garage; the piece of glass on the floor. There was nothing tangible to indicate a crime. Still, he knew that if MacDonald had kidnapped her, he had to act quickly.

The problem, of course, was that his prime suspect was the Sheriff of New Orleans. If he called in the police and it turned out he was wrong, the fallout might force him to leave the city. He knew that under normal circumstances he would have gone to MacDonald's house on his own, but that wasn't an option any more and he realized how vulnerable he felt without a gun. He had to proceed carefully and try to keep the situation controlled in case he was overreacting.

There was only one option that made sense. He picked up the phone and dialed Captain DeRoche's cell number.

"Sassy?" DeRoche answered.

"No, Captain, it's me, Michel," Michel replied.

"Oh," DeRoche responded less than enthusiastically. "What can I do for you, Michel?"

"I think something may have happened to Sassy," Michel replied quickly. "I'm at her place now and she's missing."

"Missing?" DeRoche replied. "What makes you think she isn't just out?"

"Her pocketbook, wallet and keys are still here," Michel replied.

DeRoche didn't respond for a few seconds.

"Are there any signs of a break-in or a struggle?" he asked finally, his voice conveying genuine concern.

"Not really," Michel replied. "Her coffee table is missing and there's some broken glass on the floor nearby, but no clear evidence. That's why I called. I didn't want to get a whole team over here in case I'm just being Chicken Little."

"I understand," DeRoche replied.

"There's something else," Michel said. "I think that Mac MacDonald may have taken her and that he's the one who killed Mose Lumley and Carl Adams."

DeRoche paused before replying.

"Is this some kind of joke?" he asked finally. "You think the Sheriff kidnapped Sassy and killed two people? Why?"

"Because I found his private office number on Eldridge Adams' phone bill from Houston," Michel replied.

"How?" DeRoche asked in a tone that suggested he wasn't sure if he really wanted to know.

"I remembered Eldridge mentioning a storage locker in Carl's apartment building," Michel explained. "Stan and I checked it out tonight and found his phone bills."

"Jesus Christ, Michel, are you out of your fucking mind?" DeRoche replied, his voice rising angrily. "Aren't you in enough trouble? Now you're withholding evidence?"

"I planned to call you in the morning," Michel replied evenly. "Look, Captain, if you want to throw me in jail after this is over, fine, but right now Sassy's life might be in danger."

"And you want me to send officers to MacDonald's house because you can't find her and Eldridge Adams called him?" DeRoche asked with a skeptical laugh.

"I'm not saying you should send officers," Michel replied in a reasoning tone, "but I need help."

There was a thoughtful pause before DeRoche replied.

"Michel, you're asking me to put my career on the line based on very shaky evidence," he said, his voice calm and measured. "You have to give me something more to go on."

Michel could tell that DeRoche was looking for an excuse to give in.

"There's broken glass under her couch, her car is here, and her wallet and keys are on the kitchen counter," he said. "That's good enough for me. If you won't help, I'll go myself."

He waited for a response, hoping his bluff would trigger DeRoche's paternal instincts.

"Wait, Michel," DeRoche replied finally with obvious reluctance. "If MacDonald really has Sassy he wouldn't have taken her to his house in the Quarter. He'd have gone to his farm. Let me come get you."

Michel felt a rush of relief and gratitude but tried to keep his tone neutral.

"But what if he did take her to the city house?" he asked.

"I'll send Al Ribodeau over there to check it out, just in case," DeRoche replied. "He can radio us in the car if he finds anything."

"Okay," Michel replied. "Thanks, Captain."

"Don't mention it," DeRoche replied. "To anyone. Ever."

Chapter 46

Lecher moved along the side of the barn to the last stall door. Like the first five, the top half was padlocked on the outside, with the bottom apparently bolted from the inside. He'd spent enough time riding horses in his youth to know that the configuration was unusual, that stables generally used just exterior sliding bolts for both sections. He felt certain that this was where MacDonald had taken his victims and wondered nervously what he would find inside.

He grabbed the handle and pulled firmly, but the door didn't give. For the sixth time he cursed himself for forgetting his master lock set.

The fence started again at the edge of the building. Lecher climbed to the top of it and dropped down quietly into the tall grass behind the barn. The moon was blocked now and he moved carefully through the shadows, worried that he might trip on an unseen rock or twist his ankle in a hole. As he walked, he ran his hands along the barn's rough plank exterior, feeling for any openings. As he'd expected, there were no doors or windows.

The ground began sloping dramatically as it neared the edge of the barn, and a stone foundation appeared below the wood siding. Lecher could feel mud sucking at his shoes with each step now and moved quickly, hoping to get to dryer ground before he lost one of his Topsiders.

As he rounded the corner at the end of the wall his foot caught on something and he stumbled forward, nearly losing his balance. He reached out frantically with his left hand and managed to catch hold of the barn's corner post to steady himself. Fuck, he thought, as he looked down at the pile of thick boards stacked at his feet. In the moonlight, he could see a half dozen nails poking up through the top plank.

He took a few deep breaths to calm himself, then looked at the side of the barn. Above the eighteen-inch foundation, an opening roughly three feet high by four feet wide had been cut out of the barn's exterior wall. It was covered over from the inside by what looked like plywood. He squatted down and ran his right hand over the surface of one of the discarded boards. It was damp and brittle to the touch, indicating the onset of dry rot.

Moving closer to the wall, he got down on his knees and pushed with both hands in the center of the plywood. It didn't give. He moved his hands a foot to the left and pushed again. This time the board flexed inward an inch. It's not nailed, he thought excitedly. He pushed the board in again, this time hooking his fingers over the left edge, and pulled hard to his right. The plywood moved an inch with a sound like sandpaper against steel.

He stood up and took a few steps back until he could see the windows of MacDonald's house. MacDonald was seated at the table in the kitchen eating. For a moment Lecher wondered if he should go back to his car and drive to the local police station. If someone was locked in the barn, he realized he might be putting their life at risk by trying to act on his own. If it came down to a showdown with MacDonald, he'd be at a tremendous disadvantage without a gun.

He made up his mind to stay. He couldn't take the chance of MacDonald coming back to the barn while he was gone and killing whoever might be inside. He walked back to the wall and hooked his fingers around the plywood again. Slowly he began sliding it aside.

*****

"You're sure you want to go through with this?" Michel asked as DeRoche's car headed down the exit ramp toward Boutte.

"As opposed to having the local police swarm the place and arrest the New Orleans Sheriff based on some pretty iffy evidence?" DeRoche responded rhetorically.

Michel gave him a wry smile.

"This is how it starts, you know," he said.

"How what starts?" DeRoche asked warily.

"First you make an accommodation outside the system to avoid a potential problem," Michel replied in a sing-song voice, "and the next thing you know you're a rogue cop without a job."

DeRoche studied him out of the corner of his eye for a moment before responding. He didn't smile at the attempted humor.

"Michel, you didn't give me any choice," he said finally.

"I know that," Michel replied quickly, "and I don't blame you. I dug my own grave and I knew I was doing it. You were just doing what you had to do."

"Okay," DeRoche replied, seeming to accept Michel's absolution.

"I'm just saying, this is how it starts," Michel added quickly under his breath.

DeRoche ignored the comment.

"By the way," he said, "just so you know, you're not as clever as you think you are. I knew you were bluffing about going to MacDonald's alone."

"What makes you think that?" Michel asked.

"Because I have your gun," DeRoche replied. "You're not stupid enough to go in unprotected."

"I don't suppose you brought it along for me?" Michel asked hopefully.

"Not a chance," DeRoche replied flatly.

Michel made an exaggerated show of sulking for a moment.

"So then why did you agree to come?" he asked finally.

"Because I trust your instincts," DeRoche replied. "Your methods may have needed some help, but your instincts were always good."

"Not always," Michel replied quietly. "What about Lady Chanel?"

"Your instinct that she wasn't guilty was right," DeRoche replied. "You couldn't have anticipated she'd be killed."

"The evidence suggested she was a suspect," Michel said. "If I'd brought her in for questioning right away she could have lead us to Clement. She'd still be alive and so would Clement's last victim."

"You can't know that," DeRoche replied. "Maybe things would have turned out worse. Maybe your friend Joel might have been killed instead."

Michel felt a chill run up his spine at the words and turned his head to look out the window.

"The fact that things didn't turn out perfectly doesn't mean your instincts were wrong or you were a bad cop," DeRoche continued. "Things may turn out very badly tonight, but that doesn't mean my judgment would have been wrong to trust you."

They drove in silence for a few minutes, each wrapped up in his own thoughts.

"So what were you planning to do with those numbers?" DeRoche asked finally.

"I just wanted to see if Sassy recognized any of them," Michel replied.

"And if she did?" DeRoche asked.

"I don't know," Michel answered honestly. "I suppose some part of me wanted to hand over the killer as a final gesture to prove I wasn't a total fuck up."

DeRoche nodded.

"And what about Stan?" he asked. "Do you think he would have been happy just to turn MacDonald over?"

"I think he'd given up on trying...," Michel started, then suddenly stopped and sat up straight.

"Oh, fuck," he said.

"What's the matter?" DeRoche asked, looking at him with concern.

"Stan said he met with MacDonald privately after Sassy told him she hadn't killed Lumley," Michel replied quickly. "What if he had MacDonald's private number and recognized it on Eldridge's phone bill?"

"You think he would have gone after him?" DeRoche asked.

"I don't know," Michel replied, trying to remember how Lecher had behaved when they found the phone bills. "If he did, though, he would have gone to the house in the Quarter, right? I doubt he'd know where MacDonald's farm is."

DeRoche shook his head.

"He knows where it is," he said. "He was there for a barbecue MacDonald threw right after he was elected."

"Shit," Michel exclaimed. "Maybe we should call the Boutte police after all."

"No," DeRoche replied as he pressed down harder on the gas pedal. "Stan would have had a huge head start on us. If he was going to kill MacDonald it's probably too late now anyhow. We'll be there in a few minutes. Let's just deal with it when we get there."

"Okay," Michel replied anxiously.

Chapter 47

Sweat ran down his face and dripped from the end of his nose as Lecher leaned his left shoulder against the edge of the plywood and gave it one final push. He'd been able to move the board easily for the first few inches, then it had jammed. Every inch from that point on had been a struggle. He sat back on his ankles and tried to catch his breath as he looked at the foot-wide gap he'd managed to open. He wished he'd brought some water and a flashlight.

After a minute he stood up and stepped away from the barn until he could see MacDonald's house again. His pulse quickened as he saw that the kitchen table was empty.

Where'd you go, you son of a bitch? he thought as he crouched down and surveyed the mostly dark windows. Suddenly a small light flared by the front corner of the house, causing his pulse to race even more. He held his breath, watching as the flickering light suddenly went out and was replaced by a tiny, pulsing red ember.

He's on the porch smoking, Lecher thought, as he stared at the glow, waiting to see if it would begin moving away from the house. After a few seconds, when he hadn't detected any movement, he hurried back to the opening in the barn wall.

If MacDonald comes up he's going to notice the plywood is moved, anyway, so I may as well go for broke, he reasoned, as he stared into the darkened hole.

He took a last look up at the moon, then began crawling into the barn.

*****

Lecher stood up behind the tractor whose wheel had been pressed again the plywood. Its back end was exposed, but the rest was covered by a heavy canvas tarp. As he looked along the wall he could see the tarp snagged on the far top corner of the plywood.

No wonder it was such a bitch to move, he thought, sourly.

He moved quietly to the left wheel of the tractor and peeked his head around the side. Through the darkness he could see what appeared to be a woman sitting against a heavy vertical support beam thirty feet away, her arms stretched over her head. Cautiously he stepped out from behind the massive rubber wheel.

"You take another step and I'm going to shoot you," a familiar voice threatened in a hushed voice.

"Sassy?" Lecher asked, straining his eyes to see her better.

"Stan?" Sassy replied with obvious surprise.

Lecher crossed the room quickly and knelt down beside her.

"Is anyone else here?" he whispered.

"If there was, I'm sure they'd have heard you whispering and killed you by now," Sassy whispered back.

"Are you okay?" Lecher asked as he examined the handcuffs and bolt securing Sassy's hands.

"I will be once you get me free and I shoot that motherfucker," Sassy replied. "You scared the shit out of me, Stan. I heard all that noise and thought you were a bear or a wild dog or something."

"Jesus, this is a thirteen-inch bolt," Lecher said, as though he hadn't heard her. "It's screwed all the way through the post. Even if I found something to turn it you'd have to spin like a ballerina to keep your cuffs from getting twisted."

"I don't think I'll be doing any pirouettes for a while," Sassy replied grimly. "Just shoot the chain and give me the gun. Even if he hears the shot, I guarantee he won't make it through the door alive."

"What gun?" Lecher asked.

"You didn't bring a gun?" Sassy asked with disbelief.

"The cops still have it...along with my cell phone," Lecher replied.

"Shit. What about a knife?" Sassy asked.

"You want me to cut your hands off?" Lecher replied, feigning misunderstanding.

"That's not even funny, and this really isn't a good time for jokes," Sassy replied with a reproachful look. "I meant for stabbing him."

Lecher shook his head.

"Jesus, Stan, what were you planning to do?" Sassy asked with dismay. "Poke him with a sharp stick?"

"Something like that," Lecher replied offhandedly as he began looking around the room for something to cut the chain.

"Where's Michel?" Sassy asked.

"I dropped him near your place about an hour and a half ago," Lecher replied, looking back at her.

"So he doesn't know I'm here?" Sassy asked.

"I didn't know you were here until I saw you," Lecher replied.

"Then what are you doing here?" Sassy asked, her tone suddenly wary.

Lecher hesitated a moment before replying.

"I came to kill MacDonald," he said finally.

"Shit, Stan, are you out of your fucking mind?" Sassy exclaimed, careful to keep her voice hushed.

"Yeah, probably," Lecher replied with a shrug.

"Listen, you need to get out of here and get to a phone or the police station," Sassy said, her tone making it clear she was giving an order.

"I can't," Lecher replied. "What if he comes back while I'm gone and kills you?"

Sassy stared at him for a few seconds then nodded.

"Good point," she said. "So what's your plan then?"

Lecher's attention fell on the row of stalls along the right wall.

"I have the element of surprise on my side," he said as he stood up and walked toward them.

"Surprise is only a good weapon until he points his gun at you," Sassy replied.

"Then I guess I'll have to make sure he doesn't have a chance to do that," Lecher replied, turning back toward her with a nervous smile.

Chapter 48

DeRoche pulled to the side of the road behind Lecher's car and turned off the lights.

"He's here," Michel said.

"Thanks, but I already figured that out without the voice-over narration," DeRoche snapped.

Michel knew the irritable response was a reaction to the tension of the situation and let it go.

"So what do you want to do, Captain?" he asked.

"I think I should drive up to the house and tell MacDonald we think that Stan might be trying to kill him and that I want to take him into protective custody," DeRoche replied.

"What?" Michel asked with a dumbfounded expression. "You just want to go up there and essentially tell him he's a murder suspect?"

"No," DeRoche replied. "I don't need to fill him in on the details. I just need him to believe that he's in danger and convince him to leave with me."

"And then what?" Michel asked skeptically.

"And then you search the property for Sassy and try to find Stan," DeRoche replied calmly. "If you find her, you call the station and leave a message for me. Then when I get there I'll put MacDonald under arrest."

Michel considered the plan for a moment. It seemed logical and appropriately cautious given the situation.

"Okay," he said, "but what if he refuses to go with you or something goes wrong?"

"If he refuses, then I'll leave and call in the Boutte police and we'll search the place," DeRoche replied. "If something goes wrong, you get out of here and get to the police."

Michel nodded.

"There's a bend in the drive," DeRoche said. "I'll drop you there and you make your way up to the house through the field in front."

"Sounds like a plan," Michel said nervously. "You sure you don't have a spare gun for me just in case?"

DeRoche gave him an admonishing look.

"I don't want you getting involved any more than necessary," he said.

"But what if I find Stan and he has other plans?" Michel pressed. "I may need protection."

"Stan's not going to shoot you," DeRoche replied dismissively.

"Fine," Michel replied morosely, "but if I get shot it's on your conscience."

*****

MacDonald had just stubbed out his cigarette when he saw headlights approaching. He took a look at the barn, then stepped off the porch and began walking toward the driveway. As a brown sedan rounded the final bend and came to a stop at the end of the walkway he felt a knot of unease in his stomach and paused. The car door opened and DeRoche stepped out.

"Captain DeRoche," MacDonald said casually as DeRoche approached him. "To what do I owe the pleasure?"

He shook DeRoche's hand heartily.

"I'm afraid we might have some trouble," DeRoche said, looking around with concern.

"What kind of trouble?" MacDonald asked, his thick eyebrows coming together and reaching forward even farther than normal.

"We think Stan Lecher may be planning to kill you?" DeRoche replied quickly.

MacDonald stared at him curiously for a moment.

"Why would Stan want to kill me?" he asked.

"Apparently he's had some sort of nervous breakdown," DeRoche bluffed with as much conviction as he could muster. "He's become convinced that you initiated the cover-up of how Iris actually died. I want to take you into protective custody."

"Protective custody?" MacDonald replied with a gruff laugh. "I don't need any protection. If Lecher comes up here looking for trouble I can take care of myself. Besides, where's this information coming from?"

"Michel Doucette," DeRoche replied, suddenly wishing that he'd chosen some unknown assassin rather than Lecher as his alibi for coming. "Stan made some comments to him that Doucette thought were reason for concern so he called me. I sent a squad car over to Lecher's house but he was gone."

"Maybe he just went bowling," MacDonald offered with an easy laugh. "Just because he's not home and made some accusations about me doesn't mean he's coming to kill me. You'll have to excuse me, but it seems to me you're overreacting a bit, Captain."

"Maybe," DeRoche replied, realizing he hadn't thought things through thoroughly enough, "but I'd rather err on the side of being overly cautious."

"Well, I appreciate that," MacDonald replied tolerantly, "but I don't think I'm going to be going anywhere tonight."

"I understand," DeRoche replied, trying to mask his disappointment.

"But since you came all the way out here, would you like to stay for a drink?" MacDonald asked, smiling cordially.

"Thanks, but I suppose I should get back in case we get any more information," DeRoche replied.

"I wish you'd stay, but I certainly understand," MacDonald said.

DeRoche hesitated for a moment, trying to think of another way to coax MacDonald into leaving with him, then nodded and shook MacDonald's hand. He turned and started toward his car.

"Oh, one other thing," he heard MacDonald say close behind him.

As he started to turn back, the grip of the gun in MacDonald's right hand connected with DeRoche's left temple. He saw bursts of light in front of his eyes and staggered back. Then the gun struck him again and his legs gave out. He fell to the ground and the blackness sucked him downward.

"I meant it when I said I wished you'd stay." MacDonald said, breathing hard.

*****

From his position in the field, Michel had watched the scene unfold. When he'd first seen MacDonald reach behind his back and pull out the gun, he'd almost called out a warning. As MacDonald lifted the gun above his head, however, he'd realized that MacDonald didn't intend to shoot DeRoche, at least for the moment, and had decided it would be better to keep his presence secret.

Now MacDonald was dragging DeRoche by the left arm toward the brown sedan. He seemed to be talking to himself, though Michel couldn't make out the words. The tone, however, was decidedly angry.

As they moved behind the car, MacDonald dropped DeRoche's arm and knelt down. He reached inside DeRoche's jacket and removed his cell phone and pistol, laying them on the ground, then took the car keys from the left pocket of DeRoche's pants. With a labored grunt, he pushed himself up using the bumper of the car for support, and opened the trunk.

Michel edged a few steps closer, keeping his head below the top of the high grass. After seeing the effort it had taken

MacDonald to stand, he realized he might have an opportunity to overpower MacDonald while MacDonald lifted DeRoche into the trunk. He braced his hands on the ground and dug the toe of his right foot into the ground, like a sprinter on the starting blocks.

MacDonald put the car keys in his pocket and straddled DeRoche's body. As he reached down and grabbed the lapels of DeRoche's jacket, Michel took a deep breath and held it, ready to make his move. Then with a sudden jerk MacDonald lifted DeRoche almost to a standing position and heaved him into the trunk of the sedan. The whole motion had taken less than three seconds. Michel froze, shocked by the apparent ease of the effort.

Whatever weakness he might have in his legs, he thought, he's one strong motherfucker. He slowly settled down onto his heels to see what would happen.

MacDonald slammed the trunk shut and dusted off the knees of his pants, then rubbed his hands together briskly. He picked up DeRoche's gun and cell phone and started walking determinedly toward the barn.

*****

When she'd heard the car pull up outside, Sassy had felt an odd mix of hope and fear. If it was Michel or another cop, she knew her ordeal might be almost over. Even if it was just one of MacDonald's friends unexpectedly stopping by it might delay him enough that he'd be forced to wait until the next night to carry out his plans. On the other hand, if it was an accomplice, then things were about to get much worse. There was no way Stan would be able to surprise and overpower two or more men.

"Stan, did you hear that?" she'd whispered.

"Yeah," he'd replied, looking over the top of the stall door next to the one holding MacDonald's horse. "I don't know if that's a good thing or a bad thing."

"Is there any way to see what's happening?" she'd asked.

"No," he'd replied. "He's got the walls of this place sealed up. The only way would be to go back out the way I came in."

"I think I'd rather take my chances with you in here," Sassy had replied.

Now as she heard footsteps approaching the barn she listened carefully, trying to discern if it was one set or two. It sounded like a single person, moving hard and fast. The door opened behind her and the lights came on, hurting her eyes again. This time she forced herself to keep them open.

MacDonald walked in front of her, holding a cell phone in his left hand and a pistol in his right. Sassy saw it was a Smith and Wesson CS9 with a silver barrel and black grip. She recognized it immediately and knew who had driven up to the house. She also knew that DeRoche wouldn't willingly have handed over his gun.

"Where's DeRoche?" she asked.

MacDonald showed mild surprise, but then his expression turned angry.

"Indisposed." he replied tersely.

He kicked Sassy hard in the left side with the toe of his boot. She felt a searing pain that caused her to gasp for air.

"You know, I really should have killed you in that hospital," MacDonald said. "It would have saved me a lot of trouble."

He punctuated the remark by leaning down and punching Sassy on her left cheek bone. Her head snapped back and rebounded off the wood post. The pain in her head had nearly disappeared, but now it came back with an explosive surge and she felt nausea welling up in her stomach. She struggled to keep it at bay and hold onto consciousness.

*****

Michel hung up the phone in MacDonald's kitchen and walked to the front door. The dispatcher had said the Boutte police would be at the farm in five minutes. MacDonald had already been in the barn for a minute and Michel wondered if Sassy had that long. He also wondered what had happened to Lecher. He opened the door and started for the barn.

*****

"Before I was going to hurt you just for fun," MacDonald said, kneeling down and tilting Sassy's head up by her chin so that she was looking at him. "Now I'm going to do it because you pissed me off."

With a quick motion he dropped his hand slightly and drove his fingertips into Sassy's throat. Sassy gagged and knew she was about to vomit. What the hell are you waiting for, Stan? she thought.

Suddenly a high pitched, warbling shriek filled the room and MacDonald pushed himself to his feet.

"What is it, girl?" he said, looking at the stall in the corner of the room.

The horse let out another frightened whinny and MacDonald chucked soothingly to calm her.

"It's okay, girl," he said as he began moving toward the stall.

Sassy swallowed hard and took quick breaths to suppress the nausea. Out of the corner of her eye she watched MacDonald approaching the stall. Her heart was racing.

"That's a good girl," MacDonald said as the horse seemed to calm down. "Did you have a bad dream?"

He was five feet from the horse when he noticed the unlatched bolt on the stall just to his left. He hesitated for a half second, then continued forward.

*****

Michel reached the barn and peered around the edge of the open door. He could see Sassy sitting on the mattress against the wood support column with her back to him. MacDonald wasn't near her. He leaned into the room and saw MacDonald walking slowly toward the stall in the right corner of the room.

Suddenly the door of the adjacent stall burst open and Lecher rushed out, brandishing a pitchfork in front of him. He lunged forward, jabbing the tines at MacDonald's chest. With surprising quickness, MacDonald stepped to his right and grabbed the handle of the pitchfork just above the tines with his left hand as it came toward him, redirectly its path harmlessly away. At he same time he pivoted to his left and threw an overhand right punch that hit Lecher squarely in the left temple. Lecher's momentum carried him forward and he stumbled, losing his hold on the pitchfork. MacDonald, however, managed to maintain his grip.

Michel stepped into the room and began running hard toward MacDonald. He could see MacDonald grab the handle of the pitchfork farther up with his right hand and step forward so that he was directly alongside Lecher's prone body. As Lecher started to push himself up to his knees, MacDonald drew the pitchfork up over the center of his back.

Michel knew MacDonald hadn't seen him yet because of the angle from which he was approaching. He also knew that if he didn't do something quickly, MacDonald would spear Lecher through the back.

"Hey," he yelled, still ten feet away.

MacDonald turned his head with a look of shock, but reacted quickly. He took a step back with his left foot, almost squaring his body toward Michel, and started to drive the pitchfork forward.

Suddenly, Lecher threw his body against MacDonald's right leg. With an audible snap, MacDonald's leg bent inward at what seemed like an impossible angle to Michel, and MacDonald began collapsing straight down, like a building that was imploding. As he fell, he drove the tines of the pitchfork into the ground.

Michel lowered his head and dove at MacDonald. His left arm caught MacDonald around the neck, higher than he'd anticipated, and MacDonald was dragged backwards over his splayed lower legs. As MacDonald fell, Michel realized he'd overestimated the force necessary to bring MacDonald down and braced himself for impact. His right collarbone slammed hard into the doorframe between the first and second stalls.

He lay on the ground for a moment, stunned but not yet feeling any pain, then tried to push himself up to a kneeling position. The pain was sudden and excruciating, starting at his collarbone and radiating across his chest and down his right arm. He let out a scream as his right arm gave way beneath him and he dropped to his side. He closed his eyes and gritted his teeth, trying to will the pain away.

Suddenly his collar tightened and he opened his eyes. MacDonald was lying in front of him, propped up on his left elbow, clutching the front of Michel's shirt with his right fist. His face was even redder than usual and his eyes were wild with rage. With a strength that seemed impossible he began to drag Michel toward him.

Michel tried to pull away but his arms felt numb, as though they were paralyzed. He rocked his body back and kicked out ineffectually with his legs. Then MacDonald let go of his shirt and closed his right hand around Michel's throat. He began to squeeze, digging his fingers into the sides of Michel's trachea.

"I'm going to kill all of you motherfuckers," MacDonald rasped, spit spraying from his lips onto Michel's face.

Michel stared helplessly into MacDonald's angry, bloodshot eyes as he felt his throat tightening and fought to breathe. He wondered for a split second if this was how he would die.

Then an arm slipped around MacDonald's neck from the left side and Michel saw Lecher's face appear over MacDonald's right shoulder. His expression was calm and focused, as though he were in the midst of an investigation rather than a life and death struggle.

Suddenly MacDonald's mouth opened and his face turned deep crimson. He began gasping for air and his grip on Michel's throat loosened. Michel rolled backward as MacDonald's hand dropped to the dirt and began spasming. Michel lay on his back, his head turned sideways, and watched as MacDonald's whole body went into convulsions.

"What the fuck is happening?" he managed, looking up at Lecher, who was now standing over MacDonald's body.

"It looks like a heart attack," Lecher answered without emotion.

"A heart attack?" Michel asked with a mix of surprise and relief.

Lecher shrugged.

"Must have been the stress," he replied matter-of-factly.

"You've got to do CPR," Michel said.

"Why?" Lecher asked, staring at him coldly.

"Because you don't have the right to decide if he should live or die," Michel replied passionately.

"No, but I don't have to intervene if God makes that decision," Lecher said.

Suddenly MacDonald's body stopped convulsing and a wet sigh escaped his lips. His shoulders slowly lowered to the ground. Michel felt sensation returning to his arms and pushed himself up to a sitting position using his left arm. The pain in his collarbone was still acute, but bearable. He looked over at Sassy, who was staring at him with a hopeful look.

"Is it over?" she asked.

"It's over," he said.

*****

Michel arrived home just before 2 a.m.. After giving a statement to the Boutte police, he'd gone to the hospital to get a brace for his broken collarbone, then to the station to give another statement and answer questions from Internal Affairs.

Although it was doubtful that he'd be reinstated, it appeared that no charges would be filed against him.

He felt drained both physically and emotionally, yet oddly wired. As he walked into the kitchen to pour a tall glass of Jack Daniels, he noticed that the red light on his answering machine was blinking. He hit the button.

"Hey, it's me," Joel's voice said. "I hope everything's okay. I'm wondering why you called me from home in the middle of the day on a Thursday and where you are now. Give me a call. It doesn't matter what time."

Michel smiled and decided to skip the drink. He picked up the phone and hit the speed dial.

Chapter 49

Michel sat on his front porch enjoying the warm, late afternoon sun as he nursed a glass of white wine. He heard a car door slam nearby and hoped it was Sassy. He'd been anxiously waiting for her for a half hour. As if on cue, she appeared on the sidewalk and walked up onto the porch.

"So what are we going to do for work now?" she asked as she poured herself a glass of wine.

"They fired you?" Michel asked incredulously.

"I quit," she replied emphatically, settling onto the porch swing beside him.

She raised her glass in a toast and took a sip.

"Why?" Michel asked.

"You think I want to break in a new partner at this point in my life?" Sassy asked, shaking her head. "I just got you trained right. I don't want a new puppy."

Michel smiled at her.

"Besides, I've got my twenty years so I'll get a full pension," she continued. "I might not be taking any cruises around the world, but I've got enough to live on."

"That makes one of us," Michel replied.

Sassy tilted her head and gave him a dubious look.

"Michel Doucette, don't even be trying to cry poor mouth with me," she said. "I know you have stacks of cash hidden away somewhere. The only things you ever spend any money on are liquor and cigarettes."

Michel laughed.

"I suppose I have a little something to live on for a while," he conceded.

"So, where's Joel?" Sassy asked.

"His place," Michel replied. "We're taking things slowly for now."

"That makes sense," Sassy said. "He's a good kid."

Michel rolled his eyes.

"Do you have to call him that?" he asked.

"Oh, don't go getting your panties in a bunch," Sassy replied. "You know I don't mean anything by it."

They each sipped their wine quietly for a moment.

"So have you heard from Stan?" Sassy asked, breaking the silence.

"He called this morning," Michel said. "He found someone to rent his place while he's in Europe."

"You think he's ever coming back?" Sassy asked.

"I don't know," Michel replied. "I'm not sure there's anything here for him anymore."

"What's he planning to do?" Sassy asked.

"He said he was thinking about teaching," Michel replied. "Maybe forensics at a college somewhere."

"I can see that," Sassy replied with a nod. "Of course, God help any student who thinks he's smarter than Stan."

"Yeah," Michel agreed with a smile. "So I was reading through all the local papers. Still nothing about MacDonald. They must have pulled some big strings to keep that quiet. I guess it was a lucky coincidence that he died of a heart attack."

Sassy was quiet for a moment. She seemed to be debating whether to say something.

"Was it?" she asked finally.

"What do you mean?" Michel asked, giving her a curious look.

Sassy reached into her jacket and took something out of the inner pocket. She held it out on the palm of her hand.

"What's that?" Michel asked.

"Looks like the cap to a syringe to me," Sassy replied.

Michel studied the elongated blue plastic tube with its domed tip.

"Where'd you find it?" he asked.

"On the ground near where you and MacDonald were fighting, just before the police arrived," Sassy replied.

Michel looked up at her with shock.

"You think Stan induced MacDonald's heart attack?"

"It's an awful long cap," Sassy replied. "Looks like the kind you'd use for a cardiac needle."

"Jesus Christ," Michel responded.

"Stan told me he went there to kill MacDonald, yet he didn't have any weapons with him," Sassy said. "I asked him if he was planning to poke MacDonald with a pointy stick and he said 'something like that.' I think this is what he meant."

"And you didn't tell DeRoche?" Michel asked, eyeing her warily.

"I told DeRoche, but just him," Sassy replied. "He thought that no interests would be served by Stan going to jail."

Michel looked away. He seemed to be staring at some distant point beyond the houses across the street.

"I'm not sure how I feel about this," he said after a minute.

"I'm not sure either," Sassy replied. "That's why I wasn't sure if I should tell you."

"Stan killed MacDonald," Michel said, as though trying to make sense of the words.

"He also saved your life," Sassy replied.

"I know," Michel replied sadly, "and I also know that it was probably better for everyone that things ended the way they did. I just have a hard time accepting that that makes it okay."

Sassy nodded.

"I understand," she said. "I struggled with the same question."

"So how did you resolve it?" Michel asked, looking at her intently.

Sassy pursed her lips thoughtfully.

"Putting aside the question of whether he deserved to die, I considered the situation from a purely procedural standpoint," she said, choosing her words carefully. "Both when MacDonald was ready to stick that pitchfork into Stan's back and when he was choking you, use of deadly force would have been justified. I'm not saying that there weren't other options, but if I hadn't been chained to a post and I'd had a gun, I would have shot to kill."

"So the fact that the end result would have been the same justifies Stan killing him?" Michel asked skeptically.

"No," Sassy replied, "but it allows me to live with not punishing Stan."

"That's some pretty sketchy situational ethics," Michel said with a sigh.

Sassy cocked an eye at him.

"What do you want from me?" she asked. "It's not like I'm a cop or something."

Michel gave a half smile in acknowledgment of her attempt to ease his conscience.

"I'm going to have to obsess on this one for a while," he said.

"I wouldn't expect anything less," Sassy replied affectionately.

They drank their wine in silence for a few minutes. Michel lit a cigarette and smoked it contemplatively.

"They've stopped, you know," Sassy said suddenly.

"What have?" Michel asked, turning his head toward her.

"The dreams," Sassy replied. "I haven't had one since that night."

"That's great," Michel said. "I guess your subconscious realizes they're of no use now."

"Yeah," Sassy replied. "All the missing pieces have been filled in."

"All except for one," Michel said.

"Which one is that?" Sassy asked, arching her left eyebrow.

"What happened to Carl and Eldridge when they were boys," Michel replied. "That's really where everything started. You, Carl, Eldridge, Lumley...you were all just caught up in the echo of whatever happened then."

"That's an interesting way to look at it," Sassy replied seriously. "I suppose that's true. MacDonald still would have done his thing, but the rest of us wouldn't have become a part of it. At least not in the same way. Life would have turned out very differently."

"And maybe not as well," Michel ventured. "You might have met some rich guy and moved to Paris and we wouldn't be here now."

"You mean sitting here on your porch getting drunk without a job between us?" Sassy asked sarcastically. "Explain to me how this is better."

"Well," Michel said with an impish smile, "at least we have each other."

Epilogue

Eldridge dropped the shovel on the ground and took a dirty white handkerchief out of the back pocket of his jeans to wipe the sweat from his forehead. He looked at his eight-year-old brother, sitting against a tree a few feet away from the makeshift grave they'd dug at the far edge of the field behind their house. In the dusky light he could see tears rimming the frail boy's large eyes.

"It ain't your fault what he done to you, Carl," he said. "You gotta believe that. He got what was coming to him."

"I know," Carl replied in a thin, frightened voice, "but won't Momma wonder where he is?"

"She'll just think he run off with another woman again," Eldridge replied, scattering leaves and twigs over the mound of dirt. "After a while she won't even miss him."

Carl stared up at him fearfully, his lower lip quivering.

"But what if someone finds out?" he asked.

"No one's gonna find out unless you tell 'em," Eldridge replied in a commanding tone that belied his youth. "Promise me you never gonna say nothing to no one."

"But why can't we tell Momma?" Carl asked, his voice rising plaintively.

"Cuz it was a bad thing I done," Eldridge replied harshly. "They'll send me away and you won't see me no more til I'm old and gray."

Carl began to cry.

"But he was hurting me," he said through gasping sobs. "Momma will understand."

"No, Carl," Eldridge said, his tone softening as he knelt down and put his right hand on his brother's shoulder. "Even if she does, she won't. It's like that sometimes. People can't let themselves know things cuz it hurts too bad. Sometimes it's best to just let sleeping dogs lie. You understand?"

Carl nodded and took a gulping breath.

"I understand," he said.

"Good," Eldridge replied, standing up. "So long as we never tell no one it'll be like it never happened. It ain't never gonna come back and bother us again."

Available April 2011
from

SECOND CHANCE

A New Michel Doucette
& Sassy Jones Novel

DAVID LENNON

Prologue

Chance surveyed the crowd gathered around his father's grave in the bright morning sun as the minister intoned about the life of a man who hadn't passed through the doors of a church in over forty years. Chance had expected his best friend, Joel, and Joel's grandparents, Pappy and Mammau Gaulthier, to be there, and perhaps a few of his father's drinking cronies if they'd been able to get out of bed in time, but there were at least three dozen people at the funeral. About half looked to be his father's age, the rest quite a bit older.

I guess that's life in a small town, he thought. People may avoid you and talk shit behind your back for your whole life, but when you die everyone turns out to pay their respects. There wasn't any bitterness in the thought. In fact Chance found the idea oddly comforting. It made explicit the connection between all these people whose lives were rooted in the local soil.

He looked at Pappy and Mammau and saw genuine sadness on their faces. He wondered if it was sadness for his father or for him. He suspected it was both. Even though his father's life had been one long downward spiral, he knew from firsthand experience that Joel's grandparents had an unwavering belief in the value of every person. They always saw the potential rather than dwelling on the mistakes. Regardless of is own many mistakes, they'd never lost faith in him.

A movement behind Pappy's right shoulder caught his attention and Chance shifted his gaze. Although he hadn't seen her in nearly fifteen years, he recognized his mother immediately.

Luanne LeDuc hadn't changed much. She was still small and trim, though her once-girlish features had grown somewhat harder. It wasn't the hardness of alcohol and anger that had ravaged the face of his father, Chance Sr., however, but rather a hardness that spoke of maturity and resolve. Though he hated to admit it, Chance thought it suited her. She looked more capable.

She was dressed in a simple, knee-length, black dress with cap sleeves and a high scoop neck that looked as though its sole purpose might be for attending funerals. Her blond hair was pulled back and knotted in a bun. Again, Chance had to admit that the warm honey color suited his mother far better than the peroxide blond she'd had the last time he'd seen her.

He quickly averted his eyes, afraid that Luanne might look up at him.

He felt a sudden swell of anxiety. Although he'd never expected his father to live past fifty, the end had been a shock. He'd always imagined a long, slow decline with his father hanging on for years, making life miserable for everyone around him—especially Chance—for as long as possible. That his father had died peacefully in his sleep of a heart attack had come as a surprise and a blessing. It was the first thing he could ever remember his father having done with grace. Still, it had stirred an unexpected mix of feelings—anger, regret, relief, guilt—that had already taken a heavy toll on him emotionally. Now to see his mother again after so many years was overwhelming him.

Luanne had left one night when Chance was seven, while his father was passed out on the sofa. She'd never come back. There'd never been any calls or any letters. It was as if she'd simply vanished.

For the first few months Chance's father had continued to say she'd be back, at first optimistically, then angrily, saying that "the bitch has no place else to go." Then he'd stopped talking about her altogether. But Chance had kept hoping. Every morning he'd wake up and run to in his parents' bedroom on the chance that she might have reappeared during the night as mysteriously as she'd disappeared.

Eventually he realized that she wouldn't be back, but he kept hoping that someday she'd send for him. Finally, by the time he'd turned thirteen, even that hope was gone and if he thought about his mother at all—which wasn't often—it was with resentment and anger.

To see her now brought all his old feelings to the surface, exacerbating his already raw emotional state. He literally wanted to scream to release the pressure.

Suddenly he became aware that the minister had stopped speaking and looked up. The other mourners were all staring at him expectantly and he realized they were waiting for him to place the first flower on his father's caskets.

He took a deep breath and forced himself to step forward, then gently placed the red carnation on the polished pine surface.

*****

"People will be coming back to the house," Mammau said. "Do you want to walk back with us?"

Chance shook his head distractedly.

"No, I just need a few minutes. Go on ahead and I'll meet you there."

"Okay," Mammau said with an understanding look.

Chance walked back to the grave and stared at the carnation-strewn coffin. He could hear the sounds of voices and tires on gravel receding into the distance behind him. So this is it, he thought.

A shadow appeared alongside his own on the side of the casket.

3

"So did you come to dance on his grave, Luanne?" Chance asked coldly without looking up.

"No," Luanne LeDuc replied in a soft voice. "I couldn't stay with him, but I never hated him."

Although it had been a long time since he'd heard it, his mother's voice was instantly familiar. The soft drawl and lilting cadence seemed like they had always been with him. He felt a momentary, reflexive sense of comfort, but pushed the feeling away and turned to face his mother.

"And what about me?" he asked, his eyes flashing with anger. "Could you just not stay with me, too?"

Luanne flinched but didn't reply.

"Because if you loved me I don't understand how you could have left me behind with him," Chance continued, his voice breaking with emotion. "Didn't you know he'd take it out on me? That he'd punish me for you leaving?"

"I'm sorry, Chance," Luanne replied quietly. "I'm so sorry."

"Well, gee, that just's makes it all better," Chance replied acidly. "Why don't we just hug now and things will all be better. No harm, no foul."

"Stop it," Luanne said, her voice suddenly more forceful. "I did what I had to do. If I'd stayed eventually he would have killed me."

"Oh, but you weren't afraid he'd kill me?" Chance asked sarcastically.

"No," Luanne replied flatly. "You were his flesh and blood. He couldn't kill you. He loved you."

Chance snorted derisively.

"Is that what you call that? Love?" he asked. "Beating me, ignoring me, acting like he could barely stand to look at me?"

Luanne was quiet for a moment. She stared at the ground as though trying to collect her thoughts. Finally she looked up at Chance and her pale blue eyes—his eyes—were kind and maternal.

"Can we sit down?" she asked, gesturing with her head

toward a wooden bench in the shade of a nearby oak tree. "There are some things I think you need to understand about your daddy."

Chance hesitated before responding. A part of him wanted to tell his mother to just fuck off and leave. At the same time, another part of him was glad to see her, and still another part was curious about why she'd come back and what she had to say.

"Okay," he replied grudgingly after a moment.

They settled on the bench and Luanne took a deep breath before speaking.

"He wasn't always the way he was when you knew him," she began. "In fact, he used to be a lot like you."

Chance felt a surge of anger that his mother would presume to know anything about him but decided to hold his tongue.

"I remember when my family moved here," Luanne continued. "I was fourteen. All the other girls told me to stay away from Chance LeDuc. They said he was crazy, that his family was no good, and that associating with his kind could only lead to trouble. But I saw something different. No doubt he had a wild streak a mile wide, but mostly what I saw was hurt. He was like a wounded animal that was lashing out, and I thought that maybe if someone showed him some kindness he'd be different.

"So after a few weeks I passed him a note in science class asking him to meet me at Miller's Pond after school."

Luanne's eyes became focused on the middle distance and her voice grew softer as though she were reliving a dream.

"I remember I was so nervous," she continued. "Chance was the most handsome boy I'd ever seen. And I was afraid he'd think I was one of *those* kinds of girls for being so forward. But when he showed up he was shy and sweet and funny, and I think I fell in love with him that very afternoon."

Chance tried to imagine the person his mother was describing.

5

"We started going steady a few days later," Luanne continued. "Everyone told me I was going to get hurt, but I didn't care because I was convinced that Chance was a good man. With other people he was mostly sullen or hostile, but I knew that was just his way of protecting himself so he wouldn't get his feelings hurt. When we were alone together he was kind and gentle, and he loved to talk about his dreams for our life together."

"Wait a second," Chance interrupted. "He had dreams?"

"Of course he had dreams," Luanne chided, breaking out of her reverie. "He was a young man."

Chance nodded in acknowledgment of her reproach.

"He always said that someday we'd get out of Natchez and that he'd get a job in a city and we'd have a nice house in the suburbs and a Cadillac," Luanne continued. "Maybe they weren't grand dreams, but they were dreams.

"But there was a darker side to your daddy, too, even then. Sometimes after he'd had a few drinks and was feeling melancholy he'd talk about 'the family curse.' He was convinced that somewhere in the past someone had done something terrible that had brought a curse on the family. He said that's why they'd lost their money and become outcasts. He was always afraid that some day the curse would touch him, too.

"You have to understand, your daddy hated his life here. He hated his daddy for the way he treated him, and he hated that he had to live in a rundown old house, and mostly he hated that people treated him like he was damaged because he was another one of 'those crazy LeDucs.'"

"I know the feeling," Chance said.

Luanne smiled sympathetically.

"The worst thing your daddy could imagine was being stuck here and ending up like his own daddy," Luanne continued. "He wanted to go somewhere where no one knew his family, where he could make a fresh start. Just like you."

Instead of anger, this time Chance felt surprise that his

6

mother did seem to know some things about him. He considered asking her how, but decided to wait.

"So why didn't you both leave?" he asked instead.

"We did," Luanne responded. "The summer before our senior year, on your daddy's 17th birthday, we packed up his truck and moved to Woodville where he'd got a job working in a lumber mill. Oh, the trouble that caused. My parents told me if I left they'd disown me. And they pretty much did for a long time."

She gave Chance a small, wistful smile, then the smile suddenly warmed.

"And about a month later I found out I was pregnant with you so we got married," she said.

Chance blinked his eyes in wonderment as he tried to reconcile the image of his parents that Luanne was describing with the people he'd known. He felt as though he'd just discovered he was adopted.

"Do you know why he wanted to name you after himself?" Luanne asked suddenly, staring meaningfully into Chance's eyes.

Chance shook his head.

"Because he said you'd be his second chance," Luanne said. "He wanted to give you all the things he never had so that your life could be different."

Chance was stunned. The father he'd known had always seemed intent on belittling him and tearing him down.

"For about a year things were good," Luanne continued. "We rented a small house and your daddy fixed up a room for you, and we even bought a new car. But that's when things started to go bad. Just after you were born your daddy hurt his back in an accident at the mill and was out of work for about a month, and then when he went back they told him they didn't need him anymore.

"We tried to make do for a while and your daddy was able to pick up some odd jobs here and there, but no steady work, and after a few months the money was gone and we had to move back here.

"After he lost the job at the mill your daddy had started to change. It was like the light was gone from his eyes and he got moody sometimes. But when we moved back in with his daddy it got much worse.

"I thought he was stronger than that, but I guess when you live with a fear for that long and then it seems to be coming true it takes a hard toll. It also didn't help that his daddy rubbed it in his face, ragging on him for thinking he was something special and that he could escape his family's past. If it'd been anyone else who'd said those things your daddy might have killed him, but your daddy was scared of his daddy. His daddy had a power over him. It was a terrible thing to see."

For the first time he could remember, Chance felt sympathy for his father.

"I think, your daddy was sort of a tortured soul," Luanne continued. "He had a struggle between doing what was good and doing what came naturally, what he'd learned from his daddy and granddaddy. He'd tried hard to overcome his worst self, but when things went bad he seemed to lose the will. It just seemed to break him and it was as if he decided that if he was cursed he might as well just become exactly what everyone expected of him.

"He stopped trying to find work, and every day his mood grew darker and he was drinking more. He started getting into fights in town, and he began..." Luanne trailed off.

"Beating you?" Chance asked softly.

Luanne nodded with a look of embarrassment.

"But there was no place for me to go. I didn't have any money, and as I said my folks had disowned me and I didn't even know where they were because they'd moved while we were in Woodville."

There was a moment of thoughtful silence, then suddenly Luanne brightened.

"So now do you understand what I meant about your daddy loving you?"

"Huh?" Chance replied.

He felt as though he'd fallen asleep during a movie and missed a crucial part.

"Weren't you paying attention?" Luanne asked with a look that suggested she'd just discovered he was simple.

"I guess not," Chance stammered.

Luanne gave an exasperated sigh.

"He treated you the way he did out of love because he was trying to protect you," she explained slowly. "He didn't want you to go through what he did, so he figured that if you didn't have any grand expectations you wouldn't be hurt when your life didn't amount to much."

"That's it?" Chance asked incredulously.

"What do you mean?" Luanne asked, giving him a perplexed look.

Chance fought a sudden urge to laugh as he realized that despite her apparent insights, his mother was still just a simple country girl whose greatest ambitions had probably been to run off with her high school sweetheart and marry him, and then later to escape him. Then he realized that his mother had inadvertently given some plausible reasons for why his father had treated him the way he had—resentment, a projection of self-loathing, bitterness about his own failure—though she'd missed the point herself. Still, he couldn't keep a small smirk from crossing his lips.

"What?" Luanne asked with a hint of testiness.

"Nothing," Chance replied, forcing himself to look serious. "I get it now. Makes perfect sense."

Luanne studied him for a moment as though trying to discern if he was telling the truth.

"Good," she said, apparently satisfied.

Again they were quiet for a moment before Luanne broke the silence again.

"So I imagine you're wondering where I've been?"

"The thought had crossed my mind," Chance replied dryly. "And also why you didn't take me with you."

"Because I knew he'd come after us," Luanne replied. "I knew he'd be angry if I left, but after a while he'd let it go. But he'd never have let me take you. Besides, I was only 22 when I left. I didn't have any money. I didn't have a job or a home for you. I figured you'd be better off with your daddy for a while because at least you'd have a roof over your head and someone around to look after you.

"I kept thinking that once I had enough money saved I'd get a two-bedroom apartment and find a lawyer and get custody of you legally. But then I got married again and had your baby sister, Daisy, but that marriage didn't work out and it wasn't legal anyway because your daddy and I were still married. So then I was on my own again and raising the baby to boot. I kept thinking I'd get you soon, but the years kept passing and after a while I figured that maybe it was best if I stayed away because I was sure by then you'd hate me."

Chance felt as though he were watching an episode of Jerry Springer. It amazed him that both of his parents had chosen to hurt him believing it would be in his best interest.

"But I kept checking up on you," Luanne continued breathlessly. "I used to call Mrs. Gaulthier every few months."

"Mammau?" Chance asked, surprised that his mother knew Joel's grandmother.

"Yeah, I ran into her in Fayette one day and she recognized me and told me that you and her grandson were best friends, so I asked her if it would be all right if I called now and again to see how you were doing. She told me about you moving to New Orleans and how you got stabbed. I went to the hospital to visit you once but your daddy was there so I didn't go in the room, and then another time..."

"Okay, okay," Chance said impatiently, holding up his right hand. "So why are you here now?"

Luanne gave him a slightly hurt look at having been interrupted so abruptly.

"Because I have to fulfill a promise I made to your great granddaddy," she replied.

She reached into her purse and took out a thick yellowed envelope, and held it out toward Chance.

"What is it?" he asked, eyeing the envelope suspiciously.

"It's your inheritance," Luanne replied.

"Inheritance?" Chance laughed. "There hasn't been any money in our family for over a hundred years."

"That's not true," Luanne replied. "Your great granddaddy had some money. You'd never have known it to look at him or by the way he lived, but he had money that'd been passed down to him."

Chance reached out slowly and took the envelope.

"But why would he leave it to me?" he asked.

"Because your great granddaddy knew that your granddaddy and your daddy would waste it," Luanne replied. "They were both big disappointments to him, and he didn't want to see what was left of the family fortune squandered.

"A few months before I left—about a year before he died— he gave me that envelope and told me to give it to when your daddy passed. He said that he hoped you'd be able to use it to make something of yourself so you could break the cycle."

Chance opened the envelope and pulled out the folded sheaves of paper. He straightened them out on his lap and began reading.

It was a trust document in his name, dated September 5, 1990. The principal amount at the time it was executed had been $175,000.

He looked up at Luanne, fighting back sudden tears.

"The Gaulthiers are having people back to the house," he said quietly. "Do you want to go with me...momma?"

11

Made in the USA
Lexington, KY
16 May 2012